The Mysterious Affair
at Styles

The Secret Adversary

AGATHA CHRISTIE

THE MYSTERIOUS AFFAIR
AT STYLES

THE SECRET ADVERSARY

AN AGATHA CHRISTIE OMNIBUS

CARROLL & GRAF PUBLISHERS, INC.
NEW YORK

First Carroll & Graf edition 1998

Carroll & Graf Publishers, Inc.
19 W. 21st Street
New York, NY 10010

Library of Congress Cataloging-in-Publication Data

Christie, Agatha, 1890–1976.
 [Mysterious affair at Styles]
 The mysterious affair at Styles ; & The secret adversary : an
Agatha Christie omnibus / Agatha Christie.—1st Carroll & Graf ed.
  p. cm.
 ISBN 0-7867-0434-9 (trade paper)
 1. Detective and mystery stories, English. I. Christie, Agatha,
1890–1976. Secret adversary. II. Title. III. Title: Secret
adversary.
 PR6005.H66A6 1998
 823'.912—dc21   97-4269
                                                       CIP

Designed by Kathleen Lake

Manufactured in the United States of America

CONTENTS

The Mysterious Affair at Styles

Contents

I

I Go to Styles

The intense interest aroused in the public by what was known at the time as "The Styles Case" has now somewhat subsided. Nevertheless, in view of the world-wide notoriety which attended it, I have been asked, both by my friend Poirot and the family themselves, to write an account of the whole story. This, we trust, will effectually silence the sensational rumours which still persist.

I will therefore briefly set down the circumstances which led to my being connected with the affair.

I had been invalided home from the Front; and, after spending some months in a rather depressing Convalescent Home, was given a month's sick leave. Having no near relations or friends, I was trying to make up my mind what to do, when I ran across John Cavendish. I had seen very little of him for some years. Indeed, I had never known him particularly well. He was a good fifteen years my senior, for one thing, though he hardly looked his forty-five years. As a boy, though, I had often stayed at Styles, his mother's place in Essex.

We had a good yarn about old times, and it ended in his

inviting me down to Styles to spend my leave there.

"The mater will be delighted to see you again—after all those years," he added.

"Your mother keeps well?" I asked.

"Oh, yes. I suppose you know that she has married again?"

I am afraid I showed my surprise rather plainly. Mrs. Cavendish, who had married John's father when he was a widower with two sons, had been a handsome woman of middle-age as I remembered her. She certainly could not be a day less than seventy now. I recalled her as an energetic, autocratic personality, somewhat inclined to charitable and social notoriety, with a fondness for opening bazaars and playing the Lady Bountiful. She was a most generous woman, and possessed a considerable fortune of her own.

Their country-place, Styles Court, had been purchased by Mr. Cavendish early in their married life. He had been completely under his wife's ascendancy, so much so that, on dying, he left the place to her for her lifetime, as well as the larger part of his income; an arrangement that was distinctly unfair to his two sons. Their stepmother, however, had always been most generous to them; indeed, they were so young at the time of their father's remarriage that they always thought of her as their own mother.

Lawrence, the younger, had been a delicate youth. He had qualified as a doctor but early relinquished the profession of medicine, and lived at home while pursuing literary ambitions; though his verses never had any marked success.

John practised for some time as a barrister, but had finally settled down to the more congenial life of a country squire. He had married two years ago, and had taken his wife to live at Styles, though I entertained a shrewd suspicion that he would have preferred his mother to increase his allowance, which would have enabled him to have a home of his own. Mrs. Cavendish, however, was a lady who liked to make her own plans, and expected other people to fall in with them, and in this case she certainly had the whip hand, namely: the purse strings.

John noticed my surprise at the news of his mother's remarriage and smiled rather ruefully.

"Rotten little bounder too!" he said savagely. "I can tell you, Hastings, it's making life jolly difficult for us. As for Evie—you remember Evie?"

"No."

"Oh, I suppose she was after your time. She's the mater's factotum, companion, Jack of all trades! A great sport—old Evie! Not precisely young and beautiful, but as game as they make them."

"You were going to say——?"

"Oh, this fellow! He turned up from nowhere, on the pretext of being a second cousin or something of Evie's, though she didn't seem particularly keen to acknowledge the relationship. The fellow is an absolute outsider, anyone can see that. He's got a great black beard, and wears patent leather boots in all weathers! But the mater cottoned to him at once, took him on as secretary—you know how she's always running a hundred societies?"

I nodded.

"Well, of course the war has turned the hundreds into thousands. No doubt the fellow was very useful to her. But you could have knocked us all down with a feather when, three months ago, she suddenly announced that she and Alfred were engaged! The fellow must be at least twenty years younger than she is! It's simply bare-faced fortune hunting; but there you are—she is her own mistress, and she's married him."

"It must be a difficult situation for you all."

"Difficult! It's damnable!"

Thus it came about that, three days later, I descended from the train at Styles St. Mary, an absurd little station, with no apparent reason for existence, perched up in the midst of green fields and country lanes. John Cavendish was waiting on the platform, and piloted me out to the car.

"Got a drop or two of petrol still, you see," he remarked. "Mainly owing to the mater's activities."

The village of Styles St. Mary was situated about two miles from the little station, and Styles Court lay a mile the other side of it. It was a still, warm day in early July. As one looked out over the flat Essex country, lying so green and peaceful under the afternoon sun, it seemed almost impossible to believe that, not so very far away, a great war was running its appointed course. I felt I had suddenly strayed into another world. As we turned in at the lodge gates, John said:

"I'm afraid you'll find it very quiet down here, Hastings."

"My dear fellow, that's just what I want."

"Oh, it's pleasant enough if you want to lead the idle life. I drill with the volunteers twice a week, and lend a hand at the farms. My wife works regularly 'on the land.' She is up at five every morning to milk, and keeps at it steadily until lunch-time. It's a jolly good life taking it all round—if it weren't for that fellow Alfred Inglethorp!" He checked the car suddenly, and glanced at his watch. "I wonder if we've time to pick up Cynthia. No, she'll have started from the hospital by now."

"Cynthia! That's not your wife?"

"No, Cynthia is a protegee of my mother's, the daughter of an old schoolfellow of hers, who married a rascally solicitor. He came a cropper, and the girl was left an orphan and penniless. My mother came to the rescue, and Cynthia has been with us nearly two years now. She works in the Red Cross Hospital at Tadminster, seven miles away."

As he spoke the last words, we drew up in front of the fine old house. A lady in a stout tweed skirt, who was bending over a flower bed, straightened herself at our approach.

"Hullo, Evie, here's our wounded hero! Mr. Hastings—Miss Howard."

Miss Howard shook hands with a hearty, almost painful, grip. I had an impression of very blue eyes in a sunburnt face. She was a pleasant-looking woman of about forty, with a deep voice, almost manly in its stentorian tones, and had a large sensible square body, with feet to match—these last encased in good thick boots. Her conversation, I soon found, was couched in the telegraphic style.

"Weeds grow like house afire. Can't keep even with 'em. Shall press you in. Better be careful."

"I'm sure I shall be only too delighted to make myself useful," I responded.

"Don't say it. Never does. Wish you hadn't later."

"You're a cynic, Evie," said John, laughing. "Where's tea to-day—inside or out?"

"Out. Too fine a day to be cooped up in the house."

"Come on then, you've done enough gardening for today. The labourer is worthy of his hire', you know. Come and be refreshed."

"Well," said Miss Howard, drawing off her gardening gloves, "I'm inclined to agree with you."

She led the way round the house to where tea was spread under the shade of a large sycamore.

A figure rose from one of the basket chairs, and came a few steps to meet us.

"My wife, Hastings," said John.

I shall never forget my first sight of Mary Cavendish. Her tall, slender form, outlined against the bright light; the vivid sense of slumbering fire that seemed to find expression only in those wonderful tawny eyes of hers, remarkable eyes, different from any other woman's that I have ever known; the intense power of stillness she possessed, which nevertheless conveyed the impression of a wild untamed spirit in an exquisitely civilised body—all these things are burnt into my memory. I shall never forget them.

She greeted me with a few words of pleasant welcome in a low clear voice, and I sank into a basket chair feeling distinctly glad that I had accepted John's invitation. Mrs. Cavendish gave me some tea, and her few quiet remarks heightened my first impression of her as a thoroughly fascinating woman. An appreciative listener is always stimulating, and I described, in a humorous manner, certain incidents of my Convalescent Home, in a way which, I flatter myself, greatly amused my hostess. John, of course, good fellow though he is, could hardly be called a brilliant conversationalist.

At that moment a well remembered voice floated through the open French window near at hand:

"Then you'll write to the Princess after tea, Alfred? I'll write to Lady Tadminster for the second day, myself. Or shall we wait until we hear from the Princess? In case of a refusal, Lady Tadminster might open it the first day, and Mrs. Crosbie the second. Then there's the Duchess—about the school fête."

There was the murmur of a man's voice, and then Mrs. Inglethorp's rose in reply:

"Yes, certainly. After tea will do quite well. You are so thoughtful, Alfred dear."

The French window swung open a little wider, and a handsome white-haired old lady, with a somewhat masterful cast of features, stepped out of it on to the lawn. A man followed her, a suggestion of deference in his manner.

Mrs. Inglethorp greeted me with effusion.

"Why, if it isn't too delightful to see you again, Mr. Hastings, after all these years. Alfred, darling, Mr. Hastings— my husband."

I looked with some curiosity at "Alfred darling." He certainly struck a rather alien note. I did not wonder at John objecting to his beard. It was one of the longest and blackest I have ever seen. He wore gold rimmed pince-nez, and had a curious impassivity of feature. It struck me that he might look natural on a stage, but was strangely out of place in real life. His voice was rather deep and unctuous. He placed a wooden hand in mine and said:

"This is a pleasure, Mr. Hastings." Then, turning to his wife:"Emily dearest, I think that cushion is a little damp."

She beamed fondly on him, as he substituted another with every demonstration of the tenderest care. Strange infatuation of an otherwise sensible woman!

With the presence of Mr. Inglethorp, a sense of constraint and veiled hostility seemed to settle down upon the company. Miss Howard, in particular, took no pains to conceal her feelings. Mrs. Inglethorp, however, seemed to notice nothing unusual. Her volubility, which I remembered of old, had lost nothing in the intervening years, and she poured out a steady flood of conversation, mainly on the subject of the forthcoming bazaar which she was organizing and which was to take place shortly. Occasionally she referred to her husband over a question of days or dates. His watchful and attentive manner never varied. From the very first I took a firm and rooted dislike to him, and I flatter myself that my first judgments are usually fairly shrewd.

Presently Mrs. Inglethorp turned to give some instructions about letters to Evelyn Howard, and her husband addressed me in his painstaking voice:

"Is soldiering your regular profession, Mr. Hastings?"

"No, before the war I was in Lloyd's."

"And you will return there after it is over?"

"Perhaps. Either that or a fresh start altogether."

Mary Cavendish leant forward.

"What would you really choose as a profession, if you could just consult your inclination?"

"Well, that depends."

"No secret hobby?" she asked. "Tell me—you're drawn to something? Every one is—usually something absurd."

"You'll laugh at me."

She smiled.

"Perhaps."

"Well, I've always had a secret hankering to be a detective!"

"The real thing—Scotland Yard? Or Sherlock Holmes?"

"Oh, Sherlock Holmes by all means. But really, seriously, I am awfully drawn to it. I came across a man in Belgium once, a very famous detective, and he quite inflamed me. He was a marvellous little fellow. He used to say that all good detective work was a mere matter of method. My system is based on his—though of course I have progressed rather further. He was a funny little man, a great dandy, but wonderfully clever."

"Like a good detective story myself," remarked Miss Howard. "Lots of nonsense written, though. Criminal discovered in last chapter. Every one dumbfounded. Real crime—you'd know at once."

"There have been a great number of undiscovered crimes," I argued.

"Don't mean the police, but the people that are right in it. The family. You couldn't really hoodwink them. They'd know."

"Then," I said, much amused, "you think that if you were mixed up in a crime, say a murder, you'd be able to spot the murderer right off?"

"Of course I should. Mightn't be able to prove it to a pack

of lawyers. But I'm certain I'd know. I'd feel it in my fingertips if he came near me."

"It might be a 'she,' " I suggested.

"Might. But murder's a violent crime. Associate it more with a man."

"Not in a case of poisoning." Mrs. Cavendish's clear voice startled me. "Dr. Bauerstein was saying yesterday that, owing to the general ignorance of the more uncommon poisons among the medical profession, there were probably countless cases of poisoning quite unsuspected."

"Why, Mary, what a gruesome conversation!" cried Mrs. Inglethorp. "It makes me feel as if a goose were walking over my grave. Oh, there's Cynthia!"

A young girl in V.A.D. uniform ran lightly across the lawn.

"Why, Cynthia, you are late to-day. This is Mr. Hastings— Miss Murdoch."

Cynthia Murdoch was a fresh-looking young creature, full of life and vigour. She tossed off her little V.A.D. cap, and I admired the great loose waves of her auburn hair, and the smallness and whiteness of the hand she held out to claim her tea. With dark eyes and eyelashes she would have been a beauty.

She flung herself down on the ground beside John, and as I handed her a plate of sandwiches she smiled up at me.

"Sit down here on the grass, do. It's ever so much nicer."

I dropped down obediently.

"You work at Tadminster, don't you, Miss Murdoch?"

She nodded.

"For my sins."

"Do they bully you, then?" I asked, smiling.

"I should like to see them!" cried Cynthia with dignity.

"I have got a cousin who is nursing," I remarked. "And she is terrified of 'Sisters.' "

"I don't wonder. Sisters *are*, you know, Mr. Hastings. They simp-ly *are*! You've no idea! But I'm not a nurse, thank heaven. I work in the dispensary."

"How many people do you poison?" I asked, smiling.

Cynthia smiled too.

"Oh, hundreds!" she said.

"Cynthia," called Mrs. Inglethorp, "do you think you could write a few notes for me?"

"Certainly, Aunt Emily."

She jumped up promptly, and something in her manner reminded me that her position was a dependent one, and that Mrs. Inglethorp, kind as she might be in the main, did not allow her to forget it.

My hostess turned to me.

"John will show you your room. Supper is at half-past seven. We have given up late dinner for some time now. Lady Tadminster, our Member's wife—she was the late Lord Abbotsbury's daughter—does the same. She agreed with me that one must set an example of economy. We are quite a war household; nothing is wasted here—every scrap of waste paper, even, is saved and sent away in sacks."

I expressed my appreciation, and John took me into the house and up the broad staircase, which forked right and left half-way to different wings of the building. My room was in the left wing, and looked out over the park.

John left me, and a few minutes later I saw him from my window walking slowly across the grass arm in arm with Cynthia Murdoch. I heard Mrs. Inglethorp call "Cynthia" impatiently, and the girl started and ran back to the house. At the same moment, a man stepped out from the shadow of a tree and walked slowly in the same direction.

He looked about forty, very dark with a melancholy clean-shaven face. Some violent emotion seemed to be mastering him. He looked up at my window as he passed, and I recognized him, though he had changed much in the fifteen years that had elapsed since we last met. It was John's younger brother, Lawrence Cavendish. I wondered what it was that had brought that singular expression to his face.

Then I dismissed him from my mind, and returned to the contemplation of my own affairs.

The evening passed pleasantly enough; and I dreamed that night of that enigmatical woman, Mary Cavendish.

The next morning dawned bright and sunny, and I was full of the anticipation of a delightful visit.

I did not see Mrs. Cavendish until lunch-time, when she volunteered to take me for a walk, and we spent a charming afternoon roaming in the woods, returning to the house about five.

As we entered the large hall, John beckoned us both into the smoking-room. I saw at once by his face that something disturbing had occurred. We followed him in, and he shut the door after us.

"Look here, Mary, there's the deuce of a mess. Evie's had a row with Alfred Inglethorp, and she's off."

"Evie? Off?"

John nodded gloomily.

"Yes; you see she went to the mater, and—Oh, here's Evie herself."

Miss Howard entered. Her lips were set grimly together, and she carried a small suit-case. She looked excited and determined, and slightly on the defensive.

"At any rate," she burst out, "I've spoken my mind!"

"My dear Evelyn," cried Mrs. Cavendish, "this can't be true!"

Miss Howard nodded grimly.

"True enough! Afraid I said some things to Emily she won't forget or forgive in a hurry. Don't mind if they've only sunk in a bit. Probably water off a duck's back, though. I said right out: 'You're an old woman, Emily, and there's no fool like an old fool. The man's twenty years younger than you, and don't you fool yourself as to what he married you for. Money! Well, don't let him have too much of it. Farmer Raikes has got a very pretty young wife. Just ask your Alfred how much time he spends over there.' She was very angry. Natural! I went on: 'I'm going to warn you, whether you like it or not. That man would as soon murder you in your bed as look at you. He's a bad lot. You can say what you like to me, but remember what I've told you. He's a bad lot!' "

"What did she say?"

Miss Howard made an extremely expressive grimace.

" 'Darling Alfred'—'dearest Alfred'—'wicked calumnies'—'wicked lies'—'wicked woman'—to accuse her 'dear husband'! The sooner I left her house the better. So I'm off."

"But not now?"

"This minute!"

For a moment we sat and stared at her. Finally John Cavendish, finding his persuasions of no avail, went off to look up the trains. His wife followed him, murmuring something about persuading Mrs. Inglethorp to think better of it.

As she left the room, Miss Howard's face changed. She leant toward me eagerly.

"Mr. Hastings, you're honest. I can trust you?"

I was a little startled. She laid her hand on my arm, and sank her voice to a whisper.

"Look after her, Mr. Hastings. My poor Emily. They're a lot of sharks—all of them. Oh, I know what I'm talking about. There isn't one of them that's not hard up and trying to get money out of her. I've protected her as much as I could. Now I'm out of the way, they'll impose upon her."

"Of course, Miss Howard," I said, "I'll do everything I can, but I'm sure you're excited and overwrought."

She interrupted me by slowly shaking her forefinger.

"Young man, trust me. I've lived in the world rather longer than you have. All I ask you is to keep your eyes open. You'll see what I mean."

The throb of the motor came through the open window, and Miss Howard rose and moved to the door. John's voice sounded outside. With her hand on the handle, she turned her head over her shoulder, and beckoned to me.

"Above all, Mr. Hastings, watch that devil—her husband!"

There was no time for more. Miss Howard was swallowed up in an eager chorus of protests and good-byes. The Inglethorps did not appear.

As the motor drove away, Mrs. Cavendish suddenly detached herself from the group, and moved across the drive to the lawn to meet a tall bearded man who had been evidently making for the house. The colour rose in her cheeks as she held out her hand to him.

"Who is that?" I asked sharply, for instinctively I distrusted the man.

"That's Dr. Bauerstein," said John shortly.

"And who is Dr. Bauerstein?"

"He's staying in the village doing a rest cure, after a bad nervous breakdown. He's a London specialist; a very clever man—one of the greatest living experts on poisons, I believe."

"And he's a great friend of Mary's," put in Cynthia, the irrepressible.

John Cavendish frowned and changed the subject.

"Come for a stroll, Hastings. This has been a most rotten business. She always had a rough tongue, but there is no stauncher friend in England than Evelyn Howard."

He took the path through the plantation, and we walked down to the village through the woods which bordered one side of the estate.

As we passed through one of the gates on our way home again, a pretty young woman of gipsy type coming in the opposite direction bowed and smiled.

"That's a pretty girl," I remarked appreciatively.

John's face hardened.

"That is Mrs. Raikes."

"The one that Miss Howard——"

"Exactly," said John, with rather unnecessary abruptness.

I thought of the white-haired old lady in the big house, and that vivid wicked little face that had just smiled into ours, and a vague chill of foreboding crept over me. I brushed it aside.

"Styles is really a glorious old place," I said to John.

He nodded rather gloomily.

"Yes, it's a fine property. It'll be mine some day—should be mine now by rights, if my father had only made a decent will. And then I shouldn't be so damned hard up as I am now."

"Hard up, are you?"

"My dear Hastings, I don't mind telling you that I'm at my wit's end for money."

"Couldn't your brother help you?"

"Lawrence? He's gone through every penny he ever had, publishing rotten verses in fancy bindings. No, we're an impecunious lot. My mother's always been awfully good to us, I must say. That is, up to now. Since her marriage, of course——" he broke off, frowning.

For the first time I felt that, with Evelyn Howard, something indefinable had gone from the atmosphere. Her presence had spelt security. Now that security was removed—

and the air seemed rife with suspicion. The sinister face of Dr. Bauerstein recurred to me unpleasantly. A vague suspicion of every one and everything filled my mind. Just for a moment I had a premonition of approaching evil.

II

THE 16TH AND 17TH OF JULY

I had arrived at Styles on the 5th of July. I come now to the events of the 16th and 17th of that month. For the convenience of the reader I will recapitulate the incidents of those days in as exact a manner as possible. They were elicited subsequently at the trial by a process of long and tedious cross-examinations.

I received a letter from Evelyn Howard a couple of days after her departure, telling me she was working as a nurse at the big hospital in Middlingham, a manufacturing town some fifteen miles away, and begging me to let her know if Mrs. Inglethorp should show any wish to be reconciled.

The only fly in the ointment of my peaceful days was Mrs. Cavendish's extraordinary, and, for my part, unaccountable preference for the society of Dr. Bauerstein. What she saw in the man I cannot imagine, but she was always asking him up to the house, and often went off for long expeditions with him. I must confess that I was quite unable to see his attraction.

The 16th of July fell on a Monday. It was a day of turmoil. The famous bazaar had taken place on Saturday, and an entertainment, in connection with the same charity, at which Mrs. Inglethorp was to recite a War poem, was to be held that night. We were all busy during the morning arranging and decorating the Hall in the village where it was to take place. We had a late luncheon and spent the afternoon resting in the garden. I noticed that John's manner was somewhat unusual. He seemed very excited and restless.

After tea, Mrs. Inglethorp went to lie down to rest before her efforts in the evening and I challenged Mary Cavendish to a single at tennis.

About a quarter to seven, Mrs. Inglethorp called to us that we should be late as supper was early that night. We had rather a scramble to get ready in time; and before the meal was over the motor was waiting at the door.

The entertainment was a great success, Mrs. Inglethorp's recitation receiving tremendous applause. There were also some tableaux in which Cynthia took part. She did not return with us, having been asked to a supper party, and to remain the night with some friends who had been acting with her in the tableaux.

The following morning, Mrs. Inglethorp stayed in bed to breakfast, as she was rather overtired; but she appeared in her briskest mood about 12:30, and swept Lawrence and myself off to a luncheon party.

"Such a charming invitation from Mrs. Rolleston. Lady Tadminster's sister, you know. The Rollestons came over with the Conqueror—one of our oldest families."

Mary had excused herself on the plea of an engagement with Dr. Bauerstein.

We had a pleasant luncheon, and as we drove away Lawrence suggested that we should return by Tadminster, which was barely a mile out of our way, and pay a visit to Cynthia in her dispensary. Mrs. Inglethorp replied that this was an excellent idea, but as she had several letters to write she would drop us there, and we could come back with Cynthia in the pony-trap.

We were detained under suspicion by the hospital porter, until Cynthia appeared to vouch for us, looking very cool and sweet in her long white overall. She took us up to her sanctum, and introduced us to her fellow dispenser, a rather awe-inspiring individual, whom Cynthia cheerily addressed as "Nibs."

"What a lot of bottles!" I exclaimed, as my eye travelled round the small room. "Do you really know what's in them all?"

"Say something original," groaned Cynthia. "Every single person who comes up here says that. We are really thinking of bestowing a prize on the first individual who does *not* say: 'What a lot of bottles!' And I know the next thing you're going to say is: 'How many people have you poisoned?' "

I pleaded guilty with a laugh.

"If you people only knew how fatally easy it is to poison some one by mistake, you wouldn't joke about it. Come on, let's have tea. We've got all sorts of secret stores in that cupboard. No, Lawrence—that's the poison cupboard. The big cupboard—that's right."

We had a very cheery tea, and assisted Cynthia to wash up afterwards. We had just put away the last tea-spoon when a knock came at the door. The countenances of Cynthia and Nibs were suddenly petrified into a stern and forbidding expression.

"Come in," said Cynthia, in a sharp professional tone. A young and rather scared looking nurse appeared with a bottle which she proffered to Nibs, who waved her towards Cynthia with the somewhat enigmatical remark:

"*I'm* not really here to-day."

Cynthia took the bottle and examined it with the severity of a judge.

"This should have been sent up this morning."

"Sister is very sorry. She forgot."

"Sister should read the rules outside the door."

I gathered from the little nurse's expression that there was not the least likelihood of her having the hardihood to retail this message to the dreaded "Sister."

"So now it can't be done until to-morrow," finished Cynthia.

"Don't you think you could possibly let us have it to-night?"

"Well," said Cynthia graciously, "we are very busy, but if we have time it shall be done."

The little nurse withdrew, and Cynthia promptly took a jar from the shelf, refilled the bottle, and placed it on the table outside the door.

I laughed.

"Discipline must be maintained?"

"Exactly. Come out on our little balcony. You can see all the outside wards there."

I followed Cynthia and her friend and they pointed out the different wards to me. Lawrence remained behind, but after a few moments Cynthia called to him over her shoulder to come and join us. Then she looked at her watch.

"Nothing more to do, Nibs?"

"No."

"All right. Then we can lock up and go."

I had seen Lawrence in quite a different light that afternoon. Compared to John, he was an astoundingly difficult person to get to know. He was the opposite of his brother in almost every respect, being unusually shy and reserved. Yet he had a certain charm of manner, and I fancied that, if one really knew him well, one could have a deep affection for him. I had always fancied that his manner to Cynthia was rather constrained, and that she on her side was inclined to be shy of him. But they were both gay enough this afternoon, and chatted together like a couple of children.

As we drove through the village, I remembered that I wanted some stamps, so accordingly we pulled up at the post office.

As I came out again, I cannoned into a little man who was just entering. I drew aside and apologised, when suddenly, with a loud exclamation, he clasped me in his arms and kissed me warmly.

"*Mon ami* Hastings!" he cried. "It is indeed *mon ami* Hastings!"

"Poirot!" I exclaimed.

I turned to the pony-trap.

"This is a very pleasant meeting for me, Miss Cynthia. This is my old friend, Monsieur Poirot, whom I have not seen for years."

"Oh, we know Monsieur Poirot," said Cynthia gaily. "But I had no idea he was a friend of yours."

"Yes, indeed," said Poirot seriously, "I know Mademoiselle Cynthia. It is by the charity of that good Mrs. Inglethorp that I am here." Then, as I looked at him inquiringly: "Yes, my friend, she had kindly extended hospitality to seven of my countrypeople who, alas, are refugees from their native land. We Belgians will always remember her with gratitude."

Poirot was an extraordinary looking little man. He was hardly more than five feet, four inches, but carried himself with great dignity. His head was exactly the shape of an egg, and he always perched it a little on one side. His moustache was very stiff and military. The neatness of his attire was almost incredible. I believe a speck of dust would have caused him more pain than a bullet wound. Yet this quaint dandified little man who, I was sorry to see, now limped badly, had been in his time one of the most celebrated members of the Belgian police. As a detective, his *flair* had been extraordinary, and he had achieved triumphs by unravelling some of the most baffling cases of the day.

He pointed out to me the little house inhabited by him and his fellow Belgians, and I promised to go and see him at an early date. Then he raised his hat with a flourish to Cynthia, and we drove away.

"He's a dear little man," said Cynthia. "I'd no idea you knew him."

"You've been entertaining a celebrity unawares," I replied.

And, for the rest of the way home, I recited to them the various exploits and triumphs of Hercule Poirot.

We arrived back in a very cheerful mood. As we entered the hall, Mrs. Inglethorp came out of her boudoir. She looked flushed and upset.

"Oh, it's you," she said.

"Is there anything the matter, Aunt Emily?" asked Cynthia.

"Certainly not," said Mrs. Inglethorp sharply. "What should there be?" Then catching sight of Dorcas, the parlourmaid, going into the dining-room, she called to her to bring some stamps into the boudoir.

"Yes, m'm." The old servant hesitated, then added diffidently: "Don't you think, m'm, you'd better get to bed? You're looking very tired."

"Perhaps you're right, Dorcas—yes—no—not now. I've some letters I must finish by post-time. Have you lighted the fire in my room as I told you?"

"Yes, m'm."

"Then I'll go to bed directly after supper."

She went into the boudoir again, and Cynthia stared after her.

"Goodness gracious! I wonder what's up?" she said to Lawrence.

He did not seem to have heard her, for without a word he turned on his heel and went out of the house.

I suggested a quick game of tennis before supper and, Cynthia agreeing, I ran upstairs to fetch my racquet.

Mrs. Cavendish was coming down the stairs. It may have been my fancy, but she, too, was looking odd and disturbed.

"Had a good walk with Dr. Bauerstein?" I asked, trying to appear as indifferent as I could.

"I didn't go," she replied abruptly. "Where is Mrs. Inglethorp?"

"In the boudoir."

Her hand clenched itself on the bannisters, then she seemed to nerve herself for some encounter, and went rapidly past me down the stairs across the hall to the boudoir, the door of which she shut behind her.

As I ran out to the tennis court a few moments later, I had to pass the open boudoir window, and was unable to help overhearing the following scrap of dialogue. Mary Cavendish was saying in the voice of a woman desperately controlling herself:

"Then you won't show it to me?"

To which Mrs. Inglethorp replied:

"My dear Mary, it has nothing to do with that matter."

"Then show it to me."

"I tell you it is not what you imagine. It does not concern you in the least."

To which Mary Cavendish replied, with a rising bitterness:

"Of course, I might have known you would shield him."

Cynthia was waiting for me, and greeted me eagerly with:

"I say! There's been the most awful row! I've got it all out of Dorcas."

"What kind of a row?"

"Between Aunt Emily and *him*. I do hope she's found him out at last!"

"Was Dorcas there, then?"

"Of course not. She 'happened to be near the door.' It was a real old bust-up. I do wish I knew what it was all about."

I thought of Mrs. Raikes's gipsy face, and Evelyn Howard's warnings, but wisely decided to hold my peace, whilst Cynthia exhausted every possible hypothesis, and cheerfully hoped, "Aunt Emily will send him away, and will never speak to him again."

I was anxious to get hold of John, but he was nowhere to be seen. Evidently something very momentous had occurred that afternoon. I tried to forget the few words I had overheard; but, do what I would, I could not dismiss them altogether from my mind. What was Mary Cavendish's concern in the matter?

Mr. Inglethorp was in the drawing-room when I came down to supper. His face was impassive as ever, and the strange unreality of the man struck me afresh.

Mrs. Inglethorp came down last. She still looked agitated, and during the meal there was a somewhat constrained silence. Inglethorp was unusually quiet. As a rule, he surrounded his wife with little attentions, placing a cushion at her back, and altogether playing the part of the devoted husband. Immediately after supper, Mrs. Inglethorp retired to her boudoir again.

"Send my coffee in here, Mary," she called. "I've just five minutes to catch the post."

Cynthia and I went and sat by the open window in the drawing-room. Mary Cavendish brought our coffee to us. She seemed excited.

"Do you young people want lights, or do you enjoy the twilight?" she asked. "Will you take Mrs. Inglethorp her coffee, Cynthia? I will pour it out."

"Do not trouble, Mary," said Inglethorp. "I will take it to Emily." He poured it out, and went out of the room carrying it carefully.

Lawrence followed him, and Mrs. Cavendish sat down by us.

We three sat for some time in silence. It was a glorious night, hot and still. Mrs. Cavendish fanned herself gently with a palm leaf.

"It's almost too hot," she murmured. "We shall have a thunderstorm."

Alas, that these harmonious moments can never endure! My paradise was rudely shattered by the sound of a well known, and heartily disliked, voice in the hall.

"Dr. Bauerstein!" exclaimed Cynthia. "What a funny time to come."

I glanced jealously at Mary Cavendish, but she seemed quite undisturbed, the delicate pallor of her cheeks did not vary.

In a few moments, Alfred Inglethorp had ushered the doctor in, the latter laughing, and protesting that he was in no fit state for a drawing-room. In truth, he presented a sorry spectacle, being literally plastered with mud.

"What have you been doing, Doctor?" cried Mrs. Cavendish.

"I must make my apologies," said the doctor. "I did not really mean to come in, but Mr. Inglethorp insisted."

"Well, Bauerstein, you are in a plight," said John, strolling in from the hall. "Have some coffee, and tell us what you have been up to."

"Thank you, I will." He laughed rather ruefully, as he described how he had discovered a very rare species of fern in an inaccessible place, and in his efforts to obtain it had lost his footing, and slipped ignominiously into a neighbouring pond.

"The sun soon dried me off," he added, "but I'm afraid my appearance is very disreputable."

At this juncture, Mrs. Inglethorp called to Cynthia from the hall, and the girl ran out.

"Just carry up my despatch-case, will you, dear? I'm going to bed."

The door into the hall was a wide one. I had risen when Cynthia did, John was close by me. There were therefore three witnesses who could swear that Mrs. Inglethorp was carrying her coffee, as yet untasted, in her hand.

My evening was utterly and entirely spoilt by the presence of Dr. Bauerstein. It seemed to me the man would never go. He rose at last, however, and I breathed a sigh of relief.

"I'll walk down to the village with you," said Mr. Inglethorp. "I must see our agent over those estate accounts." He turned to John. "No one need sit up. I will take the latchkey."

III

THE NIGHT OF THE TRAGEDY

To make this part of my story clear, I append the following plan of the first floor of Styles.

The servants' rooms are reached through the door B. They have no communication with the right wing, where the Inglethorps' rooms were situated.

It seemed to be the middle of the night when I was awakened by Lawrence Cavendish. He had a candle in his hand, and the agitation of his face told me at once that something was seriously wrong.

"What's the matter?" I asked, sitting up in bed, and trying to collect my scattered thoughts.

"We are afraid my mother is very ill. She seems to be having some kind of fit. Unfortunately she has locked herself in."

"I'll come at once."

I sprang out of bed; and, pulling on a dressing-gown, followed Lawrence along the passage and the gallery to the right wing of the house.

John Cavendish joined us, and one or two of the servants were standing round in a state of awe-stricken excitement. Lawrence turned to his brother.

"What do you think we had better do?"

Never, I thought, had his indecision of character been more apparent.

John rattled the handle of Mrs. Inglethorp's door violently, but with no effect. It was obviously locked or bolted on the inside. The whole household was aroused by now. The most alarming sounds were audible from the interior of the room. Clearly something must be done.

"Try going through Mr. Inglethorp's room, sir," cried Dorcas. "Oh, the poor mistress!"

Suddenly I realized that Alfred Inglethorp was not with us—that he alone had given no sign of his presence. John opened the door of his room. It was pitch dark, but Lawrence was following with the candle, and by its feeble light we saw that the bed had not been slept in, and that there was no sign of the room having been occupied.

We went straight to the connecting door. That, too, was locked or bolted on the inside. What was to be done?

"Oh, dear, sir," cried Dorcas, wringing her hands, "what ever shall we do?"

"We must try and break the door in, I suppose. It'll be a

tough job, though. Here, let one of the maids go down and wake Baily and tell him to go for Dr. Wilkins at once. Now then, we'll have a try at the door. Half a moment, though, isn't there a door into Miss Cynthia's room?"

"Yes, sir, but that's always bolted. It's never been undone."

"Well, we might just see."

He ran rapidly down the corridor to Cynthia's room. Mary Cavendish was there, shaking the girl—who must have been an unusually sound sleeper—and trying to wake her.

In a moment or two he was back.

"No good. That's bolted too. We must break in the door. I think this one is a shade less solid than the one in the passage."

We strained and heaved together. The framework of the door was solid, and for a long time it resisted our efforts, but at last we felt it give beneath our weight, and finally, with a resounding crash, it was burst open.

We stumbled in together, Lawrence still holding his candle. Mrs. Inglethorp was lying on the bed, her whole form agitated by violent convulsions, in one of which she must have overturned the table beside her. As we entered, however, her limbs relaxed, and she fell back upon the pillows.

John strode across the room, and lit the gas. Turning to Annie, one of the housemaids, he sent her downstairs to the dining-room for brandy. Then he went across to his mother whilst I unbolted the door that gave on the corridor.

I turned to Lawrence, to suggest that I had better leave them now that there was no further need of my services, but the words were frozen on my lips. Never have I seen such a ghastly look on any man's face. He was white as chalk, the candle he held in his shaking hand was sputtering onto the carpet, and his eyes, petrified with terror, or some such kindred emotion, stared fixedly over my head at a point on the further wall. It was as though he had seen something that turned him to stone. I instinctively followed the direction of his eyes, but I could see nothing unusual. The still feebly flickering ashes in the grate, and the row of prim ornaments on the mantelpiece, were surely harmless enough.

The violence of Mrs. Inglethorp's attack seemed to be passing. She was able to speak in short gasps.

"Better now—very sudden—stupid of me—to lock myself in."

A shadow fell on the bed and, looking up, I saw Mary Cavendish standing near the door with her arm around Cynthia. She seemed to be supporting the girl, who looked utterly dazed and unlike herself. Her face was heavily flushed, and she yawned repeatedly.

"Poor Cynthia is quite frightened," said Mrs. Cavendish in a low clear voice. She herself, I noticed, was dressed in her white land smock. Then it must be later than I thought. I saw that a faint streak of daylight was showing through the curtains of the windows, and that the clock on the mantelpiece pointed to close upon five o'clock.

A strangled cry from the bed startled me. A fresh access of pain seized the unfortunate old lady. The convulsions were of a violence terrible to behold. Everything was confusion. We thronged round her, powerless to help or alleviate. A final convulsion lifted her from the bed, until she appeared to rest upon her head and her heels, with her body arched in an extraordinary manner. In vain Mary and John tried to administer more brandy. The moments flew. Again the body arched itself in that peculiar fashion.

At that moment, Dr. Bauerstein pushed his way authoritatively into the room. For one instant he stopped dead, staring at the figure on the bed, and, at the same instant, Mrs. Inglethorp cried out in a strangled voice, her eyes fixed on the doctor:

"Alfred—Alfred—" Then she fell back motionless on the pillows.

With a stride, the doctor reached the bed, and seizing her arms worked them energetically, applying what I knew to be artificial respiration. He issued a few short sharp orders to the servants. An imperious wave of his hand drove us all to the door. We watched him, fascinated, though I think we all knew in our hearts that it was too late, and that nothing could be done now. I could see by the expression on his face that he himself had little hope.

Finally he abandoned his task, shaking his head gravely.

At that moment, we heard footsteps outside, and Dr. Wilkins, Mrs. Inglethorp's own doctor, a portly, fussy little man, came bustling in.

In a few words Dr. Bauerstein explained how he had happened to be passing the lodge gates as the car came out, and had run up to the house as fast as he could, whilst the car went on to fetch Dr. Wilkins. With a faint gesture of the hand, he indicated the figure on the bed.

"Ve—ry sad. Ve—ry sad," murmured Dr. Wilkins. "Poor dear lady. Always did far too much—far too much—against my advice. I warned her. Her heart was far from strong. 'Take it easy,' I said to her. 'Take—it—easy'. But no—her zeal for good works was too great. Nature rebelled. Na—ture—re—belled."

Dr. Bauerstein, I noticed, was watching the local doctor narrowly. He still kept his eyes fixed on him as he spoke.

"The convulsions were of a peculiar violence, Dr. Wilkins. I am sorry you were not here in time to witness them. They were quite—tetanic in character."

"Ah!" said Dr. Wilkins wisely.

"I should like to speak to you in private," said Dr. Bauerstein. He turned to John. "You do not object?"

"Certainly not."

We all trooped out into the corridor, leaving the two doctors alone, and I heard the key turned in the lock behind us.

We went slowly down the stairs. I was violently excited. I have a certain talent for deduction, and Dr. Bauerstein's manner had started a flock of wild surmises in my mind. Mary Cavendish laid her hand upon my arm.

"What is it? Why did Dr. Bauerstein seem so—peculiar?"

I looked at her.

"Do you know what I think?"

"What?"

"Listen!" I looked round, the others were out of earshot. I lowered my voice to a whisper. "I believe she has been poisoned! I'm certain Dr. Bauerstein suspects it."

"What?" She shrank against the wall, the pupils of her eyes dilating wildly. Then, with a sudden cry that startled me, she cried out: "No, no—not that—not that!" And breaking from me, fled up the stairs. I followed her, afraid that

she was going to faint. I found her leaning against the bannisters, deadly pale. She waved me away impatiently.

"No, no—leave me. I'd rather be alone. Let me just be quiet
for a moment or two. Go down to the others."

I obeyed her reluctantly. John and Lawrence were in the
dining-room. I joined them. We were all silent, but I suppose
I voiced the thoughts of us all when I at last broke it by
saying:

"Where is Mr. Inglethorp?"

John shook his head.

"He's not in the house."

Our eyes met. Where *was* Alfred Inglethorp? His absence
was strange and inexplicable. I remembered Mrs. Inglethorp's dying words. What lay beneath them? What more
could she have told us, if she had had time?

At last we heard the doctors descending the stairs. Dr.
Wilkins was looking important and excited, and trying to
conceal an inward exultation under a manner of decorous
calm. Dr. Bauerstein remained in the background, his grave
bearded face unchanged. Dr. Wilkins was the spokesman
for the two. He addressed himself to John:

"Mr. Cavendish, I should like your consent to a postmor-
tem."

"Is that necessary?" asked John gravely. A spasm of pain
crossed his face.

"Absolutely," said Dr. Bauerstein.

"You mean by that——?"

"That neither Dr. Wilkins nor myself could give a death
certificate under the circumstances."

John bent his head.

"In that case, I have no alternative but to agree."

"Thank you," said Dr. Wilkins briskly. "We propose that
it should take place to-morrow night—or rather to-night."
And he glanced at the daylight. "Under the circumstances,
I am afraid an inquest can hardly be avoided—these for-
malities are necessary, but I beg that you won't distress
yourselves."

There was a pause, and then Dr. Bauerstein drew two
keys from his pocket, and handed them to John.

"These are the keys of the two rooms. I have locked them

and, in my opinion, they would be better kept locked for the present."

The doctors then departed.

I had been turning over an idea in my head, and I felt that the moment had now come to broach it. Yet I was a little chary of doing so. John, I knew, had a horror of any kind of publicity, and was an easy going optimist, who preferred never to meet trouble half-way. It might be difficult to convince him of the soundness of my plan. Lawrence, on the other hand, being less conventional, and having more imagination, I felt I might count upon as an ally. There was no doubt that the moment had come for me to take the lead.

"John," I said, "I am going to ask you something."

"Well?"

"You remember my speaking of my friend Poirot? The Belgian who is here? He has been a most famous detective."

"Yes."

"I want you to let me call him in—to investigate this matter."

"What—now? Before the post-mortem?"

"Yes, time is an advantage if—if—there has been foul play."

"Rubbish!" cried Lawrence angrily. "In my opinion the whole thing is a mare's nest of Bauerstein's! Wilkins hadn't an idea of such a thing, until Bauerstein put it into his head. But, like all specialists, Bauerstein's got a bee in his bonnet. Poisons are his hobby, so of course he sees them everywhere."

I confess that I was surprised by Lawrence's attitude. He was so seldom vehement about anything.

John hesitated.

"I can't feel as you do, Lawrence," he said at last. "I'm inclined to give Hastings a free hand, though I should prefer to wait a bit. We don't want any unnecessary scandal."

"No, no," I cried eagerly, "you need have no fear of that. Poirot is discretion itself."

"Very well, then, have it your own way. I leave it in your hands. Though, if it is as we suspect, it seems a clear enough case. God forgive me if I am wronging him!"

I looked at my watch. It was six o'clock. I determined to lose no time.

Five minutes' delay, however, I allowed myself. I spent it in ransacking the library until I discovered a medical book which gave a description of strychnine poisoning.

IV

POIROT INVESTIGATES

The house which the Belgians occupied in the village was quite close to the park gates. One could save time by taking a narrow path through the long grass, which cut off the detours of the winding drive. So I, accordingly, went that way. I had nearly reached the lodge, when my attention was arrested by the running figure of a man approaching me. It was Mr. Inglethorp. Where had he been? How did he intend to explain his absence?

He accosted me eagerly.

"My God! This is terrible! My poor wife! I have only just heard."

"Where have you been?" I asked.

"Denby kept me late last night. It was one o'clock before we'd finished. Then I found that I'd forgotten the latch-key after all. I didn't want to arouse the household, so Denby gave me a bed."

"How did you hear the news?" I asked.

"Wilkins knocked Denby up to tell him. My poor Emily! She was so self-sacrificing—such a noble character. She overtaxed her strength."

A wave of revulsion swept over me. What a consummate hypocrite the man was!

"I must hurry on," I said, thankful that he did not ask me whither I was bound.

In a few minutes I was knocking at the door of Leastways Cottage.

Getting no answer, I repeated my summons impatiently. A window above me was cautiously opened, and Poirot himself looked out.

He gave an exclamation of surprise at seeing me. In a few brief words, I explained the tragedy that had occurred, and that I wanted his help.

"Wait, my friend, I will let you in, and you shall recount to me the affair whilst I dress."

In a few moments he had unbarred the door, and I followed him up to his room. There he installed me in a chair, and I related the whole story, keeping back nothing, and omitting no circumstance, however insignificant, whilst he himself made a carcful and deliberate toilet.

I told him of my awakening, of Mrs. Inglethorp's dying words, of her husband's absence, of the quarrel the day before, of the scrap of conversation between Mary and her mother-in-law that I had overheard, of the former quarrel between Mrs. Inglethorp and Evelyn Howard, and of the latter's innuendoes.

I was hardly as clear as I could wish. I repeated myself several times, and occasionally had to go back to some detail that I had forgotten. Poirot smiled kindly on me.

"The mind is confused? Is it not so? Take time, *mon ami.* You are agitated; you are excited—it is but natural. Presently, when we are calmer, we will arrange the facts, neatly, each in his proper place. We will examine—and reject. Those of importance we will put on one side; those of no importance, poof!"—he screwed up his cherub-like face, and puffed comically enough—"blow them away!"

"That's all very well," I objected, "but how are you going to decide what is important, and what isn't. That always seems the difficulty to me."

Poirot shook his head energetically. He was now arranging his moustache with exquisite care.

"Not so. *Voyons!* One fact leads to another—so we continue. Does the next fit in with that? *A merville!* Good! We can proceed. This next little fact—no! Ah, that is curious! There is something missing—a link in the chain that is not there. We examine. We search. And that little curious fact, that possibly paltry little detail that will not tally, we put it here!" He made an extravagant gesture with his hand. "It is significant! It is tremendous!"

"Y—es—"

"Ah!" Poirot shook his forefinger so fiercely at me that I quailed before it. "Beware! Peril to the detective who says: 'It is so small—it does not matter. It will not agree. I will forget it.' That way lies confusion! Everything matters."

"I know. You always told me that. That's why I have gone into all the details of this thing whether they seemed to me relevant or not."

"And I am pleased with you. You have a good memory, and you have given me the facts faithfully. Of the order in which you present them, I say nothing—truly, it is deplorable! But I make allowances—you are upset. To that I attribute the circumstance that you have omitted one fact of paramount importance."

"What is that?" I asked.

"You have not told me if Mrs. Inglethorp ate well last night."

I stared at him. Surely the war had affected the little man's brain. He was carefully engaged in brushing his coat before putting it on, and seemed wholly engrossed in the task.

"I don't remember," I said. "And, anyway, I don't see——"

"You do not see? But it is of the first importance."

"I can't see why," I said, rather nettled. "As far as I can remember, she didn't eat much. She was obviously upset, and it had taken her appetite away. That was only natural."

"Yes," said Poirot thoughtfully, "it was only natural."

He opened a drawer, and took out a small despatch-case, then turned to me.

"Now I am ready. We will proceed to the château, and study matters on the spot. Excuse me, *mon ami*, you dressed in haste, and your tie is on one side. Permit me." With a deft gesture, he rearranged it.

"*Ça y est!* Now, shall we start?"

We hurried up the village, and turned in at the lodge gates. Poirot stopped for a moment, and gazed sorrowfully over the beautiful expanse of park, still glittering with morning dew.

"So beautiful, so beautiful, and yet, the poor family, plunged in sorrow, prostrated with grief."

He looked at me keenly as he spoke, and I was aware that I reddened under his prolonged gaze.

Was the family prostrated by grief? Was the sorrow at Mrs. Inglethorp's death so great? I realized that there was an emotional lack in the atmosphere. The dead woman had not the gift of commanding love. Her death was a shock and a distress, but she would not be passionately regretted.

Poirot seemed to follow my thoughts. He nodded his head gravely.

"No, you are right," he said, "it is not as though there was a blood tie. She has been kind and generous to these Cavendishes, but she was not their own mother. Blood tells— always remember that—blood tells."

"Poirot," I said, "I wish you would tell me why you wanted to know if Mrs. Inglethorp ate well last night? I have been turning it over in my mind, but I can't see how it has anything to do with the matter."

He was silent for a minute or two as we walked along, but finally, he said:

"I do not mind telling you—though, as you know, it is not my habit to explain until the end is reached. The present contention is that Mrs. Inglethorp died of strychnine poisoning, presumably administered in her coffee."

"Yes?"

"Well, what time was the coffee served?"

"About eight o'clock."

"Therefore she drank it between then and half-past eight— certainly not much later. Well, strychnine is a fairly rapid poison. Its effects would be felt very soon, probably in about an hour. Yet, in Mrs. Inglethorp's case, the symptoms do not manifest themselves until five o'clock the next morning: nine hours! But a heavy meal, taken at about the same time as the poison, might retard its effects, though hardly to that extent. Still, it is a possibility to be taken into account. But, according to you, she ate very little for supper, and yet the symptoms do not develop until early the next morning! Now that is a curious circumstance, my friend. Something may arise at the autopsy to explain it. In the meantime, remember it."

As we neared the house, John came out and met us. His face looked weary and haggard.

"This is a very dreadful business, Monsieur Poirot," he said. "Hastings has explained to you that we are anxious for no publicity?"

"I comprehend perfectly."

"You see, it is only suspicion so far. We have nothing to go upon."

"Precisely. It is a matter of precaution only."

John turned to me, taking out his cigarette-case, and lighting a cigarette as he did so.

"You know that fellow Inglethorp is back?"

"Yes. I met him."

John flung the match into an adjacent flower bed, a proceeding which was too much for Poirot's feelings. He retrieved it, and buried it neatly.

"It's jolly difficult to know how to treat him."

"That difficulty will not exist long," pronounced Poirot quietly.

John looked puzzled, not quite understanding the portent of this cryptic saying. He handed the two keys which Dr. Bauerstein had given him to me.

"Show Monsieur Poirot everything he wants to see."

"The rooms are locked?" asked Poirot.

"Dr. Bauerstein considered it advisable."

Poirot nodded thoughtfully.

"Then he is very sure. Well, that simplifies matters for us."

We went up together to the room of the tragedy. For convenience I append a plan of the room and the principal articles of furniture in it.

Poirot locked the door on the inside, and proceeded to a minute inspection of the room. He darted from one object to the other with the agility of a grasshopper. I remained by the door, fearing to obliterate any clues. Poirot, however, did not seem grateful to me for my forbearance.

MRS. INGLETHORP'S BEDROOM
A.—Door into Passage
B.—Door into Mr. Inglethorp's Room
C.—Door into Cynthia's Room

"What have you, my friend," he cried, "that you remain there like—how do you say it?—ah, yes, the stuck pig?"

I explained that I was afraid of obliterating any foot-marks.

"Foot-marks? But what an idea! There has already been practically an army in the room! What foot-marks are we likely to find? No, come here and aid me in my search. I will put down my little case until I need it."

He did so, on the round table by the window, but it was an ill-advised proceeding; for, the top of it being loose, it tilted up, and precipitated the despatch-case on to the floor.

"En voilà une table!" cried Poirot. "Ah, my friend, one may live in a big house and yet have no comfort."

After which piece of moralizing, he resumed his search.

A small purple despatch-case, with a key in the lock, on the writing-table, engaged his attention for some time. He took out the key from the lock, and passed it to me to inspect. I saw nothing peculiar, however. It was an ordinary key of the Yale type, with a bit of twisted wire through the handle.

Next, he examined the framework of the door we had broken in, assuring himself that the bolt had really been shot. Then he went to the door opposite leading into Cynthia's room. That door was also bolted, as I had stated. However, he went to the length of unbolting it, and opening and shutting it several times; this he did with the utmost precaution against making any noise. Suddenly something in the bolt itself seemed to rivet his attention. He examined it carefully, and then, nimbly whipping out a pair of small forceps from his case, he drew out some minute particle which he carefully sealed up in a tiny envelope.

On the chest of drawers there was a tray with a spirit lamp and a small saucepan on it. A small quantity of a dark fluid remained in the saucepan, and an empty cup and saucer that had been drunk out of stood near it.

I wondered how I could have been so unobservant as to overlook this. Here was a clue worth having. Poirot delicately dipped his finger into the liquid, and tasted it gingerly. He made a grimace.

"Coco—with—I think—rum in it."

He passed on to the debris on the floor, where the table by the bed had been overturned. A reading-lamp, some books, matches, a bunch of keys, and the crushed fragments of a coffee-cup lay scattered about.

"Ah, this is curious," said Poirot.

"I must confess that I see nothing particularly curious about it."

"You do not? Observe the lamp—the chimney is broken in two places; they lie there as they fell. But see, the coffee cup is absolutely smashed to powder."

"Well," I said wearily, "I suppose some one must have stepped on it."

"Exactly," said Poirot, in an odd voice. "Some one stepped on it."

He rose from his knees, and walked slowly across to the mantelpiece, where he stood abstractedly fingering the ornaments, and straightening them—a trick of his when he was agitated.

"Mon ami," he said, turning to me, "somebody stepped on

that cup, grinding it to powder, and the reason they did so was either because it contained strychnine or—which is far more serious—because it did not contain strychnine!"

I made no reply. I was bewildered, but I knew that it was no good asking him to explain. In a moment or two he roused himself, and went on with his investigations. He picked up the bunch of keys from the floor; and twirling them round in his fingers finally selected one, very bright and shining, which he tried in the lock of the purple despatch-case. It fitted, and he opened the box, but after a moment's hesitation, closed and relocked it, and slipped the bunch of keys, as well as the key that had originally stood in the lock, into his own pocket.

"I have no authority to go through these papers. But it should be done—at once!"

He then made a very careful examination of the drawers of the wash-stand. Crossing the room to the left-hand window, a round stain, hardly visible on the dark brown carpet, seemed to interest him particularly. He went down on his knees, examining it minutely—even going so far as to smell it.

Finally, he poured a few drops of the coco into a test tube, sealing it up carefully. His next proceeding was to take out a little notebook.

"We have found in this room," he said, writing busily, "six points of interest. Shall I enumerate them, or will you?"

"Oh, you," I replied hastily.

"Very well, then. One, a coffee-cup that has been ground into powder; two, a despatch-case with a key in the lock; three, a stain on the floor."

"That may have been done some time ago," I interrupted.

"No, for it is still perceptibly damp and smells of coffee. Four, a fragment of some dark green fabric—only a thread or two, but recognizable."

"Ah!" I cried. "That was what you sealed up in the envelope."

"Yes. It may turn out to be a piece of one of Mrs. Inglethorp's own dresses, and quite unimportant. We shall see. Five, *this*!" With a dramatic gesture, he pointed to a large splash of candle grease on the floor by the writing-table. "It must have been done since yesterday, otherwise a good housemaid would have at once removed it with blotting-paper and a hot iron. One of my best hats once—but that is not to the point.

"It was very likely done last night. We were very agitated. Or perhaps Mrs. Inglethorp herself dropped her candle."

"You brought only one candle into the room?"

"Yes. Lawrence Cavendish was carrying it. But he was very upset. He seemed to see something over here"—I indicated the mantelpiece—"that absolutely paralysed him."

"That is interesting," said Poirot quickly. "Yes, it is suggestive"—his eye sweeping the whole length of the wall—"but it was not his candle that made this great patch, for you perceive that this is white grease; whereas Monsieur Lawrence's candle, which is still on the dressing-table, is pink. On the other hand, Mrs. Inglethorp had no candlestick in the room, only a reading-lamp."

"Then," I said, "what do you deduce?"

To which my friend only made a rather irritating reply, urging me to use my own natural faculties.

"And the sixth point?" I asked. "I suppose it is the sample of coco."

"No," said Poirot thoughtfully, "I might have included that in the six, but I did not. No, the sixth point I will keep to myself for the present."

He looked quickly round the room. "There is nothing more to be done here, I think, unless"—he stared earnestly and long at the dead ashes in the grate. "The fire burns—and it destroys. But by chance—there might be—let us see!"

Deftly, on hands and knees, he began to sort the ashes from the grate into the fender, handling them with the greatest caution. Suddenly, he gave a faint exclamation.

"The forceps, Hastings!"

I quickly handed them to him, and with skill he extracted a small piece of half charred paper.

"There, *mon ami!*" he cried. "What do you think of that?"

I scrutinized the fragment. This is an exact reproduction of it:

I was puzzled. It was unusually thick, quite unlike ordinary notepaper. Suddenly an idea struck me.

"Poirot!" I cried. "This is a fragment of a will!"

"Exactly."

I looked up at him sharply.

"You are not surprised?"

"No," he said gravely, "I expected it."

I relinquished the piece of paper, and watched him put it away in his case, with the same methodical care that he bestowed on everything. My brain was in a whirl. What was this complication of a will? Who had destroyed it? The person who had left the candle grease on the floor? Obviously. But how had anyone gained admission? All the doors had been bolted on the inside.

"Now, my friend," said Poirot briskly, "we will go. I should like to ask a few questions of the parlourmaid—Dorcas, her name is, is it not?"

We passed through Alfred Inglethorp's room, and Poirot delayed long enough to make a brief but fairly comprehensive examination of it. We went out through that door, locking both it and that of Mrs. Inglethorp's room as before.

I took him down to the boudoir which he had expressed a wish to see, and went myself in search of Dorcas.

When I returned with her, however, the boudoir was empty.

"Poirot," I cried, "where are you?"

"I am here, my friend."

He had stepped outside the French window, and was standing, apparently, lost in admiration, before the various shaped flower beds.

"Admirable!" he murmured. "Admirable! What symmetry! Observe that crescent; and those diamonds—their neatness rejoices the eye. The spacing of the plans, also, is perfect. It has been recently done; is it not so?"

"Yes, I believe they were at it yesterday afternoon. But come in—Dorcas is here."

"*Eh bien, eh bien!* Do not grudge me a moment's satisfaction of the eye."

"Yes, but this affair is more important."

"And how do you know that these fine begonias are not of equal importance?"

I shrugged my shoulders. There was really no arguing with him if he chose to take that line.

"You do not agree? But such things have been. Well, we will come in and interview the brave Dorcas."

Dorcas was standing in the boudoir, her hands folded in front of her, and her grey hair rose in stiff waves under her white cap. She was the very model and picture of a good old-fashioned servant.

In her attitude towards Poirot, she was inclined to be suspicious, but he soon broke down her defences. He drew forward a chair.

"Pray be seated, mademoiselle."

"Thank you, sir."

"You have been with your mistress many years, is it not so?"

"Ten years, sir."

"That is a long time, and very faithful service. You were much attached to her, were you not?"

"She was a very good mistress to me, sir."

"Then you will not object to answering a few questions. I put them to you with Mr. Cavendish's full approval."

"Oh, certainly, sir."

"Then I will begin by asking you about the events of yesterday afternoon. Your mistress had a quarrel?"

"Yes, sir. But I don't know that I ought——" Dorcas hesitated.

Poirot looked at her keenly.

"My good Dorcas, it is necessary that I should know every detail of that quarrel as fully as possible. Do not think that you are betraying your mistress's secrets. Your mistress lies dead, and it is necessary that we should know all—if we are to avenge her. Nothing can bring her back to life, but we do hope, if there has been foul play, to bring the murderer to justice."

"Amen to that," said Dorcas fiercely. "And, naming no names, there's *one* in this house that none of us could ever abide! And an ill day it was when first *he* darkened the threshold."

Poirot waited for her indignation to subside, and then, resuming his business-like tone, he asked:

"Now, as to this quarrel? What is the first you heard of it?"

"Well, sir, I happened to be going along the hall outside yesterday——"

"What time was that?"

"I couldn't say exactly, sir, but it wasn't teatime by a long way. Perhaps four o'clock—or it may have been a bit later. Well, sir, as I said, I happened to be passing along, when I heard voices very loud and angry in here. I didn't exactly mean to listen, but—well, there it is. I stopped. The door was shut, but the mistress was speaking very sharp and clear, and I heard what she said quite plainly. 'You have lied to me, and deceived me,' she said. I didn't hear what Mr. Inglethorp replied. He spoke a good bit lower than she did— but she answered: 'How dare you? I have kept you and clothed you and fed you! You owe everything to me! And this is how you repay me! By bringing disgrace upon our name!' Again I didn't hear what he said, but she went on: 'Nothing that you can say will make any difference. I see my duty clearly. My mind is made up. You need not think that any fear of publicity or scandal between husband and wife will deter me.' Then I thought I heard them coming out, so I went off quickly."

"You are sure it was Mr. Inglethorp's voice you heard?"

"Oh, yes, sir, whose else's could it be?"

"Well, what happened next?"

"Later, I came back to the hall; but it was all quiet. At five o'clock, Mrs. Inglethorp rang the bell and told me to bring her a cup of tea—nothing to eat—to the boudoir. She was looking dreadful—so white and upset. 'Dorcas,' she says, 'I've had a great shock.' 'I'm sorry for that, m'm,' I says. 'You'll feel better after a nice hot cup of tea, m'm.' She had something in her hand. I don't know if it was a letter, or just a piece of paper, but it had writing on it, and she kept staring at it, almost as if she couldn't believe what was written there. She whispered to herself, as though she had forgotten I was there: 'These few words—and everything's changed.' And then she says to me: 'Never trust a man, Dorcas, they're not worth it!' I hurried off, and got her a good strong cup of tea, and she thanked me, and said she'd feel better when she'd drunk it. 'I don't know what to do,' she says. 'Scandal between husband and wife is a dreadful thing, Dorcas. I'd rather hush it up if I could.' Mrs. Cavendish came in just then, so she didn't say any more."

"She still had the letter, or whatever it was, in her hand?"

"Yes, sir."

"What would she be likely to do with it afterwards?"

"Well, I don't know, sir, I expect she would lock it up in that purple case of hers."

"Is that where she usually kept important papers?"

"Yes, sir. She brought it down with her every morning, and took it up every night."

"When did she lose the key of it?"

"She missed it yesterday at lunch-time, sir, and told me to look carefully for it. She was very much put out about it."

"But she had a duplicate key?"

"Oh, yes, sir."

Dorcas was looking very curiously at him and, to tell the truth, so was I. What was all this about a lost key? Poirot smiled.

"Never mind, Dorcas, it is my business to know things. Is this the key that was lost?" He drew from his pocket the key that he had found in the lock of the despatch-case upstairs.

Dorcas's eyes looked as though they would pop out of her head.

"That's it, sir, right enough. But where did you find it? I looked everywhere for it."

"Ah, but you see it was not in the same place yesterday as it was today. Now, to pass to another subject, had your mistress a dark green dress in her wardrobe?"

Dorcas was rather startled by the unexpected question.

"No, sir."

"Are you quite sure?"

"Oh, yes, sir."

"Has anyone else in the house got a green dress?"

Dorcas reflected.

"Miss Cynthia has a green evening dress."

"Light or dark green?"

"A light green, sir; a sort of chiffon, they call it."

"Ah, that is not what I want. And nobody else has anything green?"

"No, sir—not that I know of."

Poirot's face did not betray a trace of whether he was disappointed or otherwise. He merely remarked:

"Good, we will leave that and pass on. Have you any reason to believe that your mistress was likely to take a sleeping powder last night?"

"Not *last* night, sir, I know she didn't."

"Why do you know so positively?"

"Because the box was empty. She took the last one two days ago, and she didn't have any more made up."

"You are quite sure of that?"

"Positive, sir."

"Then that is cleared up! By the way, your mistress didn't ask you to sign any paper yesterday?"

"To sign a paper? No, sir."

"When Mr. Hastings and Mr. Lawrence came in yesterday evening, they found your mistress busy writing letters. I suppose you can give me no idea to whom these letters were addressed?"

"I'm afraid I couldn't, sir. I was out in the evening. Perhaps Annie could tell you, though she's a careless girl. Never cleared the coffee cups away last night. That's what happens when I'm not here to look after things."

Poirot lifted his hand.

"Since they have been left, Dorcas, leave them a little longer, I pray you. I should like to examine them."

"Very well, sir."

"What time did you go out last evening?"

"About six o'clock, sir."

"Thank you, Dorcas, that is all I have to ask you." He rose and strolled to the window. "I have been admiring these flower beds. How many gardeners are employed here, by the way?"

"Only three now, sir. Five, we had, before the war, when it was kept as a gentleman's place should be. I wish you could have seen it then, sir. A fair sight it was. But now there's only old Manning, and young William, and a new-fashioned woman gardener in breeches and such-like. Ah, these are dreadful times!"

"The good times will come again, Dorcas. At least, we hope so. Now, will you send Annie to me here?"

"Yes, sir. Thank you, sir."

"How did you know that Mrs. Inglethorp took sleeping powders?" I asked, in lively curiosity, as Dorcas left the room. "And about the lost key and the duplicate?"

"One thing at a time. As to the sleeping powders, I knew by this." He suddenly produced a small cardboard box, such as chemists use for powders.

"Where did you find it?"

"In the wash-stand drawer in Mrs. Inglethorp's bedroom. It was Number Six of my catalogue."

"But I suppose, as the last powder was taken two days ago, it is not of much importance?"

"Probably not, but do you notice anything that strikes you as peculiar about this box?"

I examined it closely.

"No, I can't say that I do."

"Look at the label."

I read the label carefully: " 'One powder to be taken at bedtime, if required. Mrs. Inglethorp.' No, I see nothing unusual."

"Not the fact that there is no chemist's name?"

"Ah!" I exclaimed. "To be sure, that is odd!"

"Have you ever known a chemist to send out a box like that, without his printed name?"

"No, I can't say that I have."

I was becoming quite excited, but Poirot damped my ardour by remarking:

"Yet the explanation is quite simple. So do not intrigue yourself, my friend."

An audible creaking proclaimed the approach of Annie, so I had no time to reply.

Annie was a fine, strapping girl, and was evidently labouring under intense excitement, mingled with a certain ghoulish enjoyment of the tragedy.

Poirot came to the point at once, with a business-like briskness.

"I sent for you, Annie, because I thought you might be able to tell me something about the letters Mrs. Inglethorp wrote last night. How many were there? And can you tell me any of the names and addresses?"

Annie considered.

"There were four letters, sir. One was to Miss Howard, and one was to Mr. Wells, the lawyer, and the other two I don't think I remember, sir—oh, yes, one was to Ross's, the caterers in Tadminster. The other one, I don't remember."

"Think," urged Poirot.

Annie racked her brains in vain.

"I'm sorry, sir, but it's clean gone. I don't think I can have noticed it."

"It does not matter," said Poirot, not betraying any sign of disappointment. "Now I want to ask you about something else. There is a saucepan in Mrs. Inglethorp's room with some coco in it. Did she have that every night?"

"Yes, sir, it was put in her room every evening, and she warmed it up in the night—whenever she fancied it."

"What was it? Plain coco?"

"Yes, sir, made with milk, with a teaspoonful of sugar, and two teaspoonfuls of rum in it."

"Who took it to her room?"

"I did, sir."

"Always?"

"Yes, sir."

"At what time?"

"When I went to draw the curtains, as a rule, sir."

"Did you bring it straight up from the kitchen then?"

"No, sir, you see there's not much room on the gas stove, so Cook used to make it early, before putting the vegetables on for supper. Then I used to bring it up, and put it on the table by the swing door, and take it into her room later."

"The swing door is in the left wing, is it not?"

"Yes, sir."

"And the table, is it on this side of the door, or on the farther—servants' side?"

"It's this side, sir."

"What time did you bring it up last night?"

"About quarter-past seven, I should say, sir."

"And when did you take it into Mrs. Inglethorp's room?"

"When I went to shut up, sir. About eight o'clock. Mrs. Inglethorp came up to bed before I'd finished."

"Then, between 7:15 and 8 o'clock, the coco was standing on the table in the left wing?"

"Yes, sir." Annie had been growing redder and redder in the face, and now she blurted out unexpectedly:

"And if there *was* salt in it, sir, it wasn't me. I never took the salt near it."

"What makes you think there was salt in it?" asked Poirot.

"Seeing it on the tray, sir."

"You saw some salt on the tray?"

"Yes. Coarse kitchen salt, it looked. I never noticed it when I took the tray up, but when I came to take it into the mistress's room I saw it at once, and I suppose I ought to have taken it down again, and asked Cook to make some fresh. But I was in a hurry, because Dorcas was out, and I thought maybe the coco itself was all right, and the salt had only gone on the tray. So I dusted it off with my apron, and took it in."

I had the utmost difficulty in controlling my excitement. Unknown to herself, Annie had provided us with an important piece of evidence. How she would have gaped if she had realized that her "coarse kitchen salt" was strychnine, one of the most deadly poisons known to mankind. I marvelled at Poirot's calm. His self-control was astonishing. I awaited his next question with impatience, but it disappointed me.

"When you went into Mrs. Inglethorp's room, was the door leading into Miss Cynthia's room bolted?"

"Oh! Yes, sir; it always was. It had never been opened."

"And the door into Mr. Inglethorp's room? Did you notice if that was bolted too?"

Annie hesitated.

"I couldn't rightly say, sir; it was shut but I couldn't say whether it was bolted or not."

"When you finally left the room, did Mrs. Inglethorp bolt the door after you?"

"No, sir, not then, but I expect she did later. She usually did lock it at night. The door into the passage, that is."

"Did you notice any candle grease on the floor when you did the room yesterday?"

"Candle grease? Oh, no, sir. Mrs. Inglethorp didn't have a candle, only a reading-lamp."

"Then, if there had been a large patch of candle grease on the floor, you think you would have been sure to have seen it?"

"Yes, sir, and I would have taken it out with a piece of blotting-paper and a hot iron."

Then Poirot repeated the question he had put to Dorcas:

"Did your mistress ever have a green dress?"

"No, sir."

"Nor a mantle, nor a cape, nor a—how do you call it?—a sports coat?"

"Not green, sir."

"Nor anyone else in the house?"

Annie reflected.

"No, sir."

"You are sure of that?"

"Quite sure."

"*Bien!* That is all I want to know. Thank you very much."

With a nervous giggle, Annie took herself creakingly out of the room. My pent up excitement burst forth.

"Poirot," I cried, "I congratulate you! This is a great discovery."

"What is a great discovery?"

"Why, that it was the coco and not the coffee that was poisoned. That explains everything! Of course it did not take effect until the early morning, since the coco was only drunk in the middle of the night."

"So you think that the coco—mark well what I say, Hastings, the *coco*—contained strychnine?"

"Of course! That salt on the tray, what else could it have been?"

"It might have been salt," replied Poirot placidly.

I shrugged my shoulders. If he was going to take the matter that way, it was no good arguing with him. The idea crossed my mind, not for the first time, that poor old Poirot was growing old. Privately I thought it lucky that he had associated with him some one of a more receptive type of mind.

Poirot was surveying me with quietly twinkling eyes.

"You are not pleased with me, *mon ami?*"

"My dear Poirot," I said coldly, "it is not for me to dictate to you. You have a right to your own opinion, just as I have to mine."

"A most admirable sentiment," remarked Poirot, rising briskly to his feet. "Now I have finished with this room. By the way, whose is the smaller desk in the corner?"

"Mr. Inglethorp's."

"Ah!" He tried the roll top tentatively. "Locked. But perhaps one of Mrs. Inglethorp's keys would open it." He tried several, twisting and turning them with a practised hand, and finally uttering an ejaculation of satisfaction. "*Voilà!* It is not the key, but it will open it at a pinch." He slid back the roll top, and ran a rapid eye over the neatly filed papers. To my surprise, he did not examine them, merely remarking approvingly as he relocked the desk: "Decidedly, he is a man of method, this Mr. Inglethorp!"

A "man of method" was, in Poirot's estimation, the highest praise that could be bestowed on any individual.

I felt that my friend was not what he had been as he rambled on disconnectedly:

"There were no stamps in his desk, but there might have been, eh, *mon ami?* There might have been? Yes"—his eyes wandered round the room—"this boudoir has nothing more to tell us. It did not yield much. Only this."

He pulled a crumpled envelope out of his pocket, and tossed it over to me. It was rather a curious document. A plain, dirty looking old envelope with a few words scrawled across it, apparently at random. The following is a facsimile of it:

possessed

I am possessed

He is possessed

I am possessed

possessed

V

"It Isn't Strychnine, Is It?"

"Where did you find this?" I asked Poirot, in lively curiosity.

"In the waste-paper basket. You recognise the handwriting?"

"Yes, it is Mrs. Inglethorp's. But what does it mean?"

Poirot shrugged his shoulders.

"I cannot say—but it is suggestive."

A wild idea flashed across me. Was it possible that Mrs. Inglethorp's mind was deranged? Had she some fantastic idea of demoniacal possession? And, if that were so, was it not also possible that she might have taken her own life?

I was about to expound these theories to Poirot, when his own words distracted me.

"Come," he said, "now to examine the coffee cups!"

"My dear Poirot! What on earth is the good of that, now that we know about the coco?"

"Oh, *là là!* That miserable coco!" cried Poirot flippantly.

He laughed with apparent enjoyment, raising his arms to heaven in mock despair, in what I could not but consider the worst possible taste.

"And, anyway," I said, with increasing coldness, "as Mrs. Inglethorp took her coffee upstairs with her, I do not see what you expect to find, unless you consider it likely that we shall discover a packet of strychnine on the coffee tray!"

Poirot was sobered at once.

"Come, come, my friend," he said, slipping his arm through mine. "*Ne vous fâchez pas!* Allow me to interest myself in my coffee cups, and I will respect your coco. There! Is it a bargain?"

He was so quaintly humorous that I was forced to laugh; and we went together to the drawing-room, where the coffee cups and tray remained undisturbed as we had left them.

Poirot made me recapitulate the scene of the night before, listening very carefully, and verifying the position of the various cups.

"So Mrs. Cavendish stood by the tray—and poured out. Yes. Then she came across to the window where you sat with Mademoiselle Cynthia. Yes. Here are the three cups. And the cup on the mantel-piece, half drunk, that would be Mr. Lawrence Cavendish's. And the one on the tray?"

"John Cavendish's. I saw him put it down there."

"Good. One, two, three, four, five—but where, then, is the cup of Mr. Inglethorp?"

"He does not take coffee."

"Then all are accounted for. One moment, my friend."

With infinite care, he took a drop or two from the grounds in each cup, sealing them up in separate test tubes, tasting each in turn as he did so. His physiognomy underwent a curious change. An expression gathered there that I can only describe as half puzzled, and half relieved.

"*Bien!*" he said at last. "It is evident! I had an idea—but clearly I was mistaken. Yes, altogether I was mistaken. Yet it is strange. But no matter!"

And, with a characteristic shrug, he dismissed whatever it was that was worrying him from his mind. I could have told him from the beginning that this obsession of his over the coffee was bound to end in a blind alley, but I restrained my tongue. After all, though he was old, Poirot had been a great man in his day.

"Breakfast is ready," said John Cavendish, coming in from the hall. "You will breakfast with us, Monsieur Poirot?"

Poirot acquiesced. I observed John. Already he was almost restored to his normal self. The shock of the events of the last night had upset him temporarily, but his equable poise soon swung back to the normal. He was a man of very little imagination, in sharp contrast with his brother, who had, perhaps, too much.

Ever since the early hours of the morning, John had been hard at work, sending telegrams—one of the first had gone to Evelyn Howard—writing notices for the papers, and generally occupying himself with the melancholy duties that a death entails.

"May I ask how things are proceeding?" he said. "Do your investigations point to my mother having died a natural death—or—or must we prepare ourselves for the worst?"

"I think, Mr. Cavendish," said Poirot gravely, "that you would do well not to buoy yourself up with any false hopes. Can you tell me the views of the other members of the family?"

"My brother Lawrence is convinced that we are making a fuss over nothing. He says that everything points to its being a simple case of heart failure."

"He does, does he? That is very interesting—very interesting," murmured Poirot softly. "And Mrs. Cavendish?"

A faint cloud passed over John's face.

"I have not the least idea what my wife's views on the subject are."

The answer brought a momentary stiffness in its train. John broke the rather awkward silence by saying with a slight effort:

"I told you, didn't I, that Mr. Inglethorp has returned?"

Poirot bent his head.

"It's an awkward position for all of us. Of course one has to treat him as usual—but, hang it all, one's gorge does rise at sitting down to eat with a possible murderer!"

Poirot nodded sympathetically.

"I quite understand. It is a very difficult situation for you, Mr. Cavendish. I would like to ask you one question. Mr. Inglethorp's reason for not returning last night was, I believe, that he had forgotten the latch-key. Is that not so?"

"Yes."

"I suppose you are quite sure that the latch-key *was* for-gotten—that he did not take it after all?"

"I have no idea. I never thought of looking. We always keep it in the hall drawer. I'll go and see if it's there now."

Poirot held up his hand with a faint smile.

"No, no, Mr. Cavendish, it is too late now. I am certain that you would find it. If Mr. Inglethorp did take it, he has had ample time to replace it by now."

"But do you think—"

"I think nothing. If anyone had chanced to look this morn-ing before his return, and seen it there, it would have been a valuable point in his favour. That is all."

John looked perplexed.

"Do not worry," said Poirot smoothly. "I assure you that you need not let it trouble you. Since you are so kind, let us go and have some breakfast."

Every one was assembled in the dining-room. Under the circumstances, we were naturally not a cheerful party. The reaction after a shock is always trying, and I think we were all suffering from it. Decorum and good breeding naturally enjoined that our demeanour should be much as usual, yet I could not help wondering if this self-control were really a matter of great difficulty. There were no red eyes, no signs of secretly indulged grief. I felt that I was right in my opinion that Dorcas was the person most affected by the personal side of the tragedy.

I pass over Alfred Inglethorp, who acted the bereaved wid-ower in a manner that I felt to be disgusting in its hypocrisy. Did he know that we suspected him, I wondered. Surely he could not be unaware of the fact, conceal it as we would. Did he feel some secret stirring of fear, or was he confident that his crime would go unpunished? Surely the suspicion in the atmosphere must warn him that he was already a marked man.

But did every one suspect him? What about Mrs. Caven-dish? I watched her as she sat at the head of the table, grace-ful, composed, enigmatic. In her soft grey frock, with white ruffles at the wrists falling over her slender hands, she looked very beautiful. When she chose, however, her face could be sphinx-like in its inscrutability. She was very silent, hardly opening her lips, and yet in some queer way I felt that the great strength of her personality was dominating us all.

And little Cynthia? Did she suspect? She looked very tired and ill, I thought. The heaviness and languor of her manner were very marked. I asked her if she were feeling ill, and she answered frankly:

"Yes, I've got the most beastly headache."

"Have another cup of coffee, mademoiselle?" said Poirot solicitously. "It will revive you. It is unparalleled for the *mal de tête.*" He jumped up and took her cup.

"No sugar," said Cynthia, watching him, as he picked up the sugar-tongs.

"No sugar? You abandon it in the war-time, eh?"

"No, I never take it in coffee."

"*Sacré!*" murmured Poirot to himself, as he brought back the replenished cup.

Only I heard him, and glancing up curiously at the little man I saw that his face was working with suppressed excitement, and his eyes were as green as a cat's. He had heard or seen something that had affected him strongly—but what was it? I do not usually label myself as dense, but I must confess that nothing out of the ordinary had attracted *my* attention.

In another moment, the door opened and Dorcas appeared.

"Mr. Wells to see you, sir," she said to John.

I remembered the name as being that of the lawyer to whom Mrs. Inglethorp had written the night before.

John rose immediately.

"Show him into my study." Then he turned to us. "My mother's lawyer," he explained. And in a lower voice: "He is also the Coroner—you understand. Perhaps you would like to come with me?"

We acquiesced and followed him out of the room. John strode on ahead and I took the opportunity of whispering to Poirot:

"There will be an inquest then?"

Poirot nodded absently. He seemed absorbed in thought; so much so that my curiosity was aroused.

"What is it? You are not attending to what I say."

"It is true, my friend. I am much worried."

"Why?"

"Because Mademoiselle Cynthia does not take sugar in her coffee."

"What? You cannot be serious?"

"But I am most serious. Ah, there is something there that I do not understand. My instinct was right."

"What instinct?"

"The instinct that led me to insist on examining those coffee cups. *Chut!* no more now!"

We followed John into his study, and he closed the door behind us.

Mr. Wells was a pleasant man of middle-age, with keen eyes, and the typical lawyer's mouth. John introduced us both, and explained the reason of our presence.

"You will understand, Wells," he added, "that this is all strictly private. We are still hoping that there will turn out to be no need for investigation of any kind."

"Quite so, quite so," said Mr. Wells soothingly. "I wish we could have spared you the pain and publicity of an inquest, but of course it's quite unavoidable in the absence of a doctor's certificate."

"Yes, I suppose so."

"Clever man, Bauerstein. Great authority on toxicology, I believe."

"Indeed," said John with a certain stiffness in his manner. Then he added rather hesitatingly: "Shall we have to appear as witnesses—all of us, I mean?"

"You, of course—and ah—er—Mr.—er—Inglethorp."

A slight pause ensued before the lawyer went on in his soothing manner:

"Any other evidence will be simply confirmatory, a mere matter of form."

"I see."

A faint expression of relief swept over John's face. It puzzled me, for I saw no occasion for it.

"If you know of nothing to the contrary," pursued Mr. Wells, "I had thought of Friday. That will give us plenty of time for the doctor's report. The post-mortem is to take place tonight, I believe?"

"Yes."

"Then that arrangement will suit you?"

"Perfectly."

"I need not tell you, my dear Cavendish, how distressed I am at this most tragic affair."

"Can you give us no help in solving it, monsieur?" interposed Poirot, speaking for the first time since we had entered the room.

"I?"

"Yes, we heard that Mrs. Inglethorp wrote to you last night. You should have received the letter this morning."

"I did, but it contains no information. It is merely a note asking me to call upon her this morning, as she wanted my advice on a matter of great importance."

"She gave you no hint as to what the matter might be?"

"Unfortunately, no."

"That is a pity," said John.

"A great pity," agreed Poirot gravely.

There was silence. Poirot remained lost in thought for a few minutes. Finally he turned to the lawyer again.

"Mr. Wells, there is one thing I should like to ask you— that is, if it is not against professional etiquette. In the event of Mrs. Inglethorp's death, who would inherit her money?"

The lawyer hesitated a moment, and then replied:

"The knowledge will be public property very soon, so if Mr. Cavendish does not object—"

"Not at all," interpolated John.

"I do not see any reason why I should not answer your question. By her last will, dated August of last year, after various unimportant legacies to servants, etc., she gave her entire fortune to her stepson, Mr. John Cavendish."

"Was not that—pardon the question, Mr. Cavendish— rather unfair to her other stepson, Mr. Lawrence Cavendish?"

"No, I do not think so. You see, under the terms of their father's will, while John inherited the property, Lawrence, at his stepmother's death, would come into a considerable sum of money. Mrs. Inglethorp left her money to her elder stepson, knowing that he would have to keep up Styles. It was, to my mind, a very fair and equitable distribution."

Poirot nodded thoughtfully.

"I see. But I am right in saying, am I not, that by your English law that will was automatically revoked when Mrs. Inglethorp remarried?"

Mr. Wells bowed his head.

"As I was about to proceed, Monsieur Poirot, that document is now null and void."

"*Hein!*" said Poirot. He reflected for a moment, and then asked: "Was Mrs. Inglethorp herself aware of that fact?"

"I do not know. She may have been."

"She was," said John unexpectedly. "We were discussing the matter of wills being revoked by marriage only yesterday."

"Ah! One more question, Mr. Wells. You say 'her last will.' Had Mrs. Inglethorp, then, made several former wills?"

"On an average, she made a new will at least once a year," said Mr. Wells imperturbably. "She was given to changing her mind as to her testamentary dispositions, now benefiting one, now another member of her family."

"Suppose," suggested Poirot, "that, unknown to you, she had made a new will in favour of some one who was not, in any sense of the word, a member of the family—we will say Miss Howard, for instance—would you be surprised?"

"Not in the least."

"Ah!" Poirot seemed to have exhausted his questions.

I drew close to him, while John and the lawyer were debating the question of going through Mrs. Inglethorp's papers.

"Do you think Mrs. Inglethorp made a will leaving all her money to Miss Howard?" I asked in a low voice, with some curiosity.

Poirot smiled.

"No."

"Then why did you ask?"

"Hush!"

John Cavendish had turned to Poirot.

"Will you come with us, Monsieur Poirot? We are going

through my mother's papers. Mr. Inglethorp is quite willing to leave it entirely to Mr. Wells and myself."

"Which simplifies matters very much," murmured the lawyer. "As technically, of course, he was entitled—" He did not finish the sentence.

"We will look through the desk in the boudoir first," explained John, "and go up to her bedroom afterwards. She kept her most important papers in a purple despatch-case, which we must look through carefully."

"Yes," said the lawyer, "it is quite possible that there may be a later will than the one in my possession."

"There *is* a later will." It was Poirot who spoke.

"What?" John and the lawyer looked at him startled.

"Or, rather," pursued my friend imperturbably, "there *was* one."

"What do you mean—there was one? Where is it now?"

"Burnt!"

"Burnt?"

"Yes. See here." He took out the charred fragment we had found in the grate in Mrs. Inglethorp's room, and handed it to the lawyer with a brief explanation of when and where he had found it.

"But possibly this is an old will?"

"I do not think so. In fact I am almost certain that it was made no earlier than yesterday afternoon."

"What?" "Impossible!" broke simultaneously from both men.

Poirot turned to John.

"If you will allow me to send for your gardener, I will prove it to you."

"Oh, of course—but I don't see—"

Poirot raised his hand.

"Do as I ask you. Afterwards you shall question as much as you please."

"Very well." He rang the bell.

Dorcas answered it in due course.

"Dorcas, will you tell Manning to come round and speak to me here."

"Yes, sir."

Dorcas withdrew.

We waited in a tense silence. Poirot alone seemed perfectly at his ease, and dusted a forgotten corner of the bookcase.

The clumping of hobnailed boots on the gravel outside proclaimed the approach of Manning. John looked questioningly at Poirot. The latter nodded.

"Come inside, Manning," said John, "I want to speak to you."

Manning came slowly and hesitatingly through the French window, and stood as near it as he could. He held his cap in his hands, twisting it very carefully round and round. His back was much bent, though he was probably not as old as he looked, but his eyes were sharp and intelligent, and belied his slow and rather cautious speech.

"Manning," said John, "this gentleman will put some questions to you which I want you to answer."

"Yessir," mumbled Manning.

Poirot stepped forward briskly. Manning's eye swept over him with a faint contempt.

"You were planting a bed of begonias round by the south side of the house yesterday afternoon, were you not, Manning?"

"Yes, sir, me and Willum."

"And Mrs. Inglethorp came to the window and called you, did she not?"

"Yes, sir, she did."

"Tell me in your own words exactly what happened after that."

"Well, sir, nothing much. She just told Willum to go on his bicycle down to the village, and bring back a form of will, or such-like—I don't know what exactly—she wrote it down for him."

"Well?"

"Well, he did, sir."

"And what happened next?"

"We went on with the begonias, sir."

"Did not Mrs. Inglethorp call you again?"

"Yes, sir, both me and Willum, she called."

"And then?"

"She made us come right in, and sign our names at the bottom of a long paper—under where she'd signed."

"Did you see anything of what was written above her signature?" asked Poirot sharply.

"No, sir, there was a bit of blotting paper over that part."

"And you signed where she told you?"

"Yes, sir, first me and then Willum."

"What did she do with it afterwards?"

"Well, sir, she slipped it into a long envelope, and put it inside a sort of purple box that was standing on the desk."

"What time was it when she first called you?"

"About four, I should say, sir."

"Not earlier? Couldn't it have been about half-past three?"

"No, I shouldn't say so, sir. It would be more likely to be a bit after four—not before it."

"Thank you, Manning, that will do," said Poirot pleasantly.

The gardener glanced at his master, who nodded, whereupon Manning lifted a finger to his forehead with a low mumble, and backed cautiously out of the window.

We all looked at each other.

"Good heavens!" murmured John. "What an extraordinary coincidence."

"How—a coincidence?"

"That my mother should have made a will on the very day of her death!"

Mr. Wells cleared his throat and remarked drily:

"Are you so sure it is a coincidence, Cavendish?"

"What do you mean?"

"Your mother, you tell me, had a violent quarrel with—some one yesterday afternoon—"

"What do you mean?" cried John again. There was a tremor in his voice, and he had gone very pale.

"In consequence of that quarrel, your mother very suddenly and hurriedly makes a new will. The contents of that will we shall never know. She told no one of its provisions. This morning, no doubt, she would have consulted me on the subject—but she had no chance. The will disappears, and she takes its secret with her to her grave. Cavendish, I much fear there is no coincidence there. Monsieur Poirot, I am sure you agree with me that the facts are very suggestive."

"Suggestive, or not," interrupted John, "we are most grateful to Monsieur Poirot for elucidating the matter. But for him, we should never have known of this will. I suppose, I may not ask you, monsieur, what first led you to suspect the fact?"

Poirot smiled and answered:

"A scribbled over old envelope, and a freshly planted bed of begonias."

John, I think, would have pressed his questions further, but at that moment the loud purr of a motor was audible, and we all turned to the windows as it swept past.

"Evie!" cried John. "Excuse me, Wells." He went hurriedly out into the hall.

Poirot looked inquiringly at me.

"Miss Howard," I explained.

"Ah, I am glad she has come. There is a woman with a head and a heart too, Hastings. Though the good God gave her no beauty!"

I followed John's example, and went out into the hall, where Miss Howard was endeavouring to extricate herself from the voluminous mass of veils that enveloped her head. As her eyes fell on me, a sudden pang of guilt shot through me. This was the woman who had warned me so earnestly, and to whose warning I had, alas, paid no heed! How soon, and how contemptuously, I had dismissed it from my mind. Now that she had been proved justified in so tragic a manner, I felt ashamed. She had known Alfred Inglethorp only too well. I wondered whether, if she had remained at Styles, the tragedy would have taken place, or would the man have feared her watchful eyes?

I was relieved when she shook me by the hand, with her well remembered painful grip. The eyes that met mine were sad, but not reproachful; that she had been crying bitterly, I could tell by the redness of her eyelids, but her manner was unchanged from its old blunt gruffness.

"Started the moment I got the wire. Just come off night duty. Hired car. Quickest way to get here."

"Have you had anything to eat this morning, Evie?" asked John.

"No."

"I thought not. Come along, breakfast not cleared away yet, and they'll make you some fresh tea." He turned to me. "Look after her, Hastings, will you? Wells is waiting for me. Oh, here's Monsieur Poirot. He's helping us, you know, Evie."

Miss Howard shook hands with Poirot, but glanced suspiciously over her shoulder at John.

"What do you mean—helping us?"

"Helping us to investigate."

"Nothing to investigate. Have they taken him to prison yet?"

"Taken who to prison?"

"Who? Alfred Inglethorp, of course!"

"My dear Evie, do be careful. Lawrence is of the opinion that my mother died from heart seizure."

"More fool, Lawrence!" retorted Miss Howard. "Of course Alfred Inglethorp murdered poor Emily—as I always told you he would."

"My dear Evie, don't shout so. Whatever we may think or suspect, it is better to say as little as possible for the present. The inquest isn't until Friday."

"Not until fiddlesticks!" The snort Miss Howard gave was truly magnificent. "You're all off your heads. The man will be out of the country by then. If he's any sense, he won't stay here tamely and wait to be hanged."

John Cavendish looked at her helplessly.

"I know what it is," she accused him, "you've been listening to the doctors. Never should. What do they know? Nothing at all—or just enough to make them dangerous. I ought to know—my own father was a doctor. That little Wilkins is about the greatest fool that even I have ever seen. Heart seizure! Sort of thing he would say. Anyone with any sense could see at once that her husband had poisoned her. I always said he'd murder her in her bed, poor soul. Now he's done it. And all you can do is to murmur silly things about 'heart seizure' and 'inquest on Friday.' You ought to be ashamed of yourself, John Cavendish."

"What do you want me to do?" asked John, unable to help a faint smile. "Dash it all, Evie, I can't haul him down to the local police station by the scruff of his neck."

"Well, you might do something. Find out how he did it. He's a crafty beggar. Dare say he soaked fly papers. Ask Cook if she's missed any."

It occurred to me very forcibly at that moment that to harbour Miss Howard and Alfred Inglethorp under the same roof, and keep the peace between them, was likely to prove a Herculean task, and I did not envy John. I could see by the expression on his face that he fully appreciated the difficulty of the position. For the moment, he sought refuge in retreat, and left the room precipitately.

Dorcas brought in fresh tea. As she left the room, Poirot came over from the window where he had been standing, and sat down facing Miss Howard.

"Mademoiselle," he said gravely, "I want to ask you something."

"Ask away," said the lady, eyeing him with some disfavour.

"I want to be able to count upon your help."

"I'll help you to hang Alfred with pleasure," she replied gruffly. "Hanging's too good for him. Ought to be drawn and quartered, like in good old times."

"We are at one then," said Poirot, "for I, too, want to hang the criminal."

"Alfred Inglethorp?"

"Him, or another."

"No question of another. Poor Emily was never murdered until *he* came along. I don't say she wasn't surrounded by sharks—she was. But it was only her purse they were after. Her life was safe enough. But along comes Mr. Alfred Inglethorp—and within two months—hey presto!"

"Believe me, Miss Howard," said Poirot very earnestly, "if Mr. Inglethorp is the man, he shall not escape me. On my honour, I will hang him as high as Haman!"

"That's better," said Miss Howard more enthusiastically.

"But I must ask you to trust me. Now your help may be very valuable to me. I will tell you why. Because, in all this house of mourning, yours are the only eyes that have wept."

Miss Howard blinked, and a new note crept into the gruffness of her voice.

"If you mean that I was fond of her—yes, I was. You know,

Emily was a selfish old woman in her way. She was very generous, but she always wanted a return. She never let people forget what she had done for them—and, that way, she missed love. Don't think she ever realized it, though, or felt the lack of it. Hope not, anyway. I was on a different footing. I took my stand from the first. 'So many pounds a year I'm worth to you. Well and good. But not a penny piece besides—not a pair of gloves, nor a theatre ticket.' She didn't understand—was very offended sometimes. Said I was foolishly proud. It wasn't that—but I couldn't explain. Anyway, I kept my self-respect. And so, out of the whole bunch, I was the only one who could allow myself to be fond of her. I watched over her. I guarded her from the lot of them. And then a glib-tongued scoundrel comes along, and pooh! all my years of devotion go for nothing."

Poirot nodded sympathetically.

"I understand, mademoiselle, I understand all you feel. It is most natural. You think that we are lukewarm—that we lack fire and energy—but trust me, it is not so."

John stuck his head in at this juncture, and invited us both to come up to Mrs. Inglethorp's room, as he and Mr. Wells had finished looking through the desk in the boudoir.

As we went up the stairs, John looked back to the dining-room door, and lowered his voice confidentially:

"Look here, what's going to happen when these two meet?"

I shook my head helplessly.

"I've told Mary to keep them apart if she can."

"Will she be able to do so?"

"The Lord only knows. There's one thing, Inglethorp himself won't be too keen on meeting her."

"You've got the keys still, haven't you, Poirot?" I asked, as we reached the door of the locked room.

Taking the keys from Poirot, John unlocked it, and we all passed in. The lawyer went straight to the desk, and John followed him.

"My mother kept most of her important papers in this despatch-case, I believe," he said.

Poirot drew out the small bunch of keys.

"Permit me. I locked it, out of precaution, this morning."

"But it's not locked now."

"Impossible!"

"See." And John lifted the lid as he spoke.

"Milles tonnerres!" cried Poirot, dumbfounded. "And I—who have both the keys in my pocket!" He flung himself upon the case. Suddenly he stiffened. *"En voilà une affaire!* This lock has been forced!"

"What?"

Poirot laid down the case again.

"But who forced it? Why should they? When? But the door was locked?" These exclamations burst from us disjointedly.

Poirot answered them categorically—almost mechanically.

"Who? That is the question. Why? Ah, if I only knew. When? Since I was here an hour ago. As to the door being locked, it is a very ordinary lock. Probably any other of the doorkeys in this passage would fit it."

We stared at one another blankly. Poirot had walked over to the mantel-piece. He was outwardly calm, but I noticed his hands, which from long force of habit were mechanically straightening the spill vases on the mantel-piece, were shaking violently.

"See here, it was like this," he said at last. "There was something in that case—some piece of evidence, slight in itself perhaps; but still enough of a clue to connect the murderer with the crime. It was vital to him that it should be destroyed before it was discovered and its significance appreciated. Therefore, he took the risk, the great risk, of coming in here. Finding the case locked, he was obliged to force it, thus betraying his presence. For him to take that risk, it must have been something of great importance."

"But what was it?"

"Ah!" cried Poirot, with a gesture of anger. "That, I do not know! A document of some kind, without doubt, possibly the scrap of paper Dorcas saw in her hand yesterday afternoon. And I"—his anger burst forth freely—"miserable animal that I am! I guessed nothing! I have behaved like an imbecile! I should never have left that case here. I should have carried it away with me. Ah, triple pig! And now it is gone. It is destroyed—but is it destroyed? Is there not yet a chance—we must leave no stone unturned—"

He rushed like a madman from the room, and I followed him as soon as I had sufficiently recovered my wits. But, by the time I had reached the top of the stairs, he was out of sight.

Mary Cavendish was standing where the staircase branched, staring down into the hall in the direction in which he had disappeared.

"What has happened to your extraordinary little friend, Mr. Hastings? He has just rushed past me like a mad bull."

"He's rather upset about something," I remarked feebly. I really did not know how much Poirot would wish me to disclose. As I saw a faint smile gather on Mrs. Cavendish's expressive mouth, I endeavoured to try and turn the conversation by saying: "They haven't met yet, have they?"

"Who?"

"Mr. Inglethorp and Miss Howard."

She looked at me in rather a disconcerting manner.

"Do you think it would be such a disaster if they did meet?"

"Well, don't you?" I said, rather taken aback.

"No." She was smiling in her quiet way. "I should like to see a good flare up. It would clear the air. At present we are all thinking so much, and saying so little."

"John doesn't think so," I remarked. "He's anxious to keep them apart."

"Oh, John!"

Something in her tone fired me, and I blurted out:

"Old John's an awfully good sort."

She studied me curiously for a moment or two, and then said, to my great surprise:

"You are loyal to your friend. I like you for that."

"Aren't you my friend too?"

"I am a very bad friend."

"Why do you say that?"

"Because it is true. I am charming to my friends one day, and forget all about them the next."

I don't know what impelled me, but I was nettled, and I said foolishly and not in the best of taste:

"Yet you seem to be invariably charming to Dr. Bauerstein!"

Instantly I regretted my word. Her face stiffened. I had the impression of a steel curtain coming down and blotting out the real woman. Without a word, she turned and went swiftly up the stairs, whilst I stood like an idiot gaping after her.

I was recalled to other matters by a frightful row going on below. I could hear Poirot shouting and expounding. I was vexed to think that my diplomacy had been in vain. The little man appeared to be taking the whole house into his confidence, a proceeding of which I, for one, doubted the wisdom. Once again I could not help regretting that my friend was so prone to lose his head in moments of excitement. I stepped briskly down the stairs. The sight of me calmed Poirot almost immediately. I drew him aside.

"My dear fellow," I said, "is this wise? Surely you don't want the whole house to know of this occurrence? You are actually playing into the criminal's hands."

"You think so, Hastings?"

"I am sure of it."

"Well, well, my friend, I will be guided by you."

"Good. Although, unfortunately, it is a little too late now."

"True."

He looked so crestfallen and abashed that I felt quite sorry, though I still thought my rebuke a just and wise one.

"Well," he said at last, "let us go, *mon ami.*"

"You have finished here?"

"For the moment, yes. You will walk back with me to the village?"

"Willingly."

He picked up his little suit-case, and we went out through the open window in the drawing-room. Cynthia Murdoch was just coming in, and Poirot stood aside to let her pass.

"Excuse me, mademoiselle, one minute."

"Yes?" she turned inquiringly.

"Did you ever make up Mrs. Inglethorp's medicines?"

A slight flush rose in her face, as she answered rather constrainedly:

"No."

"Only her powders?"

The flush deepened as Cynthia replied:

"Oh, yes, I did make up some sleeping powders for her once."

"These?"

Poirot produced the empty box which had contained powders.

She nodded.

"Can you tell me what they were? Sulphonal? Veronal?"

"No, they were bromide powders."

"Ah! Thank you, mademoiselle; good morning."

As we walked briskly away from the house, I glanced at him more than once. I had often before noticed that, if anything excited him, his eyes turned green like a cat's. They were shining like emeralds now.

"My friend," he broke out at last, "I have a little idea, a very strange, and probably utterly impossible idea. And yet—it fits in."

I shrugged my shoulders. I privately thought that Poirot was rather too much given to these fantastic ideas. In this case, surely, the truth was only too plain and apparent.

"So that is the explanation of the blank label on the box," I remarked. "Very simple, as you said. I really wonder that I did not think of it myself."

Poirot did not appear to be listening to me.

"They have made one more discovery, là-bas," he observed, jerking his thumb over his shoulder in the direction of Styles. "Mr. Wells told me as we were going upstairs."

"What was it?"

"Locked up in the desk in the boudoir, they found a will of Mrs. Inglethorp's, dated before her marriage, leaving her fortune to Alfred Inglethorp. It must have been made just at the time they were engaged. It came quite as a surprise to Wells—and to John Cavendish also. It was written on one of those printed will forms, and witnessed by two of the servants—not Dorcas."

"Did Mr. Inglethorp know of it?"

"He says not."

"One might take that with a grain of salt," I remarked sceptically. "All these wills are very confusing. Tell me, how did those scribbled words on the envelope help you to discover that a will was made yesterday afternoon?"

Poirot smiled.

"*Mon ami*, have you ever, when writing a letter, been arrested by the fact that you did not know how to spell a certain word?"

"Yes, often. I suppose every one has."

"Exactly. And have you not, in such a case, tried the word once or twice on the edge of the blotting-paper, or a spare scrap of paper, to see if it looked right? Well, that is what Mrs. Inglethorp did. You will notice that the word 'possessed' is spelt first with one 's' and subsequently with two—correctly. To make sure, she had further tried it in a sentence, thus: 'I am possessed.' Now, what did that tell me? It told me that Mrs. Inglethorp had been writing the word 'possessed' that afternoon, and, having the fragment of paper found in the grate fresh in my mind, the possibility of a will—(a document almost certain to contain that word)—occurred to me at once. This possibility was confirmed by a further circumstance. In the general confusion, the boudoir had not been swept that morning, and near the desk were several traces of brown mould and earth. The weather had been perfectly fine for some days, and no ordinary boots would have left such a heavy deposit.

"I strolled to the window, and saw at once that the begonia beds had been newly planted. The mould in the beds was exactly similar to that on the floor of the boudoir, and also I learnt from you that they *had* been planted yesterday afternoon. I was now sure that one, or possibly both of the gardeners—for there were two sets of footprints in the bed—had entered the boudoir, for if Mrs. Inglethorp had merely wished to speak to them she would in all probability have stood at the window, and they would not have come into the room at all. I was now quite convinced that she had made a fresh will, and had called the two gardeners in to witness her signature. Events proved that I was right in my supposition."

"That was very ingenious," I could not help admitting. "I must confess that the conclusions I drew from those few scribbled words were quite erroneous."

He smiled.

"You gave too much rein to your imagination. Imagination is a good servant, and a bad master. The simplest explanation is always the most likely."

"Another point—how did you know that the key of the despatch-case had been lost?"

"I did not know it. It was a guess that turned out to be correct. You observed that it had a piece of twisted wire through the handle. That suggested to me at once that it had possibly been wrenched off a flimsy key-ring. Now, if it had been lost and recovered, Mrs. Inglethorp would at once have replaced it on her bunch; but on her bunch I found what was obviously the duplicate key, very new and bright, which led me to the hypothesis that somebody else had inserted the original key in the lock of the despatch-case."

"Yes," I said, "Alfred Inglethorp, without doubt."

Poirot looked at me curiously.

"You are very sure of his guilt?"

"Well, naturally. Every fresh circumstance seems to establish it more clearly."

"On the contrary," said Poirot quietly, "there are several points in his favour."

"Oh, come now!"

"Yes."

"I see only one."

"And that?"

"That he was not in the house last night."

" 'Bad shot!' as you English say! You have chosen the one point that to my mind tells against him."

"How is that?"

"Because if Mr. Inglethorp knew that his wife would be poisoned last night, he would certainly have arranged to be away from the house. His excuse was an obviously trumped up one. That leaves us two possibilities: either he knew what was going to happen or he had a reason of his own for his absence."

"And that reason?" I asked sceptically.

Poirot shrugged his shoulders.

"How should I know? Discreditable, without doubt. This Mr. Inglethorp, I should say, is somewhat of a scoundrel—

but that does not of necessity make him a murderer."

I shook my head, unconvinced.

"We do not agree, eh?" said Poirot. "Well, let us leave it. Time will show which of us is right. Now let us turn to other aspects of the case. What do you make of the fact that all the doors of the bedroom were bolted on the inside?"

"Well—" I considered. "One must look at it logically."

"True."

"I should put it this way. The doors *were* bolted—our own eyes have told us that—yet the presence of the candle grease on the floor, and the destruction of the will, prove that during the night some one entered the room. You agree so far?"

"Perfectly. Put with admirable clearness. Proceed."

"Well," I said, encouraged, "as the person who entered did not do so by the window, nor by miraculous means, it follows that the door must have been opened from inside by Mrs. Inglethorp herself. That strengthens the conviction that the person in question was her husband. She would naturally open the door to her own husband."

Poirot shook his head.

"Why should she? She had bolted the door leading into his room—a most unusual proceeding on her part—she had had a most violent quarrel with him that very afternoon. No, he was the last person she would admit."

"But you agree with me that the door must have been opened by Mrs. Inglethorp herself?"

"There is another possibility. She may have forgotten to bolt the door into the passage when she went to bed, and have got up later, towards morning, and bolted it then."

"Poirot, is that seriously your opinion?"

"No, I do not say it is so, but it might be. Now, to turn to another feature, what do you make of the scrap of conversation you overheard between Mrs. Cavendish and her mother-in-law?"

"I had forgotten that," I said thoughtfully. "That is as enigmatical as ever. It seems incredible that a woman like Mrs. Cavendish, proud and reticent to the last degree, should interfere so violently in what was certainly not her affair."

"Precisely. It was an astonishing thing for a woman of her breeding to do."

"It is certainly curious," I agreed. "Still, it is unimportant, and need not be taken into account."

A groan burst from Poirot.

"What have I always told you? Everything must be taken into account. If the fact will not fit the theory—let the theory go."

"Well, we shall see," I said, nettled.

"Yes, we shall see."

We had reached Leastways Cottage, and Poirot ushered me upstairs to his own room. He offered me one of the tiny Russian cigarettes he himself occasionally smoked. I was amused to notice that he stowed away the used matches most carefully in a little china pot. My momentary annoyance vanished.

Poirot had placed our two chairs in front of the open window which commanded a view of the village street. The fresh air blew in warm and pleasant. It was going to be a hot day.

Suddenly my attention was arrested by a weedy looking young man rushing down the street at a great pace. It was the expression on his face that was extraordinary—a curious mingling of terror and agitation.

"Look, Poirot!" I said.

He leant forward.

"*Tiens!*" he said. "It is Mr. Mace, from the chemist's shop. He is coming here."

The young man came to a halt before Leastways Cottage, and, after hesitating a moment, pounded vigorously at the door.

"A little minute," cried Poirot from the window. "I come."

Motioning to me to follow him, he ran swiftly down the stairs and opened the door. Mr. Mace began at once.

"Oh, Mr. Poirot, I'm sorry for the inconvenience, but I heard that you'd just come back from the Hall?"

"Yes, we have."

The young man moistened his dry lips. His face was working curiously.

"It's all over the village about old Mrs. Inglethorp dying so suddenly. They do say"—he lowered his voice cautiously—"that it's poison?"

Poirot's face remained quite impassive.

"Only the doctors can tell us that, Mr. Mace."

"Yes, exactly—of course—" The young man hesitated, and then his agitation was too much for him. He clutched Poirot by the arm, and sank his voice to a whisper: "Just tell me this, Mr. Poirot, it isn't—it isn't strychnine, is it?"

I hardly heard what Poirot replied. Something evidently of a non-committal nature. The young man departed, and as he closed the door Poirot's eyes met mine.

"Yes," he said nodding gravely. "He will have evidence to give at the inquest."

We went slowly upstairs again. I was opening my lips, when Poirot stopped me with a gesture of his hand.

"Not now, not now, *mon ami.* I have need of reflection. My mind is in some disorder—which is not well."

For about ten minutes he sat in dead silence, perfectly still, except for several expressive motions of his eyebrows, and all the time his eyes grew steadily greener. At last he heaved a deep sigh.

"It is well. The bad moment has passed. Now all is arranged and classified. One must never permit confusion. The case is not clear yet—no. For it is of the most complicated! It puzzles *me. Me,* Hercule Poirot! There are two facts of significance."

"And what are they?"

"The first is the state of the weather yesterday. That is very important."

"But it was a glorious day!" I interrupted. "Poirot, you're pulling my leg!"

"Not at all. The thermometer registered 80° in the shade. Do not forget that, my friend. It is the key to the whole riddle!"

"And the second point?" I asked.

"The important fact that Monsieur Inglethorp wears very peculiar clothes, has a black beard, and uses glasses."

"Poirot, I cannot believe you are serious."

"I am absolutely serious, my friend."

"But this is childish!"

"No, it is very momentous."

"And supposing the Coroner's jury returns a verdict of

Wilful Murder against Alfred Inglethorp. What becomes of your theories, then?"

"They would not be shaken because twelve stupid men had happened to make a mistake! But that will not occur. For one thing, a country jury is not anxious to take responsibility upon itself, and Mr. Inglethorp stands practically in the position of local squire. Also," he added placidly, "I should not allow it!"

"*You* would not allow it?"

"No."

I looked at the extraordinary little man, divided between annoyance and amusement. He was so tremendously sure of himself. As though he read my thoughts, he nodded gently.

"Oh, yes, *mon ami*, I would do what I say." He got up and laid his hand on my shoulder. His physiognomy underwent a complete change. Tears came into his eyes. "In all this, you see, I think of that poor Mrs. Inglethorp who is dead. She was not extravagantly loved—no. But she was very good to us Belgians—I owe her a debt."

I endeavoured to interrupt, but Poirot swept on.

"Let me tell you this, Hastings. She would never forgive me if I let Alfred Inglethorp, her husband, be arrested *now*— when a word from me could save him!"

VI

THE INQUEST

In the interval before the inquest, Poirot was unfailing in his activity. Twice he was closeted with Mr. Wells. He also took long walks into the country. I rather resented his not taking me into his confidence, the more so as I could not in the least guess what he was driving at.

It occurred to me that he might have been making inquiries at Raikes's farm; so, finding him out when I called at Leastways Cottage on Wednesday evening, I walked over there by the fields, hoping to meet him. But there was no sign of him, and I hesitated to go right up to the farm itself. As I walked away, I met an aged rustic, who leered at me cunningly.

"You'm from the Hall, bain't you?" he asked.

"Yes. I'm looking for a friend of mine whom I thought might have walked this way."

"A little chap? As waves his hands when he talks? One of them Belgies from the village?"

"Yes," I said eagerly. "He has been here, then?"

"Oh, ay, he's been here, right enough. More'n once too. Friend of yours, is he? Ah, you gentlemen from the Hall—

you'n a pretty lot!" And he leered more jocosely than ever.

"Why, do the gentlemen from the Hall come here often?" I asked, as carelessly as I could.

He winked at me knowingly.

"*One* does, mister. Naming no names, mind. And a very liberal gentleman too! Oh, thank you, sir, I'm sure."

I walked on sharply. Evelyn Howard had been right then, and I experienced a sharp twinge of disgust, as I thought of Alfred Inglethorp's liberality with another woman's money. Had that piquant gipsy face been at the bottom of the crime, or was it the baser mainspring of money? Probably a judicious mixture of both.

On one point, Poirot seemed to have a curious obsession. He once or twice observed to me that he thought Dorcas must have made an error in fixing the time of the quarrel. He suggested to her repeatedly that it was 4:30, and not 4 o'clock when she had heard the voices.

But Dorcas was unshaken. Quite an hour, or even more, had elapsed between the time when she had heard the voices and 5 o'clock, when she had taken tea to her mistress.

The inquest was held on Friday at the Stylites Arms in the village. Poirot and I sat together, not being required to give evidence.

The preliminaries were gone through. The jury viewed the body, and John Cavendish gave evidence of identification.

Further questioned, he described his awakening in the early hours of the morning, and the circumstances of his mother's death.

The medical evidence was next taken. There was a breathless hush, and every eye was fixed on the famous London specialist, who was known to be one of the greatest authorities of the day on the subject of toxicology.

In a few brief words, he summed up the result of the post-mortem. Shorn of its medical phraseology and technicalities, it amounted to the fact that Mrs. Inglethorp had met her death as the result of strychnine poisoning. Judging from the quantity recovered, she must have taken not less than three-quarters of a grain of strychnine, but probably one grain or slightly over.

"Is it possible, that she could have swallowed the poison by accident?" asked the Coroner.

"I should consider it very unlikely. Strychnine is not used for domestic purposes, as some poisons are, and there are restrictions placed on its sale."

"Does anything in your examination lead you to determine how the poison was administered?"

"No."

"You arrived at Styles before Dr. Wilkins, I believe?"

"That is so. The motor met me just outside the lodge gates, and I hurried there as fast as I could."

"Will you relate to us exactly what happened next?"

"I entered Mrs. Inglethorp's room. She was at that moment in a typical tetanic convulsion. She turned towards me, and gasped out: 'Alfred—Alfred—' "

"Could the strychnine have been administered in Mrs. Inglethorp's after-dinner coffee which was taken to her by her husband?"

"Possibly, but strychnine is a fairly rapid drug in its action. The symptoms appear from one to two hours after it has been swallowed. It is retarded under certain conditions, none of which, however, appear to have been present in this case. I presume Mrs. Inglethorp took the coffee after dinner about eight o'clock, whereas the symptoms did not manifest themselves until the early hours of the morning, which, on the face of it, points to the drug having been taken much later in the evening."

"Mrs. Inglethorp was in the habit of drinking a cup of coco in the middle of the night. Could the strychnine have been administered in that?"

"No, I myself took a sample of the coco remaining in the saucepan and had it analysed. There was no strychnine present."

I heard Poirot chuckle softly beside me.

"How did you know?" I whispered.

"Listen."

"I should say"—the doctor was continuing—"that I would have been considerably surprised at any other result."

"Why?"

"Simply because strychnine has an unusually bitter taste.

It can be detected in a solution of 1 in 70,000, and can only be disguised by some strongly flavoured substance. Coco would be quite powerless to mask it."

One of the jury wanted to know if the same objection applied to coffee.

"No. Coffee has a bitter taste of its own which would probably cover the taste of the strychnine."

"Then you consider it more likely that the drug was administered in the coffee, but that for some unknown reason its action was delayed."

"Yes, but, the cup being completely smashed, there is no possibility of analysing its contents."

This concluded Dr. Bauerstein's evidence. Dr. Wilkins corroborated it on all points. Sounded as to the possibilities of suicide, he repudiated it utterly. The deceased, he said, suffered from a weak heart, but otherwise enjoyed perfect heath, and was of a cheerful and well balanced disposition. She would be one of the last people to take her own life.

Lawrence Cavendish was next called. His evidence was quite unimportant, being a mere repetition of that of his brother. Just as he was about to step down, he paused, and said rather hesitatingly:

"I should like to make a suggestion if I may?"

He glanced deprecatingly at the Coroner, who replied briskly:

"Certainly, Mr. Cavendish, we are here to arrive at the truth of this matter, and welcome anything that may lead to further elucidation."

"It is just an idea of mine," explained Lawrence. "Of course I may be quite wrong, but it still seems to me that my mother's death might be accounted for by natural means."

"How do you make that out, Mr. Cavendish?"

"My mother, at the time of her death, and for some time before it, was taking a tonic containing strychnine."

"Ah!" said the Coroner.

The jury looked up, interested.

"I believe," continued Lawrence, "that there have been cases where the cumulative effect of a drug, administered for some time, has ended by causing death. Also, is it not possible that she may have taken an overdose of her medicine by accident?"

"This is the first we have heard of the deceased taking strychnine at the time of her death. We are much obliged to you, Mr. Cavendish."

Dr. Wilkins was recalled and ridiculed the idea.

"What Mr. Cavendish suggests is quite impossible. Any doctor would tell you the same. Strychnine is, in a certain sense, a cumulative poison, but it would be quite impossible for it to result in sudden death in this way. There would have to be a long period of chronic symptoms which would at once have attracted my attention. The whole thing is absurd."

"And the second suggestion? That Mrs. Inglethorp may have inadvertently taken an overdose?"

"Three, or even four doses, would not have resulted in death. Mrs. Inglethorp always had an extra large amount of medicine made up at a time, as she dealt with Coot's, the Cash Chemists in Tadminster. She would have had to take very nearly the whole bottle to account for the amount of strychnine found at the post-mortem."

"Then you consider that we may dismiss the tonic as not being in any way instrumental in causing her death?"

"Certainly. The supposition is ridiculous."

The same juryman who had interrupted before here suggested that the chemist who made up the medicine might have committed an error.

"That, of course, is always possible," replied the doctor.

But Dorcas, who was the next witness called, dispelled even that possibility. The medicine had not been newly made up. On the contrary, Mrs. Inglethorp had taken the last dose on the day of her death.

So the question of the tonic was finally abandoned, and the Coroner proceeded with his task. Having elicited from Dorcas how she had been awakened by the violent ringing of her mistress's bell, and had subsequently roused the household, he passed to the subject of the quarrel on the preceding afternoon.

Dorcas's evidence on this point was substantially what Poirot and I had already heard, so I will not repeat it here.

The next witness was Mary Cavendish. She stood very upright, and spoke in a low, clear, and perfectly composed voice. In answer to the Coroner's question, she told how, her alarm clock having aroused her at 4:30 as usual, she was dressing, when she was startled by the sound of something heavy falling.

"That would have been the table by the bed?" commented the Coroner.

"I opened my door," continued Mary, "and listened. In a few minutes a bell rang violently. Dorcas came running down and woke my husband, and we all went to my mother-in-law's room, but it was locked—"

The Coroner interrupted her.

"I really do not think we need trouble you further on that point. We know all that can be known of the subsequent happenings. But I should be obliged if you would tell us all you overheard of the quarrel the day before."

"I?"

There was a faint insolence in her voice. She raised her hand and adjusted the ruffle of lace at her neck, turning her head a little as she did so. And quite spontaneously the thought flashed across my mind: "She is gaining time!"

"Yes. I understand," continued the Coroner deliberately, "that you were sitting reading on the bench just outside the long window of the boudoir. That is so, is it not?"

This was news to me and glancing sideways at Poirot, I fancied that it was news to him as well.

There was the faintest pause, the mere hesitation of a moment, before she answered:

"Yes, that is so."

"And the boudoir window was open, was it not?"

Surely her face grew a little paler as she answered:

"Yes."

"Then you cannot have failed to hear the voices inside, especially as they were raised in anger. In fact, they would be more audible where you were than in the hall."

"Possibly."

"Will you repeat to us what you overheard of the quarrel?"

"I really do not remember hearing anything."

"Do you mean to say you did not hear voices?"

"Oh, yes, I heard the voices, but I did not hear what they

said." A faint spot of colour came into her cheek. "I am not in the habit of listening to private conversations."

The Coroner persisted.

"And you remember nothing at all? *Nothing*, Mrs. Cavendish? Not one stray word or phrase to make you realize that it *was* a private conversation?"

She paused, and seemed to reflect, still outwardly as calm as ever.

"Yes; I remember, Mrs. Inglethorp said something—I do not remember exactly what—about causing scandal between husband and wife."

"Ah!" The Coroner leant back satisfied. "That corresponds with what Dorcas heard. But excuse me, Mrs. Cavendish, although you realized it was a private conversation, you did not move away? You remained where you were?"

I caught the momentary gleam of her tawny eyes as she raised them. I felt certain that at that moment she would willingly have torn the little lawyer, with his insinuations, into pieces, but she replied quietly enough:

"No. I was very comfortable where I was. I fixed my mind on my book."

"And that is all you can tell us?"

"That is all."

The examination was over, though I doubted if the Coroner was entirely satisfied with it. I think he suspected that Mary Cavendish could tell more if she chose.

Amy Hill, shop assistant, was next called, and deposed to having sold a will form on the afternoon of the 17th to William Earl, under-gardener at Styles.

William Earl and Manning succeeded her, and testified to witnessing a document. Manning fixed the time at about 4:30, William was of the opinion that it was rather earlier.

Cynthia Murdoch came next. She had, however, little to tell. She had known nothing of the tragedy, until awakened by Mrs. Cavendish.

"You did not hear the table fall?"

"No. I was fast asleep."

The Coroner smiled.

"A good conscience makes a sound sleeper," he observed. "Thank you, Miss Murdoch, that is all."

"Miss Howard."

Miss Howard produced the letter written to her by Mrs. Inglethorp on the evening of the 17th. Poirot and I had, of course, already seen it. It added nothing to our knowledge of the tragedy. The following is a facsimile:

July 17th

Styles Court

Essex

My dear Evelyn

Can we not bury the hatchet? I have found it hard to forgive the things you said against my dear husband but I am an old woman & very fond of you

Yours affectionately

Emily Inglethorp

It was handed to the jury who scrutinized it attentively. "I fear it does not help us much," said the Coroner, with a sigh. "There is no mention of any of the events of that afternoon."

"Plain as a pikestaff to me," said Miss Howard shortly. "It shows clearly enough that my poor old friend had just found out she'd been made a fool of!"

"It says nothing of the kind in the letter," the Coroner pointed out.

"No, because Emily never could bear to put herself in the wrong. But *I* know her. She wanted me back. But she wasn't going to own that I'd been right. She went round about. Most people do. Don't believe in it myself."

Mr. Wells smiled faintly. So, I noticed, did several of the jury. Miss Howard was obviously quite a public character.

"Anyway, all this tomfoolery is a great waste of time," continued the lady, glancing up and down the jury disparagingly. "Talk—talk—talk! When all the time we know perfectly well—"

The Coroner interrupted her in an agony of apprehension: "Thank you, Miss Howard, that is all."

I fancy he breathed a sigh of relief when she complied.

Then came the sensation of the day. The Coroner called Albert Mace, chemist's assistant.

It was our agitated young man of the pale face. In answer to the Coroner's questions, he explained that he was a qualified pharmacist, but had only recently come to this particular shop, as the assistant formerly there had just been called up for the army.

These preliminaries completed, the Coroner proceeded to business.

"Mr. Mace, have you lately sold strychnine to any unauthorized person?"

"Yes, sir."

"When was this?"

"Last Monday night."

"Monday? Not Tuesday?"

"No, sir, Monday, the 16th."

"Will you tell us to whom you sold it?"

You could have heard a pin drop.

"Yes, sir. It was to Mr. Inglethorp."

Every eye turned simultaneously to where Alfred Inglethorp was sitting, impassive and wooden. He started slightly, as the damning words fell from the young man's lips. I half thought he was going to rise from his chair, but he remained seated, although a remarkably well acted expression of astonishment rose on his face.

"You are sure of what you say?" asked the Coroner sternly.

"Quite sure, sir."

"Are you in the habit of selling strychnine indiscriminately over the counter?"

The wretched young man wilted visibly under the Coroner's frown.

"Oh, no, sir—of course not. But, seeing it was Mr. Inglethorp of the Hall, I thought there was no harm in it. He said it was to poison a dog."

Inwardly I sympathized. It was only human nature to endeavour to please "The Hall"—especially when it might result in custom being transferred from Coot's to the local establishment.

"Is it not customary for anyone purchasing poison to sign a book?"

"Yes, sir, Mr. Inglethorp did so."

"Have you got the book here?"

"Yes, sir."

It was produced; and, with a few words of stern censure, the Coroner dismissed the wretched Mr. Mace.

Then, amidst a breathless silence, Alfred Inglethorp was called. Did he realize, I wondered, how closely the halter was being drawn around his neck?

The Coroner went straight to the point.

"On Monday evening last, did you purchase strychnine for the purpose of poisoning a dog?"

Inglethorp replied with perfect calmness:

"No, I did not. There is no dog at Styles, except an outdoor sheepdog, which is in perfect health."

"You deny absolutely having purchased strychnine from Albert Mace on Monday last?"

"I do."

"Do you also deny *this*?"

The Coroner handed him the register in which his signature was inscribed.

"Certainly I do. The hand-writing is quite different from mine. I will show you."

He took an old envelope out of his pocket, and wrote his name on it, handing it to the jury. It was certainly utterly dissimilar.

"Then what is your explanation of Mr. Mace's statement?"

Alfred Inglethorp replied imperturbably:

"Mr. Mace must have been mistaken."

The Coroner hesitated for a moment, and then said:

"Mr. Inglethorp, as a mere matter of form, would you mind telling us where you were on the evening of Monday, July 16th?"

"Really—I cannot remember."

"That is absurd, Mr. Inglethorp," said the Coroner sharply. "Think again."

Inglethorp shook his head.

"I cannot tell you. I have an idea that I was out walking."

"In what direction?"

"I really can't remember."

The Coroner's face grew graver.

"Were you in company with anyone?"

"No."

"Did you meet anyone on your walk?"

"No."

"That is a pity," said the Coroner dryly. "I am to take it then that you decline to say where you were at the time that Mr. Mace positively recognized you as entering the shop to purchase strychnine?"

"If you like to take it that way, yes."

"Be careful, Mr. Inglethorp."

Poirot was fidgeting nervously.

"*Sacré!*" he murmured. "Does this imbecile of a man *want* to be arrested?"

Inglethorp was indeed creating a bad impression. His futile denials would not have convinced a child. The Coroner, however, passed briskly to the next point, and Poirot drew a deep breath of relief.

"You had a discussion with your wife on Tuesday afternoon?"

"Pardon me," interrupted Alfred Inglethorp, "you have
been misinformed. I had no quarrel with my dear wife. The
whole story is absolutely untrue. I was absent from the
house the entire afternoon."

"Have you anyone who can testify to that?"

"You have my word," said Inglethorp haughtily.

The Coroner did not trouble to reply.

"There are two witnesses who will swear to having heard
your disagreement with Mrs. Inglethorp."

"Those witnesses were mistaken."

I was puzzled. The man spoke with such quiet assurance
that I was staggered. I looked at Poirot. There was an expression of exultation on his face which I could not understand. Was he at last convinced of Alfred Inglethorp's guilt?

"Mr. Inglethorp," said the Coroner, "you have heard your
wife's dying words repeated here. Can you explain them in
any way?"

"Certainly I can."

"You can?"

"It seems to me very simple. The room was dimly lighted.
Dr. Bauerstein is much of my height and build, and, like
me, wears a beard. In the dim light, and suffering as she
was, my poor wife mistook him for me."

"Ah!" murmured Poirot to himself. "But it is an idea, that!"

"You think it is true?" I whispered.

"I do not say that. But it is truly an ingenious supposition."

"You read my wife's last words as an accusation"—Inglethorp was continuing—"they were, on the contrary, an appeal to me."

The Coroner reflected a moment, then he said:

"I believe, Mr. Inglethorp, that you yourself poured out the
coffee, and took it to your wife that evening?"

"I poured it out, yes. But I did not take it to her. I meant
to do so, but I was told that a friend was at the hall door, so
I laid down the coffee on the hall table. When I came through
the hall again a few minutes later, it was gone."

This statement might, or might not, be true, but it did not

seem to me to improve matters much for Inglethorp. In any case, he had had ample time to introduce the poison.

At that point, Poirot nudged me gently, indicating two men were sitting together near the door. One was a little, sharp, dark, ferret faced man, the other was tall and fair.

I questioned Poirot mutely. He put his lips to my ear.

"Do you know who that little man is?"

I shook my head.

"That is Detective Inspector James Japp of Scotland Yard—Jimmy Japp. The other man is from Scotland Yard too. Things are moving quickly, my friend."

I stared at the two men intently. There was certainly nothing of the policeman about them. I should never have suspected them of being official personages.

I was still staring, when I was startled and recalled by the verdict being given:

"Wilful Murder against some person or persons unknown."

VII

POIROT PAYS HIS DEBTS

As we came out of the Stylites Arms, Poirot drew me aside by a gentle pressure of the arm. I understood his object. He was waiting for the Scotland Yard men.

In a few moments, they emerged, and Poirot at once stepped forward, and accosted the shorter of the two.

"I fear you do not remember me, Inspector Japp."

"Why, if it isn't Mr. Poirot!" cried the Inspector. He turned to the other man. "You've heard me speak of Mr. Poirot? It was in 1904 he and I worked together—the Abercrombie forgery case—you remember, he was run down in Brussels. Ah, those were great days, moosier. Then, do you remember 'Baron' Altara? There was a pretty rogue for you! He eluded the clutches of half the police in Europe. But we nailed him in Antwerp—thanks to Mr. Poirot here."

As these friendly reminiscences were being indulged in, I drew nearer, and was introduced to Detective-Inspector Japp, who in his turn, introduced us both to his companion, Superintendent Summerhaye.

"I need hardly ask what you are doing here, gentlemen," remarked Poirot.

Japp closed one eye knowingly.

"No, indeed. Pretty clear case I should say."

But Poirot answered gravely:

"There I differ from you."

"Oh, come!" said Summerhaye, opening his lips for the first time. "Surely the whole thing is clear as daylight. The man's caught redhanded. How he could be such a fool beats me!"

But Japp was looking attentively at Poirot.

"Hold your fire, Summerhaye," he remarked jocularly. "Me and Moosier here have met before—and there's no man's judgment I'd sooner take than his. If I'm not greatly mistaken, he's got something up his sleeve. Isn't that so, moosier?"

Poirot smiled.

"I have drawn certain conclusions—yes."

Summerhaye was still looking rather sceptical, but Japp continued his scrutiny of Poirot.

"It's this way," he said, "so far, we've only seen the case from the outside. That's where the Yard's at a disadvantage in a case of this kind, where the murder's only out, so to speak, after the inquest. A lot depends on being on the spot first thing, and that's where Mr. Poirot's had the start of us. We shouldn't have been here as soon as this even, if it hadn't been for the fact that there was a smart doctor on the spot, who gave us the tip through the Coroner. But you've been on the spot from the first, and you may have picked up some little hints. From the evidence at the inquest, Mr. Inglethorp murdered his wife as sure as I stand here, and if anyone but you hinted the contrary I'd laugh in his face. I must say I was surprised the jury didn't bring it in Wilful Murder against him right off. I think they would have, if it hadn't been for the Coroner—he seemed to be holding them back."

"Perhaps, though, you have a warrant for his arrest in your pocket now," suggested Poirot.

A kind of wooden shutter of officialdom came down from Japp's expressive countenance.

"Perhaps I have, and perhaps I haven't," he remarked dryly.

Poirot looked at him thoughtfully.

"I am very anxious, Messieurs, that he should not be arrested."

"I dare say," observed Summerhaye sarcastically.

Japp was regarding Poirot with comical perplexity. "Can't you go a little further, Mr. Poirot? A wink's as good as a nod—from you. You've been on the spot—and the Yard doesn't want to make any mistakes, you know."

Poirot nodded gravely.

"That is exactly what I thought. Well, I will tell you this. Use your warrant: Arrest Mr. Inglethorp. But it will bring you no kudos—the case against him will be dismissed at once! *Comme ça!*" And he snapped his fingers expressively.

Japp's face grew grave, though Summerhaye gave an incredulous snort.

As for me, I was literally dumb with astonishment. I could only conclude that Poirot was mad.

Japp had taken out a handkerchief, and was gently dabbing his brow.

"I daren't do it, Mr. Poirot. I'd take your word, but there's others over me who'll be asking what the devil I mean by it. Can't you give me a little more to go on?"

Poirot reflected a moment.

"It can be done," he said at last. "I admit I do not wish it. It forces my hand. I would have preferred to work in the dark just for the present, but what you say is very just—the word of a Belgian policeman, whose day is past, is not enough! And Alfred Inglethorp must not be arrested. That I have sworn, as my friend Hastings here knows. See, then, my good Japp, you go at once to Styles?"

"Well, in about half an hour. We're seeing the Coroner and the doctor first."

"Good. Call for me in passing—the last house in the village. I will go with you. At Styles, Mr. Inglethorp will give you, or if he refuses—as is probable—I will give you such proofs that shall satisfy you that the case against him could not possibly be sustained. Is that a bargain?"

"That's a bargain," said Japp heartily. "And, on behalf of the Yard, I'm much obliged to you, though I'm bound to confess I can't at present see the faintest possible loop-hole in the evidence, but you always were a marvel! So long, then, moosier."

The two detectives strode away, Summerhaye with an incredulous grin on his face.

"Well, my friend," cried Poirot, before I could get in a word, "what do you think? *Mon Dieu!* I had some warm moments in that court; I did not figure to myself that the man would be so pigheaded as to refuse to say anything at all. Decidedly, it was the policy of an imbecile."

"H'm! There are other explanations besides that of imbecility," I remarked. "For, if the case against him is true, how could he defend himself except by silence?"

"Why, in a thousand ingenious ways," cried Poirot. "See; say that it is I who have committed this murder, I can think of seven most plausible stories! Far more convincing than Mr. Inglethorp's stony denials!"

I could not help laughing.

"My dear Poirot, I am sure you are capable of thinking of seventy! But, seriously, in spite of what I heard you say to the detectives, you surely cannot still believe in the possibility of Alfred Inglethorp's innocence?"

"Why not now as much as before? Nothing has changed."

"But the evidence is so conclusive."

"Yes, too conclusive."

We turned in at the gate of Leastways Cottage, and proceeded up the now familiar stairs.

"Yes, yes, too conclusive," continued Poirot, almost to himself. "Real evidence is usually vague and unsatisfactory. It has to be examined—sifted. But here the whole thing is cut and dried. No, my friend, this evidence has been very cleverly manufactured—so cleverly that it has defeated its own ends."

"How do you make that out?"

"Because, so long as the evidence against him was vague and intangible, it was very hard to disprove. But, in his anxiety, the criminal has drawn the net so closely that one cut will set Inglethorp free."

I was silent. And in a minute or two, Poirot continued:

"Let us look at the matter like this. Here is a man, let us say, who sets out to poison his wife. He has lived by his wits as the saying goes. Presumably, therefore, he has some wits. He is not altogether a fool. Well, how does he set about it? He goes boldly to the village chemist's and purchases strychnine under his own name, with a trumped up story about a dog which is bound to be proved absurd. He does not employ the poison that night. No, he waits until he has had a violent quarrel with her, of which the whole household is cognisant, and which naturally directs their suspicions upon him. He prepares no defence—no shadow of an alibi, yet he knows the chemist's assistant must necessarily come forward with the facts. Bah! do not ask me to believe that any man could be so idiotic! Only a lunatic, who wished to commit suicide by causing himself to be hanged, would act so!"

"Still—I do not see—" I began.

"Neither do I see. I tell you, *mon ami*, it puzzles me. Me—Hercule Poirot!"

"But if you believe him innocent, how do you explain his buying the strychnine?"

"Very simply. He did *not* buy it."

"But Mace recognized him!"

"I beg your pardon, he saw a man with a black beard like Mr. Inglethorp's, and wearing glasses like Mr. Inglethorp, and dressed in Mr. Inglethorp's rather noticeable clothes. He could not recognize a man whom he had probably only seen in the distance, since, you remember, he himself had only been in the village a fortnight, and Mrs. Inglethorp dealt principally with Coot's in Tadminster."

"Then you think—"

"*Mon ami*, do you remember the two points I laid stress upon? Leave the first one for the moment, what was the second?"

" 'The important fact that Alfred Inglethorp wears peculiar clothes, has a black beard, and uses glasses,' " I quoted.

"Exactly. Now suppose anyone wished to pass himself off as John or Lawrence Cavendish. Would it be easy?"

"No," I said thoughtfully. "Of course an actor——"

But Poirot cut me short ruthlessly.

"And why would it not be easy? I will tell you, my friend: Because they are both clean-shaven men. To make up successfully as one of these two in broad daylight, it would need an actor of genius, and a certain initial facial resemblance. But in the case of Alfred Inglethorp, all that is changed. His clothes, his beard, the glasses which hide his eyes—those are the salient points about his personal appearance. Now, what is the first instinct of the criminal? To divert suspicion from himself, is it not so? And how can he best do that? By throwing it on some one else. In this instance, there was a man ready to his hand. Everybody was predisposed to believe in Mr. Inglethorp's guilt. It was a foregone conclusion that he would be suspected; but, to make it a sure thing there must be tangible proof—such as the actual buying of the poison, and that, with a man of the peculiar appearance of Mr. Inglethorp, was not difficult. Remember, this young Mace had never actually spoken to Mr. Inglethorp. How should he doubt that the man in his clothes, with his beard and his glasses, was not Alfred Inglethorp?"

"It may be so," I said, fascinated by Poirot's eloquence. "But, if that was the case, why does he not say where he was at six o'clock on Monday evening?"

"Ah, why indeed?" said Poirot, calming down. "If he were arrested, he probably would speak, but I do not want it to come to that. I must make him see the gravity of his position. There is, of course, something discreditable behind his silence. If he did not murder his wife, he is, nevertheless, a scoundrel, and has something of his own to conceal, quite apart from the murder."

"What can it be?" I mused, won over to Poirot's views for the moment, although still retaining a faint conviction that the obvious deduction was the correct one.

"Can you not guess?" asked Poirot, smiling.

"No, can you?"

"Oh, yes, I had a little idea sometime ago—and it has turned out to be correct."

"You never told me," I said reproachfully.

Poirot spread out his hands apologetically.

"Pardon me, *mon ami*, you were not precisely *sympathique*." He turned to me earnestly. "Tell me—you see now that he must not be arrested?"

"Perhaps," I said doubtfully, for I was really quite indifferent to the fate of Alfred Inglethorp, and thought that a good fright would do him no harm.

Poirot, who was watching me intently, gave a sigh.

"Come, my friend," he said, changing the subject, "apart from Mr. Inglethorp, how did the evidence at the inquest strike you?"

"Oh, pretty much what I expected."

"Did nothing strike you as peculiar about it?"

My thoughts flew to Mary Cavendish, and I hedged:

"In what way?"

"Well, Mr. Lawrence Cavendish's evidence for instance?"

I was relieved.

"Oh, Lawrence! No, I don't think so. He's always a nervous chap."

"His suggestion that his mother might have been poisoned accidentally by means of the tonic she was taking, that did not strike you as strange—*hein*?"

"No, I can't say it did. The doctors ridiculed it of course. But it was quite a natural suggestion for a layman to make."

"But Monsieur Lawrence is not a layman. You told me yourself that he had started by studying medicine, and that he had taken his degree."

"Yes, that's true. I never thought of that." I was rather startled. "It *is* odd."

Poirot nodded.

"From the first, his behaviour has been peculiar. Of all the household, he alone would be likely to recognize the symptoms of strychnine poisoning, and yet we find him the only member of the family to uphold strenuously the theory of death from natural causes. If it had been Monsieur John, I could have understood it. He has no technical knowledge, and is by nature unimaginative. But Monsieur Lawrence—no! And now, to-day, he puts forward a suggestion that he himself must have known was ridiculous. There is food for thought in this, *mon ami*!"

"It's very confusing," I agreed.

"Then there is Mrs. Cavendish," continued Poirot. "That's another who is not telling all she knows! What do you make of her attitude?"

"I don't know what to make of it. It seems inconceivable

that she should be shielding Alfred Inglethorp. Yet that is what it looks like."

Poirot nodded reflectively.

"Yes, it is queer. One thing is certain, she overheard a good deal more of that 'private conversation' than she was willing to admit."

"And yet she is the last person one would accuse of stooping to eavesdrop!"

"Exactly. One thing her evidence *has* shown me. I made a mistake. Dorcas was quite right. The quarrel did take place earlier in the afternoon, about four o'clock, as she said."

I looked at him curiously. I had never understood his insistence on that point.

"Yes, a good deal that was peculiar came out to-day," continued Poirot. "Dr. Bauerstein, now, what was *he* doing up and dressed at that hour in the morning? It is astonishing to me that no one ever commented on the fact."

"He has insomnia, I believe," I said doubtfully.

"Which is a very good, or a very bad explanation," remarked Poirot. "It covers everything, and explains nothing. I shall keep my eye on our clever Dr. Bauerstein."

"Any more faults to find with the evidence?" I inquired satirically.

"*Mon ami,*" replied Poirot gravely, "when you find that people are not telling you the truth—look out! Now, unless I am much mistaken, at this inquest to-day only one—at most, two persons were speaking the truth without reservation or subterfuge."

"Oh, come now, Poirot! I won't cite Lawrence, or Mrs. Cavendish. But there's John—and Miss Howard, surely they were speaking the truth?"

"Both of them, my friend? One, I grant you, but both——!"

His words gave me an unpleasant shock. Miss Howard's evidence, unimportant as it was, had been given in such a downright straightforward manner that it had never occurred to me to doubt her sincerity. Still, I had a great respect for Poirot's sagacity—except on the occasions when he was what I described to myself as "foolishly pig-headed."

"Do you really think so?" I asked. "Miss Howard had

always seemed to me so essentially honest—almost uncomfortably so."

Poirot gave me a curious look, which I could not quite fathom. He seemed to speak, and then checked himself.

"Miss Murdoch too," I continued, "there's nothing untruthful about *her.*"

"No. But it was strange that she never heard a sound, sleeping next door; whereas Mrs. Cavendish, in the other wing of the building, distinctly heard the table fall."

"Well, she's young. And she sleeps soundly."

"Ah, yes, indeed! She must be a famous sleeper, that one!"

I did not quite like the tone of his voice, but at that moment a smart knock reached our ears, and looking out of the window we perceived the two detectives waiting for us below.

Poirot seized his hat, gave a ferocious twist to his moustache, and, carefully brushing an imaginary speck of dust from his sleeve, motioned me to precede him down the stairs; there we joined the detectives and set out for Styles.

I think the appearance of the two Scotland Yard men was rather a shock—especially to John, though of course, after the verdict, he had realized that it was only a matter of time. Still, the presence of the detectives brought the truth home to him more than anything else could have done.

Poirot had conferred with Japp in a low tone on the way up, and it was the latter functionary who requested that the household, with the exception of the servants, should be assembled together in the drawing-room. I realized the significance of this. It was up to Poirot to make his boast good.

Personally, I was not sanguine. Poirot might have excellent reasons for his belief in Inglethorp's innocence, but a man of the type of Summerhaye would require tangible proofs, and these I doubted if Poirot could supply.

Before very long we had all trooped into the drawing-room, the door of which Japp closed. Poirot politely set chairs for every one. The Scotland Yard men were the cynosure of all eyes. I think that for the first time we realized that the thing was not a bad dream, but a tangible reality. We had read of such things—now we ourselves were actors in the drama.

To-morrow the daily papers, all over England, would blazon
out the news in staring headlines:

"MYSTERIOUS TRAGEDY IN ESSEX"
"WEALTHY LADY POISONED"

There would be pictures of Styles, snap-shots of "The family
leaving the Inquest"—the village photographer had not been
idle! All the things that one had read a hundred times—
things that happen to other people, not to oneself. And now,
in this house, a murder had been committed. In front of us
were "the detectives in charge of the case." The well known
glib phraseology passed rapidly through my mind in the interval before Poirot opened the proceedings.

I think every one was a little surprised that it should be
he and not one of the official detectives who took the initia-
tive.

"*Mesdames* and *messieurs*," said Poirot, bowing as
though he were a celebrity about to deliver a lecture, "I have
asked you to come here all together, for a certain object.
That object, it concerns Mr. Alfred Inglethorp."

Inglethorp was sitting a little by himself—I think, unconsciously, every one had drawn his chair slightly away from
him—and he gave a faint start as Poirot pronounced his
name.

"Mr. Inglethorp," said Poirot, addressing him directly, "a
very dark shadow is resting on this house—the shadow of
murder."

Inglethorp shook his head sadly.

"My poor wife," he murmured. "Poor Emily! It is terrible."

"I do not think, monsieur," said Poirot pointedly, "that you
quite realize how terrible it may be—for you." And as Inglethorp did not appear to understand, he added: "Mr. Inglethorp, you are standing in very grave danger."

The two detectives fidgeted. I saw the official caution "Anything you say will be used in evidence against you," actually
hovering on Summerhaye's lips. Poirot went on. "Do you understand now, monsieur?"

"No. What do you mean?"

"I mean," said Poirot deliberately, "that you are suspected of poisoning your wife."

A little gasp ran round the circle at this plain speaking.

"Good heavens!" cried Inglethorp, starting up. "What a monstrous idea! I—poison my dearest Emily!"

"I do not think"—Poirot watched him narrowly—"that you quite realize the unfavourable nature of your evidence at the inquest. Mr. Inglethorp, knowing what I have now told you, do you still refuse to say where you were at six o'clock on Monday afternoon?"

With a groan, Alfred Inglethorp sank down again and buried his face in his hands. Poirot approached and stood over him.

"Speak!" he cried menacingly.

With an effort, Inglethorp raised his face from his hands. Then, slowly and deliberately, he shook his head.

"You will not speak?"

"No. I do not believe that anyone could be so monstrous as to accuse me of what you say."

Poirot nodded thoughtfully, like a man whose mind is made up.

"*Soit!*" he said. "Then I must speak for you."

Alfred Inglethorp sprang up again.

"You? How can you speak? You do not know——" He broke off abruptly.

Poirot turned to face us. "*Mesdames* and *messieurs*! I speak! Listen! I, Hercule Poirot, affirm that the man who entered the chemist's shop, and purchased strychnine at six o'clock on Monday last was not Mr. Inglethorp, for at six o'clock on that day Mr. Inglethorp was escorting Mrs. Raikes back to her home from a neighbouring farm. I can produce no less than five witnesses to swear to having seen them together, either at six or just after and, as you may know, the Abbey Farm, Mrs. Raikes's home, is at least two and a half miles distant from the village. There is absolutely no question as to the alibi!"

VIII

FRESH SUSPICIONS

There was a moment's stupefied silence. Japp, who was the least surprised of any of us, was the first to speak.

"My word," he cried, "you're the goods! And no mistake, Mr. Poirot! These witnesses of yours are all right, I suppose?"

"*Voilà!* I have prepared a list of them—names and addresses. You must see them, of course. But you will find it all right."

"I'm sure of that." Japp lowered his voice. "I'm much obliged to you. A pretty mare's nest arresting him would have been." He turned to Inglethorp. "But, if you'll excuse me, sir, why couldn't you say all this at the inquest?"

"I will tell you why," interrupted Poirot. "There was a certain rumour——"

"A most malicious and utterly untrue one," interrupted Alfred Inglethorp in an agitated voice.

"And Mr. Inglethorp was anxious to have no scandal revived just at present. Am I right?"

"Quite right." Inglethorp nodded. "With my poor Emily not

yet buried, can you wonder I was anxious that no more lying rumours should be started."

"Between you and me, sir," remarked Japp, "I'd sooner have any amount of rumours than be arrested for murder. And I venture to think your poor lady would have felt the same. And, if it hadn't been for Mr. Poirot here, arrested you would have been, as sure as eggs is eggs!"

"I was foolish, no doubt," murmured Inglethorp. "But you do not know, Inspector, how I have been persecuted and maligned." And he shot a baleful glance at Evelyn Howard.

"Now, sir," said Japp, turning briskly to John, "I should like to see the lady's bedroom, please, and after that I'll have a little chat with the servants. Don't you bother about anything. Mr. Poirot, here, will show me the way."

As they all went out of the room, Poirot turned and made me a sign to follow him upstairs. There he caught me by the arm, and drew me aside.

"Quick, go to the other wing. Stand there—just this side of the baize door. Do not move till I come." Then, turning rapidly, he rejoined the two detectives.

I followed his instructions, taking up my position by the baize door, and wondering what on earth lay behind the request. Why was I to stand in this particular spot on guard? I looked thoughtfully down the corridor in front of me. An idea struck me. With the exception of Cynthia Murdoch's, every one's room was in this left wing. Had that anything to do with it? Was I to report who came or went? I stood faithfully at my post. The minutes passed. Nobody came. Nothing happened.

It must have been quite twenty minutes before Poirot rejoined me.

"You have not stirred?"

"No, I've stuck here like a rock. Nothing's happened."

"Ah!" Was he pleased, or disappointed? "You've seen nothing at all?"

"No."

"But you have probably heard something? A big bump—eh, *mon ami?*"

"No."

"Is it possible? Ah, but I am vexed with myself! I am not usually clumsy. I made but a slight gesture"—I know Poirot's gestures—"with the left hand, and over went the table by the bed!"

He looked so childishly vexed and crest-fallen that I hastened to console him.

"Never mind, old chap. What does it matter? Your triumph downstairs excited you. I can tell you, that was a surprise to us all. There must be more in this affair of Inglethorp's with Mrs. Raikes than we thought, to make him hold his tongue so persistently. What are you going to do now? Where are the Scotland Yard fellows?"

"Gone down to interview the servants. I showed them all our exhibits. I am disappointed in Japp. He has no method!"

"Hullo!" I said, looking out of the window. "Here's Dr. Bauerstein. I believe you're right about that man, Poirot. I don't like him."

"He is clever," observed Poirot meditatively.

"Oh, clever as the devil! I must say I was overjoyed to see him in the plight he was in on Tuesday. You never saw such a spectacle!" And I described the doctor's adventure. "He looked a regular scarecrow! Plastered with mud from head to foot."

"You saw him, then?"

"Yes. Of course, he didn't want to come in—it was just after dinner—but Mr. Inglethorp insisted."

"What?" Poirot caught me violently by the shoulders. "Was Dr. Bauerstein here on Tuesday evening? Here? And you never told me? Why did you not tell me? Why? Why?"

He appeared to be in an absolute frenzy.

"My dear Poirot," I expostulated, "I never thought it would interest you. I didn't know it was of any importance."

"Importance? It is of the first importance! So Dr. Bauerstein was here on Tuesday night—the night of the murder. Hastings, do you not see? That alters everything—everything!"

I had never seen him so upset. Loosening his hold of me, he mechanically straightened a pair of candlesticks, still murmuring to himself: "Yes, that alters everything—everything."

Suddenly he seemed to come to a decision.

"Allons!" he said. "We must act at once. Where is Mr. Cavendish?"

John was in the smoking-room. Poirot went straight to him.

"Mr. Cavendish, I have some important business in Tadminster. A new clue. May I take your motor?"

"Why, of course. Do you mean at once?"

"If you please."

John rang the bell, and ordered round the car. In another ten minutes, we were racing down the park and along the high road to Tadminster.

"Now, Poirot," I remarked resignedly, "perhaps you will tell me what all this is about?"

"Well, *mon ami,* a good deal you can guess for yourself. Of course you realize that, now Mr. Inglethorp is out of it, the whole position is greatly changed. We are face to face with an entirely new problem. We know now that there is one person who did not buy the poison. We have cleared away the manufactured clues. Now for the real ones. I have ascertained that anyone in the household, with the exception of Mrs. Cavendish, who was playing tennis with you, could have personated Mr. Inglethorp on Monday evening. In the same way, we have his statement that he put the coffee down in the hall. No one took much notice of that at the inquest—but now it has a very different significance. We must find out who did take that coffee to Mrs. Inglethorp eventually, or who passed through the hall whilst it was standing there. From your account, there are only two people whom we can positively say did not go near the coffee— Mrs. Cavendish, and Mademoiselle Cynthia."

"Yes, that is so." I felt an inexpressible lightening of the heart. Mary Cavendish could certainly not rest under suspicion.

"In clearing Alfred Inglethorp," continued Poirot, "I have been obliged to show my hand sooner than I intended. As long as I might be thought to be pursuing him, the criminal would be off his guard. Now, he will be doubly careful. Yes— doubly careful." He turned to me abruptly. "Tell me, Hastings, you yourself—have you no suspicions of anybody?"

I hesitated. To tell the truth, an idea, wild and extravagant in itself, had once or twice that morning flashed through my brain. I had rejected it as absurd, nevertheless it persisted.

"You couldn't call it a suspicion," I murmured. "It's so utterly foolish."

"Come now," urged Poirot encouragingly. "Do not fear. Speak your mind. You should always pay attention to your instincts."

"Well then," I blurted out, "it's absurd—but I suspect Miss Howard of not telling all she knows!"

"Miss Howard?"

"Yes—you'll laugh at me——"

"Not at all. Why should I?"

"I can't help feeling," I continued blunderingly, "that we've rather left her out of the possible suspects, simply on the strength of her having been away from the place. But, after all, she was only fifteen miles away. A car would do it in half an hour. Can we say positively that she was away from Styles on the night of the murder?"

"Yes, my friend," said Poirot unexpectedly, "we can. One of my first actions was to ring up the hospital where she was working."

"Well?"

"Well, I learnt that Miss Howard had been on afternoon duty on Tuesday, and that—a convoy coming in unexpectedly—she had kindly offered to remain on night duty, which offer was gratefully accepted. That disposes of that."

"Oh!" I said, rather nonplussed. "Really," I continued, "it's her extraordinary vehemence against Inglethorp that started me off suspecting her. I can't help feeling she'd do anything against him. And I had an idea she might know something about the destroying of the will. She might have burnt the new one, mistaking it for the earlier one in his favour. She is so terribly bitter against him."

"You consider her vehemence unnatural?"

"Y—es. She is so very violent. I wonder really whether she is quite sane on that point."

Poirot shook his head energetically.

"No, no, you are on a wrong tack there. There is nothing weak-minded or degenerate about Miss Howard. She is an excellent specimen of well balanced English beef and brawn. She is sanity itself."

"Yet her hatred of Inglethorp seems almost a mania. My idea was—a very ridiculous one, no doubt—that she had intended to poison him—and that, in some way, Mrs. Inglethorp got hold of it by mistake. But I don't at all see how it could have been done. The whole thing is absurd and ridiculous to the last degree."

"Still you are right in one thing. It is always wiser to suspect everybody until you can prove logically, and to your own satisfaction, that they are innocent. Now, what reasons are there against Miss Howard's having deliberately poisoned Mrs. Inglethorp?"

"Why, she was devoted to her!" I exclaimed.

"Tcha! Tcha!" cried Poirot irritably. "You argue like a child. If Miss Howard were capable of poisoning the old lady, she would be quite capable of simulating devotion. No, we must look elsewhere. You are perfectly correct in your assumption that her vehemence against Alfred Inglethorp is too violent to be natural; but you are quite wrong in the deduction you draw from it. I have drawn my own deductions, which I believe to be correct, but I will not speak of them at present." He paused a minute, then went on. "Now, to my way of thinking, there is one insuperable objection to Miss Howard's being the murderess."

"And that is?"

"That in no possible way could Mrs. Inglethorp's death benefit Miss Howard. Now there is no murder without a motive."

I reflected.

"Could not Mrs. Inglethorp have made a will in her favour?"

Poirot shook his head.

"But you yourself suggested that possibility to Mr. Wells?"

Poirot smiled.

"That was for a reason. I did not want to mention the name of the person who was actually in my mind. Miss Howard occupied very much the same position, so I used her name instead."

"Still, Mrs. Inglethorp might have done so. Why, that will,

made on the afternoon of her death may——"

But Poirot's shake of the head was so energetic that I stopped.

"No, my friend. I have certain little ideas of my own about that will. But I can tell you this much—it was not in Miss Howard's favour."

I accepted his assurance, though I did not really see how he could be so positive about the matter.

"Well," I said, with a sigh, "we will acquit Miss Howard, then. It is partly your fault that I ever came to suspect her. It was what you said about her evidence at the inquest that set me off."

Poirot looked puzzled.

"What did I say about her evidence at the inquest?"

"Don't you remember? When I cited her and John Cavendish as being above suspicion?"

"Oh—ah—yes." He seemed a little confused, but recovered himself. "By the way, Hastings, there is something I want you to do for me."

"Certainly. What is it?"

"Next time you happen to be alone with Lawrence Cavendish, I want you to say this to him. 'I have a message for you, from Poirot. He says: "Find the extra coffee cup, and you can rest in peace!"' Nothing more. Nothing less."

"'Find the extra coffee cup, and you can rest in peace.' Is that right?" I asked, much mystified.

"Excellent."

"But what does it mean?"

"Ah, that I will leave you to find out. You have access to the facts. Just say that to him, and see what he says."

"Very well—but it's all extremely mysterious."

We were running into Tadminster now, and Poirot directed the car to the "Analytical Chemist."

Poirot hopped down briskly, and went inside. In a few minutes he was back again.

"There," he said. "That is all my business."

"What were you doing there?" I asked, in lively curiosity.

"I left something to be analysed."

"Yes, but what?"

"The sample of coco I took from the saucepan in the bedroom."

"But that has already been tested!" I cried, stupefied. "Dr. Bauerstein had it tested, and you yourself laughed at the possibility of there being strychnine in it."

"I know Dr. Bauerstein had it tested," replied Poirot quietly.

"Well, then?"

"Well, I have a fancy for having it analysed again, that is all."

And not another word on the subject could I drag out of him.

This proceeding of Poirot's, in respect of the coco, puzzled me intensely. I could see neither rhyme nor reason in it. However, my confidence in him, which at one time had rather waned, was fully restored since his belief in Alfred Inglethorp's innocence had been so triumphantly vindicated.

The funeral of Mrs. Inglethorp took place the following day, and on Monday, as I came down to a late breakfast, John drew me aside, and informed me that Mr. Inglethorp was leaving that morning, to take up his quarters at the Stylites Arms until he should have completed his plans.

"And really it's a great relief to think he's going, Hastings," continued my honest friend. "It was bad enough before, when we thought he'd done it, but I'm hanged if it isn't worse now, when we all feel guilty for having been so down on the fellow. The fact is, we've treated him abominably. Of course, things did look black against him. I don't see how anyone could blame us for jumping to the conclusions we did. Still, there it is, we were in the wrong, and now there's a beastly feeling that one ought to make amends; which is difficult, when one doesn't like the fellow a bit better than one did before. The whole thing's damned awkward! And I'm thankful he's had the tact to take himself off. It's a good thing Styles wasn't the mater's to leave to him. Couldn't bear to think of the fellow lording it here. He's welcome to her money."

"You'll be able to keep up the place all right?" I asked.

"Oh, yes. There are the death duties, of course, but half

my father's money goes with the place, and Lawrence will stay with us for the present, so there is his share as well. We shall be pinched at first, of course, because, as I once told you, I am in a bit of a hole financially myself. Still, the Johnnies will wait now."

In the general relief at Inglethorp's approaching departure, we had the most genial breakfast we had experienced since the tragedy. Cynthia, whose young spirits were naturally buoyant, was looking quite her pretty self again, and we all, with the exception of Lawrence, who seemed unalterably gloomy and nervous, were quietly cheerful, at the opening of a new and hopeful future.

The papers, of course, had been full of the tragedy. Glaring headlines, sandwiched biographies of every member of the household, subtle innuendoes, the usual familiar tag about the police having a clue. Nothing was spared us. It was a slack time. The war was momentarily inactive, and the newspapers seized with avidity on this crime in fashionable life: "The Mysterious Affair at Styles" was the topic of the moment.

Naturally it was very annoying for the Cavendishes. The house was constantly besieged by reporters, who were consistently denied admission, but who continued to haunt the village and the grounds, where they lay in wait with cameras, for any unwary members of the household. We all lived in a blast of publicity. The Scotland Yard men came and went, examining, questioning, lynx-eyed and reserved of tongue. Towards what end they were working, we did not know. Had they any clue, or would the whole thing remain in the category of unsolved crimes?

After breakfast, Dorcas came up to me rather mysteriously, and asked if she might have a few words with me.

"Certainly. What is it, Dorcas?"

"Well, it's just this, sir. You'll be seeing the Belgian gentleman to-day perhaps?" I nodded. "Well, sir, you know how he asked me so particular if the mistress, or anyone else, had a green dress?"

"Yes, yes. You have found one?" My interest was aroused.

"No, not that, sir. But since then I've remembered what the young gentlemen"—John and Lawrence were still the "young gentlemen" to Dorcas—"call the 'dressing-up box.' It's up in the front attic, sir. A great chest, full of old clothes and fancy dresses, and what not. And it came to me sudden like that there might be a green dress amongst them. So, if you'd tell the Belgian gentleman——"

"I will tell him, Dorcas," I promised.

"Thank you very much, sir. A very nice gentleman he is, sir. And quite a different class from them two detectives from London, what goes prying about, and asking questions. I don't hold with foreigners as a rule, but from what the newspapers says I make out as how these brave Belges isn't the ordinary run of foreigners, and certainly he's a most polite spoken gentleman."

Dear old Dorcas! As she stood there, with her honest face upturned to mine, I thought what a fine specimen she was of the old-fashioned servant that is so fast dying out.

I thought I might as well go down to the village at once, and look up Poirot; but I met him half-way, coming up to the house, and at once gave him Dorcas's message.

"Ah, the brave Dorcas! We will look at the chest, although—but no matter—we will examine it all the same."

We entered the house by one of the windows. There was no one in the hall, and we went straight up to the attic.

Sure enough, there was the chest, a fine old piece, all studded with brass nails, and full to overflowing with every imaginable type of garment.

Poirot bundled everything out on the floor with scant ceremony. There were one or two green fabrics of varying shades; but Poirot shook his head over them all. He seemed somewhat apathetic in the search, as though he expected no great results from it. Suddenly he gave an exclamation.

"What is it?"

"Look!"

The chest was nearly empty, and there, reposing right at the bottom, was a magnificent black beard.

"*Ohó!*" said Poirot. "*Ohó!*" He turned it over in his hands, examining it closely. "New," he remarked. "Yes, quite new."

After a moment's hesitation, he replaced it in the chest, heaped all the other things on top of it as before, and made his way briskly downstairs. He went straight to the pantry, where we found Dorcas busily polishing her silver.

Poirot wished her good morning with Gallic politeness, and went on:

"We have been looking through that chest, Dorcas. I am much obliged to you for mentioning it. There is, indeed, a fine collection there. Are they often used, may I ask?"

"Well, sir, not very often nowadays, though from time to time we do have what the young gentlemen call 'a dress-up night.' And very funny it is sometimes, sir. Mr. Lawrence, he's wonderful. Most comic! I shall never forget the night he came down as the Char of Persia, I think he called it—a sort of Eastern King it was. He had the big paper knife in his hand, and 'Mind, Dorcas,' he says, 'you'll have to be very respectful. This is my specially sharpened scimitar, and it's off with your head if I'm at all displeased with you!' Miss Cynthia, she was what they call an Apache, or some such name—a Frenchified sort of cut-throat, I take it to be. A real sight she looked. You'd never have believed a pretty young lady like that could have made herself into such a ruffian. Nobody would have known her."

"These evenings must have been great fun," said Poirot genially. "I suppose Mr. Lawrence wore that fine black beard in the chest upstairs, when he was Shah of Persia?"

"He did have a beard, sir," replied Dorcas, smiling. "And well I know it, for he borrowed two skeins of my black wool to make it with! And I'm sure it looked wonderfully natural at a distance. I didn't know as there was a beard up there at all. It must have been got quite lately, I think. There was a red wig, I know, but nothing else in the way of hair. Burnt corks they use mostly—though 'tis messy getting it off again. Miss Cynthia was a nigger once, and, oh, the trouble she had."

"So Dorcas knows nothing about that black beard," said Poirot thoughtfully, as we walked out into the hall again.

"Do you think it is *the* one?" I whispered eagerly.

Poirot nodded.

"I do. You noticed it had been trimmed?"

"No."

"Yes. It was cut exactly the shape of Mr. Inglethorp's, and

I found one or two snipped hairs. Hastings, this affair is very deep."

"Who put it in the chest, I wonder?"

"Some one with a good deal of intelligence," remarked Poirot drily. "You realize that he chose the one place in the house to hide it where its presence would not be remarked? Yes, he is intelligent. But we must be more intelligent. We must be so intelligent that he does not suspect us of being intelligent at all."

I acquiesced.

"There, *mon ami*, you will be of great assistance to me."

I was pleased with the compliment. There had been times when I hardly thought that Poirot appreciated me at my true worth.

"Yes," he continued, staring at me thoughtfully, "you will be invaluable."

This was naturally gratifying, but Poirot's next words were not so welcome.

"I must have an ally in the house," he observed reflectively.

"You have me," I protested.

"True, but you are not sufficient."

I was hurt, and showed it. Poirot hurried to explain himself.

"You do not quite take my meaning. You are known to be working with me. I want somebody who is not associated with us in any way."

"Oh, I see. How about John?"

"No, I think not."

"The dear fellow isn't perhaps very bright," I said thoughtfully.

"Here comes Miss Howard," said Poirot suddenly. "She is the very person. But I am in her black books, since I cleared Mr. Inglethorp. Still, we can but try."

With a nod that was barely civil, Miss Howard assented to Poirot's request for a few minutes' conversation.

We went into the little morning-room, and Poirot closed the door.

"Well, Monsieur Poirot," said Miss Howard impatiently, "what is it? Out with it. I'm busy."

"Do you remember, mademoiselle, that I once asked you to help me?"

"Yes, I do." The lady nodded. "And I told you I'd help you with pleasure—to hang Alfred Inglethorp."

"Ah!" Poirot studied her seriously. "Miss Howard, I will ask you one question. I beg of you to reply to it truthfully."

"Never tell lies," replied Miss Howard.

"It is this. Do you still believe that Mrs. Inglethorp was poisoned by her husband?"

"What do you mean?" she asked sharply. "You needn't think your pretty explanations influence me in the slightest. I'll admit that it wasn't he who bought strychnine at the chemist's shop. What of that? I dare say he soaked fly paper, as I told you at the beginning."

"That is arsenic—not strychnine," said Poirot mildly.

"What does that matter? Arsenic would put poor Emily out of the way just as well as strychnine. If I'm convinced he did it, it doesn't matter a jot to me *how* he did it."

"Exactly. *If* you are convinced he did it," said Poirot quietly. "I will put my question in another form. Did you ever in your heart of hearts believe that Mrs. Inglethorp was poisoned by her husband?"

"Good heavens!" cried Miss Howard. "Haven't I always told you the man is a villain? Haven't I always told you he would murder her in her bed? Haven't I always hated him like poison?"

"Exactly," said Poirot. "That bears out my little idea entirely."

"What little idea?"

"Miss Howard, do you remember a conversation that took place on the day of my friend's arrival here? He repeated it to me, and there is a sentence of yours that has impressed me very much. Do you remember affirming that if a crime had been committed, and anyone you loved had been murdered, you felt certain that you would know by instinct who the criminal was, even if you were quite unable to prove it?"

"Yes, I remember saying that. I believe it too. I suppose you think it nonsense?"

"Not at all."

"And yet you will pay no attention to my instinct against Alfred Inglethorp?"

"No," said Poirot curtly. "Because your instinct is not against Mr. Inglethorp."

"What?"

"No. You wish to believe he committed the crime. You believe him capable of committing it. But your instinct tells you he did not commit it. It tells you more—shall I go on?"

She was staring at him, fascinated, and made a slight affirmative movement of the hand.

"Shall I tell you why you have been so vehement against Mr. Inglethorp? It is because you have been trying to believe what you wish to believe. It is because you are trying to drown and stifle your instinct, which tells you another name——"

"No, no, no!" cried Miss Howard wildly, flinging up her hands. "Don't say it! Oh, don't say it! It isn't true! It can't be true. I don't know what put such a wild—such a dreadful—idea into my head!"

"I am right, am I not?" asked Poirot.

"Yes, yes; you must be a wizard to have guessed. But it can't be so—it's too monstrous, too impossible. It *must* be Alfred Inglethorp."

Poirot shook his head gravely.

"Don't ask me about it," continued Miss Howard, "because I shan't tell you. I won't admit it, even to myself. I must be mad to think of such a thing."

Poirot nodded, as if satisfied.

"I will ask you nothing. It is enough for me that it is as I thought. And I—I, too, have an instinct. We are working together towards a common end."

"Don't ask me to help you, because I won't. I wouldn't lift a finger to—to——" She faltered.

"You will help me in spite of yourself. I ask you nothing—but you will be my ally. You will not be able to help yourself. You will do the only thing that I want of you."

"And that is?"

"You will watch!"

Evelyn Howard bowed her head.

"Yes, I can't help doing that. I am always watching—always hoping I shall be proved wrong."

"If we are wrong, well and good," said Poirot. "No one will be more pleased than I shall. But, if we are right? If we are right, Miss Howard, on whose side are you then?"

"I don't know, I don't know——"

"Come now."

"It could be hushed up."

"There must be no hushing up."

"But Emily herself——" She broke off.

"Miss Howard," said Poirot gravely, "this is unworthy of you."

Suddenly she took her face from her hands.

"Yes," she said quietly, "that was not Evelyn Howard who spoke!" She flung her head up proudly. "This is Evelyn Howard! And she is on the side of Justice! Let the cost be what it may." And with these words, she walked firmly out of the room.

"There," said Poirot, looking after her, "goes a very valuable ally. That woman, Hastings, has got brains as well as a heart."

I did not reply.

"Instinct is a marvellous thing," mused Poirot. "It can neither be explained nor ignored."

"You and Miss Howard seem to know what you are talking about," I observed coldly. "Perhaps you don't realize that *I* am still in the dark."

"Really? Is that so, *mon ami*?"

"Yes. Enlighten me, will you?"

Poirot studied me attentively for a moment or two. Then, to my intense surprise, he shook his head decidedly.

"No, my friend."

"Oh, look here, why not?"

"Two is enough for a secret."

"Well, I think it is very unfair to keep back facts from me."

"I am not keeping back facts. Every fact that I know is in your possession. You can draw your own deductions from them. This time it is a question of ideas."

"Still, it would be interesting to know."

Poirot looked at me very earnestly, and again shook his head.

"You see," he said sadly, "*you* have no instincts."

"It was intelligence you were requiring just now," I pointed out.

"The two often go together," said Poirot enigmatically.

The remark seemed so utterly irrelevant that I did not even take the trouble to answer it. But I decided that if I made any interesting and important discoveries—as no doubt I should—I would keep them to myself, and surprise Poirot with the ultimate result.

There are times when it is one's duty to assert oneself.

IX

DR. BAUERSTEIN

I had had no opportunity as yet of passing on Poirot's message to Lawrence. But now, as I strolled out on the lawn, still nursing a grudge against my friend's high-handedness, I saw Lawrence on the croquet lawn, aimlessly knocking a couple of very ancient balls about, with a still more ancient mallet.

It struck me that it would be a good opportunity to deliver my message. Otherwise, Poirot himself might relieve me of it. It was true that I did not quite gather its purport, but I flattered myself that by Lawrence's reply, and perhaps a little skillful cross-examination on my part, I should soon perceive its significance. Accordingly I accosted him.

"I've been looking for you," I remarked untruthfully.

"Have you?"

"Yes. The truth is, I've got a message for you—from Poirot."

"Yes?"

"He told me to wait until I was alone with you," I said, dropping my voice significantly, and watching him intently out of the corner of my eye. I have always been rather good at what is called, I believe, creating an atmosphere.

"Well?"

There was no change of expression in the dark melancholic face. Had he any idea of what I was about to say?

"This is the message." I dropped my voice still lower. " 'Find the extra coffee cup, and you can rest in peace.' "

"What on earth does he mean?" Lawrence stared at me in quite unaffected astonishment.

"Don't you know?"

"Not in the least. Do you?"

I was compelled to shake my head.

"What extra coffee cup?"

"I don't know."

"He'd better ask Dorcas, or one of the maids, if he wants to know about coffee cups. It's their business, not mine. I don't know anything about the coffee cups, except that we've got some that are never used, which are a perfect dream! Old Worcester. You're not a connoisseur, are you, Hastings?"

I shook my head.

"You miss a lot. A really perfect bit of old china—it's pure delight to handle it, or even to look at it."

"Well, what am I to tell Poirot?"

"Tell him I don't know what he's talking about. It's double Dutch to me."

"All right."

I was moving off towards the house again when he suddenly called me back.

"I say, what was the end of that message? Say it over again, will you?"

" 'Find the extra coffee cup, and you can rest in peace.' Are you sure you don't know what it means?" I asked him earnestly.

He shook his head.

"No," he said musingly, "I don't. I—I wish I did."

The boom of the gong sounded from the house, and we went in together. Poirot had been asked by John to remain to lunch, and was already seated at the table.

By tacit consent, all mention of the tragedy was barred. We conversed on the war, and other outside topics. But after the cheese and biscuits had been handed round, and Dorcas had left the room, Poirot suddenly leant forward to Mrs. Cavendish.

"Pardon me, madame, for recalling unpleasant memories, but I have a little idea"—Poirot's "little ideas" were becoming a perfect byword—"and would like to ask one or two questions."

"Of me? Certainly."

"You are too amiable, madame. What I want to ask is this: the door leading into Mrs. Inglethorp's room from that of Mademoiselle Cynthia, it was bolted, you say?"

"Certainly it was bolted," replied Mary Cavendish, rather surprised. "I said so at the inquest."

"Bolted?"

"Yes." She looked perplexed.

"I mean," explained Poirot, "you are sure it was bolted, and not merely locked?"

"Oh, I see what you mean. No, I don't know. I said bolted, meaning that it was fastened, and I could not open it, but I believe all the doors were found bolted on the inside."

"Still, as far as you are concerned, the door might equally well have been locked?"

"Oh, yes."

"You yourself did not happen to notice, madame, when you entered Mrs. Inglethorp's room, whether that door was bolted or not?"

"I—I believe it was."

"But you did not see it?"

"No. I—never looked."

"But *I* did," interrupted Lawrence suddenly. "I happened to notice that it *was* bolted."

"Ah, that settles it." And Poirot looked crestfallen.

I could not help rejoicing that, for once, one of his "little ideas" had come to naught.

After lunch Poirot begged me to accompany him home. I consented rather stiffly.

"You are annoyed, is it not so?" he asked anxiously, as we walked through the park.

"Not at all," I said coldly.

"That is well. That lifts a great load from my mind."

This was not quite what I had intended. I had hoped that he would have observed the stiffness of my manner. Still, the fervour of his words went towards the appeasing of my just displeasure. I thawed.

"I gave Lawrence your message," I said.

"And what did he say? He was entirely puzzled?"

"Yes. I am quite sure he had no idea of what you meant."

I had expected Poirot to be disappointed; but, to my surprise, he replied that that was as he had thought, and that he was very glad. My pride forbade me to ask any questions.

Poirot switched off on another tack.

"Mademoiselle Cynthia was not at lunch today? How was that?"

"She is at the hospital again. She resumed work today."

"Ah, she is an industrious little demoiselle. And pretty too. She is like pictures I have seen in Italy. I would rather like to see that dispensary of hers. Do you think she would show it to me?"

"I am sure she would be delighted. It's an interesting little place."

"Does she go there every day?"

"She has all Wednesdays off, and comes back to lunch on Saturdays. Those are her only times off."

"I will remember. Women are doing great work nowadays, and Mademoiselle Cynthia is clever—oh, yes, she has brains, that little one."

"Yes. I believe she has passed quite a stiff exam."

"Without doubt. After all, it is very responsible work. I suppose they have very strong poisons there?"

"Yes, she showed them to us. They are kept locked up in a little cupboard. I believe they have to be very careful. They always take out the key before leaving the room."

"Indeed. It is near the window, this cupboard?"

"No, right the other side of the room. Why?"

Poirot shrugged his shoulders.

"I wondered. That is all. Will you come in?"

We had reached the cottage.

"No. I think I'll be getting back. I shall go round the long way through the woods."

The woods round Styles were very beautiful. After the

walk across the open park, it was pleasant to saunter lazily through the cool glades. There was hardly a breath of wind, the very chirp of the birds was faint and subdued. I strolled on a little way, and finally flung myself down at the foot of a grand old beech-tree. My thoughts of mankind were kindly and charitable. I even forgave Poirot for his absurd secrecy. In fact, I was at peace with the world. Then I yawned.

I thought about the crime, and it struck me as being very unreal and far off.

I yawned again.

Probably, I thought, it really never happened. Of course, it was all a bad dream. The truth of the matter was that it was Lawrence who had murdered Alfred Inglethorp with a croquet mallet. But it was absurd of John to make such a fuss about it, and to go shouting out: "I tell you I won't have it!"

I woke up with a start.

At once I realized that I was in a very awkward predicament. For, about twelve feet away from me, John and Mary Cavendish were standing facing each other, and they were evidently quarrelling. And, quite as evidently, they were unaware of my vicinity, for before I could move or speak John repeated the words which had aroused me from my dream.

"I tell you, Mary, I won't have it."

Mary's voice came, cool and liquid:

"Have *you* any right to criticize my actions?"

"It will be the talk of the village! My mother was only buried on Saturday, and here you are gadding about with the fellow."

"Oh," she shrugged her shoulders, "if it is only village gossip that you mind!"

"But it isn't. I've had enough of the fellow hanging about. He's a Polish Jew, anyway."

"A tinge of Jewish blood is not a bad thing. It leavens the"—she looked at him—"stolid stupidity of the ordinary Englishman."

Fire in her eyes, ice in her voice. I did not wonder that the blood rose to John's face in a crimson tide.

"Mary!"

"Well?" Her tone did not change.

The pleading died out of his voice.

"Am I to understand that you will continue to see Bauerstein against my express wishes?"

"If I choose."

"You defy me?"

"No, but I deny your right to criticize my actions. Have *you* no friends of whom I should disapprove?"

John fell back a pace. The colour ebbed slowly from his face.

"What do you mean?" he said, in an unsteady voice.

"You see!" said Mary quietly. "You do see, don't you, that *you* have no right to dictate to *me* as to the choice of my friends?"

John glanced at her pleadingly, a stricken look in his face.

"No right? Have I *no* right, Mary?" he said unsteadily. He stretched out his hands. "Mary——"

For a moment, I thought she wavered. A softer expression came over her face, then suddenly she turned almost fiercely away.

"None!"

She was walking away when John sprang after her, and caught her by the arm.

"Mary"—his voice was very quiet now—"are you in love with this fellow Bauerstein?"

She hesitated, and suddenly there swept across her face a strange expression, old as the hills, yet with something eternally young about it. So might some Egyptian sphinx have smiled.

She freed herself quietly from his arm, and spoke over her shoulder.

"Perhaps," she said; and then swiftly passed out of the little glade, leaving John standing there as though he had been turned to stone.

Rather ostentatiously, I stepped forward, crackling some dead branches with my feet as I did so. John turned. Luckily, he took it for granted that I had only just come upon the scene.

"Hullo, Hastings. Have you seen the little fellow safely back to his cottage? Quaint little chap! Is he any good, though, really?"

"He was considered one of the finest detectives of his day."

"Oh, well, I suppose there must be something in it, then. What a rotten world it is, though!"

"You find it so?" I asked.

"Good Lord, yes! There's this terrible business to start with. Scotland Yard men in and out of the house like a jack-in-the-box! Never know where they won't turn up next. Screaming headlines in every paper in the country—damn all journalists, I say! Do you know there was a whole crowd staring in at the lodge gates this morning. Sort of Madame Tussaud's chamber of horrors business that can be seen for nothing. Pretty thick, isn't it?"

"Cheer up, John!" I said soothingly. "It can't last for ever."

"Can't it, though? It can last long enough for us never to be able to hold up our heads again."

"No, no, you're getting morbid on the subject."

"Enough to make a man morbid, to be stalked by beastly journalists and stared at by gaping moon-faced idiots, wherever he goes! But there's worse than that."

"What?"

John lowered his voice:

"Have you ever thought, Hastings—it's a nightmare to me—who did it? I can't help feeling sometimes it must have been an accident. Because—because—who could have done it? Now Inglethorp's out of the way, there's no one else; no one, I mean, except—one of us."

Yes, indeed, that was nightmare enough for any man! One of us? Yes, surely it must be so, unless——

A new idea suggested itself to my mind. Rapidly, I considered it. The light increased. Poirot's mysterious doings, his hints—they all fitted in. Fool that I was not to have thought of this possibility before, and what a relief for us all.

"No, John," I said, "it isn't one of us. How could it be?"

"I know, but, still, who else is there?"

"Can't you guess?"

"No."

I looked cautiously round, and lowered my voice.

"Dr. Bauerstein!" I whispered.

"Impossible!"

"Not at all."

"But what earthly interest could he have in my mother's death?"

"That I don't see," I confessed, "but I'll tell you this: Poirot thinks so."

"Poirot? Does he? How do you know?"

I told him of Poirot's intense excitement on hearing that Dr. Bauerstein had been at Styles on the fatal night, and added:

"He said twice: 'That alters everything.' And I've been thinking. You know Inglethorp said he had put down the coffee in the hall? Well, it was just then that Bauerstein arrived. Isn't it possible that, as Inglethorp brought him through the hall, the doctor dropped something into the coffee in passing?"

"H'm," said John. "It would have been very risky."

"Yes, but it was possible."

"And then, how could he know it was her coffee? No, old fellow, I don't think that will wash."

But I had remembered something else.

"You're quite right. That wasn't how it was done. Listen." And I then told him of the coco sample which Poirot had taken to be analysed.

John interrupted just as I had done.

"But, look here, Bauerstein had had it analysed already?"

"Yes yes, that's the point. I didn't see it either until now. Don't you understand? Bauerstein had it analysed—that's just it! If Bauerstein's the murderer, nothing could be simpler than for him to substitute some ordinary coco for his sample, and send that to be tested. And of course they would find no strychnine! But no one would dream of suspecting Bauerstein, or think of taking another sample—except Poirot," I added, with belated recognition.

"Yes, but what about the bitter taste that coco won't disguise?"

"Well, we've only his word for that. And there are other possibilities. He's admittedly one of the world's greatest toxicologists——"

"One of the world's greatest what? Say it again."

"He knows more about poisons than almost anybody," I explained. "Well, my idea is, that perhaps he's found some way of making strychnine tasteless. Or it may not have been strychnine at all, but some obscure drug no one has ever heard of, which produces much the same symptoms."

"H'm, yes, that might be," said John. "But look here, how could he have got at the coco? That wasn't downstairs?"

"No, it wasn't," I admitted reluctantly.

And then, suddenly, a dreadful possibility flashed through my mind. I hoped and prayed it would not occur to John also. I glanced sideways at him. He was frowning perplexedly, and I drew a deep breath of relief, for the terrible thought that had flashed across my mind was this: that Dr. Bauerstein might have had an accomplice.

Yet surely it could not be ! Surely no woman as beautiful as Mary Cavendish could be a murderess. Yet beautiful women had been known to poison.

And suddenly I remembered that first conversation at tea on the day of my arrival, and the gleam in her eyes as she had said that poison was a woman's weapon. How agitated she had been on that fatal Tuesday evening! Had Mrs. Inglethorp discovered something between her and Bauerstein, and threatened to tell her husband? Was it to stop that denunciation that the crime had been committed?

Then I remembered that enigmatical conversation between Poirot and Evelyn Howard. Was this what they had meant? Was this the monstrous possibility that Evelyn had tried not to believe?

Yes, it all fitted in.

No wonder Miss Howard had suggested "hushing it up." Now I understood that unfinished sentence of hers: "Emily herself——" And in my heart I agreed with her. Would not Mrs. Inglethorp have preferred to go unavenged rather than have such terrible dishonor fall upon the name of Cavendish?

"There's another thing," said John suddenly, and the unexpected sound of his voice made me start guiltily. "Something which makes me doubt if what you say can be true."

"What's that?" I asked, thankful that he had gone away from the subject of how the poison could have been introduced into the coco.

"Why, the fact that Bauerstein demanded a post-mortem.

He needn't have done so. Little Wilkins would have been quite content to let it go at heart disease."

"Yes," I said doubtfully. "But we don't know. Perhaps he thought it safer in the long run. Some one might have talked afterwards. Then the Home Office might have ordered exhumation. The whole thing would have come out, then, and he would have been in an awkward position, for no one would have believed that a man of his reputation could have been deceived into calling it heart disease."

"Yes, that's possible," admitted John. "Still," he added, "I'm blest if I can see what his motive could have been."

I trembled.

"Look here," I said, "I may be altogether wrong. And, remember, all this is in confidence."

"Oh, of course—that goes without saying."

We had walked, as we talked, and now we passed through the little gate into the garden. Voices rose near at hand, for tea was spread out under the sycamore-tree, as it had been on the day of my arrival.

Cynthia was back from the hospital, and I placed my chair beside her, and told her of Poirot's wish to visit the dispensary.

"Of course! I'd love him to see it. He'd better come to tea there one day. I must fix it up with him. He's such a dear little man! But he is funny. He made me take the brooch out of my tie the other day, and put it in again, because he said it wasn't straight."

I laughed.

"It's quite a mania with him."

"Yes, isn't it?"

We were silent for a minute or two, and then, glancing in the direction of Mary Cavendish, and dropping her voice, Cynthia said:

"Mr. Hastings."

"Yes?"

"After tea, I want to talk to you."

Her glance at Mary had set me thinking. I fancied that between these two there existed very little sympathy. For the first time, it occurred to me to wonder about the girl's future. Mrs. Inglethorp had made no provision of any kind for her, but I imagined that John and Mary would probably insist on her making her home with them—at any rate until the end of the war. John, I knew, was very fond of her, and would be sorry to let her go.

John, who had gone into the house, now reappeared. His good-natured face wore an unaccustomed frown of anger.

"Confound those detectives! I can't think what they're after! They've been in every room in the house—turning things inside out, and upside down. It really is too bad! I suppose they took advantage of our all being out. I shall go for that fellow Japp, when I next see him!"

"Lot of Paul Prys," grunted Miss Howard.

Lawrence opined that they had to make a show of doing something.

Mary Cavendish said nothing.

After tea, I invited Cynthia to come for a walk, and we sauntered off into the woods together.

"Well?" I inquired, as soon as we were protected from prying eyes by the leafy screen.

With a sigh, Cynthia flung herself down, and tossed off her hat. The sunlight, piercing through the branches, turned the auburn of her hair to quivering gold.

"Mr. Hastings—you are always so kind, and you know such a lot."

It struck me at this moment that Cynthia was really a very charming girl! Much more charming than Mary, who never said things of that kind.

"Well?" I asked benignantly, as she hesitated.

"I want to ask your advice. What shall I do?"

"Do?"

"Yes. You see, Aunt Emily always told me I should be provided for. I suppose she forgot, or didn't think she was likely to die—anyway, I am not provided for! And I don't know what to do. Do you think I ought to go away from here at once?"

"Good heavens, no! They don't want to part with you, I'm sure."

Cynthia hesitated a moment, plucking up the grass with her tiny hands. Then she said: "Mrs. Cavendish does. She hates me."

"Hates you?" I cried, astonished.

Cynthia nodded.

"Yes. I don't know why, but she can't bear me; and he can't, either."

"There I know you're wrong," I said warmly. "On the contrary, John is very fond of you."

"Oh, yes—*John*. I meant Lawrence. Not, of course, that I care whether Lawrence hates me or not. Still, it's rather horrid when no one loves you, isn't it?"

"But they do, Cynthia dear," I said earnestly. "I'm sure you are mistaken. Look, there is John—and Miss Howard—"

Cynthia nodded rather gloomily. "Yes, John likes me, I think, and of course Evie, for all her gruff ways, wouldn't be unkind to a fly. But Lawrence never speaks to me if he can help it, and Mary can hardly bring herself to be civil to me. She wants Evie to stay on, is begging her to, but she doesn't want me, and—and—I don't know what to do." Suddenly the poor child burst out crying.

I don't know what possessed me. Her beauty, perhaps, as she sat there, with the sunlight glinting down on her head; perhaps the sense of relief at encountering someone who so obviously could have no connection with the tragedy; perhaps honest pity for her youth and loneliness. Anyway, I leant forward, and taking her little hand, I said awkwardly:

"Marry me, Cynthia."

Unwittingly, I had hit upon a sovereign remedy for her tears. She sat up at once, drew her hand away, and said, with some asperity:

"Don't be silly!"

I was a little annoyed.

"I'm not being silly. I am asking you to do me the honour of becoming my wife."

To my intense surprise, Cynthia burst out laughing, and called me a "funny dear".

"It's perfectly sweet of you," she said, "but you know you don't want to!"

"Yes, I do. I've got—"

"Never mind what you've got. You don't really want to—and I don't either."

"Well, of course, that settles it," I said stiffly. "But I don't see anything to laugh at. There's nothing funny about a proposal."

"No, indeed," said Cynthia. "Somebody might accept you next time. Good-bye, you've cheered me up *very* much."

And, with a final uncontrollable burst of merriment, she vanished through the trees.

Thinking over the interview, it struck me as being profoundly unsatisfactory.

It occurred to me suddenly that I would go down to the village, and look up Bauerstein. Somebody ought to be keeping an eye on the fellow. At the same time, it would be wise to allay any suspicions he might have as to his being suspected. I remembered how Poirot had relied on my diplomacy. Accordingly, I went to the little house with the "Apartments" card inserted in the window, where I knew he lodged, and tapped on the door.

An old woman came and opened it.

"Good afternoon," I said pleasantly. "Is Dr. Bauerstein in?"

She stared at me.

"Haven't you heard?"

"Heard what?"

"About him."

"What about him?"

"He's took."

"Took? Dead?"

"No, took by the perlice."

"By the police!" I gasped. "Do you mean they've arrested him?"

"Yes, that's it, and—"

I waited to hear no more, but tore up the village to find Poirot.

X

THE ARREST

To my extreme annoyance, Poirot was not in, and the old Belgian who answered my knock informed me that he believed he had gone to London.

I was dumbfounded. What on earth could Poirot be doing in London! Was it a sudden decision on his part, or had he already made up his mind when he parted from me a few hours earlier?

I retraced my steps to Styles in some annoyance. With Poirot away, I was uncertain how to act. Had he foreseen this arrest? Had he not, in all probability, been the cause of it? Those questions I could not resolve. But in the meantime what was I to do? Should I announce the arrest openly at Styles, or not? Though I did not acknowledge it to myself, the thought of Mary Cavendish was weighing on me. Would it not be a terrible shock to her? For the moment, I set aside utterly any suspicions of her. She could not be implicated— otherwise I should have heard some hint of it.

Of course, there was no possibility of being able permanently to conceal Dr. Bauerstein's arrest from her. It would be announced in every newspaper on the morrow. Still, I shrank from blurting it out. If only Poirot had been accessible, I could have asked his advice. What possessed him to go posting off to London in this unaccountable way?

In spite of myself, my opinion of his sagacity was immeasurably heightened. I would never have dreamt of suspecting the doctor, had not Poirot put it into my head. Yes, decidedly, the little man was clever.

After some reflecting, I decided to take John into my confidence, and leave him to make the matter public or not, as he thought fit.

He gave vent to a prodigious whistle, as I imparted the news.

"Great Scot! You *were* right, then. I couldn't believe it at the time."

"No, it is astonishing until you get used to the idea, and see how it makes everything fit in. Now, what are we to do? Of course, it will be generally known to-morrow."

John reflected.

"Never mind," he said at last, "we won't say anything at present. There is no need. As you say, it will be known soon enough."

But to my intense surprise, on getting down early the next morning, and eagerly opening the newspapers, there was not a word about the arrest! There was a column of mere padding about "The Styles Poisoning Case," but nothing further. It was rather inexplicable, but I supposed that, for some reason or other, Japp wished to keep it out of the papers. It worried me just a little, for it suggested the possibility that there might be further arrests to come.

After breakfast, I decided to go down to the village, and see if Poirot had returned yet; but, before I could start, a well known face blocked one of the windows, and the well known voice said:

"*Bon jour, mon ami!*"

"Poirot," I exclaimed, with relief, and seizing him by both hands, I dragged him into the room. "I was never so glad to see anyone. Listen, I have said nothing to anybody but John. Is that right?"

"My friend," replied Poirot, "I do not know what you are talking about."

"Dr. Bauerstein's arrest, of course," I answered impatiently.

"Is Bauerstein arrested, then?"

"Did you not know it?"

"Not the least in the world." But, pausing a moment, he added: "Still, it does not surprise me. After all, we are only four miles from the coast."

"The coast?" I asked, puzzled. "What has that got to do with it?"

Poirot shrugged his shoulders.

"Surely, it is obvious!"

"Not to me. No doubt I am very dense, but I cannot see what the proximity of the coast has got to do with the murder of Mrs. Inglethorp."

"Nothing at all, of course," replied Poirot, smiling. "But we are speaking of the arrest of Dr. Bauerstein."

"Well, he is arrested for the murder of Mrs. Inglethorp—"

"What?" cried Poirot, in apparently lively astonishment. "Dr. Bauerstein arrested for the murder of Mrs. Inglethorp?"

"Yes."

"Impossible! That would be too good a farce! Who told you that, my friend?"

"Well, no one exactly told me," I confessed. "But he is arrested."

"Oh, yes, very likely. But for espionage, *mon ami.*"

"Espionage?" I gasped.

"Precisely."

"Not for poisoning Mrs. Inglethorp?"

"Not unless our friend Japp has taken leave of his senses," replied Poirot placidly.

"But—but I thought you thought so too?"

Poirot gave me one look, which conveyed a wondering pity, and his full sense of the utter absurdity of such an idea.

"Do you mean to say," I asked, slowly adapting myself to the new idea, "that Dr. Bauerstein is a spy?"

Poirot nodded.

"Have you never suspected it?"

"It never entered my head."

"It did not strike you as peculiar that a famous London doctor should bury himself in a little village like this, and should be in the habit of walking about at all hours of the night, fully dressed?"

"No," I confessed, "I never thought of such a thing."

"He is, of course, a German by birth," said Poirot thoughtfully, "though he has practised so long in this country that nobody thinks of him as anything but an Englishman. He was naturalized about fifteen years ago. A very clever man."

"The blackguard!" I cried indignantly.

"Not at all. He is, on the contrary, a patriot. Think what he stands to lose. I admire the man myself."

But I could not look at it in Poirot's philosophical way.

"And this is the man with whom Mrs. Cavendish has been wandering about all over the country!" I cried indignantly.

"Yes. I should fancy he had found her very useful," remarked Poirot. "So long as gossip busied itself in coupling their names together, any other vagaries of the doctor's passed unobserved."

"Then you think he never really cared for her?" I asked eagerly—rather too eagerly, perhaps, under the circumstances.

"That, of course, I cannot say, but—shall I tell you my own private opinion, Hastings?"

"Yes."

"Well, it is this: that Mrs. Cavendish does not care, and never has cared one little jot about Dr. Bauerstein!"

"Do you really think so?" I could not disguise my pleasure.

"I am quite sure of it. And I will tell you why."

"Yes?"

"Because she cares for some one else, *mon ami.*"

"Oh!" What did he mean? In spite of myself, an agreeable warmth spread over me. I am not a vain man where women are concerned, but I remembered certain evidences, too lightly thought of at the time, perhaps, but which certainly seemed to indicate——

My pleasing thoughts were interrupted by the sudden entrance of Miss Howard. She glanced round hastily to make sure there was no one else in the room, and quickly produced an old sheet of brown paper. This she handed to Poirot, murmuring as she did so the cryptic words:

"On top of the wardrobe." Then she hurriedly left the room.

Poirot unfolded the sheet of paper eagerly, and uttered an exclamation of satisfaction. He spread it out on the table.

"Come here, Hastings. Now tell me, what is that initial— J. or L.?"

It was a medium sized sheet of paper, rather dusty, as though it had lain by for some time. But it was the label that was attracting Poirot's attention. At the top, it bore the printed stamp of Messrs. Parkson's, the well known theatrical costumiers, and it was addressed to "—(the debatable initial) Cavendish, Esq., Styles Court, Styles St. Mary, Essex."

"It might be T., or it might be L.," I said, after studying the thing for a minute or two. "It certainly isn't a J."

"Good," replied Poirot, folding up the paper again. "I, also, am of your way of thinking. It is an L., depend upon it!"

"Where did it come from?" I asked curiously. "Is it important?"

"Moderately so. It confirms a surmise of mine. Having deduced its existence, I set Miss Howard to search for it, and, as you see, she has been successful."

"What did she mean by 'On the top of the wardrobe'?"

"She meant," replied Poirot promptly, "that she found it on top of a wardrobe."

"A funny place for a piece of brown paper," I mused.

"Not at all. The top of a wardrobe is an excellent place for brown paper and cardboard boxes. I have kept them there myself. Neatly arranged, there is nothing to offend the eye."

"Poirot," I asked earnestly, "have you made up your mind about this crime?"

"Yes—that is to say, I believe I know how it was committed."

"Ah!"

"Unfortunately, I have no proof beyond my surmise, unless—" With sudden energy, he caught me by the arm, and whirled me down the hall, calling out in French in his excitement: "Mademoiselle Dorcas, Mademoiselle Dorcas, *un moment, s'il vous plaît!*"

Dorcas, quite flurried by the noise, came hurrying out of the pantry.

"My good Dorcas, I have an idea—a little idea—if it should prove justified, what magnificent chance! Tell me, on Monday, not Tuesday, Dorcas, but Monday, the day before the tragedy, did anything go wrong with Mrs. Inglethorp's bell?"

Dorcas looked very surprised.

"Yes, sir, now you mention it, it did; though I don't know how you came to hear of it. A mouse, or some such, must have nibbled the wire through. The man came and put it right on Tuesday morning."

With a long drawn exclamation of ecstasy, Poirot led the way back to the morning-room.

"See you, one should not ask for outside proof—no, reason should be enough. But the flesh is weak, it is consolation to find that one is on the right track. Ah, my friend, I am like a giant refreshed. I run! I leap!"

And, in very truth, run and leap he did, gambolling wildly down the stretch of lawn outside the long window.

"What is your remarkable little friend doing?" asked a voice behind me, and I turned to find Mary Cavendish at my elbow. She smiled, and so did I. "What is it all about?"

"Really, I can't tell you. He asked Dorcas some question about a bell, and appeared so delighted with her answer that he is capering about as you see!"

Mary laughed.

"How ridiculous! He's going out of the gate. Isn't he coming back today?"

"I don't know. I've given up trying to guess what he'll do next."

"Is he quite mad, Mr. Hastings?"

"I honestly don't know. Sometimes, I feel sure he is as mad as a hatter; and then, just as he is at his maddest, I find there is method in his madness."

"I see."

In spite of her laugh, Mary was looking thoughtful this morning. She seemed grave, almost sad.

It occurred to me that it would be a good opportunity to tackle her on the subject of Cynthia. I began rather tactfully,

I thought, but I had not gone far before she stopped me authoritatively.

"You are an excellent advocate, I have no doubt, Mr. Hastings, but in this case your talents are quite thrown away. Cynthia will run no risk of encountering any unkindness from me."

I began to stammer feebly that I hoped she hadn't thought—But again she stopped me, and her words were so unexpected that they quite drove Cynthia, and her troubles, out of my mind.

"Mr. Hastings," she said, "do you think I and my husband are happy together?"

I was considerably taken aback, and murmured something about it not being my business to think anything of the sort.

"Well," she said quietly, "whether it is your business or not, I will tell you that we are *not* happy."

I said nothing, for I saw that she had not finished.

She began slowly, walking up and down the room, her head a little bent, and that slim, supple figure of hers swaying gently as she walked. She stopped suddenly, and looked up at me.

"You don't know anything about me, do you?" she asked. "Where I come from, who I was before I married John—anything, in fact? Well, I will tell you. I will make a father confessor of you. You are kind, I think—yes, I am sure you are kind."

Somehow, I was not quite as elated as I might have been. I remembered that Cynthia had begun her confidences in much the same way. Besides, a father confessor should be elderly, it is not at all the rôle for a young man.

"My father was English," said Mrs. Cavendish, "but my mother was a Russian."

"Ah," I said, "now I understand—"

"Understand what?"

"A hint of something foreign—different—that there has always been about you."

"My mother was very beautiful, I believe. I don't know, because I never saw her. She died when I was quite a little child. I believe there was some tragedy connected with her death—she took an overdose of some sleeping draught by mistake. However that may be, my father was broken-hearted. Shortly afterwards, he went into the Consular Service. Everywhere he went, I went with him. When I was twenty-three, I had been nearly all over the world. It was a splendid life—I loved it."

There was a smile on her face, and her head was thrown back. She seemed living in the memory of those old glad days.

"Then my father died. He left me very badly off. I had to go and live with some old aunts in Yorkshire." She shuddered. "You will understand me when I say that it was a deadly life for a girl brought up as I had been. The narrowness, the deadly monotony of it, almost drove me mad." She paused a minute, and added in a different tone: "And then I met John Cavendish."

"Yes?"

"You can imagine that, from my aunts' point of view, it was a very good match for me. But I can honestly say it was not this fact which weighed with me. No, he was simply a way of escape from the insufferable monotony of my life."

I said nothing, and after a moment, she went on:

"Don't misunderstand me. I was quite honest with him. I told him, what was true, that I liked him very much, that I hoped to come to like him more, but that I was not in any way what the world calls 'in love' with him. He declared that that satisfied him, and so—we were married."

She waited a long time, a little frown had gathered on her forehead. She seemed to be looking back earnestly into those past days.

"I think—I am sure—he cared for me at first. But I suppose we were not well matched. Almost at once, we drifted apart. He—it is not a pleasing thing for my pride, but it is the truth—tired of me very soon." I must have made some murmur of dissent, for she went on quickly: "Oh, yes, he did! Not that it matters now—now that we've come to the parting of the ways."

"What do you mean?"

She answered quietly:

"I mean that I am not going to remain at Styles."

"You and John are not going to live here?"

"John may live here, but I shall not."

"You are going to leave him?"

"Yes."

"But why?"

She paused a long time, and said at last:

"Perhaps—because I want to be—free!"

And, as she spoke, I had a sudden vision of broad spaces, virgin tracts of forests, untrodden lands—and a realization of what freedom would mean to such a nature as Mary Cavendish. I seemed to see her for a moment as she was, a proud wild creature, as untamed by civilization as some shy bird of the hills. A little cry broke from her lips:

"You don't know, you don't know, how this hateful place has been prison to me!"

"I understand," I said, "but—but don't do anything rash."

"Oh, rash!" Her voice mocked at my prudence.

Then suddenly I said a thing I could have bitten out my tongue for:

"You know that Dr. Bauerstein has been arrested?"

An instant coldness passed like a mask over her face, blotting out all expression.

"John was so kind as to break that to me this morning."

"Well, what do you think?" I asked feebly.

"Of what?"

"Of the arrest?"

"What should I think? Apparently he is a German spy; so the gardener had told John."

Her face and voice were absolutely cold and expressionless. Did she care, or did she not?

She moved away a step or two, and fingered one of the flower vases.

"These are quite dead. I must do them again. Would you mind moving—thank you, Mr. Hastings." And she walked quietly past me out of the window, with a cool little nod of dismissal.

No, surely she could not care for Bauerstein. No woman could act her part with that icy unconcern.

Poirot did not make his appearance the following morning, and there was no sign of the Scotland Yard men.

But, at lunch-time, there arrived a new piece of evidence—or rather lack of evidence. We had vainly tried to trace the fourth letter, which Mrs. Inglethorp had written on the evening preceding her death. Our efforts having been in vain, we had abandoned the matter, hoping that it might turn up of itself one day. And this is just what did happen, in the shape of a communication, which arrived by the second post from a firm of French music publishers, acknowledging Mrs. Inglethorp's cheque, and regretting they had been unable to trace a certain series of Russian folk-songs. So the last hope of solving the mystery, by means of Mrs. Inglethorp's correspondence on the fatal evening, had to be abandoned.

Just before tea, I strolled down to tell Poirot of the new disappointment, but found, to my annoyance, that he was once more out.

"Gone to London again?"

"Oh, no, monsieur, he has but taken the train to Tadminster. 'To see a young lady's dispensary,' he said."

"Silly ass!" I ejaculated. "I told him Wednesday was the one day she wasn't there! Well, tell him to look us up tomorrow morning, will you?"

"Certainly, monsieur."

But, on the following day, no sign of Poirot. I was getting angry. He was really treating us in the most cavalier fashion.

After lunch, Lawrence drew me aside, and asked if I was going down to see him.

"No, I don't think I shall. He can come up here if he wants to see us."

"Oh!" Lawrence looked indeterminate. Something unusually nervous and excited in his manner roused my curiosity.

"What is it?" I asked. "I could go if there's anything special."

"It's nothing much, but—well, if you are going, will you tell him"—he dropped his voice to a whisper—"I think I've found the extra coffee cup!"

I had almost forgotten that enigmatical message of Poirot's, but now my curiosity was aroused afresh.

Lawrence would say no more, so I decided that I would

descend from my high horse, and once more seek out Poirot at Leastways Cottage.

This time I was received with a smile. Monsieur Poirot was within. Would I mount? I mounted accordingly.

Poirot was sitting by the table, his head buried in his hands. He sprang up at my entrance.

"What is it?" I asked solicitously. "You are not ill, I trust?"

"No, no, not ill. But I decide an affair of great moment."

"Whether to catch the criminal or not?" I asked facetiously.

But, to my great surprise, Poirot nodded gravely.

" 'To speak or not to speak,' as your so great Shakespeare says, 'that is the question.' "

I did not trouble to correct the quotation.

"You are not serious, Poirot?"

"I am of the most serious. For the most serious of all things hangs in the balance."

"And that is?"

"A woman's happiness, *mon ami*," he said gravely.

I did not quite know what to say.

"The moment has come," said Poirot thoughtfully, "and I do not know what to do. For, you see, it is a big stake for which I play. No one but I, Hercule Poirot, would attempt it!" And he tapped himself proudly on the breast.

After pausing a few minutes respectfully, so as not to spoil his effect, I gave him Lawrence's message.

"Aha!" he cried. "So he has found the extra coffee cup. That is good. He has more intelligence than would appear, this long-faced Monsieur Lawrence of yours!"

I did not myself think very highly of Lawrence's intelligence; but I forbore to contradict Poirot, and gently took him to task for forgetting my instructions as to which were Cynthia's days off.

"It is true. I have the head of a sieve. However, the other young lady was most kind. She was sorry for my disappointment, and showed me everything in the kindest way."

"Oh, well, that's all right, then, and you must go to tea with Cynthia another day."

I told him about the letter.

"I am sorry for that," he said. "I always had hopes of that

letter. But no, it was not to be. This affair must all be un-ravelled from within." He tapped his forehead. "These little grey cells. It is 'up to them'—as you say over here." Then, suddenly, he asked: "Are you a judge of finger-marks, my friend?"

"No," I said, rather surprised, "I know that there are no two finger-marks alike, but that's as far as my science goes."

"Exactly."

He unlocked a little drawer, and took out some photo-graphs which he laid on the table.

"I have numbered them, 1, 2, 3. Will you describe them to me?"

I studied the proofs attentively.

"All greatly magnified, I see. No. 1, I should say, are a man's finger-prints; thumb and first finger. No. 2 are a lady's; they are much smaller, and quite different in every way. No. 3"—I paused for some time—"there seem to be a lot of confused finger-marks, but here, very distinctly, are No. 1's."

"Overlapping the others?"

"Yes."

"You recognize them beyond fail?"

"Oh, yes; they are identical."

Poirot nodded, and gently taking the photographs from me locked them up again.

"I suppose," I said, "that as usual, you are not going to explain?"

"On the contrary. No. 1 were the finger-prints of Monsieur Lawrence. No. 2 were those of Mademoiselle Cynthia. They are not important. I merely obtained them for comparison. No. 3 is a little more complicated."

"Yes?"

"It is, as you see, highly magnified. You may have noticed a sort of blur extending all across the picture. I will not de-scribe to you the special apparatus, dusting powder, etc., which I used. It is a well known process to the police, and by means of it you can obtain a photograph of the finger-prints on any object in a very short space of time. Well, my friend, you have seen the finger-marks—it remains to tell you the particular object on which they had been left."

"Go on—I am really excited."

"*Eh bien!* Photo No. 3 represents the highly magnified surface of a tiny bottle in the top poison cupboard of the dispensary in the Red Cross Hospital at Tadminster—which sounds like the house that Jack built!"

"Good heavens!" I exclaimed. "But what were Lawrence Cavendish's finger-marks doing on it? He never went near the poison cupboard the day we were there?"

"Oh, yes, he did!"

"Impossible! We were all together the whole time."

Poirot shook his head.

"No, my friend, there was a moment when you were not all together. There was a moment when you could not have been all together, or it would not have been necessary to call to Monsieur Lawrence to come and join you on the balcony."

"I'd forgotten that," I admitted. "But it was only for a moment."

"Long enough."

"Long enough for what?"

Poirot's smile became rather enigmatical.

"Long enough for a gentleman who had once studied medicine to gratify a very natural interest and curiosity."

Our eyes met. Poirot's were pleasantly vague. He got up and hummed a little tune. I watched him suspiciously.

"Poirot," I said, "what was in this particular little bottle?"

Poirot looked out of the window.

"Hydro-chloride of Strychnine," he said, over his shoulder, continuing to hum.

"Good heavens!" I said it quite quietly. I was not surprised. I had expected that answer.

"They use the pure Hydro-chloride of Strychnine very little—only occasionally for pills. It is the official solution, Liq. Strychnine Hydro-clor. that is used in most medicines. That is why the finger-marks have remained undisturbed since then."

"How did you manage to take this photograph?"

"I dropped my hat from the balcony," explained Poirot simply. "Visitors were not permitted below at that hour, so, in spite of my many apologies, Mademoiselle Cynthia's colleague had to go down and fetch it for me."

"Then you knew what you were going to find?"

"No, not at all. I merely realized that it was possible, from your story, for Monsieur Lawrence to go to the poison cupboard. The possibility had to be confirmed, or eliminated."

"Poirot," I said, "your gaiety does not deceive me. This is a very important discovery."

"I do not know," said Poirot. "But one thing does strike me. No doubt it has struck you too."

"What is that?"

"Why, that there is altogether too much strychnine about this case. This is the third time we have run up against it. There was strychnine in Mrs. Inglethorp's tonic. There is the strychnine sold across the counter at Styles St. Mary by Mace. Now we have more strychnine, handled by one of the household. It is confusing; and, as you know, I do not like confusion."

Before I could reply, one of the other Belgians opened the door and stuck his head in.

"There is a lady below, asking for Mr. Hastings."

"A lady?"

I jumped up. Poirot followed me down the narrow stairs. Mary Cavendish was standing in the doorway.

"I have been visiting an old woman in the village," she explained, "and as Lawrence told me you were with Monsieur Poirot I thought I would call for you."

"Alas, madame," said Poirot, "I thought you had come to honour me with a visit!"

"I will some day, if you ask me," she promised him, smiling.

"That is well. If you should need a father confessor, madame"—she started ever so slightly—"remember, Papa Poirot is always at your service."

She stared at him for a few minutes, as though seeking to read some deeper meaning into his words. Then she turned abruptly away.

"Come, will you not walk back with us too, Monsieur Poirot?"

"Enchanted, madame."

All the way to Styles, Mary talked fast and feverishly. It struck me that in some way she was nervous of Poirot's eyes.

The weather had broken, and the sharp wind was almost autumnal in its shrewishness. Mary shivered a little, and buttoned her black sports coat closer. The wind through the trees made a mournful noise, like some great giant sighing.

We walked up to the great door of Styles, and at once the knowledge came to us that something was wrong.

Dorcas came running out to meet us. She was crying and wringing her hands. I was aware of other servants huddled together in the background, all eyes and tears.

"Oh, m'am! Oh, m'am! I don't know how to tell you—"

"What is it, Dorcas?" I asked impatiently. "Tell us at once."

"It's those wicked detectives. They've arrested him—they've arrested Mr. Cavendish!"

"Arrested Lawrence?" I gasped.

I saw a strange look come into Dorcas's eyes.

"No, sir. Not Mr. Lawrence—Mr. John."

Behind me, with a wild cry, Mary Cavendish fell heavily against me, and as I turned to catch her I met the quiet triumph in Poirot's eyes.

XI

THE CASE FOR THE PROSECUTION

The trial of John Cavendish for the murder of his step-mother took place two months later.

Of the intervening weeks I will say little, but my admiration and sympathy went out unfeignedly to Mary Cavendish. She ranged herself passionately on her husband's side, scorning the mere idea of his guilt, and fought for him tooth and nail.

I expressed my admiration to Poirot, and he nodded thoughtfully.

"Yes, she is of those women who show at their best in adversity. It brings out all that is sweetest and truest in them. Her pride and her jealousy have—"

"Jealousy?" I queried.

"Yes. Have you not realized that she is an unusually jealous woman? As I was saying, her pride and jealousy have been laid aside. She thinks of nothing but her husband, and the terrible fate that is hanging over him."

He spoke very feelingly, and I looked at him earnestly, remembering that last afternoon, when he had been deliberating whether or no to speak. With his tenderness for "a woman's happiness," I felt glad that the decision had been taken out of his hands.

"Even now," I said, "I can hardly believe it. You see, up to the very last minute, I thought it was Lawrence!"

Poirot grinned.

"I know you did."

"But John! My old friend John!"

"Every murderer is probably somebody's old friend," observed Poirot philosophically. "You cannot mix up sentiment and reason."

"I must say I think you might have given me a hint."

"Perhaps, *mon ami*, I did not do so, just because he *was* your old friend."

I was rather disconcerted by this, remembering how I had busily passed on to John what I believed to be Poirot's views concerning Bauerstein. He, by the way, had been acquitted of the charge brought against him. Nevertheless, although he had been too clever for them this time, and the charge of espionage could not be brought home to him, his wings were pretty well clipped for the future.

I asked Poirot whether he thought John would be condemned. To my intense surprise, he replied that, on the contrary, he was extremely likely to be acquitted.

"But, Poirot—" I protested.

"Oh, my friend, have I not said to you all along that I have no proofs. It is one thing to know that a man is guilty, it is quite another matter to prove him so. And, in this case, there is terribly little evidence. That is the whole trouble. I, Hercule Poirot, know, but I lack the last link in my chain. And unless I can find that missing link—" He shook his head gravely.

"When did you first suspect John Cavendish?" I asked, after a minute or two.

"Did you not suspect him at all?"

"No, indeed."

"Not after the fragment of conversation you overheard between Mrs. Cavendish and her mother-in-law, and her subsequent lack of frankness at the inquest?"

"No."

"Did you not put two and two together, and reflect that if

it was not Alfred Inglethorp who was quarrelling with his wife—and you remember, he strenuously denied it at the inquest—it must be either Lawrence or John. Now, if it was Lawrence, Mary Cavendish's conduct was just as inexplicable. But if, on the other hand, it was John, the whole thing was explained quite naturally."

"So," I cried, a light breaking in upon me, "it was John who quarrelled with his mother that afternoon?"

"Exactly."

"And you have known this all along?"

"Certainly. Mrs. Cavendish's behaviour could only be explained that way."

"And yet you say he may be acquitted?"

Poirot shrugged his shoulders.

"Certainly I do. At the police court proceedings, we shall hear the case for the prosecution, but in all probability his solicitors will advise him to reserve his defence. That will be sprung upon us at the trial. And—ah, by the way, I have a word of caution to give you, my friend. I must not appear in the case."

"What?"

"No. Officially, I have nothing to do with it. Until I have found that last link in my chain, I must remain behind the scenes. Mrs. Cavendish must think I am working for her husband, not against him."

"I say, that's playing it a bit low down," I protested.

"Not at all. We have to deal with a most clever and unscrupulous man, and we must use any means in our power—otherwise he will slip through our fingers. That is why I have been careful to remain in the background. All the discoveries have been made by Japp, and Japp will take all the credit. If I am called upon to give evidence at all"—he smiled broadly—"it will probably be as a witness for the defence."

I could hardly believe my ears.

"It is quite *en règle*," continued Poirot. "Strangely enough, I can give evidence that will demolish one contention of the prosecution."

"Which one?"

"The one that relates to the destruction of the will. John Cavendish did not destroy that will."

Poirot was a true prophet. I will not go into the details of the police court proceedings, as it involves many tiresome repetitions. I will merely state baldly that John Cavendish reserved his defence, and was duly committed for trial.

September found us all in London. Mary took a house in Kensington, Poirot being included in the family party.

I myself had been given a job at the War Office, so was able to see them continually.

As the weeks went by, the state of Poirot's nerves grew worse and worse. That "last link" he talked about was still lacking. Privately, I hoped it might remain so, for what happiness could there be for Mary, if John were not acquitted?

On September 15th John Cavendish appeared in the dock at the Old Bailey, charged with "The Wilful Murder of Emily Agnes Inglethorp," and pleaded "Not Guilty."

Sir Ernest Heavywether, the famous K. C., had been engaged to defend him.

Mr. Philips, K. C., opened the case for the Crown.

The murder, he said, was a most premeditated and cold-blooded one. It was neither more nor less than the deliberate poisoning of a fond and trusting woman by the stepson to whom she had been more than a mother. Ever since his boyhood, she had supported him. He and his wife had lived at Styles Court in every luxury, surrounded by her care and attention. She had been their kind and generous benefactress.

He proposed to call witnesses to show how the prisoner, a profligate and spendthrift, had been at the end of his financial tether, and had also been carrying on an intrigue with a certain Mrs. Raikes, a neighbouring farmer's wife. This having come to his stepmother's ears, she taxed him with it on the afternoon before her death, and a quarrel ensued, part of which was overheard. On the previous day, the prisoner had purchased strychnine at the village chemist's shop, wearing a disguise by means of which he hoped to throw the onus of the crime upon another man—to wit, Mrs. Inglethorp's husband, of whom he had been bitterly jealous.

Luckily for Mr. Inglethorp, he had been able to produce an unimpeachable alibi.

On the afternoon of July 17th, continued Counsel, immediately after the quarrel with her son, Mrs. Inglethorp made a new will. This will was found destroyed in the grate of her bedroom the following morning, but evidence had come to light which showed that it had been drawn up in favour of her husband. Deceased had already made a will in his favour before her marriage, but—and Mr. Philips wagged an expressive forefinger—the prisoner was not aware of that. What had induced the deceased to make a fresh will, with the old one still extant, he could not say. She was an old lady, and might possibly have forgotten the former one; or—this seemed to him more likely—she may have had an idea that it was revoked by her marriage, as there had been some conversation on the subject. Ladies were not always very well versed in legal knowledge. She had, about a year before, executed a will in favour of the prisoner. He would call evidence to show that it was the prisoner who ultimately handed his stepmother her coffee on the fatal night. Later in the evening, he had sought admission to her room, on which occasion, no doubt, he found an opportunity of destroying the will which, as far as he knew, would render the one in his favour valid.

The prisoner had been arrested in consequence of the discovery, in his room, by Detective Inspector Japp—a most brilliant officer—of the identical phial of strychnine which had been sold at the village chemist's to the supposed Mr. Inglethorp on the day before the murder. It would be for the jury to decide whether or no these damning facts constituted an overwhelming proof of the prisoner's guilt.

And, subtly implying that a jury which did not so decide was quite unthinkable, Mr. Philips sat down and wiped his forehead.

The first witnesses for the prosecution were mostly those who had been called at the inquest, the medical evidence being again taken first.

Sir Ernest Heavywether, who was famous all over England for the unscrupulous manner in which he bullied witnesses, only asked two questions.

"I take it, Dr. Bauerstein, that strychnine, as a drug, acts quickly?"

"Yes."

"And that you are unable to account for the delay in this case?"

"Yes."

"Thank you."

Mr. Mace identified the phial handed him by Counsel as that sold by him to "Mr. Inglethorp." Pressed, he admitted that he only knew Mr. Inglethorp by sight. He had never spoken to him. The witness was not cross-examined.

Alfred Inglethorp was called, and denied having purchased the poison. He also denied having quarrelled with his wife. Various witnesses testified to the accuracy of these statements.

The gardeners' evidence, as to the witnessing of the will, was taken, and then Dorcas was called.

Dorcas, faithful to her "young gentlemen," denied strenuously that it could have been John's voice she heard, and resolutely declared, in the teeth of everything, that it was Mr. Inglethorp who had been in the boudoir with her mistress. A rather wistful smile passed across the face of the prisoner in the dock. He knew only too well how useless her gallant defiance was, since it was not the object of the defence to deny this point. Mrs. Cavendish, of course, could not be called upon to give evidence against her husband.

After various questions on other matters, Mr. Philips asked:

"In the month of June last, do you remember a parcel arriving for Mr. Lawrence Cavendish from Parkson's?"

Dorcas shook her head.

"I don't remember, sir. It may have done, but Mr. Lawrence was away from home part of June."

"In the event of a parcel arriving for him whilst he was away, what would be done with it?"

"It would either be put in his room or sent on after him."

"By you?"

"No, sir, I should leave it on the hall table. It would be Miss Howard who would attend to anything like that."

Evelyn Howard was called and, after being examined on

other points, was questioned as to the parcel.

"Don't remember. Lots of parcels come. Can't remember one special one."

"You do not know if it was sent after Mr. Lawrence Cavendish to Wales, or whether it was put in his room?"

"Don't think it was sent after him. Should have remembered it if it was."

"Supposing a parcel arrived addressed to Mr. Lawrence Cavendish, and afterwards it disappeared, should you remark its absence?"

"No, don't think so. I should think some one had taken charge of it."

"I believe, Miss Howard, that it was you who found this sheet of brown paper?" He held up the same dusty piece which Poirot and I had examined in the morning-room at Styles.

"Yes, I did."

"How did you come to look for it?"

"The Belgian detective who was employed on the case asked me to search for it."

"Where did you eventually discover it?"

"On the top of—of—a wardrobe."

"On top of the prisoner's wardrobe?"

"I—I believe so."

"Did you not find it yourself?"

"Yes."

"Then you must know where you found it?"

"Yes, it was on the prisoner's wardrobe."

"That is better."

An assistant from Parkson's, Theatrical Costumiers, testified that on June 29th, they had supplied a black beard to Mr. L. Cavendish, as requested. It was ordered by letter, and a postal order was enclosed. No, they had not kept the letter. All transactions were entered in their books. They had sent the beard, as directed, to "L. Cavendish, Esq., Styles Court."

Sir Ernest Heavywether rose ponderously.

"Where was the letter written from?"

"From Styles Court."

"The same address to which you sent the parcel?"

"Yes."

"And the letter came from there?"

"Yes."

Like a beast of prey, Heavywether fell upon him:

"How do you know?"

"I—I don't understand."

"How do you know that letter came from Styles? Did you notice the postmark?"

"No—but—"

"Ah, you did *not* notice the postmark! And yet you affirm so confidently that it came from Styles. It might, in fact, have been any postmark?"

"Y—es."

"In fact, the letter, though written on stamped notepaper, might have been posted from anywhere? From Wales, for instance?"

The witness admitted that such might be the case, and Sir Ernest signified that he was satisfied.

Elizabeth Wells, second housemaid at Styles, stated that after she had gone to bed she remembered that she had bolted the front door, instead of leaving it on the latch as Mr. Inglethorp had requested. She had accordingly gone downstairs again to rectify her error. Hearing a slight noise in the West wing, she had peeped along the passage, and had seen Mr. John Cavendish knocking at Mrs. Inglethorp's door.

Sir Ernest Heavywether made short work of her, and under his unmerciful bullying she contradicted herself hopelessly, and Sir Ernest sat down again with a satisfied smile on his face.

With the evidence of Annie, as to the candle grease on the floor, and as to seeing the prisoner take the coffee into the boudoir, the proceedings were adjourned until the following day.

As we went home, Mary Cavendish spoke bitterly against the prosecuting counsel.

"That hateful man! What a net he has drawn around my poor John! How he twisted every little fact until he made it seem what it wasn't!"

"Well," I said consolingly, "it will be the other way around to-morrow."

"Yes," she said meditatively; then suddenly dropped her voice. "Mr. Hastings, you do not think—surely it could not have been Lawrence—Oh, no, that could not be!"

But I myself was puzzled, and as soon as I was alone with Poirot I asked him what he thought Sir Ernest was driving at.

"Ah!" said Poirot appreciatively. "He is a clever man, that Sir Ernest."

"Do you think he believes Lawrence guilty?"

"I do not think he believes or cares anything! No, what he is trying for is to create such confusion in the minds of the jury that they are divided in their opinion as to which brother did it. He is endeavouring to make out that there is quite as much evidence against Lawrence as against John—and I am not at all sure that he will not succeed."

Detective-Inspector Japp was the first witness called when the trial was reopened, and gave his evidence succinctly and briefly. After relating the earlier events, he proceeded:

"Acting on information received, Superintendent Summerhaye and myself searched the prisoner's room, during his temporary absence from the house. In his chest of drawers, hidden beneath some underclothing, we found: first, a pair of gold-rimmed pince-nez similar to those worn by Mr. Inglethorp"—these were exhibited—"secondly, this phial."

The phial was that already recognized by the chemist's assistant, a tiny bottle of blue glass, containing a few grains of white crystalline powder, and labelled: "Strychnine Hydrochloride. POISON."

A fresh piece of evidence discovered by the detectives since the police court proceedings was a long, almost new piece of blotting-paper. It had been found in Mrs. Inglethorp's cheque book, and on being reversed at a mirror, showed clearly the words: ". . . erything of which I die possessed I leave to my beloved husband Alfred Ing . . ." This placed beyond question the fact that the destroyed will had been in favour of the deceased lady's husband. Japp then produced the charred fragment of paper recovered from the grate, and this, with the discovery of the beard in the attic, completed his evidence.

But Sir Ernest's cross-examination was yet to come.

"What day was it when you searched the prisoner's room?"

"Tuesday, the 24th of July."

"Exactly a week after the tragedy?"

"Yes."

"You found these two objects, you say in the chest of drawers. Was the drawer unlocked?"

"Yes."

"Does it not strike you as unlikely that a man who had committed a crime should keep the evidence of it in an unlocked drawer for anyone to find?"

"He might have stowed them there in a hurry."

"But you have just said it was a whole week since the crime. He would have had ample time to remove them and destroy them."

"Perhaps."

"There is no perhaps about it. Would he, or would he not have had plenty of time to remove and destroy them?"

"Yes."

"Was the pile of underclothes under which the things were hidden heavy or light?"

"Heavyish."

"In other words, it was winter underclothing. Obviously, the prisoner would not be likely to go to that drawer?"

"Perhaps not."

"Kindly answer my question. Would the prisoner, in the hottest week of a hot summer, be likely to go to a drawer containing winter underclothing. Yes, or no?"

"No."

"In that case, is it not possible that the articles in question might have been put there by a third person, and that the prisoner was quite unaware of their presence?"

"I should not think it likely."

"But it is possible?"

"Yes."

"That is all."

More evidence followed. Evidence as to the financial difficulties in which the prisoner had found himself at the end of July. Evidence as to his intrigue with Mrs. Raikes—poor

Mary, that must have been bitter hearing for a woman of her pride. Evelyn Howard had been right in her facts, though her animosity against Alfred Inglethorp had caused her to jump to the conclusion that he was the person concerned.

Lawrence Cavendish was then put into the box. In a low voice, in answer to Mr. Philips' questions, he denied having ordered anything from Parkson's in June. In fact, on June 29th, he had been staying away, in Wales.

Instantly, Sir Ernest's chin was shooting pugnaciously forward.

"You deny having ordered a black beard from Parkson's on June 29th?"

"I do."

"Ah! In the event of anything happening to your brother, who will inherit Styles Court?"

The brutality of the question called a flush to Lawrence's pale face. The judge gave vent to a faint murmur of disapprobation, and the prisoner in the dock leant forward angrily.

Heavywether cared nothing for his client's anger.

"Answer my question, if you please."

"I suppose," said Lawrence quietly, "that I should."

"What do you mean by you 'suppose'? Your brother has no children. You *would* inherit it, wouldn't you?"

"Yes."

"Ah, that's better," said Heavywether, with ferocious geniality. "And you'd inherit a good slice of money too, wouldn't you?"

"Really, Sir Ernest," protested the judge, "these questions are not relevant."

Sir Ernest bowed, and having shot his arrow proceeded.

"On Tuesday, the 17th July, you went, I believe, with another guest, to visit the dispensary at the Red Cross Hospital in Tadminster?"

"Yes."

"Did you—while you happened to be alone for a few seconds—unlock the poison cupboard, and examine some of the bottles?"

"I—I—may have done so."

"I put it to you that you did do so?"

"Yes."

Sir Ernest fairly shot the next question at him.

"Did you examine one bottle in particular?"

"No, I do not think so."

"Be careful, Mr. Cavendish. I am referring to a little bottle of Hydro-chloride of Strychnine."

Lawrence was turning a sickly greenish colour.

"N—o—I am sure I didn't."

"Then how do you account for the fact that you left the unmistakable impress of your fingerprints on it?"

The bullying manner was highly efficacious with a nervous disposition.

"I—I suppose I must have taken up the bottle."

"I suppose so too! Did you abstract any of the contents of the bottle?"

"Certainly not."

"Then why did you take it up?"

"I once studied to be a doctor. Such things naturally interest me."

"Ah! So poisons 'naturally interest' you, do they? Still, you waited to be alone before gratifying that 'interest' of yours?"

"That was pure chance. If the others had been there, I should have done just the same."

"Still, as it happens, the others were not there?"

"No, but—"

"In fact, during the whole afternoon, you were only alone for a couple of minutes, and it happened—I say, it happened—to be during those two minutes that you displayed your 'natural interest' in Hydro-chloride of Strychnine?"

Lawrence stammered pitiably.

"I—I—"

With a satisfied and expressive countenance, Sir Ernest observed:

"I have nothing more to ask you, Mr. Cavendish."

This bit of cross-examination had caused great excitement in court. The heads of the many fashionably attired women present were busily laid together, and their whispers became so loud that the judge angrily threatened to have the court cleared if there was not immediate silence.

There was little more evidence. The handwriting experts

were called upon for their opinion of the signature of "Alfred Inglethorp" in the chemist's poison register. They all declared unanimously that it was certainly not his handwriting, and gave it as their view that it might be that of the prisoner disguised. Cross-examined, they admitted that it might be the prisoner's hand-writing cleverly counterfeited.

Sir Ernest Heavywether's speech in opening the case for the defence was not a long one, but it was backed by the full force of his emphatic manner. Never, he said, in the course of his long experience, had he known a charge of murder to rest on slighter evidence. Not only was it entirely circumstantial, but the greater part of it was practically unproved. Let them take the testimony they had heard and sift it impartially. The strychnine had been found in a drawer in the prisoner's room. That drawer was an unlocked one, as he had pointed out, and he submitted that there was no evidence to prove that it was the prisoner who had concealed the poison there. It was, in fact, a wicked and malicious attempt on the part of some third person to fix the crime on the prisoner. The prosecution had been unable to produce a shred of evidence in support of their contention that it was the prisoner who ordered the black beard from Parkson's. The quarrel which had taken place between the prisoner and his stepmother was freely admitted, but both it and his financial embarrassments had been grossly exaggerated.

His learned friend—Sir Ernest nodded carelessly at Mr. Philips—had stated that if the prisoner were an innocent man, he would have come forward at the inquest to explain that it was he, and not Mr. Inglethorp, who had been the participator in the quarrel. He thought the facts had been misrepresented. What had actually occurred was this. The prisoner, returning to the house on Tuesday evening, had been authoritatively told that there had been a violent quarrel between Mr. and Mrs. Inglethorp. No suspicion had entered the prisoner's head that anyone could possibly have mistaken his voice for that of Mr. Inglethorp. He naturally concluded that his stepmother had had two quarrels.

The prosecution averred that on Monday, July 16th, the prisoner had entered the chemist's shop in the village, disguised as Mr. Inglethorp. The prisoner, on the contrary, was at that time at a lonely spot called Marston's Spinney, where he had been summoned by an anonymous note, couched in blackmailing terms, and threatening to reveal certain matters to his wife unless he complied with its demands. The prisoner had, accordingly, gone to the appointed spot, and after waiting there vainly for half an hour had returned home. Unfortunately, he had met with no one on the way there or back who could vouch for the truth of his story, but luckily he had kept the note, and it would be produced as evidence.

As for the statement relating to the destruction of the will, the prisoner had formerly practised at the Bar, and was perfectly well aware that the will made in his favour a year before was automatically revoked by his stepmother's remarriage. He would call evidence to show who did destroy the will, and it was possible that that might open up quite a new view of the case.

Finally, he would point out to the jury that there was evidence against other people besides John Cavendish. He would direct their attention to the fact that the evidence against Mr. Lawrence Cavendish was quite as strong, if not stronger than that against his brother.

He would now call the prisoner.

John acquitted himself well in the witness-box. Under Sir Ernest's skilful handling, he told his tale credibly and well. The anonymous note received by him was produced, and handed to the jury to examine. The readiness with which he admitted his financial difficulties, and the disagreement with his stepmother, lent value to his denials.

At the close of his examination, he paused, and said:

"I should like to make one thing clear. I utterly reject and disapprove of Sir Ernest Heavywether's insinuations against my brother. My brother, I am convinced, had no more to do with the crime than I have."

Sir Ernest merely smiled, and noted with a sharp eye that John's protest had produced a very favourable impression on the jury.

Then the cross-examination began.

"I understand you to say that it never entered your head that the witnesses at the inquest could possibly have mistaken your voice for that of Mr. Inglethorp. Is not that very surprising?"

"No, I don't think so. I was told there had been a quarrel between my mother and Mr. Inglethorp, and it never occurred to me that such was not really the case."

"Not when the servant Dorcas repeated certain fragments of the conversation—fragments which you must have recognized?"

"I did not recognize them."

"Your memory must be unusually short!"

"No, but we were both angry, and, I think, said more than we meant. I paid very little attention to my mother's actual words."

Mr. Philips' incredulous sniff was a triumph of forensic skill. He passed on to the subject of the note.

"You have produced this note very opportunely. Tell me, is there nothing familiar about the handwriting of it?"

"Not that I know of."

"Do you think that it bears a marked resemblance to your own hand-writing—carelessly disguised?"

"No, I do not think so."

"I put it to you that it is your own hand-writing!"

"No."

"I put it to you that, anxious to prove an alibi, you conceived the idea of a fictitious and rather incredible appointment, and wrote this note yourself in order to bear out your statement!"

"No."

"Is it not a fact that, at the time you claim to have been waiting about at a solitary and unfrequented spot, you were really in the chemist's shop in Styles St. Mary, where you purchased strychnine in the name of Alfred Inglethorp?"

"No, that is a lie."

"I put it to you that, wearing a suit of Mr. Inglethorp's clothes, with a black beard trimmed to resemble his, you were there—and signed the register in his name!"

"That is absolutely untrue."

"Then I will leave the remarkable similarity of handwriting between the note, the register, and your own, to the consideration of the jury," said Mr. Philips, and sat down with the air of a man who has done his duty, but who was nevertheless horrified by such deliberate perjury.

After this, as it was growing late, the case was adjourned till Monday.

Poirot, I noticed, was looking profoundly discouraged. He had that little frown between the eyes that I knew so well.

"What is it, Poirot?" I inquired.

"Ah, *mon ami*, things are going badly, badly."

In spite of myself, my heart gave a leap of relief. Evidently there was a likelihood of John Cavendish being acquitted.

When we reached the house, my little friend waved aside Mary's offer of tea.

"No, I thank you, madame. I will mount to my room."

I followed him. Still frowning, he went across to the desk and took out a small pack of patience cards. Then he drew up a chair to the table, and, to my utter amazement, began solemnly to build card houses!

My jaw dropped involuntarily, and he said at once:

"No, *mon ami*, I am not in my second childhood! I steady my nerves, that is all. This employment requires precision of the fingers. With precision of the fingers goes precision of the brain. And never have I needed that more than now!"

"What is the trouble?" I asked.

With a great thump on the table, Poirot demolished his carefully built up edifice.

"It is this, *mon ami*! That I can build card houses seven stories high, but I cannot"—thump—"find"—thump—"that last link of which I spoke to you."

I could not quite tell what to say, so I held my peace, and he began slowly building up the cards again, speaking in jerks as he did so.

"It is done—so! By placing—one card—on another—with mathematical—precision!"

I watched the card house rising under his hands, story by story. He never hesitated or faltered. It was really almost like a conjuring trick.

"What a steady hand you've got," I remarked. "I believe I've only seen your hand shake once."

"On an occasion when I was enraged, without doubt," observed Poirot, with great placidity.

"Yes indeed! You were in a towering rage. Do you remember? It was when you discovered that the lock of the despatch-case in Mrs. Inglethorp's bedroom had been forced. You stood by the mantelpiece, twiddling the things on it in your usual fashion, and your hand shook like a leaf! I must say——"

But I stopped suddenly. For Poirot, uttering a hoarse and inarticulate cry, again annihilated his masterpiece of cards, and putting his hands over his eyes swayed backwards and forwards, apparently suffering the keenest agony.

"Good heavens, Poirot!" I cried. "What is the matter? Are you taken ill?"

"No, no," he gasped. "It is—it is—that I have an idea!"

"Oh!" I exclaimed, much relieved. "One of your 'little ideas'?"

"Ah, *ma foi*, no!" replied Poirot frankly. "This time it is an idea gigantic! Stupendous! And you—*you*, my friend, have given it to me!"

Suddenly clasping me in his arms, he kissed me warmly on both cheeks, and before I had recovered from my surprise ran headlong from the room.

Mary Cavendish entered at that moment.

"What *is* the matter with Monsieur Poirot? He rushed past me crying out: 'A garage! For the love of Heaven, direct me to a garage, madame!' And, before I could answer, he had dashed out into the street."

I hurried to the window. True enough, there he was, tearing down the street, hatless, and gesticulating as he went. I turned to Mary with a gesture of despair.

"He'll be stopped by a policeman in another minute. There he goes, round the corner!"

Our eyes met, and we stared helplessly at one another.

"What can be the matter?"

I shook my head.

"I don't know. He was building card houses, when suddenly he said he had an idea, and rushed off as you saw."

"Well," said Mary, "I expect he will be back before dinner."

But night fell, and Poirot had not returned.

XII

The Last Link

Poirot's abrupt departure had intrigued us all greatly. Sunday morning wore away, and still he did not reappear. But about three o'clock a ferocious and prolonged hooting outside drove us to the window, to see Poirot alighting from a car, accompanied by Japp and Summerhaye. The little man was transformed. He radiated an absurd complacency. He bowed with exaggerated respect to Mary Cavendish.

"Madame, I have your permission to hold a little *réunion* in the *salon*? It is necessary for every one to attend."

Mary smiled sadly.

"You know, Monsieur Poirot, that you have *carte blanche* in every way."

"You are too amiable, madame."

Still beaming, Poirot marshalled us all into the drawing-room, bringing forward chairs as he did so.

"Miss Howard—here. Mademoiselle Cynthia. Monsieur Lawrence. The good Dorcas. And Annie. *Bien!* We must delay our proceedings a few minutes until Mr. Inglethorp arrives. I have sent him a note."

Miss Howard rose immediately from her seat.

"If that man comes into the house, I leave it!"

"No, no!" Poirot went up to her and pleaded in a low voice. Finally Miss Howard consented to return to her chair. A few minutes later Alfred Inglethorp entered the room.

The company once assembled, Poirot rose from his seat with the air of a popular lecturer, and bowed politely to his audience.

"*Messieurs, mesdames,* as you all know, I was called in by Monsieur John Cavendish to investigate this case. I at once examined the bedroom of the deceased which, by the advice of the doctors, had been kept locked, and was consequently exactly as it had been when the tragedy occurred. I found: first, a fragment of green material; secondly, a stain on the carpet near the window, still damp; thirdly, an empty box of bromide powders.

"To take the fragment of green material first, I found it caught in the bolt of the communicating door between that room and the adjoining one occupied by Mademoiselle Cynthia. I handed the fragment over to the police who did not consider it of much importance. Nor did they recognize it for what it was—a piece torn from a green land armlet."

There was a little stir of excitement.

"Now there was only one person at Styles who worked on the land—Mrs. Cavendish. Therefore it must have been Mrs. Cavendish who entered the deceased's room through the door communicating with Mademoiselle Cynthia's room."

"But that door was bolted on the inside!" I cried.

"When I examined the room, yes. But in the first place we have only her word for it, since it was she who tried that particular door and reported it fastened. In the ensuing confusion she would have had ample opportunity to shoot the bolt across. I took an early opportunity of verifying my conjectures. To begin with, the fragment corresponds exactly with a tear in Mrs. Cavendish's armlet. Also, at the inquest, Mrs. Cavendish declared that she had heard, from her own room, the fall of the table by the bed. I took an early opportunity of testing that statement by stationing my friend Monsieur Hastings, in the left wing of the building, just outside Mrs. Cavendish's door. I myself, in company with the police, went to the deceased's room, and whilst there I, apparently accidentally, knocked over the table in question, but found that, as I had expected, Monsieur Hastings had heard no sound at all. This confirmed my belief that Mrs. Cavendish was not speaking the truth when she declared that she had been dressing in her room at the time of the tragedy. In fact, I was convinced that, far from having been in her own room, Mrs. Cavendish was actually in the deceased's room when the alarm was given."

I shot a quick glance at Mary. She was very pale, but smiling.

"I proceeded to reason on that assumption. Mrs. Cavendish is in her mother-in-law's room. We will say that she is seeking for something and has not yet found it. Suddenly Mrs. Inglethorp awakens and is seized with an alarming paroxysm. She flings out her arm, overturning the bed table, and then pulls desperately at the bell. Mrs. Cavendish, startled, drops her candle, scattering the grease on the carpet. She picks it up, and retreats quickly to Mademoiselle Cynthia's room, closing the door behind her. She hurries out into the passage, for the servants must not find her where she is. But it is too late! Already footsteps are echoing along the gallery which connects the two wings. What can she do? Quick as thought, she hurries back to the young girl's room, and starts shaking her awake. The hastily aroused household come trooping down the passage. They are all busily battering at Mrs. Inglethorp's door. It occurs to nobody that Mrs. Cavendish has not arrived with the rest, but—and this is significant—I can find no one who saw her come from the other wing." He looked at Mary Cavendish. "Am I right, madame?"

She bowed her head.

"Quite right, monsieur. You understand that, if I had thought I would do my husband any good by revealing these facts, I would have done so. But it did not seem to me to bear upon the question of his guilt or innocence."

"In a sense, that is correct, madame. But it cleared my mind of many misconceptions, and left me free to see other facts in their true significance."

"The will!" cried Lawrence. "Then it was you, Mary, who destroyed the will?"

She shook her head, and Poirot shook his also.

"No," he said quietly. "There is only one person who could possibly have destroyed that will—Mrs. Inglethorp herself!"

"Impossible!" I exclaimed. "She had only made it out that very afternoon!"

"Nevertheless, *mon ami*, it was Mrs. Inglethorp. Because, in no other way can you account for the fact that, on one of the hottest days of the year, Mrs. Inglethorp ordered a fire to be lighted in her room."

I gave a gasp. What idiots we had been never to think of that fire as being incongruous! Poirot was continuing:

"The temperature on that day, messieurs, was 80° in the shade. Yet Mrs. Inglethorp ordered a fire! Why? Because she wished to destroy something, and could think of no other way. You will remember that, in consequence of the War economies practised at Styles, no waste paper was thrown away. There was therefore no means of destroying a thick document such as a will. The moment I heard of a fire being lighted in Mrs. Inglethorp's room, I leaped to the conclusion that it was to destroy some important document—possibly a will. So the discovery of the charred fragment in the grate was no surprise to me. I did not, of course, know at the time that the will in question had only been made that afternoon, and I will admit that, when I learnt that fact, I fell into a grievous error. I came to the conclusion that Mrs. Inglethorp's determination to destroy her will arose as a direct consequence of the quarrel she had that afternoon, and that therefore the quarrel took place after, and not before the making of the will.

"Here, as we know, I was wrong, and I was forced to abandon that idea. I faced the problem from a new standpoint. Now, at 4 o'clock, Dorcas overheard her mistress saying angrily: 'You need not think that any fear of publicity, or scandal between husband and wife will deter me.' I conjectured, and conjectured rightly, that these words were addressed, not to her husband, but to Mr. John Cavendish. At 5 o'clock, an hour later, she uses almost the same words, but the standpoint is different. She admits to Dorcas, 'I don't know what to do; scandal between husband and wife is a dreadful thing.' At 4 o'clock she has been angry, but completely mistress of herself. At 5 o'clock she is in violent distress, and speaks of having had 'a great shock.'

"Looking at the matter psychologically, I drew one deduction which I was convinced was correct. The second 'scandal' she spoke of was not the same as the first—and it concerned herself!

"Let us reconstruct. At 4 o'clock, Mrs. Inglethorp quarrels with her son, and threatens to denounce him to his wife—who, by the way, overheard the greater part of the conversation. At 4:30, Mrs. Inglethorp, in consequence of a conversation on the validity of wills, makes a will in favour of her husband, which the two gardeners witness. At 5 o'clock, Dorcas finds her mistress in a state of considerable agitation, with a slip of paper—'a letter,' Dorcas thinks—in her hand, and it is then that she orders the fire in her room to be lighted. Presumably, then, between 4:30 and 5 o'clock, something has occurred to occasion a complete revolution of feeling, since she is now as anxious to destroy the will, as she was before to make it. What was that something?

"As far as we know, she was quite alone during that half-hour. Nobody entered or left that boudoir. What then occasioned this sudden change of sentiment?

"One can only guess, but I believe my guess to be correct. Mrs. Inglethorp had no stamps in her desk. We know this, because later she asked Dorcas to bring her some. Now in the opposite corner of the room stood her husband's desk—locked. She was anxious to find some stamps, and, according to my theory, she tried her own keys in the desk. That one of them fitted I know. She therefore opened the desk, and in searching for the stamps she came across something else—that slip of paper which Dorcas saw in her hand, and which assuredly was never meant for Mrs. Inglethorp's eyes. On the other hand, Mrs. Cavendish believed that the slip of paper to which her mother-in-law clung so tenaciously was a written proof of her own husband's infidelity. She demanded it from Mrs. Inglethorp who assured her, quite truly, that it had nothing to do with that matter. Mrs. Cavendish did not believe her. She thought that Mrs. Inglethorp was shielding her stepson. Now Mrs. Cavendish is a very resolute woman, and, behind her mask of reserve, she was madly jealous of her husband. She determined to get hold of that paper at all costs, and in this resolution chance came to her aid. She happened to pick up the key of Mrs. Inglethorp's despatch-case, which had been lost that morning. She knew that her mother-in-law invariably kept all important papers in this particular case.

"Mrs. Cavendish, therefore, made her plans as only a woman driven desperate through jealousy could have done. Some time in the evening she unbolted the door leading into Mademoiselle Cynthia's room. Possibly she applied oil to the hinges, for I found that it opened quite noiselessly when I tried it. She put off her project until the early hours of the morning as being safer, since the servants were accustomed to hearing her move about her room at that time. She dressed completely in her land kit, and made her way quietly through Mademoiselle Cynthia's room into that of Mrs. Inglethorp."

He paused a moment, and Cynthia interrupted:

"But I should have woken up if anyone had come through my room?"

"Not if you were drugged, mademoiselle."

"Drugged?"

"Mais, oui!"

"You remember"—he addressed us collectively again—"that through all the tumult and noise next door Mademoiselle Cynthia slept. That admitted of two possibilities. Either her sleep was feigned—which I did not believe—or her unconsciousness was induced by artificial means.

"With this latter idea in my mind, I examined all the coffee cups most carefully, remembering that it was Mrs. Cavendish who had brought Mademoiselle Cynthia her coffee the night before. I took a sample from each cup, and had them analysed—with no result. I had counted the cups carefully, in the event of one having been removed. Six persons had taken coffee, and six cups were duly found. I had to confess myself mistaken.

"Then I discovered that I had been guilty of a very grave oversight. Coffee had been brought in for seven persons, not

six, for Dr. Bauerstein had been there that evening. This changed the face of the whole affair, for there was now one cup missing. The servants noticed nothing, since Annie, the housemaid, who took in the coffee, brought in seven cups, not knowing that Mr. Inglethorp never drank it, whereas Dorcas, who cleared them away the following morning, found six as usual—or strictly speaking she found five, the sixth being the one found broken in Mrs. Inglethorp's room.

"I was confident that the missing cup was that of Mademoiselle Cynthia. I had an additional reason for that belief in the fact that all the cups found contained sugar, which Mademoiselle Cynthia never took in her coffee. My attention was attracted by the story of Annie about some 'salt' on the tray of coco which she took every night to Mrs. Inglethorp's room. I accordingly secured a sample of that coco, and sent it to be analysed."

"But that had already been done by Dr. Bauerstein," said Lawrence quickly.

"Not exactly. The analyst was asked by him to report whether strychnine was, or was not, present. He did not have it tested, as I did, for a narcotic."

"For a narcotic?"

"Yes. Here is the analyst's report. Mrs. Cavendish administered a safe, but effectual, narcotic to both Mrs. Inglethorp and Mademoiselle Cynthia. And it is possible that she had a *mauvais quart d'heure* in consequence! Imagine her feelings when her mother-in-law is suddenly taken ill and dies, and immediately after she hears the word 'Poison'! She has believed that the sleeping draught she administered was perfectly harmless, but there is no doubt that for one terrible moment she must have feared that Mrs. Inglethorp's death lay at her door. She is seized with panic, and under its influence she hurries downstairs, and quickly drops the coffee cup and saucer used by Mademoiselle Cynthia into a large brass vase, where it is discovered later by Monsieur Lawrence. The remains of the coco she dare not touch. Too many eyes are upon her. Guess at her relief when strychnine is mentioned, and she discovers that after all the tragedy is not her doing.

"We are now able to account for the symptoms of strych-

nine poisoning being so long in making their appearance. A narcotic taken with strychnine will delay the action of the poison for some hours."

Poirot paused. Mary looked up at him, the colour slowly rising in her face.

"All you have said is quite true, Monsieur Poirot. It was the most awful hour of my life. I shall never forget it. But you are wonderful. I understand now——"

"What I meant when I told you that you could safely confess to Papa Poirot, eh? But you would not trust me."

"I see everything now," said Lawrence. "The drugged coco, takcn on top of the poisoned coffee, amply accounts for the delay."

"Exactly. But was the coffee poisoned, or was it not? We come to a little difficulty here, since Mrs. Inglethorp never drank it."

"What?" The cry of surprise was universal.

"No. You will remember my speaking of a stain on the carpet in Mrs. Inglethorp's room? There were some peculiar points about that stain. It was still damp, it exhaled a strong odour of coffee, and imbedded in the nap of the carpet I found some little splinters of china. What had happened was plain to me, for not two minutes before I had placed my little case on the table near the window, and the table, tilting up, had deposited it upon the floor on precisely the identical spot. In exactly the same way, Mrs. Inglethorp had laid down her cup of coffee on reaching her room the night before, and the treacherous table had played her the same trick.

"What happened next is mere guess work on my part, but I should say that Mrs. Inglethorp picked up the broken cup and placed it on the table by the bed. Feeling in need of a stimulant of some kind, she heated up her coco, and drank it off then and there. Now we are faced with a new problem. We know the coco contained no strychnine. The coffee was never drunk. Yet the strychnine must have been administered between seven and nine o'clock that evening. What third medium was there—a medium so suitable for disguising the taste of strychnine that it is extraordinary no one has thought of it?" Poirot looked round the room, and then answered himself impressively. "Her medicine!"

"Do you mean that the murderer introduced the strychnine into her tonic?" I cried.

"There was no need to introduce it. It was already there—in the mixture. The strychnine that killed Mrs. Inglethorp was the identical strychnine prescribed by Dr. Wilkins. To make that clear to you, I will read you an extract from a book on dispensing which I found in the Dispensary of the Red Cross Hospital at Tadminster":

"The following prescription has become famous in text books:

    Strychninae Sulph............................ gr. I
    Potass Bromide................................... ^{3}vi
    Aqua ad .... ^{3}viii
    Fiat Mistura

This solution deposits in a few hours the greater part of the strychnine salt as an insoluble bromide in transparent crystals. A lady in England lost her life by taking a similar mixture: the precipitated strychnine collected at the bottom, and in taking the last dose she swallowed nearly all of it!

"Now there was, of course, no bromide in Dr. Wilkins' prescription, but you will remember that I mentioned an empty box of bromide powders. One or two of those powders introduced into the full bottle of medicine would effectually precipitate the strychnine, as the book describes, and cause it to be taken in the last dose. You will learn later that the person who usually poured out Mrs. Inglethorp's medicine was always extremely careful not to shake the bottle, but to leave the sediment at the bottom of it undisturbed.

"Throughout the case, there have been evidences that the tragedy was intended to take place on Monday evening. On that day, Mrs. Inglethorp's bell wire was neatly cut, and on Monday evening Mademoiselle Cynthia was spending the night with friends, so that Mrs. Inglethorp would have been quite alone in the right wing, completely shut off from help of any kind, and would have died, in all probability, before medical aid could have been summoned. But in her hurry to be in time for the village entertainment Mrs. Inglethorp forgot to take her medicine, and the next day she lunched away from home, so that the last—and fatal—dose was actually taken twenty-four hours later than had been anticipated by the murderer; and it is owing to that delay that the final proof—the last link of the chain—is now in my hands."

Amid breathless excitement, he held out three thin strips of paper.

"A letter in the murderer's own handwriting, *mes amis!* Had it been a little clearer in its terms, it is possible that Mrs. Inglethorp, warned in time, would have escaped. As it was, she realized her danger, but not the manner of it."

In the deathly silence, Poirot pieced together the slips of paper and, clearing his throat, read:

" 'Dearest Evelyn:
     'You will be anxious at hearing nothing. It is all right— only it will be to-night instead of last night. You under- stand. There's a good time coming once the old woman is dead and out of the way. No one can possibly bring home the crime to me. That idea of yours about the bromides was a stroke of genius! But we must be very circumspect. A false step—'

"Here, my friends, the letter breaks off. Doubtless the writer was interrupted; but there can be no question as to his identity. We all know this handwriting and—"

A howl that was almost a scream broke the silence.

"You devil! How did you get it?"

A chair was overturned. Poirot skipped nimbly aside. A quick movement on his part, and his assailant fell with a crash.

"*Messieurs, mesdames,*" said Poirot, with a flourish, "let me introduce you to the murderer, Mr. Alfred Inglethorp!"

XIII

POIROT EXPLAINS

"Poirot, you old villain," I said, "I've half a mind to strangle you! What do you mean by deceiving me as you have done?"

We were sitting in the library. Several hectic days lay behind us. In the room below, John and Mary were together once more, while Alfred Inglethorp and Miss Howard were in custody. Now at last, I had Poirot to myself, and could relieve my still burning curiosity.

Poirot did not answer me for a moment, but at last he said:

"I did not deceive you, *mon ami*. At most, I permitted you to deceive yourself."

"Yes, but why?"

"Well, it is difficult to explain. You see, my friend, you have a nature so honest, and a countenance so transparent, that—*enfin*, to conceal your feelings is impossible! If I had told you my ideas, the very first time you saw Mr. Alfred Inglethorp that astute gentleman would have—in your so expressive idiom—'smelt a rat'! And then, *bon jour* to our chances of catching him!"

"I think that I have more diplomacy than you give me credit for."

"My friend," besought Poirot, "I implore you, do not enrage yourself! Your help has been of the most invaluable. It is but the extremely beautiful nature that you have, which made me pause."

"Well," I grumbled, a little mollified. "I still think you might have given me a hint."

"But I did, my friend. Several hints. You would not take them. Think now, did I ever say to you that I believed John Cavendish guilty? Did I not, on the contrary, tell you that he would almost certainly be acquitted?"

"Yes, but——"

"And did I not immediately afterwards speak of the difficulty of bringing the murderer to justice? Was it not plain to you that I was speaking of two entirely different persons?"

"No," I said, "it was not plain to me!"

"Then again," continued Poirot, "at the beginning, did I not repeat to you several times that I didn't want Mr. Inglethorp arrested *now*? That should have conveyed something to you."

"Do you mean to say you suspected him as long ago as that?"

"Yes. To begin with, whoever else might benefit by Mrs. Inglethorp's death, her husband would benefit the most. There was no getting away from that. When I went up to Styles with you that first day, I had no idea as to how the crime had been committed, but from what I knew of Mr. Inglethorp I fancied that it would be very hard to find anything to connect him with it. When I arrived at the château, I realized at once that it was Mrs. Inglethorp who had burnt the will; and there, by the way, you cannot complain, my friend, for I tried my best to force on you the significance of that bedroom fire in midsummer."

"Yes, yes," I said impatiently. "Go on."

"Well, my friend, as I say, my views as to Mr. Inglethorp's guilt were very much shaken. There was, in fact, so much evidence against him that I was inclined to believe that he had not done it."

"When did you change your mind?"

"When I found that the more efforts I made to clear him, the more efforts he made to get himself arrested. Then, when I discovered that Inglethorp had nothing to do with Mrs. Raikes, and that in fact it was John Cavendish who was interested in that quarter, I was quite sure."

"But why?"

"Simply this. If it had been Inglethorp who was carrying on an intrigue with Mrs. Raikes, his silence was perfectly comprehensible. But, when I discovered that it was known all over the village that it was John who was attracted by the farmer's pretty wife, his silence bore quite a different interpretation. It was nonsense to pretend that he was afraid of the scandal, as no possible scandal could attach to him. This attitude of his gave me furiously to think, and I was slowly forced to the conclusion that Alfred Inglethorp wanted to be arrested. *Eh bien!* from that moment, I was equally determined that he should not be arrested."

"Wait a moment. I don't see why he wished to be arrested?"

"Because, *mon ami,* it is the law of your country that a man once acquitted can never be tried again for the same offence. Aha! but it was clever—his idea! Assuredly, he is a man of method. See here, he knew that in his position he was bound to be suspected, so he conceived the exceedingly clever idea of preparing a lot of manufactured evidence against himself. He wished to be suspected. He wished to be arrested. He would then produce his irreproachable alibi— and, hey presto, he was safe for life!"

"But I still don't see how he managed to prove his alibi, and yet go to the chemist's shop?"

Poirot stared at me in surprise.

"Is it possible? My poor friend! You have not yet realized that it was Miss Howard who went to the chemist's shop?"

"Miss Howard?"

"But, certainly. Who else? It was most easy for her. She is of a good height, her voice is deep and manly; moreover, remember, she and Inglethorp are cousins, and there is a distinct resemblance between them, especially in their gait and bearing. It was simplicity itself. They are a clever pair!"

"I am still a little fogged as to how exactly the bromide business was done," I remarked.

"*Bon!* I will reconstruct for you as far as possible. I am inclined to think that Miss Howard was the master mind in that affair. You remember her once mentioning that her father was a doctor? Possibly she dispensed his medicines for him, or she may have taken the idea from one of the many books lying about when Mademoiselle Cynthia was studying for her exam. Anyway, she was familiar with the fact that the addition of a bromide to a mixture containing strychnine would cause the precipitation of the latter. Probably the idea came to her quite suddenly. Mrs. Inglethorp had a box of bromide powders, which she occasionally took at night. What could be easier quietly than to dissolve one or more of those powders in Mrs. Inglethorp's large sized bottle of medicine when it came from Coot's? The risk is practically nil. The tragedy will not take place until nearly a fortnight later. If anyone has seen either of them touching the medicine, they will have forgotten it by that time. Miss Howard will have engineered her quarrel, and departed from the house. The lapse of time, and her absence, will defeat all suspicion. Yes, it was a clever idea! If they had left it alone, it is possible the crime might never have been brought home to them. But they were not satisfied. They tried to be too clever—and that was their undoing."

Poirot puffed at his tiny cigarette, his eyes fixed on the ceiling.

"They arranged a plan to throw suspicion on John Cavendish, by buying strychnine at the village chemist's, and signing the register in his handwriting.

"On Monday Mrs. Inglethorp will take the last dose of her medicine. On Monday, therefore, at six o'clock, Alfred Inglethorp arranges to be seen by a number of people at a spot far removed from the village. Miss Howard has previously made up a cock and bull story about him and Mrs. Raikes to account for his holding his tongue afterwards. At six o'clock, Miss Howard, disguised as Alfred Inglethorp, enters the chemist's shop, with her story about a dog, obtains the strychnine, and writes the name of Alfred Inglethorp in

John's handwriting, which she had previously studied carefully.

"But, as it will never do if John, too, can prove an alibi, she writes him an anonymous note—still copying his handwriting—which takes him to a remote spot where it is exceedingly unlikely that anyone will see him.

"So far, all goes well. Miss Howard goes back to Middlingham. Alfred Inglethorp returns to Styles. There is nothing that can compromise him in any way, since it is Miss Howard who has the strychnine, which, after all, is only wanted as a blind to throw suspicion on John Cavendish.

"But now a hitch occurs. Mrs. Inglethorp does not take her medicine that night. The broken bell, Cynthia's absence—arranged by Inglethorp through his wife—all these are wasted. And then—he makes his slip.

"Mrs. Inglethorp is out, and he sits down to write to his accomplice, who, he fears, may be in a panic at the nonsuccess of their plan. It is probable that Mrs. Inglethorp returned earlier than he expected. Caught in the act, and somewhat flurried, he hastily shuts and locks his desk. He fears that if he remains in the room he may have to open it again, and that Mrs. Inglethorp might catch sight of the letter before he could snatch it up. So he goes out and walks in the woods, little dreaming that Mrs. Inglethorp will open his desk, and discover the incriminating document.

"But this, as we know, is what happened. Mrs. Inglethorp reads it, and becomes aware of the perfidy of her husband and Evelyn Howard, though, unfortunately, the sentence about the bromides conveys no warning to her mind. She knows that she is in danger—but is ignorant of where the danger lies. She decides to say nothing to her husband, but sits down and writes to her solicitor, asking him to come on the morrow, and she also determines to destroy immediately the will which she has just made. She keeps the fatal letter."

"It was to discover that letter, then, that her husband forced the lock of the despatch-case?"

"Yes, and from the enormous risk he ran we can see how fully he realized its importance. That letter excepted, there was absolutely nothing to connect him with the crime."

"There's only one thing I can't make out, why didn't he destroy it at once when he got hold of it?"

"Because he did not dare take the biggest risk of all—that of keeping it on his own person."

"I don't understand."

"Look at it from his point of view. I have discovered that there were only five short minutes in which he could have taken it—the five minutes immediately before our own arrival on the scene, for before that time Annie was brushing the stairs, and would have seen anyone who passed going to the right wing. Figure to yourself the scene! He enters the room, unlocking the door by means of one of the other door-keys—they were all much alike. He hurries to the despatch-case—it is locked, and the keys are nowhere to be seen. That is a terrible blow to him, for it means that his presence in the room cannot be concealed as he had hoped. But he sees clearly that everything must be risked for the sake of that damning piece of evidence. Quickly, he forces the lock with a penknife, and turns over the papers until he finds what he is looking for.

"But now a fresh dilemma arises: he dare not keep that piece of paper on him. He may be seen leaving the room—he may be searched. If the paper is found on him, it is certain doom. Probably, at this minute, too, he hears the sounds below of Mr. Wells and John leaving the boudoir. He must act quickly. Where can he hide this terrible slip of paper? The contents of the waste-paper-basket are kept and in any case, are sure to be examined. There are no means of destroying it; and he dare not keep it. He looks round, and he sees—what do you think, *mon ami*?"

I shook my head.

"In a moment, he has torn the letter into long thin strips, and rolling them up into spills he thrusts them hurriedly in amongst the other spills in the vase on the mantelpiece."

I uttered an exclamation.

"No one would think of looking there," Poirot continued. "And he will be able, at his leisure, to come back and destroy this solitary piece of evidence against him."

"Then, all the time, it was in the spill vase in Mrs. Inglethorp's bedroom, under our very noses?" I cried.

Poirot nodded.

"Yes, my friend. That is where I discovered my 'last link,' and I owe that very fortunate discovery to you."

"To me?"

"Yes. Do you remember telling me that my hand shook as I was straightening the ornaments on the mantelpiece?"

"Yes, but I don't see——"

"No, but I saw. Do you know, my friend, I remembered that earlier in the morning, when we had been there together, I had straightened all the objects on the mantelpiece. And, if they were already straightened, there would be no need to straighten them again, unless, in the meantime, some one else had touched them."

"Dear me," I murmured, "so that is the explanation of your extraordinary behaviour. You rushed down to Styles, and found it still there?"

"Yes, and it was a race for time."

"But I still can't understand why Inglethorp was such a fool as to leave it there when he had plenty of opportunity to destroy it."

"Ah, but he had no opportunity. *I* saw to that."

"You?"

"Yes. Do you remember reproving me for taking the household into my confidence on the subject?"

"Yes."

"Well, my friend, I saw there was just one chance. I was not sure then if Inglethorp was the criminal or not, but if he was I reasoned that he would not have the paper on him, but would have hidden it somewhere, and by enlisting the sympathy of the household I could effectually prevent his destroying it. He was already under suspicion, and by making the matter public I secured the services of about ten amateur detectives, who would be watching him unceasingly, and being himself aware of their watchfulness he would not dare seek further to destroy the document. He was therefore forced to depart from the house, leaving it in the spill vase."

"But surely Miss Howard had ample opportunities of aiding him."

"Yes, but Miss Howard did not know of the paper's existence. In accordance with their prearranged plan, she never spoke to Alfred Inglethorp. They were supposed to be deadly enemies, and until John Cavendish was safely convicted they neither of them dared risk a meeting. Of course I had a watch kept on Mr. Inglethorp, hoping that sooner or later he would lead me to the hiding-place. But he was too clever to take any chances. The paper was safe where it was; since no one had thought of looking there in the first week, it was not likely they would do so afterwards. But for your lucky remark, we might never have been able to bring him to justice."

"I understand that now; but when did you first begin to suspect Miss Howard?"

"When I discovered that she had told a lie at the inquest about the letter she had received from Mrs. Inglethorp."

"Why, what was there to lie about?"

"You saw that letter? Do you recall its general appearance?"

"Yes—more or less."

"You will recollect, then, that Mrs. Inglethorp wrote a very distinctive hand, and left large clear spaces between her words. But if you look at the date at the top of the letter you will notice that 'July 17th' is quite different in this respect. Do you see what I mean?"

"No," I confessed, "I don't."

"You do not see that that letter was not written on the 17th, but on the 7th—the day after Miss Howard's departure? The '1' was written in before the '7' to turn it into the '17th'."

"But why?"

"That is exactly what I asked myself. Why does Miss Howard suppress the letter written on the 17th, and produce this faked one instead? Because she did not wish to show the letter of the 17th. Why, again? And at once a suspicion dawned in my mind. You will remember my saying that it was wise to beware of people who were not telling you the truth."

"And yet," I cried indignantly, "after that, you gave me two reasons why Miss Howard could not have committed the crime!"

"And very good reasons too," replied Poirot. "For a long

time they were a stumbling-block to me until I remembered a very significant fact: that she and Alfred Inglethorp were cousins. She could not have committed the crime single-handed, but the reasons against that did not debar her from being an accomplice. And, then, there was that rather over-vehement hatred of hers! It concealed a very opposite emo-tion. There was, undoubtedly, a tie of passion between them long before he came to Styles. They had already arranged their infamous plot—that he should marry this rich, but rather foolish old lady, induce her to make a will leaving her money to him, and then gain their ends by a very cleverly conceived crime. If all had gone as they planned, they would probably have left England, and lived together on their poor victim's money.

"They are a very astute and unscrupulous pair. While sus-picion was to be directed against him, she would be making quiet preparations for a very different *dénouement*. She ar-rives from Middlingham with all the compromising items in her possession. No suspicion attaches to her. No notice is paid to her coming and going in the house. She hides the strychnine and glasses in John's room. She puts the beard in the attic. She will see to it that sooner or later they are duly discovered."

"I don't quite see why they tried to fix the blame on John," I remarked. "It would have been much easier for them to bring the crime home to Lawrence."

"Yes, but that was mere chance. All the evidence against him arose out of pure accident. It must, in fact, have been distinctly annoying to the pair of schemers."

"His manner was unfortunate," I observed thoughtfully.

"Yes. You realize, of course, what was at the back of that?"

"No."

"You did not understand that he believed Mademoiselle Cynthia guilty of the crime?"

"No," I exclaimed, astonished. "Impossible!"

"Not at all. I myself nearly had the same idea. It was in my mind when I asked Mr. Wells that first question about the will. Then there were the bromide powders which she had made up, and her clever male impersonations, as Dorcas recounted them to us. There was really more evidence against her than anyone else."

"You are joking, Poirot!"

"No. Shall I tell you what made Monsieur Lawrence turn so pale when he first entered his mother's room on the fatal night? It was because, whilst his mother lay there, obviously poisoned, he saw, over your shoulder, that the door into Mademoiselle Cynthia's room was unbolted."

"But he declared that he saw it bolted?" I cried.

"Exactly," said Poirot dryly. "And that was just what confirmed my suspicion that it was not. He was shielding Mademoiselle Cynthia."

"But why should he shield her?"

"Because he is in love with her."

I laughed.

"There, Poirot, you are quite wrong! I happen to know for a fact that, far from being in love with her, he positively dislikes her."

"Who told you that, *mon ami?*"

"Cynthia herself."

"*La pauvre petite!* And she was concerned?"

"She said that she did not mind at all."

"Then she certainly did mind very much," remarked Poirot. "They are like that—*les femmes!*"

"What you say about Lawrence is a great surprise to me," I said.

"But why? It was most obvious. Did not Monsieur Lawrence make the sour face every time Mademoiselle Cynthia spoke and laughed with his brother? He had taken it into his long head that Mademoiselle Cynthia was in love with Monsieur John. When he entered his mother's room, and saw her obviously poisoned, he jumped to the conclusion that Mademoiselle Cynthia knew something about the matter. He was nearly driven desperate. First he crushed the coffee cup to powder under his feet, remembering that *she* had gone up with his mother the night before, and he determined that there should be no chance of testing its contents. Thenceforward, he strenuously, and quite uselessly, upheld the theory of 'Death from natural causes.' "

"And what about the 'extra coffee cup?' "

"I was fairly certain that it was Mrs. Cavendish who had hidden it, but I had to make sure. Monsieur Lawrence did not know at all what I meant; but, on reflection, he came to the conclusion that if he could find an extra coffee cup anywhere his lady love would be cleared of suspicion. And he was perfectly right."

"One thing more. What did Mrs. Inglethorp mean by her dying words?"

"They were, of course, an accusation against her husband."

"Dear me, Poirot," I said with a sigh, "I think you have explained everything. I am glad it has all ended so happily. Even John and his wife are reconciled."

"Thanks to me."

"How do you mean—thanks to you?"

"My dear friend, do you not realize that it was simply and solely the trial which has brought them together again? That John Cavendish still loved his wife, I was convinced. Also, that she was equally in love with him. But they had drifted very far apart. It all arose from a misunderstanding. She married him without love. He knew it. He is a sensitive man in his way, he would not force himself upon her if she did not want him. And, as he withdrew, her love awoke. But they are both unusually proud, and their pride held them inexorably apart. He drifted into an entanglement with Mrs. Raikes, and she deliberately cultivated the friendship of Dr. Bauerstein. Do you remember the day of John Cavendish's arrest, when you found me deliberating over a big decision?"

"Yes, I quite understood your distress."

"Pardon me, mon ami, but you did not understand it in the least. I was trying to decide whether or not I would clear John Cavendish at once. I could have cleared him—though it might have meant a failure to convict the real criminals. They were entirely in the dark as to my real attitude up to the very last moment—which partly accounts for my success."

"Do you mean that you could have saved John Cavendish from being brought to trial?"

"Yes, my friend. But I eventually decided in favour of 'a woman's happiness.' Nothing but the great danger through which they have passed could have brought these two proud souls together again."

I looked at Poirot in silent amazement. The colossal cheek of the little man! Who on earth but Poirot would have thought of a trial for murder as a restorer of conjugal happiness!

"I perceive your thoughts, *mon ami*," said Poirot, smiling at me. "No one but Hercule Poirot would have attempted such a thing! And you are wrong in condemning it. The happiness of one man and one woman is the greatest thing in all the world."

His words took me back to earlier events. I remembered Mary as she lay white and exhausted on the sofa, listening, listening. There had come the sound of the bell below. She had started up. Poirot had opened the door, and meeting her agonized eyes had nodded gently. "Yes, madame," he said. "I have brought him back to you." He had stood aside, and as I went out I had seen the look in Mary's eyes, as John Cavendish had caught his wife in his arms.

"Perhaps you are right, Poirot," I said gently. "Yes, it is the greatest thing in the world."

Suddenly, there was a tap at the door, and Cynthia peeped in.

"I—I—only——"

"Come in," I said, springing up.

She came in, but did not sit down.

"I—only wanted to tell you something——"

"Yes?"

Cynthia fidgeted with a little tassel for some moments, then, suddenly exclaiming: "You dears!," kissed first me and then Poirot, and rushed out of the room again.

"What on earth does this mean?" I asked, surprised.

It was very nice to be kissed by Cynthia, but the publicity of the salute rather impaired the pleasure.

"It means that she has discovered Monsieur Lawrence does not dislike her as much as she thought," replied Poirot philosophically.

"But——"

"Here he is."

Lawrence at that moment passed the door.

"Eh! Monsieur Lawrence," called Poirot. "We must congratulate you, is it not so?"

Lawrence blushed, and then smiled awkwardly. A man in love is a sorry spectacle. Now Cynthia had looked charming.

I sighed.

"What is it, *mon ami*?"

"Nothing," I said sadly. "They are two delightful women!"

"And neither of them is for you?" finished Poirot. "Never mind. Console yourself, my friend. We may hunt together again, who knows? And then——"

THE SECRET ADVERSARY

To all those who lead
monotonous lives
In the hope that they may experience
at second hand
the delights and dangers of
adventure

CONTENTS

PROLOGUE

It was 2 p.m. on the afternoon of May 7, 1915. The *Lusitania* had been struck by two torpedoes in succession and was sinking rapidly, while the boats were being launched with all possible speed. The women and children were being lined up awaiting their turn. Some still clung desperately to husbands and fathers; others clutched their children closely to their breasts. One girl stood alone, slightly apart from the rest. She was quite young, not more than eighteen. She did not seem afraid, and her grave, steadfast eyes looked straight ahead.

"I beg your pardon."

A man's voice beside her made her start and turn. She had noticed the speaker more than once amongst the first-class passengers. There had been a hint of mystery about him which had appealed to her imagination. He spoke to no one. If anyone spoke to him he was quick to rebuff the overture. Also he had a nervous way of looking over his shoulder with a swift, suspicious glance.

She noticed now that he was greatly agitated. There were beads of perspiration on his brow. He was evidently in a state of overmastering fear. And yet he did not strike her as the kind of man who would be afraid to meet death!

"Yes?" Her grave eyes met his inquiringly.

He stood looking at her with a kind of desperate irresolution.

"It must be!" he muttered to himself. "Yes—it is the only way." Then aloud he said abruptly: "You are an American?"

"Yes."

"A patriotic one?"

The girl flushed.

"I guess you've no right to ask such a thing! Of course I am!"

"Don't be offended. You wouldn't be if you knew how much there was at stake. But I've got to trust some one—and it must be a woman."

"Why?"

"Because of 'women and children first.' " He looked round and lowered his voice. "I'm carrying papers—vitally important papers. They may make all the difference to the Allies in the war. You understand? These papers have *got* to be saved! They've more chance with you than with me. Will you take them?"

The girl held out her hand.

"Wait—I must warn you. There may be a risk—if I've been followed. I don't think I have, but one never knows. If so, there will be danger. Have you the nerve to go through with it?"

The girl smiled.

"I'll go through with it all right. And I'm real proud to be chosen! What am I to do with them afterwards?"

"Watch the newspapers! I'll advertise in the personal column of the *Times*, beginning 'Shipmate.' At the end of three days if there's nothing—well, you'll know I'm down and out. Then take the packet to the American Embassy, and deliver it into the Ambassador's own hands. Is that clear?"

"Quite clear."

"Then be ready—I'm going to say good-bye." He took her hand in his. "Good-bye. Good luck to you," he said in a louder tone.

Her hand closed on the oilskin packet that had lain in his palm.

The *Lusitania* settled with a more decided list to starboard. In answer to a quick command, the girl went forward to take her place in the boat.

I
_____

THE YOUNG ADVENTURERS, LTD.

"Tommy, old thing!"
    "Tuppence, old bean!"
The two young people greeted each other affectionately,
and momentarily blocked the Dover Street Tube exit in doing so. The adjective "old" was misleading. Their united ages
would certainly not have totalled forty-five.

"Not seen you for simply centuries," continued the young
man. "Where are you off to? Come and chew a bun with me.
We're getting a bit unpopular here—blocking the gangway
as it were. Let's get out of it."

The girl assenting, they started walking down Dover Street
towards Piccadilly.

"Now then," said Tommy, "where shall we go?"

The very faint anxiety which underlay his tone did not escape the astute ears of Miss Prudence Cowley, known to her
intimate friends for some mysterious reason as "Tuppence."
She pounced at once.

"Tommy, you're stony!"

"Not a bit of it," declared Tommy unconvincingly. "Rolling
in cash."

"You always were a shocking liar," said Tuppence severely, "though you did once persuade Sister Greenbank
that the doctor had ordered you beer as a tonic, but forgotten to write it on the chart. Do you remember?"

Tommy chuckled.

"I should think I did! Wasn't the old cat in a rage when
she found out? Not that she was a bad sort really, old Mother
Greenbank! Good old hospital—demobbed like everything
else, I suppose?"

Tuppence sighed.

"Yes. You too?"

Tommy nodded.

"Two months ago."

"Gratuity?" hinted Tuppence.

"Spent."

"Oh, Tommy!"

"No, old thing, not in riotous dissipation. No such luck!
The cost of living—ordinary plain, or garden living nowadays is, I assure you, if you do not know——"

"My dear child," interrupted Tuppence, "there is nothing
I do *not* know about the cost of living. Here we are at Lyons',
and we will each of us pay for our own. That's that!" And
Tuppence led the way upstairs.

The place was full, and they wandered about looking for
a table, catching odds and ends of conversation as they did
so.

"And—do you know, she sat down and *cried* when I told
her she couldn't have the flat after all." "It was simply a *bargain*, my dear! Just like the one Mabel Lewis brought from
Paris——"

"Funny scraps one does overhear," murmured Tommy. "I
passed two Johnnies in the street to-day talking about some
one called Jane Finn. Did you ever hear such a name?"

But at that moment two elderly ladies rose and collected
parcels, and Tuppence deftly ensconced herself in one of the
vacant seats.

Tommy ordered tea and buns. Tuppence ordered tea and
buttered toast.

"And mind the tea comes in separate teapots," she added
severely.

Tommy sat down opposite her. His bared head revealed a shock of exquisitely slicked-back red hair. His face was pleasantly ugly—nondescript, yet unmistakably the face of a gentleman and a sportsman. His brown suit was well cut, but perilously near the end of its tether.

They were an essentially modern-looking couple as they sat there. Tuppence had no claim to beauty, but there was character and charm in the elfin lines of her little face, with its determined chin and large, wide-apart grey eyes that looked mistily out from under straight, black brows. She wore a small bright green toque over her black bobbed hair, and her extremely short and rather shabby skirt revealed a pair of uncommonly dainty ankles. Her appearance presented a valiant attempt at smartness.

The tea came at last, and Tuppence, rousing herself from a fit of meditation, poured it out.

"Now then," said Tommy, taking a large bite of bun, "let's get up-to-date. Remember, I haven't seen you since that time in hospital in 1916."

"Very well." Tuppence helped herself liberally to buttered toast. "Abridged biography of Miss Prudence Cowley, fifth daughter of Archdeacon Cowley of Little Missendell, Suffolk. Miss Cowley left the delights (and drudgeries) of her home life early in the war and came up to London, where she entered an officers' hospital. First month: Washed up six hundred and forty-eight plates every day. Second month: Promoted to drying aforesaid plates. Third month: Promoted to peeling potatoes. Fourth month: Promoted to cutting bread and butter. Fifth month: Promoted one floor up to duties of wardmaid with mop and pail. Sixth month: Promoted to waiting at table. Seventh month: Pleasing appearance and nice manners so striking that am promoted to waiting on the Sisters! Eighth month: Slight check in career. Sister Bond ate Sister Westhaven's egg! Grand row! Wardmaid clearly to blame! Inattention in such important matters cannot be too highly censured. Mop and pail again! How are the mighty fallen! Ninth month: Promoted to sweeping out wards, where I found a friend of my childhood in Lieutenant Thomas Beresford (bow, Tommy!), whom I had not seen for five long years. The meeting was affecting! Tenth month: Reproved by matron for visiting the pictures in company with one of the patients, namely: the aforementioned Lieutenant Thomas Beresford. Eleventh and twelfth months: Parlour-maid duties resumed with entire success. At the end of the year left hospital in a blaze of glory. After that, the talented Miss Cowley drove successively a trade delivery van, a mo-tor-lorry and a general. The last was the pleasantest. He was quite a young general!"

"What blighter was that?" inquired Tommy. "Perfectly sickening the way those brass hats drove from the War Of-fice to the Savoy, and from the Savoy to the War Office!"

"I've forgotten his name now," confessed Tuppence. "To resume, that was in a way the apex of my career. I next en-tered a Government office. We had several very enjoyable tea parties. I had intended to become a land girl, a postwoman, and a bus conductress by way of rounding off my career—but the Armistice intervened! I clung to the office with the true limpet touch for many long months, but, alas, I was combed out at last. Since then I've been looking for a job. Now then—your turn."

"There's not so much promotion in mine," said Tommy regretfully, "and a great deal less variety. I went out to France again, as you know. Then they sent me to Mesopo-tamia, and I got wounded for the second time, and went into hospital out there. Then I got stuck in Egypt till the Armi-stice happened, kicked my heels there some time longer, and, as I told you, finally got demobbed. And, for ten long, weary months I've been job hunting! There aren't any jobs! And, if there were, they wouldn't give 'em to me. What good am I? What do I know about business? Nothing."

Tuppence nodded gloomily.

"What about the colonies?" she suggested.

Tommy shook his head.

"I shouldn't like the colonies—and I'm perfectly certain they wouldn't like me!"

"Rich relations?"

Again Tommy shook his head.

"Oh, Tommy, not even a great-aunt?"

"I've got an old uncle who's more or less rolling, but he's no good."

"Why not?"

"Wanted to adopt me once. I refused."

"I think I remember hearing about it," said Tuppence slowly. "You refused because of your mother—"

Tommy flushed.

"Yes, it would have been a bit rough on the mater. As you know, I was all she had. Old boy hated her—wanted to get me away from her. Just a bit of spite."

"Your mother's dead, isn't she?" said Tuppence gently.

Tommy nodded.

Tuppence's large grey eyes looked misty.

"You're a good sort, Tommy. I always knew it."

"Rot!" said Tommy hastily. "Well, that's my position. I'm just about desperate."

"So am I! I've hung out as long as I could. I've touted round. I've answered advertisements. I've tried every mortal blessed thing. I've screwed and saved and pinched! But it's no good. I shall have to go home!"

"Don't you want to?"

"Of course I don't want to! What's the good of being sentimental? Father's a dear—I'm awfully fond of him—but you've no idea how I worry him! He has that delightful early Victorian view that short skirts and smoking are immoral. You can imagine what a thorn in the flesh I am to him! He just heaved a sigh of relief when the war took me off. You see, there are seven of us at home. It's awful! All housework and mothers' meetings! I have always been the changeling. I don't want to go back, but—oh, Tommy, what else is there to do?"

Tommy shook his head sadly. There was a silence, and then Tuppence burst out:

"Money, money, money! I think about money morning, noon and night! I dare say it's mercenary of me, but there it is!"

"Same here," agreed Tommy with feeling.

"I've thought over every imaginable way of getting it too," continued Tuppence. "There are only three! To be left it, to marry it, or to make it. First is ruled out. I haven't got any rich elderly relatives. Any relatives I have are in homes for decayed gentlewomen! I always help old ladies over crossings, and pick up parcels for old gentlemen, in case they should turn out to be eccentric millionaires. But not one of them has ever asked me my name—and quite a lot never said 'Thank you.' "

There was a pause.

"Of course," resumed Tuppence, "marriage is my best chance. I made up my mind to marry money when I was quite young. Any thinking girl would! I'm not sentimental, you know." She paused. "Come now, you can't say I'm sentimental," she added sharply.

"Certainly not," agreed Tommy hastily. "No one would ever think of sentiment in connection with you."

"That's not very polite," replied Tuppence. "But I dare say you mean it all right. Well, there it is! I'm ready and willing—but I never meet any rich men! All the boys I know are about as hard up as I am."

"What about the general?" inquired Tommy.

"I fancy he keeps a bicycle shop in time of peace," explained Tuppence. "No, there it is! Now *you* could marry a rich girl."

"I'm like you. I don't know any."

"That doesn't matter. You can always get to know one. Now, if I see a man in a fur coat come out of the Ritz I can't rush up to him and say: 'Look here, you're rich. I'd like to know you.' "

"Do you suggest that I should do that to a similarly garbed female?"

"Don't be silly. You tread on her foot, or pick up her handkerchief, or something like that. If she thinks you want to know her she's flattered, and will manage it for you somehow."

"You overrate my manly charms," murmured Tommy.

"On the other hand," proceeded Tuppence, "my millionaire would probably run for his life! No—marriage is fraught with difficulties. Remains—to *make* money!"

"We've tried that, and failed," Tommy reminded her.

"We've tried all the orthodox ways, yes. But suppose we try the unorthodox. Tommy, let's be adventurers!"

"Certainly," replied Tommy cheerfully. "How do we begin?"

"That's the difficulty. If we could make ourselves known, people might hire us to commit crimes for them."

"Delightful," commented Tommy. "Especially coming from a clergyman's daughter!"

"The moral guilt," Tuppence pointed out, "would be theirs—not mine. You must admit that there's a difference between stealing a diamond necklace for yourself and being hired to steal it."

"There wouldn't be the least difference if you were caught!"

"Perhaps not. But I shouldn't be caught. I'm so clever."

"Modesty always was your besetting sin," remarked Tommy.

"Don't rag. Look here, Tommy, shall we really? Shall we form a business partnership?"

"Form a company for the stealing of diamond necklaces?"

"That was only an illustration. Let's have a—what do you call it in book-keeping?"

"Don't know. Never did any."

"I have—but I always got mixed up, and used to put credit entries on the debit side, and vice versa—so they fired me out. Oh, I know—a joint venture! It struck me as such a romantic phrase to come across in the middle of musty old figures. It's got an Elizabethan flavour about it—makes one think of galleons and doubloons. A joint venture!"

"Trading under the name of the Young Adventurers, Ltd.? Is that your idea, Tuppence?"

"It's all very well to laugh, but I feel there might be something in it."

"How do you propose to get in touch with your would-be employers?"

"Advertisement," replied Tuppence promptly. "Have you got a bit of paper and a pencil? Men usually seem to have. Just like we have hairpins and powder-puffs."

Tommy handed over a rather shabby green notebook, and Tuppence began writing busily.

"Shall we begin: 'Young officer, twice wounded in the war—' "

"Certainly not."

"Oh, very well, my dear boy. But I can assure you that

that sort of thing might touch the heart of an elderly spin-
ster, and she might adopt you, and then there would be no
need for you to be a young adventurer at all."

"I don't want to be adopted."

"I forgot you had a prejudice against it. I was only ragging
you! The papers are full up to the brim with that type of
thing. Now listen—how's this? 'Tow young adventurers for
hire. Willing to do anything, go anywhere. Pay must be
good.' (We might as well make that clear from the start.)
Then we might add: 'No reasonable offer refused'—like flats
and furniture."

"I should think any offer we get in answer to that would
be a pretty *un*reasonable one!"

"Tommy! You're a genius! That's ever so much more chic.
'No unreasonable offer refused—if pay is good.' How's that?"

"I shouldn't mention pay again. It looks rather eager."

"It couldn't look as eager as I feel! But perhaps you are
right. Now I'll read it straight through. 'Two young adventurers for hire. Willing to do anything, go anywhere. Pay
must be good. No unreasonable offer refused.' How would
that strike you if you read it?"

"It would strike me as either being a hoax, or else written
by a lunatic."

"It's not half so insane as a thing I read this morning beginning 'Petunia' and signed 'Best Boy.' " She tore out the
leaf and handed it to Tommy. "There you are. *Times*, I think.
Reply to Box so-and-so. I expect it will be about five shillings. Here's half a crown for my share."

Tommy was holding the paper thoughtfully. His face
burned a deeper red.

"Shall we really try it?" he said at last. "Shall we, Tuppence? Just for the fun of the thing?"

"Tommy, you're a sport! I knew you would be! Let's drink
to success." She poured some cold dregs of tea into the two
cups.

"Here's to our joint venture, and may it prosper!"

"The Young Adventurers, Ltd.!" responded Tommy.

They put down the cups and laughed rather uncertainly.
Tuppence rose.

"I must return to my palatial suite at the hostel."

"Perhaps it is time I strolled round to the Ritz," agreed Tommy with a grin. "Where shall we meet? And when?"

"Twelve o'clock to-morrow. Piccadilly Tube station. Will that suit you?"

"My time is my own," replied Mr. Beresford magnificently. "So long, then."

"Good-bye, old thing."

The two young people went off in opposite directions. Tuppence's hostel was situated in what was charitably called Southern Belgravia. For reasons of economy she did not take a bus.

She was half-way across St. James's Park, when a man's voice behind her made her start.

"Excuse me," it said. "But may I speak to you for a moment?"

II

Mr. Whittington's Offer

Tuppence turned sharply, but the words hovering on the tip of her tongue remained unspoken, for the man's appearance and manner did not bear out her first and most natural assumption. She hesitated. As if he read her thoughts, the man said quickly:

"I can assure you I mean no disrespect."

Tuppence believed him. Although she disliked and distrusted him instinctively, she was inclined to acquit him of the particular motive which she had at first attributed to him. She looked him up and down. He was a big man, clean shaven, with a heavy jowl. His eyes were small and cunning, and shifted their glance under her direct gaze.

"Well, what is it?" she asked.

The man smiled.

"I happened to overhear part of your conversation with the young gentleman in Lyons'."

"Well—what of it?"

"Nothing—except that I think I may be of some use to you."

Another inference forced itself into Tuppence's mind:

"You followed me here?"

"I took that liberty."

"And in what way do you think you could be of use to me?"

The man took a card from his pocket and handed it to her with a bow.

Tuppence took it and scrutinized it carefully. It bore the inscription, "Mr. Edward Whittington." Below the name were the words "Esthonia Glassware Co.," and the address of a city office. Mr. Whittington spoke again:

"If you will call upon me to-morrow morning at eleven o'clock, I will lay the details of my proposition before you."

"At eleven o'clock?" said Tuppence doubtfully.

"At eleven o'clock."

Tuppence made up her mind.

"Very well. I'll be there."

"Thank you. Good evening."

He raised his hat with a flourish, and walked away. Tuppence remained for some minutes gazing after him. Then she gave a curious movement of her shoulders, rather as a terrier shakes himself.

"The adventures have begun," she murmured to herself. "What does he want me to do, I wonder? There's something about you, Mr. Whittington, that I don't like at all. But, on the other hand, I'm not the least bit afraid of you. And as I've said before, and shall doubtless say again, little Tuppence can look after herself, thank you!"

And with a short, sharp nod of her head she walked briskly onward. As a result of further meditations, however, she turned aside from the direct route and entered a post office. There she pondered for some moments, a telegraph form in her hand. The thought of a possible five shillings spent unnecessarily spurred her to action, and she decided to risk the waste of ninepence.

Disdaining the spiky pen and thick, black treacle which a beneficent Government had provided, Tuppence drew out Tommy's pencil which she had retained and wrote rapidly: "Don't put in advertisement. Will explain to-morrow." She addressed it to Tommy at his club, from which in one short month he would have to resign, unless a kindly fortune permitted him to renew his subscription.

"It may catch him," she murmured. "Anyway, it's worth trying."

After handing it over the counter she set out briskly for home, stopping at a baker's to buy three penny-worth of new buns.

Later, in her tiny cubicle at the top of the house she munched buns and reflected on the future. What was the Esthonia Glassware Co., and what earthly need could it have for her services? A pleasurable thrill of excitement made Tuppence tingle. At any rate, the country vicarage had retreated into the background again. The morrow held possibilities.

It was a long time before Tuppence went to sleep that night, and, when at length she did, she dreamed that Mr. Whittington had set her to washing up a pile of Esthonia glassware, which bore an unaccountable resemblance to hospital plates!

It wanted some five minutes to eleven when Tuppence reached the block of buildings in which the offices of the Esthonia Glassware Co. were situated. To arrive before the time would look over-eager. So Tuppence decided to walk to the end of the street and back again. She did so. On the stroke of eleven she plunged into the recesses of the building. The Esthonia Glassware Co. was on the top floor. There was a lift, but Tuppence chose to walk up.

Slightly out of breath, she came to a halt outside the ground glass door with the legend painted across it "Esthonia Glassware Co."

Tuppence knocked. In response to a voice from within, she turned the handle and walked into a small, rather dirty outer office.

A middle-aged clerk got down from a high stool at a desk near the window and came towards her inquiringly.

"I have an appointment with Mr. Whittington," said Tuppence.

"Will you come this way, please." He crossed to a partition door with "Private" on it, knocked, then opened the door and stood aside to let her pass in.

Mr. Whittington was seated behind a large desk covered with papers. Tuppence felt her previous judgment confirmed. There was something wrong about Mr. Whittington. The combination of his sleek prosperity and his shifty eye was not attractive.

He looked up and nodded.

"So you've turned up all right? That's good. Sit down, will you?"

Tuppence sat down on the chair facing him. She looked particularly small and demure this morning. She sat there meekly with downcast eyes whilst Mr. Whittington sorted and rustled amongst his papers. Finally he pushed them away, and leaned over the desk.

"Now, my dear young lady, let us come to business." His large face broadened into a smile. "You want work? Well, I have work to offer you. What should you say now to £100 down, and all expenses paid?" Mr. Whittington leaned back in his chair, and thrust his thumbs into the arm-holes of his waistcoat.

Tuppence eyed him warily.

"And the nature of the work?" she demanded.

"Nominal—purely nominal. A pleasant trip, that is all."

"Where to?"

Mr. Whittington smiled again.

"Paris."

"Oh!" said Tuppence thoughtfully. To herself she said: "Of course, if father heard that he would have a fit! But somehow I don't see Mr. Whittington in the rôle of the gay deceiver."

"Yes," continued Whittington. "What could be more delightful? To put the clock back a few years—a very few, I am sure—and re-enter one of those charming *pensionnats de jeunes filles* with which Paris abounds——"

Tuppence interrupted him.

"A *pensionnat?*"

"Exactly. Madame Colombier's in the Avenue de Neuilly."

Tuppence knew the name well. Nothing could have been more select. She had had several American friends there. She was more than ever puzzled.

"You want me to go to Madame Colombier's? For how long?"

"That depends. Possibly three months."

"And that is all? There are no other conditions?"

"None whatever. You would, of course, go in the character of my ward, and you would hold no communication with your friends. I should have to request absolute secrecy for the time being. By the way, you are English, are you not?"

"Yes."

"Yet you speak with a slight American accent?"

"My great pal in hospital was a little American girl. I dare say I picked it up from her. I can soon get out of it again."

"On the contrary, it might be simpler for you to pass as an American. Details about your past life in England might be more difficult to sustain. Yes, I think that would be de-cidedly better. Then——"

"One moment, Mr. Whittington! You seem to be taking my consent for granted."

Whittington looked surprised.

"Surely you are not thinking of refusing? I can assure you that Madame Colombier's is a most high-class and orthodox establishment. And the terms are most liberal."

"Exactly," said Tuppence. "That's just it. The terms are almost too liberal, Mr. Whittington. I cannot see any way in which I can be worth that amount of money to you."

"No?" said Whittington softly. "Well, I will tell you. I could doubtless obtain some one else for very much less. What I am willing to pay for is a young lady with sufficient intelli-gence and presence of mind to sustain her part well, and also one who will have sufficient discretion not to ask too many questions."

Tuppence smiled a little. She felt that Whittington had scored.

"There's another thing. So far there has been no mention of Mr. Beresford. Where does he come in?"

"Mr. Beresford?"

"My partner," said Tuppence with dignity. "You saw us together yesterday."

"Ah, yes. But I'm afraid we shan't require his services."

"Then it's off!" Tuppence rose. "It's both or neither. Sorry—but that's how it is. Good morning, Mr. Whittington."

"Wait a minute. Let us see if something can't be managed. Sit down again, Miss——" He paused interrogatively.

Tuppence's conscience gave her a passing twinge as she remembered the archdeacon. She seized hurriedly on the first name that came into her head.

"Jane Finn," she said hastily; and then paused open-mouthed at the effect of those two simple words.

All the geniality had faded out of Whittington's face. It was purple with rage, and the veins stood out on the forehead. And behind it all there lurked a sort of incredulous dismay. He leaned forward and hissed savagely:

"So that's your little game, is it?"

Tuppence, though utterly taken aback, nevertheless kept her head. She had not the faintest comprehension of his meaning, but she was naturally quick-witted, and felt it imperative to "keep her end up" as she phrased it.

Whittington went on:

"Been playing with me, have you, all the time, like a cat and mouse? Knew all the time what I wanted you for, but kept up the comedy. Is that it, eh?" He was cooling down. The red colour was ebbing out of his face. He eyed her keenly. "Who's been blabbing? Rita?"

Tuppence shook her head. She was doubtful as to how long she could sustain this illusion, but she realized the importance of not dragging an unknown Rita into it.

"No," she replied with perfect truth. "Rita knows nothing about me."

His eyes still bored into her like gimlets.

"How much do you know?" he shot out.

"Very little indeed," answered Tuppence, and was pleased to note that Whittington's uneasiness was augmented instead of allayed. To have boasted that she knew a lot might have raised doubts in his mind.

"Anyway," snarled Whittington, "you knew enough to come in here and plump out that name."

"It might be my own name," Tuppence pointed out.

"It's likely, isn't it, that there would be two girls with a name like that?"

"Or I might just have hit upon it by chance," continued Tuppence, intoxicated with the success of truthfulness.

Mr. Whittington brought his fist down upon the desk with a bang.

"Quit fooling! How much do you know? And how much do you want?"

The last five words took Tuppence's fancy mightily, especially after a meagre breakfast and a supper of buns the night before. Her present part was of the adventuress rather than the adventurous order, but she did not deny its possibilities. She sat up and smiled with the air of one who has the situation thoroughly well in hand.

"My dear Mr. Whittington," she said, "let us by all means lay our cards upon the table. And pray do not be so angry. You heard me say yesterday that I proposed to live by my wits. It seems to me that I have now proved I have some wits to live by! I admit I have knowledge of a certain name, but perhaps my knowledge ends there."

"Yes—and perhaps it doesn't," snarled Whittington.

"You insist on misjudging me," said Tuppence, and sighed gently.

"As I said once before," said Whittington angrily, "quit fooling, and come to the point. You can't play the innocent with me. You know a great deal more than you're willing to admit."

Tuppence paused a moment to admire her own ingenuity, and then said softly:

"I shouldn't like to contradict you, Mr. Whittington."

"So we come to the usual question—how much?"

Tuppence was in a dilemma. So far she had fooled Whittington with complete success, but to mention a palpably impossible sum might awaken his suspicions. An idea flashed across her brain.

"Suppose we say a little something down, and a fuller discussion of the matter later?"

Whittington gave her an ugly glance.

"Blackmail, eh?"

Tuppence smiled sweetly.

"Oh no! Shall we say payment of services in advance?"

Whittington grunted.

"You see," explained Tuppence still sweetly, "I'm so very fond of money!"

"You're about the limit, that's what you are," growled Whittington, with a sort of unwilling admiration. "You took me in all right. Thought you were quite a meek little kid with just enough brains for my purpose."

"Life," moralized Tuppence, "is full of surprises."

"All the same," continued Whittington, "some one's been talking. You say it isn't Rita. Was it—? Oh, come in."

The clerk followed his discreet knock into the room, and laid a paper at his master's elbow.

"Telephone message just come for you, sir."

Whittington snatched it up and read it. A frown gathered on his brow.

"That'll do, Brown. You can go."

The clerk withdrew, closing the door behind him. Whittington turned to Tuppence.

"Come to-morrow at the same time. I'm busy now. Here's fifty to go on with."

He rapidly sorted out some notes, and pushed them across the table to Tuppence, then stood up, obviously impatient for her to go.

The girl counted the notes in a business-like manner, secured them in her handbag, and rose.

"Good morning, Mr. Whittington," she said politely. "At least, *au revoir*, I should say."

"Exactly. *Au revoir!*" Whittington looked almost genial again, a reversion that aroused in Tuppence a faint misgiving. "*Au revoir*, my clever and charming young lady."

Tuppence sped lightly down the stairs. A wild elation possessed her. A neighbouring clock showed the time to be five minutes to twelve.

"Let's give Tommy a surprise!" murmured Tuppence, and hailed a taxi.

The cab drew up outside the tube station. Tommy was just within the entrance. His eyes opened to their fullest extent as he hurried forward to assist Tuppence to alight. She smiled at him affectionately, and remarked in a slightly affected voice:

"Pay the thing, will you, old bean? I've got nothing smaller than a five-pound note!"

III

A SET BACK

The moment was not quite so triumphant as it ought to have been. To begin with, the resources of Tommy's pockets were somewhat limited. In the end the fare was managed, the lady recollecting a plebeian twopence, and the driver, still holding the varied assortment of coins in his hand, was prevailed upon to move on, which he did after one last hoarse demand as to what the gentleman thought he was giving him.

"I think you've given him too much, Tommy," said Tuppence innocently. "I fancy he wants to give some of it back."

It was possibly this remark which induced the driver to move away.

"Well," said Mr. Beresford, at length able to relieve his feelings, "what the—dickens, did you want to take a taxi for?"

"I was afraid I might be late and keep you waiting," said Tuppence gently.

"Afraid—you—might—be—late! Oh, Lord, I give it up!" said Mr. Beresford.

"And really and truly," continued Tuppence, opening her

eyes very wide, "I haven't got anything smaller than a five-pound note."

"You did that part of it very well, old bean, but all the same the fellow wasn't taken in—not for a moment!"

"No," said Tuppence thoughtfully, "he didn't believe it. That's the curious part about speaking the truth. No one does believe it. I found that out this morning. Now let's go to lunch. How about the Savoy?"

Tommy grinned.

"How about the Ritz?"

"On second thoughts, I prefer the Piccadilly. It's nearer. We shan't have to take another taxi. Come along."

"Is this a new brand of humour? Or is your brain really unhinged?" inquired Tommy.

"Your last supposition is the correct one. I have come into money, and the shock has been too much for me! For that particular form of mental trouble an eminent physician recommends unlimited *hors d'œuvre*, Lobster *à l'américane*, Chicken Newberg, and Pêche Melba! Let's go and get them!"

"Tuppence, old girl, what has really come over you?"

"Oh, unbelieving one!" Tuppence wrenched open her bag. "Look here, and here, and here!"

"Great Jehoshaphat! My dear girl, don't wave Fishers aloft like that!"

"They're not Fishers. They're five times better than Fishers, and this one's ten times better!"

Tommy groaned.

"I must have been drinking unawares! Am I dreaming, Tuppence, or do I really behold a large quantity of five-pound notes being waved about in a dangerous fashion?"

"Even so, O King! *Now*, will you come and have lunch?"

"I'll come anywhere. But what have you been doing! Holding up a bank?"

"All in good time. What an awful place Piccadilly Circus is. There's a huge bus bearing down on us. It would be too terrible if they killed the five-pound notes!"

"Grill room?" inquired Tommy, as they reached the opposite pavement in safety.

"The other's more expensive," demurred Tuppence.

"That's mere wicked wanton extravagance. Come on below."

"Are you sure I can get all the things I want there?"

"That extremely unwholesome menu you were outlining just now? Of course you can—or as much as is good for you, anyway."

"And now tell me," said Tommy, unable to restrain his pent-up curiosity any longer, as they sat in state surrounded by the many hors d'œuvre of Tuppence's dreams.

Miss Cowley told him.

"And the curious part of it is," she ended, "that I really did invent the name of Jane Finn! I didn't want to give my own because of poor father—in case I should get mixed up in anything shady."

"Perhaps that's so," said Tommy slowly. "But you didn't invent it."

"What?"

"No. I told it to you. Don't you remember, I said yesterday I'd overheard two people talking about a female called Jane Finn? That's what brought the name into your mind so pat."

"So you did. I remember now. How extraordinary—" Tuppence tailed off into silence. Suddenly she aroused herself. "Tommy!"

"Yes?"

"What were they like, the two men you passed?"

Tommy frowned in an effort at remembrance.

"One was a big fat sort of chap. Clean shaven, I think—and dark."

"That's him," cried Tuppence, in an ungrammatical squeal. "That's Whittington! What was the other man like?"

"I can't remember. I didn't notice him particularly. It was really the outlandish name that caught my attention."

"And people say that coincidences don't happen!" Tuppence tackled her Pêche Melba happily.

But Tommy had become serious.

"Look here, Tuppence, old girl, what is this going to lead to?"

"More money," replied his companion.

"I know that. You've only got one idea in your head. What

I mean is, what about the next step? How are you going to keep the game up?"

"Oh!" Tuppence laid down her spoon. "You're right, Tommy, it is a bit of a poser."

"After all, you know, you can't bluff him forever. You're sure to slip up sooner or later. And, anyway, I'm not at all sure that it isn't actionable—blackmail, you know."

"Nonsense. Blackmail is saying you'll tell unless you are given money. Now, there's nothing I could tell, because I don't really know anything."

"Hm," said Tommy doubtfully. "Well, anyway, what *are* we going to do? Whittington was in a hurry to get rid of you this morning, but next time he'll want to know something more before he parts with his money. He'll want to know how much *you* know, and where you got your information from, and a lot of other things that you can't cope with. What are you going to do about it?"

Tuppence frowned severely.

"We must think. Order some Turkish coffee, Tommy. Stimulating to the brain. Oh, dear, what a lot I have eaten!"

"You have made rather a hog of yourself! So have I for that matter, but I flatter myself that my choice of dishes was more judicious than yours. Two coffees." (This was to the waiter.) "One Turkish, one French."

Tuppence sipped her coffee with a deeply reflective air, and snubbed Tommy when he spoke to her.

"Be quiet. I'm thinking."

"Shades of Pelmanism!" said Tommy, and relapsed into silence.

"There!" said Tuppence at last. "I've got a plan. Obviously what we've got to do is to find out more about it all."

Tommy applauded.

"Don't jeer. We can only find out through Whittington. We must discover where he lives, what he does—sleuth him, in fact! Now I can't do it, because he knows me, but he only saw you for a minute or two in Lyons'. He's not likely to recognize you. After all, one young man is much like another."

"I repudiate that remark utterly. I'm sure my pleasing features and distinguished appearance would single me out from any crowd."

"My plan is this," Tuppence went on calmly, "I'll go alone to-morrow. I'll put him off again like I did to-day. It doesn't matter if I don't get any more money at once. Fifty pounds ought to last us a few days."

"Or even longer!"

"You'll hang about outside. When I come out I shan't speak to you in case he's watching. But I'll take up my stand somewhere near, and when he comes out of the building I'll drop a handkerchief or something, and off you go!"

"Off I go where?"

"Follow him, of course, silly! What do you think of the idea?"

"Sort of thing one reads about in books. I somehow feel that in real life one will feel a bit of an ass standing in the street for hours with nothing to do. People will wonder what I'm up to."

"Not in the city. Every one's in such a hurry. Probably no one will even notice you at all."

"That's the second time you've made that sort of remark. Never mind, I forgive you. Anyway, it will be rather a lark. What are you doing this afternoon?"

"Well," said Tuppence meditatively. "I *had* thought of hats! Or perhaps silk stockings! Or perhaps—"

"Hold hard," admonished Tommy. "There's a limit to fifty pounds! But let's do dinner and a show tonight at all events."

"Rather."

The day passed pleasantly. The evening even more so. Two of the five-pound notes were now irretrievably dead.

They met by arrangement the following morning and proceeded citywards. Tommy remained on the opposite side of the road while Tuppence plunged into the building.

Tommy strolled slowly down to the end of the street, then back again. Just as he came abreast of the buildings, Tuppence darted across the road.

"Tommy!"

"Yes. What's up?"

"The place is shut. I can't make any one hear."

"That's odd."

"Isn't it? Come with me, and let's try again."

Tommy followed her. As they passed the third floor landing a young clerk came out of an office. He hesitated a moment, then addressed himself to Tuppence.

"Were you wanting the Esthonia Glassware?"

"Yes, please."

"It's closed down. Since yesterday afternoon. Company being wound up, they say. Not that I've ever heard of it myself. But anyway the office is to let."

"Th—thank you," faltered Tuppence. "I suppose you don't know Mr. Whittington's address?"

"Afraid I don't. They left rather suddenly."

"Thank you very much," said Tommy. "Come on, Tuppence."

They descended to the street again where they gazed at one another blankly.

"That's torn it," said Tommy at length.

"And I never suspected it," wailed Tuppence.

"Cheer up, old thing, it can't be helped."

"Can't it, though!" Tuppence's little chin shot out defiantly. "Do you think this is the end? If so, you're wrong. It's just the beginning!"

"The beginning of what?"

"Of our adventure! Tommy, don't you see, if they are scared enough to run away like this, it shows that there must be a lot in this Jane Finn business! Well, we'll get to the bottom of it. We'll run them down! We'll be sleuths in earnest!"

"Yes, but there's no one left to sleuth."

"No, that's why we'll have to start all over again. Lend me that bit of pencil. Thanks. Wait a minute—don't interrupt. There!" Tuppence handed back the pencil, and surveyed the piece of paper on which she had written with a satisfied eye:

"What's that?"

"Advertisement."

"You're not going to put that thing in after all?"

"No, it's a different one." She handed him the slip of paper. Tommy read the words on it aloud:

"WANTED, any information respecting Jane Finn. Apply Y. A."

IV

WHO IS JANE FINN?

The next day passed slowly. It was necessary to curtail expenditure. Carefully husbanded, forty pounds will last a long time. Luckily the weather was fine, and "walking is cheap," dictated Tuppence. An outlying picture house provided them with recreation for the evening.

The day of disillusionment had been a Wednesday. On Thursday the advertisement had duly appeared. On Friday letters might be expected to arrive at Tommy's rooms.

He had been bound by an honourable promise not to open any such letters if they did arrive, but to repair to the National Gallery, where his colleague would meet him at ten o'clock.

Tuppence was first at the rendezvous. She ensconced herself on a red velvet seat, and gazed at the Turners with unseeing eyes until she saw the familiar figure enter the room.

"Well?"

"Well," returned Mr. Beresford provokingly. "Which is your favourite picture?"

"Don't be a wretch. Aren't there *any* answers?"

Tommy shook his head with a deep and somewhat over-acted melancholy.

"I didn't want to disappoint you, old thing, by telling you right off. It's too bad. Good money wasted." He sighed. "Still, there it is. The advertisement has appeared, and there are only two answers!"

"Tommy, you devil!" almost screamed Tuppence. "Give them to me. How could you be so mean!"

"Your language, Tuppence, your language! They're very particular at the National Gallery. Government show, you know. And do remember, as I have pointed out to you before, that as a clergyman's daughter——"

"I ought to be on the stage!" finished Tuppence with a snap.

"That is not what I intended to say. But if you are sure that you have enjoyed to the full the reaction of joy after despair with which I have kindly provided you free of charge, let us get down to our mail, as the saying goes."

Tuppence snatched the two precious envelopes from him unceremoniously, and scrutinized them carefully.

"Thick paper, this one. It looks rich. We'll keep it to the last and open the other first."

"Right you are. One, two, three, go!"

Tuppence's little thumb ripped open the envelope, and she extracted the contents.

"DEAR SIR,

Referring to your advertisement in this morning's paper, I may be able to be of some use to you. Perhaps you could call and see me at the above address at eleven o'clock to-morrow morning.

                              Yours truly,
                              A. CARTER."

"27 Carshalton Gardens," said Tuppence, referring to the address. "That's Gloucester Road way. Plenty of time to get there if we tube."

"The following," said Tommy, "is the plan of campaign. It is my turn to assume the offensive. Ushered into the presence of Mr. Carter, he and I wish each other good morning

as is customary. He then says; 'Please take a seat, Mr.—er?'
To which I reply promptly and significantly: 'Edward Whittington!' Whereupon Mr. Carter turns purple in the face and
gasps out: 'How much?' Pocketing the usual fee of fifty
pounds, I rejoin you in the road outside, and we proceed to
the next address and repeat the performance."

"Don't be absurd, Tommy. Now for the other letter. Oh,
this is from the Ritz!"

"A hundred pounds instead of fifty!"

"I'll read it:

"DEAR SIR,
Re your advertisement, I should be glad if you would call
round somewhere about lunch-time.
Yours truly,
JULIUS P. HERSHEIMMER."

"Ha!" said Tommy. "Do I smell a Boche? Or only an American millionaire of unfortunate ancestry? At all events we'll
call at lunch-time. It's a good time—frequently leads to free
food for two."

Tuppence nodded assent.

"Now for Carter. We'll have to hurry."

Carshalton Terrace proved to be an unimpeachable row
of what Tuppence called "ladylike looking houses." They
rang the bell at No. 27, and a neat maid answered the door.
She looked so respectable that Tuppence's heart sank. Upon
Tommy's request for Mr. Carter, she showed them into a
small study on the ground floor where she left them. Hardly
a minute elapsed, however, before the door opened, and a
tall man with a lean hawklike face and a tired manner entered the room.

"Mr. Y. A.?" he said, and smiled. His smile was distinctly
attractive. "Do sit down, both of you."

They obeyed. He himself took a chair opposite to Tuppence and smiled at her encouragingly. There was something in the quality of his smile that made the girl's usual
readiness desert her.

As he did not seem inclined to open the conversation, Tuppence was forced to begin.

"We wanted to know—that is, would you be so kind as to tell us anything you know about Jane Finn?"

"Jane Finn? Ah!" Mr. Carter appeared to reflect. "Well, the question is, what do *you* know about her?"

Tuppence drew herself up.

"I don't see that that's got anything to do with it."

"No? But it has, you know, really it has." He smiled again in his tired way, and continued reflectively. "So that brings us down to it again. What do *you* know about Jane Finn?

"Come now," he continued, as Tuppence remained silent. "You must know *something* to have advertised as you did?" He leaned forward a little, his weary voice held a hint of persuasiveness. "Suppose you tell me. . . ."

There was something very magnetic about Mr. Carter's personality. Tuppence seemed to shake herself free of it with an effort, as she said:

"We couldn't do that, could we, Tommy?"

But to her surprise, her companion did not back her up. His eyes were fixed on Mr. Carter, and his tone when he spoke held an unusual note of deference.

"I dare say the little we know won't be any good to you, sir. But such as it is, you're welcome to it."

"Tommy!" cried out Tuppence in surprise.

Mr. Carter slewed round in his chair. His eyes asked a question.

Tommy nodded.

"Yes, sir, I recognized you at once. Saw you in France when I was with the Intelligence. As soon as you came into the room, I knew——"

Mr. Carter held up his hand.

"No names, please. I'm known as Mr. Carter here. It's my cousin's house, by the way. She's willing to lend it to me sometimes when it's a case of working on strictly unofficial lines. Well, now"—he looked from one to the other—"who's going to tell me the story?"

"Fire ahead, Tuppence," directed Tommy. "It's your yarn."

"Yes, little lady, out with it."

And obediently Tuppence did out with it, telling the whole story from the forming of the Young Adventurers, Ltd., downwards.

Mr. Carter listened in silence with a resumption of his tired manner. Now and then he passed his hand across his lips as though to hide a smile. When she had finished he nodded gravely.

"Not much. But suggestive. Quite suggestive. If you'll excuse my saying so, you're a curious young couple. I don't know—you might succeed where others have failed. . . . I believe in luck, you know—always have. . . ."

He paused a moment, and then went on.

"Well, how about it? You're out for adventure. How would you like to work for me? All quite unofficial, you know. Expenses paid, and a moderate screw?"

Tuppence gazed at him, her lips parted, her eyes growing wider and wider.

"What should we have to do?" she breathed.

Mr. Carter smiled.

"Just go on with what you're doing now. *Find Jane Finn.*"

"Yes, but—who *is* Jane Finn?"

Mr. Carter nodded gravely.

"Yes, you're entitled to know that, I think."

He leaned back in his chair, crossed his legs, brought the tips of his fingers together, and began in a low monotone:

"Secret diplomacy (which, by the way, is nearly always bad policy!) does not concern you. It will be sufficient to say that in the early days of 1915 a certain document came into being. It was the draft of a secret agreement—treaty—call it what you like. It was drawn up ready for signature by the various representatives, and drawn up in America—at that time a neutral country. It was dispatched to England by a special messenger selected for that purpose, a young fellow called Danvers. It was hoped that the whole affair had been kept so secret that nothing would have leaked out. That kind of hope is usually disappointed. Somebody always talks!

"Danvers sailed for England on the *Lusitania.* He carried the precious papers in an oilskin packet which he wore next his skin. It was on that particular voyage that the *Lusitania* was torpedoed and sunk. Danvers was among the list of those missing. Eventually his body was washed ashore, and identified beyond any possible doubt. But the oilskin packet was missing!

"The question was, had it been taken from him, or had he himself passed it on into another's keeping? There were a few incidents that strengthened the possibility of the latter theory. After the torpedo struck the ship, in the few moments during the launching of the boats, Danvers was seen speaking to a young American girl. No one actually saw him pass anything to her, but he might have done so. It seems to me quite likely that he entrusted the papers to this girl, believing that she, as a woman, had a greater chance of bringing them safely to shore.

"But if so, where was the girl, and what had she done with the papers? By later advice from America it seemed likely that Danvers had been closely shadowed on the way over. Was this girl in league with his enemies? Or had she, in her turn, been shadowed and either tricked or forced into handing over the precious packet?

"We set to work to trace her out. It proved unexpectedly difficult. Her name was Jane Finn, and it duly appeared among the list of the survivors, but the girl herself seemed to have vanished completely. Inquiries into her antecedents did little to help us. She was an orphan, and had been what we should call over here a pupil teacher in a small school out West. Her passport had been made out for Paris, where she was going to join the staff of a hospital. She had offered her services voluntarily, and after some correspondence they had been accepted. Having seen her name in the list of the saved from the *Lusitania*, the staff of the hospital were naturally very surprised at her not arriving to take up her billet, and at not hearing from her in any way.

"Well, every effort was made to trace the young lady—but all in vain. We tracked her across Ireland, but nothing could be heard of her after she set foot in England. No use was made of the draft treaty—as might very easily have been done—and we therefore came to the conclusion that Danvers had, after all, destroyed it. The war entered on another phase, the diplomatic aspect changed accordingly, and the treaty was never redrafted. Rumours as to its existence were emphatically denied. The disappearance of Jane Finn was forgotten and the whole affair was lost in oblivion."

Mr. Carter paused, and Tuppence broke in impatiently:

"But why has it all cropped up again? The war's over."

A hint of alertness came into Mr. Carter's manner.

"Because it seems that the papers were not destroyed after all, and that they might be resurrected to-day with a new and deadly significance."

Tuppence stared. Mr. Carter nodded.

"Yes, five years ago, that draft treaty was a weapon in our hands; to-day it is a weapon against us. It was a gigantic blunder. If its terms were made public, it would mean disaster. . . . It might possibly bring about another war—not with Germany this time! That is an extreme possibility, and I do not believe in its likelihood myself, but that document undoubtedly implicates a number of our statesmen whom we cannot afford to have discredited in any way at the present moment. As a party cry for Labour it would be irresistible, and a Labour Government at this juncture would, in my opinion, be a grave disability for British trade, but that is a mere nothing to the *real* danger."

He paused, and then said quietly:

"You may perhaps have heard or read that there is Bolshevist influence at work behind the present labour unrest?"

Tuppence nodded.

"That is the truth. Bolshevist gold is pouring into this country for the specific purpose of procuring a revolution. And there is a certain man, a man whose real name is unknown to us, who is working in the dark for his own ends. The Bolshevists are behind the Labour unrest—but this man is *behind the Bolshevists.* Who is he? We do not know. He is always spoken of by the unassuming title of 'Mr. Brown.' But one thing is certain, he is the master criminal of this age. He controls a marvellous organization. Most of the Peace propaganda during the war was originated and financed by him. His spies are everywhere."

"A naturalized German?" asked Tommy.

"On the contrary, I have every reason to believe he is an Englishman. He was pro-German, as he would have been pro-Boer. What he seeks to attain we do not know—probably supreme power for himself, of a kind unique in history. We have no clue as to his real personality. It is reported that even his own followers are ignorant of it. Where we have come across his tracks, he has always played a secondary part. Somebody else assumes the chief rôle. But afterwards we always find that there has been some nonentity, a servant or a clerk, who has remained in the background unnoticed, and that the elusive Mr. Brown has escaped us once more."

"Oh!" Tuppence jumped. "I wonder——"

"Yes?"

"I remember in Mr. Whittington's office. The clerk—he called him Brown. You don't think——"

Carter nodded thoughtfully.

"Very likely. A curious point is that the name is usually mentioned. An idiosyncrasy of genius. Can you describe him at all?"

"I really didn't notice. He was quite ordinary—just like any one else."

Mr. Carter sighed in his tired manner.

"That is the invariable description of Mr. Brown! Brought a telephone message to the man Whittington, did he? Notice a telephone in the outer office?"

Tuppence thought.

"No, I don't think I did."

"Exactly. That 'message' was Mr. Brown's way of giving an order to his subordinate. He overheard the whole conversation of course. Was it after that that Whittington handed you over the money, and told you to come the following day?"

Tuppence nodded.

"Yes, undoubtedly the hand of Mr. Brown!" Mr. Carter paused. "Well, there it is, you see what you are pitting yourselves against? Possibly the finest criminal brain of the age. I don't quite like it, you know. You're such young things, both of you. I shouldn't like anything to happen to you."

"It won't," Tuppence assured him positively.

"I'll look after her, sir," said Tommy.

"And I'll look after *you*," retorted Tuppence, resenting the manly assertion.

"Well, then, look after each other," said Mr. Carter, smiling. "Now let's get back to business. There's something mysterious about this draft treaty that we haven't fathomed yet. We've been threatened with it—in plain and unmistakable terms. The Revolutionary element as good as declare that it's in their hands, and that they intend to produce it at a given moment. On the other hand, they are clearly at fault about many of its provisions. The Government consider it as mere bluff on their part, and, rightly or wrongly, have stuck to the policy of absolute denial. I'm not so sure. There have been hints, indiscreet allusions, that seem to indicate that the menace is a real one. The position is much as though they had got hold of an incriminating document, but couldn't read it because it was in cipher—but we know that the draft treaty wasn't in cipher—couldn't be in the nature of things—so that won't wash. But there's *something*. Of course, Jane Finn may be dead for all we know—but I don't think so. The curious thing is that *they're trying to get information about the girl from us.*"

"What?"

"Yes. One or two little things have cropped up. And your story, little lady, confirms my idea. They know we're looking for Jane Finn. Well, they'll produce a Jane Finn of their own—say at a *pensionnat* in Paris." Tuppence gasped, and Mr. Carter smiled. "No one knows in the least what she looks like, so that's all right. She's primed with a trumped-up tale, and her real business is to get as much information as possible out of us. See the idea?"

"Then you think"—Tuppence paused to grasp the supposition fully—"that it *was* as Jane Finn that they wanted me to go to Paris?"

Mr. Carter smiled more wearily than ever.

"I believe in coincidences, you know," he said.

V

Mr. Julius P. Hersheimmer

"Well," said Tuppence, recovering herself, "it really seems as though it were meant to be."

Carter nodded.

"I know what you mean. I'm superstitious myself. Luck, and all that sort of thing. Fate seems to have chosen you out to be mixed up in this."

Tommy indulged in a chuckle.

"My word! I don't wonder Whittington got the wind up when Tuppence plumped out that name! I should have myself. But look here, sir, we're taking up an awful lot of your time. Have you any tips to give us before we clear out?"

"I think not. My experts, working in stereotyped ways, have failed. You will bring imagination and an open mind to the task. Don't be discouraged if that too does not succeed. For one thing there is a likelihood of the pace being forced."

Tuppence frowned uncomprehendingly.

"When you had that interview with Whittington, they had time before them. I have information that the big *coup* was planned for early in the new year. But the Government is contemplating legislative action which will deal effectually with the strike menace. They'll get wind of it soon, if they haven't already, and it's possible that that may bring things to a head. I hope it will myself. The less time they have to mature their plans the better. I'm just warning you that you haven't much time before you, and that you needn't be cast down if you fail. It's not an easy proposition anyway. That's all."

Tuppence rose.

"I think we ought to be business-like. What exactly can we count upon you for, Mr. Carter?"

Mr. Carter's lips twitched slightly, but he replied succinctly:

"Funds within reason, detailed information on any point, and *no official recognition.* I mean that if you get yourselves into trouble with the police, I can't officially help you out of it. You're on your own."

Tuppence nodded sagely.

"I quite understand that. I'll write out a list of the things I want to know when I've had time to think. Now—about money—"

"Yes, Miss Tuppence. Do you want to say how much?"

"Not exactly. We've got plenty to go with for the present, but when we want more—"

"It will be waiting for you."

"Yes, but—I'm sure I don't want to be rude about the Government if you've got anything to do with it, but you know one really has the devil of a time getting anything out of it! And if we have to fill up a blue form and send it in, and then, after three months, they send us a green one, and so on— well, that won't be much use, will it?"

Mr. Carter laughed outright.

"Don't worry, Miss Tuppence. You will send a personal demand to me here, and the money, in notes, shall be sent by return of post. As to salary, shall we say at the rate of three hundred a year? And an equal sum for Mr. Beresford, of course."

Tuppence beamed upon him.

"How lovely. You are kind. I do love money! I'll keep beautiful accounts of our expenses—all debit and credit, and the balance on the right side, and a red line drawn sideways with the totals the same at the bottom. I really know how to do it when I think."

"I'm sure you do. Well, good-bye, and good luck to you both."

He shook hands with them, and in another minute they were descending the steps of 27 Carshalton Terrace with their heads in a whirl.

"Tommy! Tell me at once, who is 'Mr. Carter?' "

Tommy murmured a name in her ear.

"Oh!" said Tuppence, impressed.

"And I can tell you, old bean, he's IT!"

"Oh!" said Tuppence again. Then she added reflectively, "I like him, don't you? He looks so awfully tired and bored, and yet you feel that underneath he's just like steel, all keen and flashing. Oh!" She gave a skip. "Pinch me, Tommy, do pinch me. I can't believe it's real!"

Mr. Beresford obliged.

"Ow! That's enough! Yes, we're not dreaming. We've got a job!"

"And what a job! The joint venture has really begun."

"It's more respectable than I thought it would be," said Tuppence thoughtfully.

"Luckily I haven't got your craving for crime! What time is it? Let's have lunch—oh!"

The same thought sprang to the minds of each. Tommy voiced it first.

"Julius P. Hersheimmer!"

"We never told Mr. Carter about hearing from him."

"Well, there wasn't much to tell—not till we've seen him. Come on, we'd better take a taxi."

"Now who's being extravagant?"

"All expenses paid, remember. Hop in."

"At any rate, we shall make a better effect arriving this way," said Tuppence, leaning back luxuriously. "I'm sure blackmailers never arrive in buses!"

"We've ceased being blackmailers," Tommy pointed out.

"I'm not sure I have," said Tuppence darkly.

On inquiring for Mr. Hersheimmer, they were at once taken up to his suite. An impatient voice cried "Come in" in answer to the page-boy's knock, and the lad stood aside to let them pass in.

Mr. Julius P. Hersheimmer was a great deal younger than either Tommy or Tuppence had pictured him. The girl put him down as thirty-five. He was of middle height, and squarely built to match his jaw. His face was pugnacious but pleasant. No one could have mistaken him for anything but an American, though he spoke with very little accent.

"Get my note? Sit down and tell me right away all you know about my cousin."

"Your cousin?"

"Sure thing. Jane Finn."

"Is she your cousin?"

"My father and her mother were brother and sister," explained Mr. Hersheimmer meticulously.

"Oh!" cried Tuppence. "Then you know where she is?"

"No!" Mr. Hersheimmer brought down his fist with a bang on the table. "I'm darned if I do! Don't you?"

"We advertised to receive information, not to give it," said Tuppence severely.

"I guess I know that. I can read. But I thought maybe it was her back history you were after, and that you'd know where she was now?"

"Well, we wouldn't mind hearing her back history," said Tuppence guardedly.

But Mr. Hersheimmer seemed to grow suddenly suspicious.

"See here," he declared. "This isn't Sicily! No demanding ransom or threatening to crop her ears if I refuse. These are the British Isles, so quit the funny business, or I'll just sing out for that beautiful big British policeman I see out there in Piccadilly."

Tommy hastened to explain.

"We haven't kidnapped your cousin. On the contrary, we're trying to find her. We're employed to do so."

Mr. Hersheimmer leant back in his chair.

"Put me wise," he said succinctly.

Tommy fell in with this demand in so far as he gave him a guarded version of the disappearance of Jane Finn, and of the possibility of her having been mixed up unawares in "some political show." He alluded to Tuppence and himself as "private inquiry agents" commissioned to find her, and added that they would therefore be glad of any details Mr. Hersheimmer could give them.

That gentleman nodded approval.

"I guess that's all right. I was just a mite hasty. But London gets my goat! I only know little old New York. Just trot out your questions and I'll answer."

For the moment this paralysed the Young Adventurers, but Tuppence, recovering herself, plunged boldly into the breach with a reminiscence culled from detective fiction.

"When did you last see the dece—your cousin, I mean?"

"Never seen her," responded Mr. Hersheimmer.

"What?" demanded Tommy astonished.

Hersheimmer turned to him.

"No, sir. As I said before, my father and her mother were brother and sister, just as you might be"—Tommy did not correct this view of their relationship—"but they didn't always get on together. And when my aunt made up her mind to marry Amos Finn, who was a poor school teacher out West, my father was just mad! Said if he made his pile, as he seemed in a fair way to do, she'd never see a cent of it. Well, the upshot was that Aunt Jane went out West and we never heard from her again.

"The old man *did* pile it up. He went into oil, and he went into steel, and he played a bit with railroads, and I can tell you he made Wall Street sit up!" He paused. "Then he died—last fall—and I got the dollars. Well, would you believe it, my conscience got busy! Kept knocking me up and saying: What about your Aunt Jane, way out West? It worried me some. You see, I figured it out that Amos Finn would never make good. He wasn't the sort. End of it was, I hired a man to hunt her down. Result, she was dead, and Amos Finn was dead, but they'd left a daughter—Jane—who'd been torpedoed in the *Lusitania* on her way to Paris. She was saved all right, but they didn't seem able to hear of her over this side. I guessed they weren't hustling any, so I thought I'd come along over, and speed things up. I phoned Scotland Yard and the Admiralty first thing. The Admiralty rather choked me off, but Scotland Yard were very civil—said they would make inquiries, even sent a man round this morning to get her photograph. I'm off to Paris to-morrow, just to see what the Prefecture is doing. I guess if I go to and fro hustling them, they ought to get busy!"

The energy of Mr. Hersheimmer was tremendous. They bowed before it.

"But say now," he ended, "you're not after her for anything? Contempt of court, or something British? A proud-spirited young American girl might find your rules and regulations in war time rather irksome, and get up against it. If that's the case, and there's such a thing as graft in this country, I'll buy her off."

Tuppence reassured him.

"That's good. Then we can work together. What about some lunch? Shall we have it up here, or go down to the restaurant?"

Tuppence expressed a preference for the latter, and Julius bowed to her decision.

Oysters had just given place to Sole Colbert when a card was brought to Hersheimmer.

"Inspector Japp, C.I.D. Scotland Yard again. Another man this time. What does he expect I can tell him that I didn't tell the first chap? I hope they haven't lost that photograph. That Western photographer's place was burned down and all his negatives destroyed—this is the only copy in existence. I got it from the principal of the college there."

An unformulated dread swept over Tuppence.

"You—you don't know the name of the man who came this morning?"

"Yes, I do. No, I don't. Half a second. It was on his card. Oh, I know! Inspector Brown. Quiet, unassuming sort of chap."

Tommy and Tuppence took up their abode forthwith at the Ritz, in order, as Tuppence put it, to keep in touch with Jane Finn's only living relation. "And put like that," she added confidentially to Tommy, "nobody could boggle at the expense!"

Nobody did, which was the great thing.

"And now," said the young lady on the morning after their installation, "to work!"

Mr. Beresford put down the *Daily Mail*, which he was reading, and applauded with somewhat unnecessary vigour. He was politely requested by his colleague not to be an ass.

"Dash it all, Tommy, we've got to *do* something for our money."

Tommy sighed.

"Yes, I fear even the dear old Government will not support us at the Ritz in idleness for ever."

"Therefore, as I said before, we must *do* something."

"Well," said Tommy, picking up the *Daily Mail* again, "do it. I shan't stop you."

"You see," continued Tuppence, "I've been thinking——"

She was interrupted by a fresh bout of applause.

"It's all very well for you to sit there being funny, Tommy. It would do you no harm to do a little brain work too."

"My union, Tuppence, my union! It does not permit me to work before 11 A.M."

"Tommy, do you want something thrown at you? It is absolutely essential that we should without delay map out a plan of campaign."

"Hear, hear!"

"Well, let's do it."

Tommy laid his paper finally aside. "There's something of the simplicity of the truly great mind about you, Tuppence. Fire ahead. I'm listening."

"To begin with," said Tuppence, "what have we to go upon?"

"Absolutely nothing," said Tommy cheerily.

"Wrong!" Tuppence wagged an energetic finger. "We have two distinct clues."

"What are they?"

"First clue, we know one of the gang."

VI

A PLAN OF CAMPAIGN

A veil might with profit be drawn over the events of the next half-hour. Suffice it to say that no such person as "Inspector Brown" was known to Scotland Yard. The photograph of Jane Finn, which would have been of the utmost value to the police in tracing her, was lost beyond recovery. Once again "Mr. Brown" had triumphed.

The immediate result of this set-back was to effect a *rapprochement* between Julius Hersheimmer and the Young Adventurers. All barriers went down with a crash, and Tommy and Tuppence felt they had known the young American all their lives. They abandoned the discreet reticence of "private inquiry agents," and revealed to him the whole history of the joint venture, whereat the young man declared himself "tickled to death."

He turned to Tuppence at the close of the narration.

"I've always had a kind of idea that English girls were just a mite moss-grown. Old-fashioned and sweet, you know, but scared to move round without a footman or a maiden aunt. I guess I'm a bit behind the times!"

The upshot of these confidential relations was tha

"Whittington?"

"Yes. I'd recognize him anywhere."

"Hum," said Tommy doubtfully. "I don't call that much of a clue. You don't know where to look for him, and it's about a thousand to one against your running against him by accident."

"I'm not so sure about that," replied Tuppence thoughtfully. "I've often noticed that once coincidences start happening they go on happening in the most extraordinary way. I dare say it's some natural law that we haven't found out. Still, as you say, we can't rely on that. But there *are* places in London where simply every one is bound to turn up sooner or later. Piccadilly Circus, for instance. One of my ideas was to take up my stand there every day with a tray of flags."

"What about meals?" inquired the practical Tommy.

"How like a man! What does mere food matter?"

"That's all very well. You've just had a thundering good breakfast. No one's got a better appetite than you have, Tuppence, and by tea-time you'd be eating the flags, pins and all. But, honestly, I don't think much of the idea. Whittington mayn't be in London at all."

"That's true. Anyway, I think clue No. 2 is more promising."

"Let's hear it."

"It's nothing much. Only a Christian name—Rita. Whittington mentioned it that day."

"Are you proposing a third advertisement: Wanted, female crook, answering to the name of Rita?"

"I am not. I propose to reason in a logical manner. That man, Danvers, was shadowed on the way over, wasn't he? And it's more likely to have been a woman than a man——"

"I don't see that at all."

"I am absolutely certain that it would be a woman, and a good-looking one," replied Tuppence calmly.

"On these technical points I bow to your decision," murmured Mr. Beresford.

"Now, obviously this woman, whoever she was, was saved."

"How do you make that out?"

"If she wasn't, how would they have known Jane Finn had got the papers?"

"Correct. Proceed, O Sherlock!"

"Now there's just a chance, I admit it's only a chance, that this woman may have been 'Rita.' "

"And if so?"

"If so, we've got to hunt through the survivors of the *Lusitania* till we find her."

"Then the first thing is to get a list of the survivors."

"I've got it. I wrote a long list of things I wanted to know, and sent it to Mr. Carter. I got his reply this morning, and among other things it encloses the official statement of those saved from the *Lusitania*. How's that for clever little Tuppence?"

"Full marks for industry, zero for modesty. But the great point is, is there a 'Rita' on the list?"

"That's just what I don't know," confessed Tuppence.

"Don't know?"

"Yes. Look here." Together they bent over the list. "You see, very few Christian names are given. They're nearly all Mrs. or Miss."

Tommy nodded.

"That complicates matters," he murmured thoughtfully.

Tuppence gave her characteristic "terrier" shake.

"Well, we've just got to get down to it, that's all. We'll start with the London area. Just note down the addresses of any of the females who live in London or roundabout, while I put on my hat."

Five minutes later the young couple emerged into Piccadilly, and a few seconds later a taxi was bearing them to The Laurels, Glendower Road, N.7, the residence of Mrs. Edgar Keith, whose name figured first in a list of seven reposing in Tommy's pocket-book.

The Laurels was a dilapidated house, standing back from the road with a few grimy bushes to support the fiction of a front garden. Tommy paid off the taxi, and accompanied Tuppence to the front door bell. As she was about to ring it, he arrested her hand.

"What are you going to say?"

"What am I going to say? Why, I shall say—Oh dear, I don't know. It's very awkward."

"I thought as much," said Tommy with satisfaction. "How like a woman! No foresight! Now just stand aside, and see how easily the mere male deals with the situation." He pressed the bell. Tuppence withdrew to a suitable spot.

A slatternly-looking servant, with an extremely dirty face and a pair of eyes that did not match, answered the door.

Tommy had produced a note-book and pencil.

"Good morning," he said briskly and cheerfully. "From the Hampstead Borough Council. The new Voting Register. Mrs. Edgar Keith lives here, does she not?"

"Yaas," said the servant.

"Christian name?" asked Tommy, his pencil poised.

"Missus's? Eleanor Jane."

"Eleanor," spelt Tommy. "Any sons or daughters over twenty-one?"

"Naow."

"Thank you." Tommy closed the notebook with a brisk snap. "Good morning."

The servant volunteered her first remark:

"I thought perhaps as you'd come about the gas," she observed cryptically, and shut the door.

Tommy rejoined his accomplice.

"You see, Tuppence," he observed. "Child's play to the masculine mind."

"I don't mind admitting that for once you've scored handsomely. I should never have thought of that."

"Good wheeze, wasn't it? And we can repeat it ad lib."

Lunch-time found the young couple attacking a steak and chips in an obscure hostelry with avidity. They had collected a Gladys Mary and a Marjorie, been baffled by one change of address, and had been forced to listen to a long lecture on universal suffrage from a vivacious American lady whose Christian name had proved to be Sadie.

"Ah!" said Tommy, imbibing a long draught of beer, "I feel better. Where's the next draw?"

The notebook lay on the table between them. Tuppence picked it up.

"Mrs. Vandemeyer," she read, "20 South Audley Mansions. Miss Wheeler, 43 Clapington Road, Battersea. She's a lady's maid, as far as I remember, so probably won't be there, and, anyway, she's not likely."

"Then the Mayfair lady is clearly indicated as the first port of call."

"Tommy, I'm getting discouraged."

"Buck up, old bean. We always knew it was an outside chance. And, anyway, we're only starting. If we draw a blank in London, there's a fine tour of England, Ireland and Scotland before us."

"True," said Tuppence, her flagging spirits reviving. "And all expenses paid! But, oh, Tommy, I do like things to happen quickly. So far, adventure has succeeded adventure, but this morning has been dull as dull."

"You must stifle this longing for vulgar sensation, Tuppence. Remember that if Mr. Brown is all he is reported to be, it's a wonder that he has not ere now done us to death. That's a good sentence, quite a literary flavour about it."

"You're really more conceited than I am—with less excuse! Ahem! But it certainly is queer that Mr. Brown has not yet wreaked vengeance upon us. (You see, I can do it too.) We pass on our way unscathed."

"Perhaps he doesn't think us worth bothering about," suggested the young man simply.

Tuppence received the remark with great disfavour.

"How horrid you are, Tommy. Just as though we didn't count."

"Sorry, Tuppence. What I meant was that we work like moles in the dark, and that he has no suspicion of our nefarious schemes. Ha ha!"

"Ha ha!" echoed Tuppence approvingly, as she rose.

South Audley Mansions was an imposing looking block of flats just off Park Lane. No. 20 was on the second floor.

Tommy had by this time the glibness born of practice. He rattled off the formula to the elderly woman, looking more like a housekeeper than a servant, who opened the door to him.

"Christian name?"

"Margaret."

Tommy spelt it, but the other interrupted him.

"No, g u e."

"Oh, Marguerite; French way, I see." He paused, then plunged boldly. "We had her down as Rita Vandemeyer, but I suppose that's incorrect?"

"She's mostly called that, sir, but Marguerite's her name."

"Thank you. That's all. Good morning."

Hardly able to contain his excitement, Tommy hurried down the stairs. Tuppence was waiting at the angle of the turn.

"You heard?"

"Yes. Oh, *Tommy!*"

Tommy squeezed her arm sympathetically.

"I know, old thing. I feel the same."

"It's—it's so lovely to think of things—and then for them really to happen!" cried Tuppence enthusiastically.

Her hand was still in Tommy's. They had reached the entrance hall. There were footsteps on the stairs above them, and voices.

Suddenly, to Tommy's complete surprise, Tuppence dragged him into the little space by the side of the lift where the shadow was deepest.

"What the—"

"Hush!"

Two men came down the stairs and passed out through the entrance. Tuppence's hand closed tighter on Tommy's arm.

"Quick—follow them. I daren't. He might recognize me. I don't know who the other man is, but the bigger of the two was Whittington."

VII

THE HOUSE IN SOHO

Whittington and his companion were walking at a good
pace. Tommy started in pursuit at once, and was in
time to see them turn the corner of the street. His vigorous
strides soon enabled him to gain upon them, and by the time
he, in his turn, reached the corner the distance between
them was sensibly lessened. The small Mayfair streets were
comparatively deserted, and he judged it wise to content
himself with keeping them in sight.

The sport was a new one to him. Though familiar with the
technicalities from a course of novel reading, he had never
before attempted to "follow" anyone, and it appeared to him
at once that, in actual practice, the proceeding was fraught
with difficulties. Supposing, for instance, that they should
suddenly hail a taxi? In books, you simply leapt into another, promised the driver a sovereign—or its modern equiv-
alent—and there you were. In actual fact, Tommy foresaw
that it was extremely likely there would be no second taxi.
Therefore he would have to run. What happened in actual
fact to a young man who ran incessantly and persistently
through the London streets? In a main road he might hope

to create the illusion that he was merely running for a bus. But in these obscure aristocratic byways he could not but feel that an officious policeman might stop him to explain matters.

At this juncture in his thoughts a taxi with flag erect turned the corner of the street ahead. Tommy held his breath. Would they hail it?

He drew a sigh of relief as they allowed it to pass unchallenged. Their course was a zigzag one designed to bring them as quickly as possible to Oxford Street. When at length they turned into it, proceeding in an easterly direction, Tommy slightly increased his pace. Little by little he gained upon them. On the crowded pavement there was little chance of his attracting their notice, and he was anxious if possible to catch a word or two of their conversation. In this he was completely foiled; they spoke low and the din of the traffic drowned their voices effectually.

Just before the Bond Street Tube station they crossed the road, Tommy, unperceived, faithfully at their heels, and entered the big Lyons'. There they went up to the first floor, and sat at a small table in the window. It was late, and the place was thinning out. Tommy took a seat at the table next to them, sitting directly behind Whittington in case of recognition. On the other hand, he had a full view of the second man and studied him attentively. He was fair, with a weak, unpleasant face, and Tommy put him down as being either a Russian or a Pole. He was probably about fifty years of age, his shoulders cringed a little as he talked, and his eyes, small and crafty, shifted unceasingly.

Having already lunched heartily, Tommy contented himself with ordering a Welsh rarebit and a cup of coffee. Whittington ordered a substantial lunch for himself and his companion; then, as the waitress withdrew, he moved his chair a little closer to the table and began to talk earnestly in a low voice. The other man joined in. Listen as he would, Tommy could only catch a word here and there; but the gist of it seemed to be some directions or orders which the big man was impressing on his companion, and with which the latter seemed from time to time to disagree. Whittington addressed the other as Boris.

Tommy caught the word "Ireland" several times, also "propaganda," but of Jane Finn there was no mention. Suddenly, in a lull in the clatter of the room, he got one phrase entire. Whittington was speaking. "Ah, but you don't know Flossie. She's a marvel. An archbishop would swear she was his own mother. She gets the voice right every time, and that's really the principal thing."

Tommy did not hear Boris's reply, but in response to it Whittington said something that sounded like: "Of course— only in an emergency. . . ."

Then he lost the thread again. But presently the phrases became distinct again whether because the other two had insensibly raised their voices, or because Tommy's ears were getting more attuned, he could not tell. But two words certainly had a most stimulating effect upon the listener. They were uttered by Boris and they were: "Mr. Brown."

Whittington seemed to remonstrate with him, but he merely laughed.

"Why not, my friend? It is a name most respectable—most common. Did he not choose it for that reason? Ah, I should like to meet him—Mr. Brown."

There was a steely ring in Whittington's voice as he replied:

"Who knows? You may have met him already."

"Bah!" retorted the other. "That is children's talk—a fable for the police. Do you know what I say to myself sometimes? That he is a fable invented by the Inner Ring, a bogy to frighten us with. It might be so."

"And it might not."

"I wonder . . . or is it indeed true that he is with us and amongst us, unknown to all but a chosen few? If so, he keeps his secret well. And the idea is a good one, yes. We never know. We look at each other—*one of us is Mr. Brown*— which? He commands—but also he serves. Among—us in the midst of us. And no one knows which he is. . . ."

With an effort the Russian shook off the vagary of his fancy. He looked at his watch.

"Yes," said Whittington. "We might as well go."

He called the waitress and asked for his bill. Tommy did

likewise, and a few moments later was following the two men down the stairs.

Outside, Whittington hailed a taxi, and directed the driver to go to Waterloo.

Taxis were plentiful here, and before Whittington's had driven off another was drawing up to the curb in obedience to Tommy's peremptory hand.

"Follow that other taxi," directed the young man. "Don't lose it."

The elderly chauffeur showed no interest. He merely grunted and jerked down his flag. The drive was uneventful. Tommy's taxi came to rest at the departure platform just after Whittington's. Tommy was behind him at the booking-office. He took a first-class single ticket to Bournemouth, Tommy did the same. As he emerged, Boris remarked, glancing up at the clock: "You are early. You have nearly half an hour."

Boris's words had aroused a new train of thought in Tommy's mind. Clearly Whittington was making the journey alone, while the other remained in London. Therefore he was left with a choice as to which he would follow. Obviously, he could not follow both of them unless—Like Boris, he glanced up at the clock, and then to the announcement board of the trains. The Bournemouth train left at 3:30. It was now ten past. Whittington and Boris were walking up and down by the bookstall. He gave one doubtful look at them, then hurried into an adjacent telephone box. He dared not waste time in trying to get hold of Tuppence. In all probability she was still in the neighbourhood of South Audley Mansions. But there remained another ally. He rang up the Ritz and asked for Julius Hersheimmer. There was a click and a buzz. Oh, if only the young American was in his room! There was another click, and then "Hello" in unmistakable accents came over the wire.

"That you, Hersheimmer? Beresford speaking. I'm at Waterloo. I've followed Whittington and another man here. No time to explain. Whittington's off to Bournemouth by the 3:30. Can you get there by then?"

The reply was reassuring.

"Sure. I'll hustle."

The telephone rang off. Tommy put back the receiver with a sigh of relief. His opinion of Julius's power of hustling was high. He felt instinctively that the American would arrive in time.

Whittington and Boris were still where he had left them. If Boris remained to see his friend off, all was well. Then Tommy fingered his pocket thoughtfully. In spite of the carte blanche assured to him, he had not yet acquired the habit of going about with any considerable sum of money on him. The taking of the first-class ticket to Bournemouth had left him with only a few shillings in his pocket. It was to be hoped that Julius would arrive better provided.

In the meantime, the minutes were creeping by: 3:15, 3: 20, 3:25, 3:27. Supposing Julius did not get there in time. 3:29. . . . Doors were banging. Tommy felt cold waves of despair pass over him. Then a hand fell on his shoulder.

"Here I am, son. Your British traffic beats description! Put me wise to the crooks right away."

"That's Whittington—there, getting in now, that big dark man. The other is the foreign chap he's talking to."

"I'm on to them. Which of the two is my bird?"

Tommy had thought out this question.

"Got any money with you?"

Julius shook his head, and Tommy's face fell.

"I guess I haven't more than three or four hundred dollars with me at the moment," explained the American.

Tommy gave a faint whoop of relief.

"Oh, Lord, you millionaires! You don't talk the same language! Climb aboard the lugger. Here's your ticket. Whittington's your man."

"Me for Whittington!" said Julius darkly. The train was just starting as he swung himself aboard. "So long, Tommy." The train slid out of the station.

Tommy drew a deep breath. The man Boris was coming along the platform towards him. Tommy allowed him to pass and then took up the chase once more.

From Waterloo Boris took the tube as far as Piccadilly Circus. Then he walked up Shaftesbury Avenue, finally turning off into the maze of mean streets round Soho. Tommy followed him at a judicious distance.

They reached at length a small dilapidated square. The houses there had a sinister air in the midst of their dirt and decay. Boris looked round, and Tommy drew back into the shelter of a friendly porch. The place was almost deserted. It was a cul-de-sac, and consequently no traffic passed that way. The stealthy way the other had looked round stimulated Tommy's imagination. From the shelter of the doorway he watched him go up the steps of a particularly evil-looking house and rap sharply, with a peculiar rhythm, on the door. It was opened promptly, he said a word or two to the doorkeeper, then passed inside. The door was shut to again.

It was at this juncture that Tommy lost his head. What he ought to have done, what any sane man would have done, was to remain patiently where he was and wait for his man to come out again. What he did do was entirely foreign to the sober common sense which was, as a rule, his leading characteristic. Something, as he expressed it, seemed to snap in his brain. Without a moment's pause for reflection he, too, went up the steps, and reproduced as far as he was able the peculiar knock.

The door swung open with the same promptness as before. A villainous-faced man with close-cropped hair stood in the doorway.

"Well?" he grunted.

It was at that moment that the full realization of his folly began to come home to Tommy. But he dared not hesitate. He seized at the first words that came into his mind.

"Mr. Brown?" he said.

To his surprise the man stood aside.

"Upstairs," he said, jerking his thumb over his shoulder, "second door on your left."

VIII

THE ADVENTURES OF TOMMY

Taken aback though he was by the man's words, Tommy did not hesitate. If audacity had successfully carried him so far, it was to be hoped it would carry him yet farther. He quietly passed into the house and mounted the ramshackle staircase. Everything in the house was filthy beyond words. The grimy paper, of a pattern now indistinguishable, hung in loose festoons from the wall. In every angle was a grey mass of cobweb.

Tommy proceeded leisurely. By the time he reached the bend of the staircase, he had heard the man below disappear into a back room. Clearly no suspicion attached to him as yet. To come to the house and ask for "Mr. Brown" appeared indeed to be a reasonable and natural proceeding.

At the top of the stairs Tommy halted to consider his next move. In front of him ran a narrow passage, with doors opening on either side of it. From the one nearest him on the left came a low murmur of voices. It was this room which he had been directed to enter. But what held his glance fascinated was a small recess immediately on his right, half concealed by a torn velvet curtain. It was directly opposite the left-handed door and, owing to its angle, it also commanded a good view of the upper part of the staircase. As a hiding-place for one or, at a pinch, two men, it was ideal, being about two feet deep and three feet wide. It attracted Tommy mightily. He thought things over in his usual slow and steady way, deciding that the mention of "Mr. Brown" was not a request for an individual, but in all probability a password used by the gang. His lucky use of it had gained him admission. So far he had aroused no suspicion. But he must decide quickly on his next step.

Suppose he were boldly to enter the room on the left of the passage. Would the mere fact of his having been admitted to the house be sufficient? Perhaps a further password would be required, or, at any rate, some proof of identity. The doorkeeper clearly did not know all the members of the gang by sight, but it might be different upstairs. On the whole it seemed to him that luck had served him very well so far, but that there was such a thing as trusting it too far. To enter that room was a colossal risk. He could not hope to sustain his part indefinitely; sooner or later he was almost bound to betray himself, and then he would have thrown away a vital chance in mere foolhardiness.

A repetition of the signal knock sounded on the door below, and Tommy, his mind made up, slipped quickly into the recess, and cautiously drew the curtain farther across so that it shielded him completely from sight. There were several rents and slits in the ancient material which afforded him a good view. He would watch events, and any time he chose could, after all, join the assembly, modelling his behaviour on that of the new arrival.

The man who came up the staircase with a furtive, soft-footed tread was quite unknown to Tommy. He was obviously of the very dregs of society. The low beetling brows, and the criminal jaw, the bestiality of the whole countenance were new to the young man, though he was a type that Scotland Yard would have recognized at a glance.

The man passed the recess, breathing heavily as he went. He stopped at the door opposite, and gave a repetition of the signal knock. A voice inside called out something, and the man opened the door and passed in, affording Tommy a momentary glimpse of the room inside. He thought there must be about four or five people seated round a long table that took up most of the space, but his attention was caught and held by a tall man with close-cropped hair and a short, pointed, naval-looking beard, who sat at the head of the table with papers in front of him. As the newcomer entered he glanced up, and with a correct, but curiously precise enunciation, which attracted Tommy's notice, he asked:

"Your number, comrade?"

"Fourteen, guv'nor," replied the other hoarsely.

"Correct."

The door shut again.

"If that isn't a Hun, I'm a Dutchman!" said Tommy to himself. "And running the show darned systematically too—as they always do. Lucky I didn't roll in. I'd have given the wrong number, and there would have been the deuce to pay. No, this is the place for me. Hullo, here's another knock."

This visitor proved to be of an entirely diffcrent type to the last. Tommy recognized in him an Irish Sinn Feiner. Certainly Mr. Brown's organization was a far-reaching concern. The common criminal, the well-bred Irish gentleman, the pale Russian, and the efficient German master of the ceremonies! Truly a strange and sinister gathering! Who was this man who held in his finger these curiously variegated links of an unknown chain?

In this case, the procedure was exactly the same. The signal knock, the demand for a number, and the reply "Correct."

Two knocks followed in quick succession on the door below. The first man was quite unknown to Tommy, who put him down as a city clerk. A quiet, intelligent-looking man, rather shabbily dressed. The second was of the working classes, and his face was vaguely familiar to the young man.

Three minutes later came another, a man of commanding appearance, exquisitely dressed, and evidently well born. His face, again, was not unknown to the watcher, though he could not for the moment put a name to it.

After his arrival there was a long wait. In fact Tommy concluded that the gathering was now complete, and was just cautiously creeping out from his hiding-place, when another knock sent him scuttling back to cover.

This last-comer came up the stairs so quietly that he was almost abreast of Tommy before the young man had realized his presence.

He was a small man, very pale, with a gentle almost womanish air. The angle of the cheek-bones hinted at his Slavonic ancestry, otherwise there was nothing to indicate his nationality. As he passed the recess, he turned his head slowly. The strange light eyes seemed to burn through the curtain; Tommy could hardly believe that the man did not know he was there and in spite of himself he shivered. He was no more fanciful than the majority of young Englishmen, but he could not rid himself of the impression that some unusually potent force emanated from the man. The creature reminded him of a venomous snake.

A moment later his impression was proved correct. The newcomer knocked on the door as all had done, but his reception was very different. The bearded man rose to his feet, and all the others followed suit. The German came forward and shook hands. His heels clicked together.

"We are honoured," he said. "We are greatly honoured. I much feared that it would be impossible."

The other answered in a low voice that had a kind of hiss in it:

"There were difficulties. It will not be possible again, I fear. But one meeting is essential—to define my policy. I can do nothing without—Mr. Brown. He is here?"

The change in the German's voice was audible as he replied with slight hesitation:

"We have received a message. It is impossible for him to be present in person." He stopped, giving a curious impression of having left the sentence unfinished.

A very slow smile overspread the face of the other. He looked round at a circle of uneasy faces.

"Ah! I understand. I have read of his methods. He works in the dark and trusts no one. But, all the same, it is possible that he is among us now. . . ." He looked round him again, and again that expression of fear swept over the group. Each man seemed eyeing his neighbour doubtfully.

The Russian tapped his cheek.

"So be it. Let us proceed."

The German seemed to pull himself together. He indicated the place he had been occupying at the head of the table. The Russian demurred, but the other insisted.

"It is the only possible place," he said, "for—Number One. Perhaps Number Fourteen will shut the door?"

In another moment Tommy was once more confronting bare wooden panels, and the voices within had sunk once more to a mere undistinguishable murmur. Tommy became restive. The conversation he had overheard had stimulated his curiosity. He felt that, by hook or by crook, he must hear more.

There was no sound from below, and it did not seem likely that the door-keeper would come upstairs. After listening intently for a minute or two, he put his head round the curtain. The passage was deserted. Tommy bent down and removed his shoes, then, leaving them behind the curtain, he walked gingerly out on his stockinged feet, and kneeling down by the closed door he laid his ear cautiously to the crack. To his intense annoyance he could distinguish little more; just a chance word here and there if a voice was raised, which merely served to whet his curiosity still farther.

He eyed the handle of the door tentatively. Could he turn it by degrees so gently and imperceptibly that those in the room would notice nothing? He decided that with great care it could be done. Very slowly, a fraction of an inch at a time, he moved it round, holding his breath in his excessive care. A little more—a little more still—would it never be finished? Ah! at last it would turn no farther.

He stayed so for a minute or two, then drew a deep breath, and pressed it ever so slightly inward. The door did not budge. Tommy was annoyed. If he had to use too much force, it would almost certainly creak. He waited until the voices rose a little, then he tried again. Still nothing happened. He increased the pressure. Had the beastly thing stuck? Finally, in desperation, he pushed with all his might. But the door remained firm, and at last the truth dawned upon him. It was locked or bolted on the inside.

For a moment or two Tommy's indignation got the better of him.

"Well, I'm damned!" he said. "What a dirty trick!"

As his indignation cooled, he prepared to face the situation. Clearly the first thing to be done was to restore the handle to its original position. If he let it go suddenly, the men inside would be almost certain to notice it, so, with the same infinite pains, he reversed his former tactics. All went well, and with a sigh of relief the young man rose to his feet. There was a certain bulldog tenacity about Tommy that made him slow to admit defeat. Checkmated for the moment, he was far from abandoning the conflict. He still intended to hear what was going on in the locked room. As one plan had failed, he must hunt about for another.

He looked round him. A little farther along the passage on the left was a second door. He slipped silently along to it. He listened for a moment or two, then tried the handle. It yielded, and he slipped inside.

The room, which was untenanted, was furnished as a bedroom. Like everything else in the house, the furniture was falling to pieces, and the dirt was, if anything, more abundant.

But what interested Tommy was the thing he had hoped to find, a communicating door between the two rooms, up on the left by the window. Carefully closing the door into the passage behind him, he stepped across to the other and examined it closely. The bolt was shot across it. It was very rusty, and had clearly not been used for some time. By gently wriggling it to and fro, Tommy managed to draw it back without making too much noise. Then he repeated his former manoeuvres with the handle—this time with complete success. The door swung open—a crack, a mere fraction, but enough for Tommy to hear what went on. There was a velvet *portière* on the inside of this door which prevented him from seeing, but he was able to recognize the voices with a reasonable amount of accuracy.

The Sinn Feiner was speaking. His rich Irish voice was unmistakable:

"That's all very well. But more money is essential. No money—no results!"

Another voice which Tommy rather thought was that of Boris replied:

"Will you guarantee that there *are* results?"

"In a month from now—sooner or later as you wish—I will guarantee you such a reign of terror in Ireland as shall shake the British Empire to its foundations."

There was a pause, and then came the soft, sibilant accents of Number One:

"Good! You shall have the money. Boris, you will see to that."

Boris asked a question:

"Via the Irish Americans, and Mr. Potter as usual?"

"I guess that'll be all right!" said a new voice, with a transatlantic intonation, "though I'd like to point out, here and now, that things are getting a mite difficult. There's not the sympathy there was, and a growing disposition to let the Irish settle their own affairs without interference from America."

Tommy felt that Boris had shrugged his shoulders as he answered:

"Does that matter, since the money only nominally comes from the States?"

"The chief difficulty is the landing of the ammunition," said the Sinn Feiner. "The money is conveyed in easily enough—thanks to our colleague here."

Another voice, which Tommy fancied was that of the tall, commanding-looking man whose face had seemed familiar to him, said:

"Think of the feelings of Belfast if they could hear you!"

"That is settled, then," said the sibilant tones. "Now, in the matter of the loan to an English newspaper, you have arranged the details satisfactorily, Boris?"

"I think so."

"That is good. An official denial from Moscow will be forthcoming if necessary."

There was a pause, and then the clear voice of the German broke the silence:

"I am directed by—Mr. Brown, to place the summaries of the reports from the different unions before you. That of the miners is most satisfactory. We must hold back the railways. There may be trouble with the A.S.E."

For a long time there was a silence, broken only by the rustle of papers and an occasional word of explanation from the German. Then Tommy heard the light tap-tap of fingers, drumming on the table.

"And—the date, my friend?" said Number One.

"The 29th."

The Russian seemed to consider:

"That is rather soon."

"I know. But it was settled by the principal Labour leaders, and we cannot seem to interfere too much. They must believe it to be entirely their own show."

The Russian laughed softly, as though amused.

"Yes, yes," he said. "That is true. They must have no inkling that we are using them for our own ends. They are honest men—and that is their value to us. It is curious—but you cannot make a revolution without honest men. The instinct of the populace is infallible." He paused, and then repeated, as though the phrase pleased him: "Every revolution has had its honest men. They are soon disposed of afterwards."

There was a sinister note in his voice.

The German resumed:

"Clymes must go. He is too far-seeing. Number Fourteen will see to that."

There was a hoarse murmur.

"That's all right, guv'nor." And then after a moment or two: "Suppose I'm nabbed."

"You will have the best legal talent to defend you," replied the German quietly. "But in any case you will wear gloves fitted with the finger-prints of a notorious housebreaker. You have little to fear."

"Oh, I ain't afraid, guv'nor. All for the good of the cause. The streets is going to run with blood, so they say." He spoke with a grim relish. "Dreams of it, sometimes, I does. And diamonds and pearls rolling about in the gutter for anyone to pick up!"

Tommy heard a chair shifted. Then Number One spoke:

"Then all is arranged. We are assured of success?"

"I—think so." But the German spoke with less than his usual confidence.

Number One's voice held suddenly a dangerous quality: "What has gone wrong?"

"Nothing; but——"

"But what?"

"The Labour leaders. Without them, as you say, we can do nothing. If they do not declare a general strike on the 29th——"

"Why should they not?"

"As you've said, they're honest. And, in spite of everything we've done to discredit the Government in their eyes, I'm not sure that they haven't got a sneaking faith and belief in it."

"But——"

"I know. They abuse it unceasingly. But, on the whole, public opinion swings to the side of the Government. They will not go against it."

Again the Russian's fingers drummed on the table.

"To the point, my friend. I was given to understand that there was a certain document in existence which assured success."

"That is so. If that document were placed before the leaders, the result would be immediate. They would publish it broadcast throughout England, and declare for the revolution without a moment's hesitation. The Government would be broken finally and completely."

"Then what more do you want?"

"The document itself," said the German bluntly.

"Ah! It is not in your possession? But you know where it is?"

"No."

"Does anyone know where it is?"

"One person—perhaps. And we are not sure of that even."

"Who is this person?"

"A girl."

Tommy held his breath.

"A girl?" The Russian's voice rose contemptuously. "And you have not made her speak? In Russia we have ways of making a girl talk."

"This case is different," said the German sullenly.

"How—different?" He paused a moment, then went on: "Where is the girl now?"

"The girl?"

"Yes."

"She is——"

But Tommy heard no more. A crashing blow descended on his head, and all was darkness.

IX

TUPPENCE ENTERS DOMESTIC SERVICE

When Tommy set forth on the trail of the two men, it took all Tuppence's self-command to refrain from accompanying him. However, she contained herself as best she might, consoled by the reflection that her reasoning had been justified by events. The two men had undoubtedly come from the second floor flat, and that one slender thread of the name "Rita" had set the Young Adventurers once more upon the track of the abductors of Jane Finn.

The question was what to do next? Tuppence hated letting the grass grow under her feet. Tommy was amply employed, and debarred from joining him in the chase, the girl felt at a loose end. She retraced her steps to the entrance hall of the mansions. It was now tenanted by a small lift-boy, who was polishing brass fittings, and whistling the latest air with a good deal of vigour and a reasonable amount of accuracy.

He glanced round at Tuppence's entry. There was a certain amount of the gamin element in the girl, at all events she invariably got on well with small boys. A sympathetic bond seemed instantly to be formed. She reflected that an ally in the enemy's camp, so to speak, was not to be despised.

"Well, William," she remarked cheerfully, in the best approved hospital-early-morning style, "getting a good shine up?"

The boy grinned responsively.

"Albert, miss," he corrected.

"Albert be it," said Tuppence. She glanced mysteriously round the hall. The effect was purposely a broad one in case Albert should miss it. She leaned towards the boy and dropped her voice: "I want a word with you, Albert."

Albert ceased operations on the fittings and opened his mouth slightly.

"Look! Do you know what this is?" With a dramatic gesture she flung back the left side of her coat and exposed a small enamelled badge. It was extremely unlikely that Albert would have any knowledge of it—indeed, it would have been fatal for Tuppence's plans, since the badge in question was the device of a local training corps originated by the archdeacon in the early days of the war. Its presence in Tuppence's coat was due to the fact that she had used it for pinning in some flowers a day or two before. But Tuppence had sharp eyes, and had noted the corner of a three-penny detective novel protruding from Albert's pocket, and the immediate enlargement of his eyes told her that her tactics were good, and that the fish would rise to the bait.

"American Detective Force!" she hissed.

Albert fell for it.

"Lord!" he murmured ecstatically.

Tuppence nodded at him with the air of one who has established a thorough understanding.

"Know who I'm after?" she inquired genially.

Albert, still round-eyed, demanded breathlessly:

"One of the flats?"

Tuppence nodded and jerked a thumb up the stairs.

"No. 20. Calls herself Vandemeyer. Vandemeyer! Ha! ha!"

Albert's hand stole to his pocket.

"A crook?" he queried eagerly.

"A crook? I should say so. Ready Rita they call her in the States."

"Ready Rita," repeated Albert deliriously. "Oh, ain't it just like the pictures!"

It was. Tuppence was a great frequenter of the kinema.

"Annie always said as how she was a bad lot," continued the boy.

"Who's Annie?" inquired Tuppence idly.

" 'Ouse-parlourmaid. She's leaving to-day. Many's the time Annie's said to me: 'Mark my words, Albert, I wouldn't wonder if the police was to come after her one of these days.' Just like that. But she's a stunner to look at, ain't she?"

"She's some peach," allowed Tuppence carelessly. "Finds it useful in her lay-out, you bet. Has she been wearing any of the emeralds, by the way?"

"Emeralds? Them's the green stones, isn't they?"

Tuppence nodded.

"That's what we're after her for. You know old man Rysdale?"

Albert shook his head.

"Peter B. Rysdale, the oil king?"

"It seems sort of familiar to me."

"The sparklers belonged to him. Finest collection of emeralds in the world. Worth a million dollars!"

"Lumme!" came ecstatically from Albert. "It sounds more like the pictures every minute."

Tuppence smiled, gratified at the success of her efforts.

"We haven't exactly proved it yet. But we're after her. And"—she produced a long-drawn-out wink—"I guess she won't get away with the goods this time."

Albert uttered another ejaculation indicative of delight.

"Mind you, sonny, not a word of this," said Tuppence suddenly. "I guess I oughtn't to have put you wise, but in the States we know a real smart lad when we see one."

"I'll not breathe a word," protested Albert eagerly. "Ain't there anything I could do? A bit of shadowing, maybe, or such like?"

Tuppence affected to consider, then shook her head.

"Not at the moment, but I'll bear you in mind, son. What's this about the girl you say is leaving?"

"Annie? Regular turn up, they 'ad. As Annie said, servants is some one nowadays, and to be treated accordingly, and, what with her passing the word round, she won't find it so easy to get another."

"Won't she?" said Tuppence thoughtfully. "I wonder——"

An idea was dawning in her brain. She thought a minute or two, then tapped Albert on the shoulder.

"See here, son, my brain's got busy. How would it be if you mentioned that you'd got a young cousin, or a friend of yours had, that might suit the place. You get me?"

"I'm there," said Albert instantly. "You leave it to me, miss, and I'll fix the whole thing up in two ticks."

"Some lad!" commented Tuppence, with a nod of approval. "You might say that the young woman could come in right away. You let me know, and if it's O.K. I'll be round to-morrow at eleven o'clock."

"Where am I to let you know to?"

"Ritz," replied Tuppence laconically. "Name of Cowley."

Albert eyed her enviously.

"It must be a good job, this tec business."

"It sure is," drawled Tuppence, "especially when old man Rysdale backs the bill. But don't fret, son. If this goes well, you shall come in on the ground floor."

With which promise she took leave of her new ally, and walked briskly away from South Audley Mansions, well pleased with her morning's work.

But there was no time to be lost. She went straight back to the Ritz and wrote a few brief words to Mr. Carter. Having dispatched this, and Tommy not having yet returned—which did not surprise her—she started off on a shopping expedition which, with an interval for tea and assorted creamy cakes, occupied her until well after six o'clock, and she returned to the hotel jaded, but satisfied with her purchases. Starting with a cheap clothing store, and passing through one or two second-hand establishments, she had finished the day at a well-known hairdresser's. Now, in the seclusion of her bedroom, she unwrapped that final purchase. Five minutes later she smiled contentedly at her reflection in the glass. With an actress's pencil she had slightly altered the line of her eyebrows, and that, taken in conjunction with the new luxuriant growth of fair hair above, so changed her appearance that she felt confident that even if she came face to face with Whittington he would not recognize her. She would wear elevators in her shoes, and the cap and apron would be an even more valuable disguise. From hospital experience she knew only too well that a nurse out of uniform is frequently unrecognized by her patients.

"Yes," said Tuppence aloud, nodding at the pert reflection in the glass, "you'll do." She then resumed her normal appearance.

Dinner was a solitary meal. Tuppence was rather surprised at Tommy's non-return. Julius, too, was absent—but that to the girl's mind was more easily explained. His "hustling" activities were not confined to London, and his abrupt appearances and disappearances were fully accepted by the Young Adventurers as part of the day's work. It was quite on the cards that Julius P. Hersheimmer had left for Constantinople at a moment's notice if he fancied that a clue to his cousin's disappearance was to be found there. The energetic young man had succeeded in making the lives of several Scotland Yard men unbearable to them, and the telephone girls at the Admiralty had learned to know and dread the familiar "Hullo!" He had spent three hours in Paris hustling the Prefecture, and had returned from there imbued with the idea, possibly inspired by a weary French official, that the true clue to the mystery was to be found in Ireland.

"I dare say he's dashed off there now," thought Tuppence. "All very well, but this is very dull for *me*! Here I am bursting with news, and absolutely no one to tell it to! Tommy might have wired, or something. I wonder where he is. Anyway, he can't have 'lost the trail' as they say. That reminds me——" And Miss Cowley broke off in her meditations, and summoned a small boy.

Ten minutes later the lady was ensconced comfortably on her bed, smoking cigarettes and deep in the perusal of *Garnaby Williams, the Boy Detective*, which, with other threepenny works of lurid fiction, she had sent out to purchase. She felt, and rightly, that before the strain of attempting further intercourse with Albert, it would be as well to fortify herself with a good supply of local colour.

The morning brought a note from Mr. Carter:

"DEAR MISS TUPPENCE,

You have made a splendid start, and I congratulate you. I feel, though, that I should like to point out to you once more the risks you are running, especially if you pursue the course you indicate. Those people are absolutely desperate and incapable of either mercy or pity. I feel that you probably underestimate the danger, and therefore warn you again that I can promise you no protection. You have given us valuable information, and if you choose to withdraw now no one could blame you. At any rate, think the matter over well before you decide.

If, in spite of my warnings, you make up your mind to go through with it, you will find everything arranged. You have lived for two years with Miss Dufferin, The Parsonage, Llanelly, and Mrs. Vandemeyer can apply to her for a reference.

May I be permitted a word or two of advice? Stick as near to the truth as possible—it minimizes the danger of 'slips.' I suggest that you should represent yourself to be what you are, a former V.A.D., who has chosen domestic service as a profession. There are many such at the present time. That explains away any incongruities of voice or manner which otherwise might awaken suspicion.

Whichever way you decide, good luck to you.

Your sincere friend,
MR. CARTER."

Tuppence's spirits rose mercurially. Mr. Carter's warnings passed unheeded. The young lady had far too much confidence in herself to pay any heed to them.

With some reluctance she abandoned the interesting part she had sketched out for herself. Although she had no doubts of her own powers to sustain a rôle indefinitely, she had too much common sense not to recognize the force of Mr. Carter's arguments.

There was still no word or message from Tommy, but the

morning post brought a somewhat dirty postcard with the words: "It's O.K." scrawled upon it.

At ten-thirty Tuppence surveyed with pride a slightly battered tin trunk containing her new possessions. It was artistically corded. It was with a slight blush that she rang the bell and ordered it to be placed in a taxi. She drove to Paddington, and left the box in the cloak room. She then repaired with a handbag to the fastnesses of the ladies' waiting-room. Then minutes later a metamorphosed Tuppence walked demurely out of the station and entered a bus.

It was a few minutes past eleven when Tuppence again entered the hall of South Audley Mansions. Albert was on the look-out, attending to his duties in a somewhat desultory fashion. He did not immediately recognize Tuppence. When he did, his admiration was unbounded.

"Blest if I'd have known you! That rig-out's top-hole."

"Glad you like it, Albert," replied Tuppence modestly. "By the way, am I your cousin, or am I not?"

"Your voice too," cried the delighted boy. "It's as English as anything! No, I said as a friend of mine knew a young gal. Annie wasn't best pleased. She's stopped on till to-day—to oblige, *she* said, but really it's so as to put you against the place."

"Nice girl," said Tuppence.

Albert suspected no irony.

"She's style about her, and keeps her silver a treat—but, my word, ain't she got a temper. Are you going up now, miss? Step inside the lift. No. 20, did you say?" And he winked.

Tuppence quelled him with a stern glance, and stepped inside.

As she rang the bell of No. 20 she was conscious of Albert's eyes slowly descending beneath the level of the floor.

A smart young woman opened the door.

"I've come about the place," said Tuppence.

"It's a rotten place," said the young woman without hesitation. "Regular old cat—always interfering. Accused me of tampering with her letters. Me! The flap was half undone anyway. There's never anything in the waste-paper basket—she burns everything. She's a wrong 'un, that's what she is.

Swell clothes, but no class. Cook knows something about her—but she won't tell—scared to death of her. And suspicious! She's on to you in a minute if you as much as speak to a fellow. I can tell you——"

But what more Annie could tell, Tuppence was never destined to learn, for at that moment a clear voice with a peculiarly steely ring to it called:

"Annie!"

The smart young woman jumped as if she had been shot.

"Yes, ma'am."

"Who are you talking to?"

"It's a young woman about the situation, ma'am."

"Show her in then. At once."

"Yes, ma'am."

Tuppence was ushered into a room on the right of the long passage. A woman was standing by the fireplace. She was no longer in her first youth, and the beauty she undeniably possessed was hardened and coarsened. In her youth she must have been dazzling. Her pale gold hair, owing a slight assistance to art, was coiled low on her neck, her eyes, of a piercing electric blue, seemed to possess a faculty of boring into the very soul of the person she was looking at. Her exquisite figure was enhanced by a wonderful gown of indigo charmeuse. And yet, despite her swaying grace, and the almost ethereal beauty of her face, you felt instinctively the presence of something hard and menacing, a kind of metallic strength that found expression in the tones of her voice and in that gimlet-like quality of her eyes.

For the first time Tuppence felt afraid. She had not feared Whittington, but this woman was different. As if fascinated, she watched the long cruel line of the red curving mouth, and again she felt that sensation of panic pass over her. Her usual self-confidence deserted her. Vaguely she felt that deceiving this woman would be very different to deceiving Whittington. Mr. Carter's warning recurred to her mind. Here, indeed, she might expect no mercy.

Fighting down that instinct of panic which urged her to turn tail and run without further delay, Tuppence returned the lady's gaze firmly and respectfully.

As though that first scrutiny had been satisfactory, Mrs. Vandemeyer motioned to a chair.

"You can sit down. How did you hear I wanted a house-parlourmaid?"

"Through a friend who knows the lift boy here. He thought the place might suit me."

Again that basilisk glance seemed to pierce her through.

"You speak like an educated girl?"

Glibly enough, Tuppence ran through her imaginary career on the lines suggested by Mr. Carter. It seemed to her, as she did so, that the tension of Mrs. Vandemeyer's attitude relaxed.

"I see," she remarked at length. "Is there anyone I can write to for a reference?"

"I lived last with a Miss Dufferin, The Parsonage, Llanelly. I was with her two years."

"And then you thought you would get more money by coming to London, I suppose? Well, it doesn't matter to me. I will give you £50—£60—whatever you want. You can come in at once?"

"Yes, ma'am. To-day, if you like. My box is at Paddington."

"Go and fetch it in a taxi, then. It's an easy place. I am out a good deal. By the way, what's your name?"

"Prudence Cooper, ma'am."

"Very well, Prudence. Go away and fetch your box. I shall be out to lunch. The cook will show you where everything is."

"Thank you, ma'am."

Tuppence withdrew. The smart Annie was not in evidence. In the hall below a magnificent hall porter had relegated Albert to the background. Tuppence did not even glance at him as she passed meekly out.

The adventure had begun, but she felt less elated than she had done earlier in the morning. It crossed her mind that if the unknown Jane Finn had fallen into the hands of Mrs. Vandemeyer, it was likely to have gone hard with her.

X

ENTER SIR JAMES PEEL EDGERTON

Tuppence betrayed no awkwardness in her new duties. The daughters of the archdeacon were well grounded in household tasks. They were also experts in training a "raw girl," the inevitable result being that the raw girl, once trained, departed elsewhere where her newly acquired knowledge commanded a more substantial remuneration than the archdeacon's meagre purse allowed.

Tuppence had therefore very little fear of proving inefficient. Mrs. Vandemeyer's cook puzzled her. She evidently went in deadly terror of her mistress. The girl thought it probable that the other woman had some hold over her. For the rest, she cooked like a *chef*, as Tuppence had an opportunity of judging that evening. Mrs. Vandemeyer was expecting a guest to dinner, and Tuppence accordingly laid the beautifully polished table for two. She was a little exercised in her own mind as to this visitor. It was highly possible that it might prove to be Whittington. Although she felt fairly confident that he would not recognize her, yet she would have been better pleased had the guest proved to be a total stranger. However, there was nothing for it but to hope for the best.

At a few minutes past eight the front door bell rang, and Tuppence went to answer it with some inward trepidation. She was relieved to see that the visitor was the second of the two men whom Tommy had taken upon himself to follow.

He gave his name as Count Stepanov. Tuppence announced him, and Mrs. Vandemeyer rose from her seat on a low divan with a quick murmur of pleasure.

"It is delightful to see you, Boris Ivanovitch," she said.

"And you, madame!" He bowed low over her hand.

Tuppence returned to the kitchen.

"Count Stepanov, or some such," she remarked, and affecting a frank and unvarnished curiosity: "Who's he?"

"A Russian gentleman, I believe."

"Come here much?"

"Once in a while. What d'you want to know for?"

"Fancied he might be sweet on the missus, that's all," explained the girl, adding with an appearance of sulkiness: "How you do take one up!"

"I'm not quite easy in my mind about the *soufflé*," explained the other.

"You know something," thought Tuppence to herself, but aloud she only said: "Going to dish up now? Right-o."

Whilst waiting at table, Tuppence listened closely to all that was said. She remembered that this was one of the men Tommy was shadowing when she had last seen him. Already, although she would hardly admit it, she was becoming uneasy about her partner. Where was he? Why had no word of any kind come from him? She had arranged before leaving the Ritz to have all letters or messages sent on at once by special messenger to a small stationer's shop near at hand where Albert was to call in frequently. True, it was only yesterday morning that she had parted from Tommy, and she told herself that any anxiety on his behalf would be absurd. Still, it was strange that he had sent no word of any kind.

But, listen as she might, the conversation presented no clue. Boris and Mrs. Vandemeyer talked on purely indifferent subjects; plays they had seen, new dances, and the lat-

est society gossip. After dinner they repaired to the small
boudoir where Mrs. Vandemeyer, stretched on the divan,
looked more wickedly beautiful than ever. Tuppence
brought in the coffee and liqueurs and unwillingly retired.
As she did so, she heard Boris say:

"New, isn't she?"

"She came in to-day. The other was a fiend. This girl
seems all right. She waits well."

Tuppence lingered a moment longer by the door which she
had carefully neglected to close, and heard him say:

"Quite safe, I suppose?"

"Really, Boris, you are absurdly suspicious. I believe she's
the cousin of the hall porter, or something of the kind. And
nobody even dreams that I have any connection with our—
mutual friend, Mr. Brown."

"For heaven's sake, be careful, Rita. That door isn't shut."

"Well, shut it then," laughed the woman.

Tuppence removed herself speedily.

She dared not absent herself longer from the back prem-
ises, but she cleared away and washed up with a breathless
speed acquired in hospital. Then she slipped quietly back to
the boudoir door. The cook, more leisurely, was still busy in
the kitchen and, if she missed the other, would only suppose
her to be turning down the beds.

Alas! The conversation inside was being carried on in too
low a tone to permit of her hearing anything of it. She dared
not reopen the door, however gently. Mrs. Vandemeyer was
sitting almost facing it, and Tuppence respected her mistress's lynx-eyed powers of observation.

Nevertheless, she felt she would give a good deal to overhear what was going on. Possibly, if anything unforeseen
had happened, she might get news of Tommy. For some moments she reflected desperately, then her face brightened.
She went quickly along the passage to Mrs. Vandemeyer's
bedroom, which had long French windows leading on to a
balcony that ran the length of the flat. Slipping quickly
through the window, Tuppence crept noiselessly along till
she reached the boudoir window. As she had thought it
stood a little ajar, and the voices within were plainly audible.

Tuppence listened attentively, but there was no mention

of anything that could be twisted to apply to Tommy. Mrs. Vandemeyer and the Russian seemed to be at variance over some matter, and finally the latter exclaimed bitterly:

"With your persistent recklessness, you will end by ruining us!"

"Bah!" laughed the woman. "Notoriety of the right kind is the best way of disarming suspicion. You will realize that one of these days—perhaps sooner than you think!"

"In the meantime, you are going about everywhere with Peel Edgerton. Not only is he, perhaps, the most celebrated K.C. in England, but his special hobby is criminology! It is madness!"

"I know that his eloquence has saved untold men from the gallows," said Mrs. Vandemeyer calmly. "What of it? I may need his assistance in that line myself some day. If so, how fortunate to have such a friend at court—or perhaps it would be more to the point to say *in* court."

Boris got up and began striding up and down. He was very excited.

"You are a clever woman, Rita; but you are also a fool! Be guided by me, and give up Peel Edgerton."

Mrs. Vandemeyer shook her head gently.

"I think not."

"You refuse?" There was an ugly ring in the Russian's voice.

"I do."

"Then, by Heaven," snarled the Russian, "we will see——"

But Mrs. Vandemeyer also rose to her feet, her eyes flashing.

"You forget, Boris," she said. "I am accountable to no one. I take my orders only from—Mr. Brown."

The other threw up his hands in despair.

"You are impossible," he muttered. "Impossible! Already it may be too late. They say Peel Edgerton can *smell* a criminal! How do we know what is at the bottom of his sudden interest in you? Perhaps even now his suspicions are aroused. He guesses——"

Mrs. Vandemeyer eyed him scornfully.

"Reassure yourself, my dear Boris. He suspects nothing.

With less than your usual chivalry, you seem to forget that I am commonly accounted a beautiful woman. I assure you that is all that interests Peel Edgerton."

Boris shook his head doubtfully.

"He has studied crime as no other man in this kingdom has studied it. Do you fancy that you can deceive him?"

Mrs. Vandemeyer's eyes narrowed.

"If he is all that you say—it would amuse me to try!"

"Good heavens, Rita——"

"Besides," added Mrs. Vandemeyer, "he is extremely rich. I am not one who despises money. The 'sinews of war,' you know, Boris!"

"Money—money! That is always the danger with you, Rita. I believe you would sell your soul for money. I believe——" He paused, then in a low, sinister voice he said slowly: "Sometimes I believe that you would sell—*us!*"

Mrs. Vandemeyer smiled and shrugged her shoulders.

"The price, at any rate, would have to be enormous," she said lightly. "It would be beyond the power of anyone but a millionaire to pay."

"Ah!" snarled the Russian. "You see, I was right!"

"My dear Boris, can you not take a joke?"

"Was it a joke?"

"Of course."

"Then all I can say is that your ideas of humour are peculiar, my dear Rita."

Mrs. Vandemeyer smiled.

"Let us not quarrel, Boris. Touch the bell. We will have some drinks."

Tuppence beat a hasty retreat. She paused a moment to survey herself in Mrs. Vandemeyer's long glass, and be sure that nothing was amiss with her appearance. Then she answered the bell demurely.

The conversation that she had overheard, although interesting in that it proved beyond doubt the complicity of both Rita and Boris, threw very little light on the present preoccupations. The name of Jane Finn had not even been mentioned.

The following morning a few brief words with Albert informed her that nothing was waiting for her at the stationer's. It seemed incredible that Tommy, if all was well with him, should not send any word to her. A cold hand seemed to close round her heart. . . . Supposing . . . She choked her fears down bravely. It was no good worrying. But she leapt at a chance offered her by Mrs. Vandemeyer.

"What day do you usually go out, Prudence?"

"Friday's my usual day, ma'am."

Mrs. Vandemeyer lifted her eyebrows.

"And to-day is Friday! But I suppose you hardly wish to go out to-day, as you only came yesterday."

"I was thinking of asking you if I might, ma'am."

Mrs. Vandemeyer looked at her a minute longer, and then smiled.

"I wish Count Stepanov could hear you. He made a suggestion about you last night." Her smile broadened, cat-like. "Your request is very—typical. I am satisfied. You do not understand all this—but you can go out to-day. It makes no difference to me, as I shall not be dining at home."

"Thank you, ma'am."

Tuppence felt a sensation of relief once she was out of the other's presence. Once again she admitted to herself that she was afraid, horribly afraid, of the beautiful woman with the cruel eyes.

In the midst of a final desultory polishing of her silver, Tuppence was disturbed by the ringing of the front door bell, and went to answer it. This time the visitor was neither Whittington nor Boris, but a man of striking appearance.

Just a shade over average height, he nevertheless conveyed the impression of a big man. His face, clean-shaven and exquisitely mobile, was stamped with an expression of power and force far beyond the ordinary. Magnetism seemed to radiate from him.

Tuppence was undecided for the moment whether to put him down as an actor or a lawyer, but her doubts were soon solved as he gave her his name: Sir James Peel Edgerton.

She looked at him with renewed interest. This, then, was the famous K.C. whose name was familiar all over England. She had heard it said that he might one day be Prime Minister. He was known to have refused office in the interests of his profession, preferring to remain a simple Member for a Scotch constituency.

Tuppence went back to her pantry thoughtfully. The great man had impressed her. She understood Boris's agitation. Peel Edgerton would not be an easy man to deceive.

In about a quarter of an hour the bell rang, and Tuppence repaired to the hall to show the visitor out. He had given her a piercing glance before. Now, as she handed him his hat and stick, she was conscious of his eyes raking her through. As she opened the door and stood aside to let him pass out, he stopped in the doorway.

"Not been doing this long, eh?"

Tuppence raised her eyes, astonished. She read in his glance kindliness, and something else more difficult to fathom.

He nodded as though she had answered.

"V.A.D. and hard up, I suppose?"

"Did Mrs. Vandemeyer tell you that?" asked Tuppence suspiciously.

"No, child. The look of you told me. Good place here?"

"Very good, thank you, sir."

"Ah, but there are plenty of good places nowadays. And a change does no harm sometimes."

"Do you mean——?" began Tuppence.

But Sir James was already on the topmost stair. He looked back with his kindly, shrewd glance.

"Just a hint," he said. "That's all."

Tuppence went back to the pantry more thoughtful than ever.

XI

JULIUS TELLS A STORY

Dressed appropriately, Tuppence duly sallied forth for her "afternoon out." Albert was in temporary abeyance, but Tuppence went herself to the stationer's to make quite sure that nothing had come for her. Satisfied on this point, she made her way to the Ritz. On inquiry she learnt that Tommy had not yet returned. It was the answer she had expected, but it was another nail in the coffin of her hopes. She resolved to appeal to Mr. Carter, telling him when and where Tommy had started on his quest, and asking him to do something to trace him. The prospect of his aid revived her mercurial spirits, and she next inquired for Julius Hersheimmer. The reply she got was to the effect that he had returned about half an hour ago, but had gone out immediately.

Tuppence's spirits revived still more. It would be something to see Julius. Perhaps he could devise some plan for finding out what had become of Tommy. She wrote her note to Mr. Carter in Julius's sitting-room, and was just addressing the envelope when the door burst open.

"What the hell——" began Julius, but checked himself

abruptly. "I beg your pardon, Miss Tuppence. Those fools down at the office would have it that Beresford wasn't here any longer—hadn't been here since Wednesday. Is that so?"

Tuppence nodded.

"You don't know where he is?" she asked faintly.

"I? How should I know? I haven't had one darned word from him, though I wired him yesterday morning."

"I expect your wire's at the office unopened."

"But where is he?"

"I don't know. I hoped you might."

"I tell you I haven't had one darned word from him since we parted at the depot on Wednesday."

"What depot?"

"Waterloo. Your London and South Western road."

"Waterloo?" frowned Tuppence.

"Why, yes. Didn't he tell you?"

"I haven't seen him either," replied Tuppence impatiently. "Go on about Waterloo. What were you doing there?"

"He gave me a call. Over the phone. Told me to get a move on, and hustle. Said he was trailing two crooks."

"Oh!" said Tuppence, her eyes opening. "I see. Go on."

"I hurried along right away. Beresford was there. He pointed out the crooks. The big one was mine, the guy you bluffed. Tommy shoved a ticket into my hand and told me to get aboard the cars. He was going to sleuth the other crook." Julius paused. "I thought for sure you'd know all this."

"Julius," said Tuppence firmly, "stop walking up and down. It makes me giddy. Sit down in that armchair, and tell me the whole story with as few fancy turns of speech as possible."

Mr. Hersheimmer obeyed.

"Sure," he said. "Where shall I begin?"

"Where you left off. At Waterloo."

"Well," began Julius, "I got into one of your dear old-fashioned first-class British compartments. The train was just off. First thing I knew a guard came along and informed me mighty politely that I wasn't in a smoking-carriage. I handed him out half a dollar, and that settled that. I did a bit of prospecting along the corridor to the next coach. Whittington was there right enough. When I saw the skunk, with his big sleek fat face, and thought of poor little Jane in his clutches, I felt real mad that I hadn't got a gun with me. I'd have tickled him up some.

"We got to Bournemouth all right. Whittington took a cab and gave the name of an hotel. I did likewise, and we drove up within three minutes of each other. He hired a room, and I hired one too. So far it was all plain sailing. He hadn't the remotest notion that any one was on to him. Well, he just sat around in the hotel lounge, reading the papers and so on, till it was time for dinner. He didn't hurry any over that either.

"I began to think that there was nothing doing, that he'd just come on the trip for his health, but I remembered that he hadn't changed for dinner, though it was by way of being a slap-up hotel, so it seemed likely enough that he'd be going out on his real business afterwards.

"Sure enough, about nine o'clock, so he did. Took a car across the town—mighty pretty place by the way, I guess I'll take Jane there for a spell when I find her—and then paid it off and struck out along those pine-woods on the top of the cliff. I was there too, you understand. We walked, maybe, for half an hour. There's a lot of villas all the way along, but by degrees they seemed to get more and more thinned out, and in the end we got to one that seemed the last of the bunch. Big house it was, with a lot of piny grounds around it.

"It was a pretty black night, and the carriage drive up to the house was dark as pitch. I could hear him ahead, though I couldn't see him. I had to walk carefully in case he might get on to it that he was being followed. I turned a curve and I was just in time to see him ring the bell and get admitted to the house. I just stopped where I was. It was beginning to rain, and I was soon pretty near soaked through. Also, it was almighty cold.

"Whittington didn't come out again, and by and by I got kind of restive, and began to mooch around. All the ground floor windows were shuttered tight, but upstairs, on the first floor (it was a two-storied house) I noticed a window with a light burning and the curtains not drawn.

"Now, just opposite to that window, there was a tree growing. It was about thirty feet away from the house, maybe, and I sort of got it into my head that, if I climbed up that tree, I'd very likely be able to see into that room. Of course, I knew there was no reason why Whittington should be in that room rather than in any other—less reason, in fact, for the betting would be on his being in one of the reception-rooms downstairs. But I guess I'd got the hump from standing so long in the rain, and anything seemed better than going on doing nothing. So I started up.

"It wasn't so easy, by a long chalk! The rain had made the boughs mighty slippery, and it was all I could do to keep a foot-hold, but bit by bit I managed it, until at last there I was level with the window.

"But then I was disappointed. I was too far to the left. I could only see sideways into the room. A bit of curtain, and a yard of wallpaper was all I could command. Well, that wasn't any manner of good to me, but just as I was going to give it up, and climb down ignominiously, some one inside moved and threw his shadow on my little bit of wall—and, by gum, it was Whittington!

"After that, my blood was up. I'd just *got* to get a look into that room. It was up to me to figure out how. I noticed that there was a long branch running out from the tree in the right direction. If I could only swarm about half-way along it, the proposition would be solved. But it was mighty uncertain whether it would bear my weight. I decided I'd just got to risk that, and I started. Very cautiously, inch by inch, I crawled along. The bough creaked and swayed in a nasty fashion, and it didn't do to think of the drop below, but at last I got safely to where I wanted to be.

"The room was medium-sized, furnished in a kind of bare hygienic way. There was a table with a lamp on it in the middle of the room, and sitting at that table, facing towards me, was Whittington right enough. He was talking to a woman dressed as a hospital nurse. She was sitting with her back to me, so I couldn't see her face. Although the blinds were up, the window itself was shut, so I couldn't catch a word of what they said. Whittington seemed to be doing all the talking, and the nurse just listened. Now and then she nodded, and sometimes she'd shake her head, as though she were answering questions. He seemed very emphatic—once or twice he beat with his fist on the table. The rain had stopped now, and the sky was clearing in that sudden way it does.

"Presently, he seemed to get to the end of what he was saying. He got up, and so did she. He looked towards the window and asked something—I guess it was whether it was raining. Anyway, she came right across and looked out. Just then the moon came out from behind the clouds. I was scared the woman would catch sight of me, for I was full in the moonlight. I tried to move back a bit. The jerk I gave was too much for that rotten old branch. With an almighty crash, down it came, and Julius P. Hersheimmer with it!"

"Oh, Julius," breathed Tuppence, "how exciting! Go on."

"Well, luckily for me, I pitched down into a good soft bed of earth—but it put me out of action for the time, sure enough. The next thing I knew, I was lying in bed with a hospital nurse (not Whittington's one) on one side of me, and a little black-bearded man with gold glasses, and medical man written all over him, on the other. He rubbed his hands together, and raised his eyebrows as I stared at him. 'Ah!' he said. 'So our young friend is coming round again. Capital. Capital.'

"I did the usual stunt. Said: 'What's happened?' And 'Where am I?' But I knew the answer to the last well enough. There's no moss growing on my brain. 'I think that'll do for the present, sister,' said the little man, and the nurse left the room in a sort of brisk well-trained way. But I caught her handing me out a look of deep curiosity as she passed through the door.

"That look of hers gave me an idea. 'Now then, doc,' I said, and tried to sit up in bed, but my right foot gave me a nasty twinge as I did so. 'A slight sprain,' explained the doctor. 'Nothing serious. You'll be about again in a couple of days.' "

"I noticed you walked lame," interpolated Tuppence.

Julius nodded, and continued:

" 'How did it happen?' I asked again. He replied dryly, 'You fell, with a considerable portion of one of my trees, into one of my newly planted flower-beds.' "

"I liked the man. He seemed to have a sense of humour. I felt sure that he, at least, was plumb straight. 'Sure, doc,' I said. 'I'm sorry about the tree, and I guess the new bulbs will be on me. But perhaps you'd like to know what I was doing in your garden?' 'I think the facts do call for an explanation,' he replied. 'Well, to begin with, I wasn't after the spoons.'

"He smiled. 'My first theory. But I soon altered my mind. By the way, you are an American, are you not?' I told him my name. 'And you?' 'I am Dr. Hall, and this, as you doubtless know, is my private nursing home.'

"I didn't know, but I wasn't going to put him wise. I was just thankful for the information. I liked the man, and I felt he was straight, but I wasn't going to give him the whole story. For one thing he probably wouldn't have believed it.

"I made up my mind in a flash. 'Why, doctor,' I said, 'I guess I feel an almighty fool, but I owe it to you to let you know that it wasn't the Bill Sikes business I was up to.' Then I went on and mumbled out something about a girl. I trotted out the stern guardian business, and a nervous breakdown, and finally explained that I had fancied I recognized her among the patients at the home, hence my nocturnal adventures.

"I guess it was just the kind of story he was expecting. 'Quite a romance,' he said genially, when I'd finished. 'Now, doc,' I went on, 'will you be frank with me? Have you here now, or have you had here at any time, a young girl called Jane Finn?' He repeated the name thoughtfully. 'Jane Finn?' he said. 'No.'

"I was chagrined, and I guess I showed it. 'You are sure?' 'Quite sure, Mr. Hersheimmer. It is an uncommon name, and I should not have been likely to forget it.'

"Well, that was flat. It laid me out for a space. I'd kind of hoped my search was at an end. 'That's that,' I said at last. 'Now, there's another matter. When I was hugging that darned branch I thought I recognized an old friend of mine talking to one of your nurses.' I purposely didn't mention any name because, of course, Whittington might be calling himself something quite different down here, but the doctor answered at once. 'Mr. Whittington, perhaps?' 'That's the fellow,' I replied. 'What's he doing down here? Don't tell me *his* nerves are out of order?'

"Dr. Hall laughed. 'No. He came down to see one of my nurses, Nurse Edith, who is a niece of his.' 'Why, fancy that!' I exclaimed. 'Is he still here?' 'No, he went back to town almost immediately.' 'What a pity!' I ejaculated. 'But perhaps I could speak to his niece—Nurse Edith, did you say her name was?'

"But the doctor shook his head. 'I'm afraid that, too, is impossible. Nurse Edith left with a patient to-night also.' 'I seem to be real unlucky,' I remarked. 'Have you Mr. Whittington's address in town? I guess I'd like to look him up when I get back.' 'I don't know his address. I can write to Nurse Edith for it if you like.' I thanked him. 'Don't say who it is wants it. I'd like to give him a little surprise.'

"That was about all I could do for the moment. Of course, if the girl was really Whittington's niccc, she might be too cute to fall into the trap, bul il was worth trying. Next thing I did was to write out a wire to Beresford saying where I was, and that I was laid up with a sprained foot, and telling him to come down if he wasn't busy. I had to be guarded in what I said. However, I didn't hear from him, and my foot soon got all right. It was only ricked, not really sprained, so to-day I said good-bye to the little doctor chap, asked him to send me word if he heard from Nurse Edith, and came right away back to town. Say, Miss Tuppence, you're looking mighty pale?"

"It's Tommy," said Tuppence. "What can have happened to him?"

"Buck up, I guess he's all right really. Why shouldn't he be? See here, it was a foreign-looking guy he went off after. Maybe they've gone abroad—to Poland, or something like that?"

Tuppence shook her head.

"He couldn't without passports and things. Besides I've seen that man, Boris Something, since. He dined with Mrs. Vandemeyer last night."

"Mrs. Who?"

"I forgot. Of course you don't know all that."

"I'm listening," said Julius, and gave vent to his favourite expression. "Put me wise."

Tuppence thereupon related the events of the last two days. Julius's astonishment and admiration were unbounded.

"Bully for you! Fancy you a menial. It just tickles me to death!" Then he added seriously: "But say now, I don't like it, Miss Tuppence, I sure don't. You're just as plucky as they make 'em, but I wish you'd keep right out of this. These crooks we're up against would as soon croak a girl as a man any day."

"Do you think I'm afraid?" said Tuppence indignantly, valiantly repressing memories of the steely glitter in Mrs. Vandemeyer's eyes.

"I said before you were darned plucky. But that doesn't alter facts."

"Oh, bother *me*!" said Tuppence impatiently. "Let's think about what can have happened to Tommy. I've written to Mr. Carter about it," she added, and told him the gist of her letter.

Julius nodded gravely.

"I guess that's good as far as it goes. But it's for us to get busy and do something."

"What can we do?" asked Tuppence, her spirits rising.

"I guess we'd better get on the track of Boris. You say he's been to your place. Is he likely to come again?"

"He might. I really don't know."

"I see. Well, I guess I'd better buy a car, a slap-up one, dress as a chauffeur and hang about outside. Then if Boris comes, you could make some kind of signal, and I'd trail him. How's that?"

"Splendid, but he mightn't come for weeks."

"We'll have to chance that. I'm glad you like the plan." He rose.

"Where are you going?"

"To buy the car, of course," replied Julius, surprised. "What make do you like? I guess you'll do some riding in it before we've finished."

"Oh," said Tuppence faintly, "I *like* Rolls-Royces, but——"

"Sure," agreed Julius. "What you say goes. I'll get one."

"But you can't at once," cried Tuppence. "People wait ages sometimes."

"Little Julius doesn't," affirmed Mr. Hersheimmer. "Don't you worry any. I'll be round in the car in half an hour."

Tuppence got up.

"You're awfully good, Julius. But I can't help feeling that it's rather a forlorn hope. I'm really pinning my faith to Mr. Carter."

"Then I shouldn't."

"Why?"

"Just an idea of mine."

"Oh; but he must do something. There's no one else. By the way, I forgot to tell you of a queer thing that happened this morning."

And she narrated her encounter with Sir James Peel Edgerton. Julius was interested.

"What did the guy mean, do you think?" he asked.

"I don't quite know," said Tuppence meditatively. "But I think that, in an ambiguous, legal, without prejudicious lawyer's way, he was trying to warn me."

"Why should he?"

"I don't know," confessed Tuppence. "But he looked kind, and simply awfully clever. I wouldn't mind going to him and telling him everything."

Somewhat to her surprise, Julius negatived the idea sharply.

"See here," he said, "we don't want any lawyers mixed up in this. That guy couldn't help us any."

"Well, I believe he could," reiterated Tuppence obstinately.

"Don't you think it. So long. I'll be back in half an hour."

Thirty-five minutes had elapsed when Julius returned. He took Tuppence by the arm, and walked her to the window.

"There she is."

"Oh!" said Tuppence with a note of reverence in her voice, as she gazed down at the enormous car.

"She's some pace-maker, I can tell you," said Julius complacently.

"How did you get it?" gasped Tuppence.

"She was just being sent home to some bigwig."

"Well?"

"I went round to his house," said Julius. "I said that I reckoned a car like that was worth every penny of twenty thousand dollars. Then I told him that it was worth just about fifty thousand dollars to me if he'd get out."

"Well?" said Tuppence, intoxicated.

"Well," returned Julius, "he got out, that's all."

XII

A Friend in Need

Friday and Saturday passed uneventfully. Tuppence had received a brief answer to her appeal from Mr. Carter. In it he pointed out that the Young Adventurers had undertaken the work at their own risk, and had been fully warned of the dangers. If anything had happened to Tommy he regretted it deeply, but he could do nothing.

This was cold comfort. Somehow, without Tommy, all the savour went out of the adventure, and, for the first time, Tuppence felt doubtful of success. While they had been together she had never questioned it for a minute. Although she was accustomed to take the lead, and to pride herself on her quick-wittedness, in reality she had relied upon Tommy more than she realized at the time. There was something so eminently sober and clear-headed about him, his common sense and soundness of vision were so unvarying, that without him Tuppence felt much like a rudderless ship. It was curious that Julius, who was undoubtedly much cleverer than Tommy, did not give her the same feeling of support. She had accused Tommy of being a pessimist, and it is certain that he always saw the disadvantages and difficulties which she herself was optimistically given to over-looking, but nevertheless she had really relied a good deal on his judgment. He might be slow, but he was very sure.

It seemed to the girl that, for the first time, she realized the sinister character of the mission they had undertaken so lightheartedly. It had begun like a page of romance. Now, shorn of its glamour, it seemed to be turning to grim reality. Tommy——that was all that mattered. Many times in the day Tuppence blinked the tears out of her eyes resolutely. "Little fool," she would apostrophize herself, "don't snivel. Of course you're fond of him. You've known him all your life. But there's no need to be sentimental about it."

In the meantime, nothing more was seen of Boris. He did not come to the flat, and Julius and the car waited in vain. Tuppence gave herself over to new meditations. Whilst admitting the truth of Julius's objections, she had nevertheless not entirely relinquished the idea of appealing to Sir James Peel Edgerton. Indeed, she had gone so far as to look up his address in the *Red Book*. Had he meant to warn her that day? If so, why? Surely she was at least entitled to demand an explanation. He had looked at her so kindly. Perhaps he might tell them something concerning Mrs. Vandemeyer which might lead to a clue to Tommy's whereabouts.

Anyway, Tuppence decided, with her usual shake of the shoulders, it was worth trying, and try it she would. Sunday was her afternoon out. She would meet Julius, persuade him to her point of view, and they would beard the lion in his den.

When the day arrived Julius needed a considerable amount of persuading, but Tuppence held firm. "It can do no harm," was what she always came back to. In the end Julius gave in, and they proceeded in the car to Carlton House Terrace.

The door was opened by an irreproachable butler. Tuppence felt a little nervous. After all, perhaps it *was* colossal cheek on her part. She had decided not to ask if Sir James was "at home," but to adopt a more personal attitude.

"Will you ask Sir James if I can see him for a few minutes? I have an important message for him."

The butler retired, returning a moment or two later. "Sir James will see you. Will you step this way?"

He ushered them into a room at the back of the house, furnished as a library. The collection of books was a magnificent one, and Tuppence noticed that all one wall was devoted to works on crime and criminology. There were several deep-padded leather arm-chairs, and an old-fashioned open hearth. In the window was a big roll-top desk strewn with papers at which the master of the house was sitting.

He rose as they entered.

"You have a message for me? Ah"—he recognized Tuppence with a smile—"it's you, is it? Brought a message from Mrs. Vandemeyer, I suppose?"

"Not exactly," said Tuppence. "In fact, I'm afraid I only said that to be quite sure of getting in. Oh, by the way, this is Mr. Hersheimmer, Sir James Peel Edgerton."

"Pleased to meet you," said the American, shooting out a hand.

"Won't you both sit down?" asked Sir James. He drew forward two chairs.

"Sir James," said Tuppence, plunging boldly, "I dare say you will think it is most awful cheek of me coming here like this. Because, of course, it's nothing whatever to do with you, and then you're a very important person, and of course Tommy and I are very unimportant." She paused for breath.

"Tommy?" queried Sir James, looking across at the American.

"No, that's Julius," explained Tuppence. "I'm rather nervous, and that makes me tell it badly. What I really want to know is what you meant by what you said to me the other day. Did you mean to warn me against Mrs. Vandemeyer? You did, didn't you?"

"My dear young lady, as far as I recollect I only mentioned that there were equally good situations to be obtained elsewhere."

"Yes, I know. But it was a hint, wasn't it?"

"Well, perhaps it was," admitted Sir James gravely.

"Well, I want to know more. I want to know just *why* you gave me a hint."

Sir James smiled at her earnestness.

"Suppose the lady brings a libel action against me for defamation of character?"

"Of course," said Tuppence. "I know lawyers are always dreadfully careful. But can't we say 'without prejudice' first, and then say just what we want to?"

"Well," said Sir James, still smiling, "without prejudice, then, if I had a young sister forced to earn her living, I should not like to see her in Mrs. Vandemeyer's service. I felt it incumbent on me just to give you a hint. It is no place for a young and inexperienced girl. That is all I can tell you."

"I see," said Tuppence thoughtfully. "Thank you very much. But I'm not *really* inexperienced, you know. I knew perfectly that she was a bad lot when I went there—as a matter of fact that's *why* I went——" She broke off, seeing some bewilderment on the lawyer's face, and went on: "I think perhaps I'd better tell you the whole story, Sir James. I've a sort of feeling that you'd know in a minute if I didn't tell the truth, and so you might as well know all about it from the beginning. What do you think, Julius?"

"As you're bent on it, I'd go right ahead with the facts," replied the American, who had so far sat in silence.

"Yes, tell me all about it," said Sir James. "I want to know who Tommy is."

Thus encouraged Tuppence plunged into her tale, and the lawyer listened with close attention.

"Very interesting," he said, when she finished. "A great deal of what you tell me, child, is already known to me. I've had certain theories of my own about this Jane Finn. You've done extraordinarily well so far, but it's rather too bad of—what do you know him as?—Mr. Carter to pitchfork you two young things into an affair of this kind. By the way, where did Mr. Hersheimmer come in originally? You didn't make that clear?"

Julius answered for himself.

"I'm Jane's first cousin," he explained, returning the lawyer's keen gaze.

"Ah!"

"Oh, Sir James," broke out Tuppence, "what do you think has become of Tommy?"

"H'm." The lawyer rose, and paced slowly up and down.

"When you arrived, young lady, I was just packing up my traps. Going to Scotland by the night train for a few days' fishing. But there are different kinds of fishing. I've a good mind to stay, and see if we can't get on the track of that young chap."

"Oh!" Tuppence clasped her hands ecstatically.

"All the same, as I said before, it's too bad of—of Carter to set you two babies on a job like this. Now, don't get offended, Miss—er——"

"Cowley. Prudence Cowley. But my friends call me Tuppence."

"Well, Miss Tuppence, then, as I'm certainly going to be a friend. Don't be offended because I think you're young. Youth is a failing only too easily outgrown. Now, about this young Tommy of yours——"

"Yes." Tuppence clasped her hands.

"Frankly, things look bad for him. He's been butting in somewhere where he wasn't wanted. Not a doubt of it. But don't give up hope."

"And you really will help us? There, Julius! He didn't want me to come," she added by way of explanation.

"H'm," said the lawyer, favouring Julius with another keen glance. "And why was that?"

"I reckoned it would be no good worrying you with a petty little business like this."

"I see." He paused a moment. "This petty little business, as you call it, bears directly on a very big business, bigger perhaps than either you or Miss Tuppence know. If this boy is alive, he may have very valuable information to give us. Therefore, we must find him."

"Yes, but how?" cried Tuppence. "I've tried to think of everything."

Sir James smiled.

"And yet there's one person quite near at hand who in all probability knows where he is, or at all events where he is likely to be."

"Who is that?" asked Tuppence, puzzled.

"Mrs. Vandemeyer."

"Yes, but she'd never tell us."

"Ah, that is where I come in. I think it quite likely that I

shall be able to make Mrs. Vandemeyer tell me what I want
to know."

"How?" demanded Tuppence, opening her eyes very wide.

"Oh, just by asking her questions," replied Sir James easily. "That's the way we do it, you know."

He tapped with his finger on the table, and Tuppence felt
again the intense power that radiated from the man.

"And if she won't tell?" asked Julius suddenly.

"I think she will. I have one or two powerful levers. Still,
in that unlikely event, there is always the possibility of brib-
ery."

"Sure. And that's where I come in!" cried Julius, bringing
his fist down on the table with a bang. "You can count on
me, if necessary, for one million dollars. Yes, sir, one million
dollars!"

Sir James sat down and subjected Julius to a long scrutiny.

"Mr. Hersheimmer," he said at last, "that is a very large
sum."

"I guess it'll have to be. These aren't the kind of folk to
offer sixpence to."

"At the present rate of exchange it amounts to considerably over two hundred and fifty thousand pounds."

"That's so. Maybe you think I'm talking through my hat,
but I can deliver the goods all right, with enough over to
spare for your fee."

Sir James flushed slightly.

"There is no question of a fee, Mr. Hersheimmer. I am not
a private detective."

"Sorry. I guess I was just a mite hasty, but I've been feeling
bad about this money question. I wanted to offer a big re-
ward for news of Jane some days ago, but your crusted in-
stitution of Scotland Yard advised me against it. Said it was
undesirable."

"They were probably right," said Sir James dryly.

"But it's all O.K. about Julius," put in Tuppence. "He's not
pulling your leg. He's got simply pots of money."

"The old man piled it up in style," explained Julius. "Now,
let's get down to it. What's your idea?"

Sir James considered for a moment or two.

"There is no time to be lost. The sooner we strike the better." He turned to Tuppence. "Is Mrs. Vandemeyer dining out tonight, do you know?"

"Yes, I think so, but she will not be out late. Otherwise, she would have taken the latchkey."

"Good. I will call upon her about ten o'clock. What time are you supposed to return?"

"About nine-thirty or ten, but I could go back earlier."

"You must not do that on any account. It might arouse suspicion if you did not stay out till the usual time. Be back by nine-thirty. I will arrive at ten. Mr. Hersheimmer will wait below in a taxi perhaps."

"He's got a new Rolls-Royce car," said Tuppence with vicarious pride.

"Even better. If I succeed in obtaining the address from her, we can go there at once, taking Mrs. Vandemeyer with us if necessary. You understand?"

"Yes." Tuppence rose to her feet with a skip of delight. "Oh, I feel so much better!"

"Don't build on it too much, Miss Tuppence. Go easy."

Julius turned to the lawyer.

"Say, then. I'll call for you in the car round about nine-thirty. Is that right?"

"Perhaps that will be the best plan. It would be unnecessary to have two cars waiting about. Now, Miss Tuppence, my advice to you is to go and have a good dinner, a *really* good one, mind. And don't think ahead more than you can help."

He shook hands with them both, and a moment later they were outside.

"Isn't he a duck?" inquired Tuppence ecstatically, as she skipped down the steps. "Oh, Julius, isn't he just a duck?"

"Well, I allow he seems to be the goods all right. And I was wrong about its being useless to go to him. Say, shall we go right away back to the Ritz?"

"I must walk a bit, I think. I feel so excited. Drop me in the park, will you? Unless you'd like to come too?"

"I want to get some petrol," he explained. "And send off a cable or two."

"All right. I'll meet you at the Ritz at seven. We'll have to dine upstairs. I can't show myself in these glad rags."

"Sure. I'll get Felix to help me choose the menu. He's some head waiter, that. So long."

Tuppence walked briskly along towards the Serpentine, first glancing at her watch. It was nearly six o'clock. She remembered that she had had no tea, but felt too excited to be conscious of hunger. She walked as far as Kensington Gardens and then slowly retraced her steps, feeling infinitely better for the fresh air and exercise. If was not so easy to follow Sir James's advice, and put the possible events of the evening out of her head. As she drew nearer and nearer to Hyde Park corner, the temptation to return to South Audley Mansions was almost irresistible.

At any rate, she decided, it would do no harm just to go and *look* at the building. Perhaps, then, she could resign herself to waiting patiently for ten o'clock.

South Audley Mansions looked exactly the same as usual. What Tuppence had expected she hardly knew, but the sight of its red brick stolidity slightly assuaged the growing and entirely unreasonable uneasiness that possessed her. She was just turning away when she heard a piercing whistle, and the faithful Albert came running from the building to join her.

Tuppence frowned. It was no part of the programme to have attention called to her presence in the neighbourhood, but Albert was purple with suppressed excitement.

"I say, miss, she's a going!"

"Who's going?" demanded Tuppence sharply.

"The crook. Ready Rita. Mrs. Vandemeyer. She's a-packing up, and she's just sent down word for me to get her a taxi."

"What?" Tuppence clutched his arm.

"It's the truth, miss. I thought maybe as you didn't know about it."

"Albert," cried Tuppence, "you're a brick. If it hadn't been for you we'd have lost her."

Albert flushed with pleasure at this tribute.

"There's no time to lose," said Tuppence, crossing the road. "I've got to stop her. At all costs I must keep her here until——" She broke off. "Albert, there's a telephone here, isn't there."

The boy shook his head.

"The flats mostly have their own, miss. But there's a box just round the corner."

"Go to it then, at once, and ring up the Ritz Hotel. Ask for Mr. Hersheimmer, and when you get him tell him to get Sir James and come on at once, as Mrs. Vandemeyer is trying to hook it. If you can't get him, ring up Sir James Peel Edgerton, you'll find his number in the book, and tell him what's happening. You won't forget the names, will you?"

Albert repeated them glibly. "You trust to me, miss, it'll be all right. But what about you? Aren't you afraid to trust yourself with her?"

"No, no, that's all right. *But go and telephone.* Be quick."

Drawing a long breath, Tuppence entered the Mansions and ran up to the door of No. 20. How she was to detain Mrs. Vandemeyer until the two men arrived, she did not know, but somehow or other it had to be done, and she must accomplish the task single-handed. What had occasioned this precipitate departure? Did Mrs. Vandemeyer suspect her?

Speculations were idle. Tuppence pressed the bell firmly. She might learn something from the cook.

Nothing happened and, after waiting some minutes, Tuppence pressed the bell again, keeping her finger on the button for some little while. At last she heard footsteps inside, and a moment later Mrs. Vandemeyer herself opened the door. She lifted her eyebrows at the sight of the girl.

"You?"

"I had a touch of toothache, ma'am," said Tuppence glibly. "So thought it better to come home and have a quiet evening."

Mrs. Vandemeyer said nothing, but she drew back and let Tuppence pass into the hall.

"How unfortunate for you," she said coldly. "You had better go to bed."

"Oh, I shall be all right in the kitchen, ma'am. Cook will——"

"Cook is out," said Mrs. Vandemeyer, in a rather disagreeable tone. "I sent her out. So you see you had better go to bed."

Suddenly Tuppence felt afraid. There was a ring in Mrs. Vandemeyer's voice that she did not like at all. Also, the other woman was slowly edging her up the passage. Tuppence turned at bay.

"I don't want——"

Then, in a flash, a rim of cold steel touched her temple, and Mrs. Vandemeyer's voice rose cold and menacing:

"You damned little fool! Do you think I don't know? No, don't answer. If you struggle or cry out, I'll shoot you like a dog."

The rim of steel pressed a little harder against the girl's temple.

"Now then, march," went on Mrs. Vandemeyer. "This way—into my room. In a minute, when I've done with you, you'll go to bed as I told you to. And you'll sleep—oh yes, my little spy, you'll sleep all right!"

There was a sort of hideous geniality in the last words which Tuppence did not at all like. For the moment there was nothing to be done, and she walked obediently into Mrs. Vandemeyer's bedroom. The pistol never left her forehead. The room was in a state of wild disorder, clothes were flung about right and left, a suit-case and a hat box, half-packed, stood in the middle of the floor.

Tuppence pulled herself together with an effort. Her voice shook a little, but she spoke out bravely.

"Come now," she said. "This is nonsense. You can't shoot me. Why, every one in the building would hear the report."

"I'd risk that," said Mrs. Vandemeyer cheerfully. "But, as long as you don't sing out for help, you're all right—and I don't think you will. You're a clever girl. You deceived *me* all right. I hadn't a suspicion of you! So I've no doubt that you understand perfectly well that this is where I'm on top and you're underneath. Now then—sit on the bed. Put your hands above your head, and if you value your life don't move them."

Tuppence obeyed passively. Her good sense told her that there was nothing else to do but accept the situation. If she shrieked for help there was very little chance of any one hearing her, whereas there was probably quite a good chance of Mrs. Vandemeyer's shooting her. In the meantime, every minute of delay gained was valuable.

Mrs. Vandemeyer laid down the revolver on the edge of the washstand within reach of her hand, and, still eyeing Tuppence like a lynx in case the girl should attempt to move, she took a little stoppered bottle from its place on the marble and poured some of its contents into a glass which she filled up with water.

"What's that?" asked Tuppence sharply.

"Something to make you sleep soundly."

Tuppence paled a little.

"Are you going to poison me?" she asked in a whisper.

"Perhaps," said Mrs. Vandemeyer, smiling agreeably.

"Then I shan't drink it," said Tuppence firmly. "I'd much rather be shot. At any rate that would make a row, and some one might hear it. But I won't be killed off quietly like a lamb."

Mrs. Vandemeyer stamped her foot.

"Don't be a little fool! Do you really think I want a hue and cry for murder out after me? If you've any sense at all, you'll realize that poisoning you wouldn't suit my book at all. It's a sleeping draught, that's all. You'll wake up to-morrow morning none the worse. I simply don't want the bother of tying you up and gagging you. That's the alternative—and you won't like it, I can tell you! I can be very rough if I choose. So drink this down like a good girl, and you'll be none the worse for it."

In her heart of hearts Tuppence believed her. The arguments she had adduced rang true. It was a simple and effective method of getting her out of the way for the time being. Nevertheless, the girl did not take kindly to the idea of being tamely put to sleep without as much as one bid for freedom. She felt that once Mrs. Vandemeyer gave them the slip, the last hope of finding Tommy would be gone.

Tuppence was quick in her mental processes. All these reflections passed through her mind in a flash, and she saw where a chance, a very problematical chance, lay, and she determined to risk all in one supreme effort.

Accordingly, she lurched suddenly off the bed and fell on

her knees before Mrs. Vandemeyer, clutching her skirts frantically.

"I don't believe it," she moaned. "It's poison—I know it's poison. Oh, don't make me drink it"—her voice rose to a shriek—"don't make me drink it!"

Mrs. Vandemeyer, glass in hand, looked down with a curling lip at this sudden collapse.

"Get up, you little idiot! Don't go on drivelling there. How you ever had the nerve to play your part as you did I can't think." She stamped her foot. "Get up, I say."

But Tuppence continued to cling and sob, interjecting her sobs with incoherent appeals for mercy. Every minute gained was to the good. Moreover, as she grovelled, she moved imperceptibly nearer to her objective.

Mrs. Vandemeyer gave a sharp impatient exclamation, and jerked the girl to her knees.

"Drink it at once!" Imperiously she pressed the glass to the girl's lips.

Tuppence gave one last despairing moan.

"You swear it won't hurt me?" she temporized.

"Of course it won't hurt you. Don't be a fool."

"Will you swear it?"

"Yes, yes," said the other impatiently. "I swear it."

Tuppence raised a trembling left hand to the glass.

"Very well." Her mouth opened meekly.

Mrs. Vandemeyer gave a sigh of relief, off her guard for the moment. Then, quick as a flash, Tuppence jerked the glass upward as hard as she could. The fluid in it splashed into Mrs. Vandemeyer's face, and during her momentary gasp, Tuppence's right hand shot out and grasped the revolver where it lay on the edge of the washstand. The next moment she had sprung back a pace, and the revolver pointed straight at Mrs. Vandemeyer's heart, with no unsteadiness in the hand that held it.

In the moment of victory, Tuppence betrayed a somewhat unsportsman-like triumph.

"Now who's on top and who's underneath?" she crowed.

The other's face was convulsed with rage. For a minute Tuppence thought she was going to spring upon her, which would have placed the girl in an unpleasant dilemma, since she meant to draw the line at actually letting off the revolver. However, with an effort Mrs. Vandemeyer controlled herself, and at last a slow evil smile crept over her face.

"Not a fool, then, after all! You did that well, girl. But you shall pay for it—oh, yes, you shall pay for it! I have a long memory!"

"I'm surprised you should have been gulled so easily," said Tuppence scornfully. "Did you really think I was the kind of girl to roll about on the floor and whine for mercy?"

"You may do—some day!" said the other significantly.

The cold malignity of her manner sent an unpleasant chill down Tuppence's spine, but she was not going to give in to it.

"Supposing we sit down," she said pleasantly. "Our present attitude is a little melodramatic. No—not on the bed. Draw a chair up to the table, that's right. Now I'll sit opposite you with the revolver in front of me—just in case of accidents. Splendid. Now, let's talk."

"What about?" said Mrs. Vandemeyer sullenly.

Tuppence eyed her thoughtfully for a minute. She was remembering several things. Boris's words, "I believe you would sell—us!" and her answer, "The price would have to be enormous," given lightly, it was true, yet might not there be a substratum of truth in it? Long ago, had not Whittington asked: "Who's been blabbing? Rita?" Would Rita Vandemeyer prove to be the weak spot in the armour of Mr. Brown?

Keeping her eyes fixed steadily on the other's face, Tuppence replied quietly:

"Money—"

Mrs. Vandemeyer started. Clearly, the reply was unexpected.

"What do you mean?"

"I'll tell you. You said just now that you had a long memory. A long memory isn't half as useful as a long purse! I dare say it relieves your feelings a good deal to plan out all sorts of dreadful things to do to me, but is that *practical*? Revenge is very unsatisfactory. Every one always says so. But money"—Tuppence warmed to her pet creed—"well, there's nothing unsatisfactory about money, is there?"

"Do you think," said Mrs. Vandemeyer scornfully, "that I am the kind of woman to sell my friends?"

"Yes," said Tuppence promptly. "If the price was big enough."

"A paltry hundred pounds or so!"

"No," said Tuppence. "I should suggest—a hundred thousand!"

Her economical spirit did not permit her to mention the whole million dollars suggested by Julius.

A flush crept over Mrs. Vandemeyer's face.

"What did you say?" she asked, her fingers playing nervously with a brooch on her breast. In that moment Tuppence knew that the fish was hooked, and for the first time she felt a horror of her own money-loving spirit. It gave her a dreadful sense of kinship to the woman fronting her.

"A hundred thousand pounds," repeated Tuppence.

The light died out of Mrs. Vandemeyer's eyes. She leaned back in her chair.

"Bah!" she said. "You haven't got it."

"No," admitted Tuppence, "I haven't—but I know some one who has."

"Who?"

"A friend of mine."

"Must be a millionaire," remarked Mrs. Vandemeyer unbelievingly.

"As a matter of fact he is. He's an American. He'll pay you that without a murmur. You can take it from me that it's a perfectly genuine proposition."

Mrs. Vandemeyer sat up again.

"I'm inclined to believe you," she said slowly.

There was silence between them for some time, then Mrs. Vandemeyer looked up.

"What does he want to know, this friend of yours?"

Tuppence went through a momentary struggle, but it was Julius's money, and his interests must come first.

"He wants to know where Jane Finn is," she said boldly.

Mrs. Vandemeyer showed no surprise.

"I'm not sure where she is at the present moment," she replied.

"But you could find out?"

"Oh, yes," returned Mrs. Vandemeyer carelessly. "There would be no difficulty about that."

"Then"—Tuppence's voice shook a little—"there's a boy, a friend of mine. I'm afraid something's happened to him, through your pal Boris."

"What's his name?"

"Tommy Beresford."

"Never heard of him. But I'll ask Boris. He'll tell me anything he knows."

"Thank you." Tuppence felt a terrific rise in her spirits. It impelled her to more audacious efforts. "There's one thing more."

"Well?"

Tuppence leaned forward and lowered her voice.

"Who is Mr. Brown?"

Her quick eyes saw the sudden paling of the beautiful face. With an effort Mrs. Vandemeyer pulled herself together and tried to resume her former manner. But the attempt was a mere parody.

She shrugged her shoulders.

"You can't have learnt much about us if you don't know that *nobody knows who Mr. Brown is.* . . ."

"You do," said Tuppence quietly.

Again the colour deserted the other's face.

"What makes you think that?"

"I don't know," said the girl truthfully. "But I'm sure."

Mrs. Vandemeyer stared in front of her for a long time.

"Yes," she said hoarsely, at last, "*I* know. I was beautiful, you see—very beautiful—"

"You are still," said Tuppence with admiration.

Mrs. Vandemeyer shook her head. There was a strange gleam in her electric-blue eyes.

"Not beautiful enough," she said in a soft dangerous voice. "Not—beautiful—enough! And sometimes, lately, I've been afraid. . . . It's dangerous to know too much!" She leaned forward across the table. "Swear that my name shan't be brought into it—that no one shall ever know."

"I swear it. And, once he's caught, you'll be out of danger."

A terrified look swept across Mrs. Vandemeyer's face.

"Shall I? Shall I ever be?" She clutched Tuppence's arm. "You're sure about the money?"

"Quite sure."

"When shall I have it? There must be no delay."

"This friend of mine will be here presently. He may have to send cables, or something like that. But there won't be any delay—he's a terrific hustler."

A resolute look settled on Mrs. Vandemeyer's face.

"I'll do it. It's a great sum of money, and besides"—she gave a curious smile—"it is not—wise to throw over a woman like me!"

For a moment or two, she remained smiling, and lightly tapping her fingers on the table. Suddenly she started, and her face blanched.

"What was that?"

"I heard nothing."

Mrs. Vandemeyer gazed round her fearfully.

"If there should be some one listening——"

"Nonsense. Who could there be?"

"Even the walls might have ears," whispered the other. "I tell you I'm frightened. You don't know him!"

"Think of the hundred thousand pounds," said Tuppence soothingly.

Mrs. Vandemeyer passed her tongue over her dried lips.

"You don't know him," she reiterated hoarsely. "He's—ah!"

With a shriek of terror she sprang to her feet. Her outstretched hand pointed over Tuppence's head. Then she swayed to the ground in a dead faint.

Tuppence looked round to see what had startled her.

In the doorway were Sir James Peel Edgerton and Julius Hersheimmer.

XIII

THE VIGIL

Sir James brushed past Julius and hurriedly bent over the fallen woman.

"Heart," he said sharply. "Seeing us so suddenly must have given her a shock. Brandy—and quickly, or she'll slip through our fingers."

Julius hurried to the washstand.

"Not there," said Tuppence over her shoulder. "In the tantalus in the dining-room. Second door down the passage."

Between them Sir James and Tuppence lifted Mrs. Vandemeyer and carried her to the bed. There they dashed water on her face, but with no result. The lawyer fingered her pulse.

"Touch and go," he muttered. "I wish that young fellow would hurry up with the brandy."

At that moment Julius re-entered the room, carrying a glass half full of the spirit which he handed to Sir James. While Tuppence lifted her head the lawyer tried to force a little of the spirit between her closed lips. Finally the woman opened her eyes feebly. Tuppence held the glass to her lips.

"Drink this."

Mrs. Vandemeyer complied. The brandy brought the colour back to her white cheeks, and revived her in a marvellous fashion. She tried to sit up—then fell back with a groan, her hand to her side.

"It's my heart," she whispered. "I mustn't talk."

She lay back with closed eyes.

Sir James kept his finger on her wrist a minute longer, then withdrew it with a nod.

"She'll do now."

All three moved away, and stood together talking in low voices. One and all were conscious of a certain feeling of anticlimax. Clearly any scheme for cross-questioning the lady was out of the question for the moment. For the time being they were baffled, and could do nothing.

Tuppence related how Mrs. Vandemeyer had declared herself willing to disclose the identity of Mr. Brown, and how she had consented to discover and reveal to them the whereabouts of Jane Finn. Julius was congratulatory.

"That's all right, Miss Tuppence. Splendid! I guess that hundred thousand pounds will look just as good in the morning to the lady as it did over night. There's nothing to worry over. She won't speak without the cash anyway, you bet!"

There was certainly a good deal of common sense in this, and Tuppence felt a little comforted.

"What you say is true," said Sir James meditatively. "I must confess, however, that I cannot help wishing we had not interrupted at the minute we did. Still, it cannot be helped, it is only a matter of waiting until the morning."

He looked across at the inert figure on the bed. Mrs. Vandemeyer lay perfectly passive with closed eyes. He shook his head.

"Well," said Tuppence, with an attempt at cheerfulness, "we must wait until the morning, that's all. But I don't think we ought to leave the flat."

"What about leaving that bright boy of yours on guard?"

"Albert? And suppose she came round again and hooked it. Albert couldn't stop her."

"I guess she won't want to make tracks away from the dollars."

"She might. She seemed very frightened of 'Mr. Brown.' "

"What? Real plumb scared of him?"

"Yes. She looked round and said even walls had ears."

"Maybe she meant a dictaphone," said Julius with interest.

"Miss Tuppence is right," said Sir James quietly. "We must not leave the flat—if only for Mrs. Vandemeyer's sake."

Julius stared at him.

"You think he'd get after her? Between now and to-morrow morning. How could he know, even?"

"You forget your own suggestion of a dictaphone," said Sir James dryly. "We have a very formidable adversary. I believe, if we exercise all due care, that there is a very good chance of his being delivered into our hands. But we must neglect no precaution. We have an important witness, but she must be safeguarded. I would suggest that Miss Tuppence should go to bed, and that you and I, Mr. Hersheimmer, should share the vigil."

Tuppence was about to protest, but happening to glance at the bed she saw Mrs. Vandemeyer, her eyes half-open, with such an expression of mingled fear and malevolence on her face that it quite froze the words on her lips.

For a moment she wondered whether the faint and the heart attack had been a gigantic sham, but remembering the deadly pallor she could hardly credit the supposition. As she looked the expression disappeared as by magic, and Mrs. Vandemeyer lay inert and motionless as before. For a moment the girl fancied she must have dreamt it. But she determined nevertheless to be on the alert.

"Well," said Julius, "I guess we'd better make a move out of here anyway."

The others fell in with his suggestion. Sir James again felt Mrs. Vandemeyer's pulse.

"Perfectly satisfactory," he said in a low voice to Tuppence. "She'll be absolutely all right after a night's rest."

The girl hesitated a moment by the bed. The intensity of the expression she had surprised had impressed her powerfully. Mrs. Vandemeyer lifted her lids. She seemed to be struggling to speak. Tuppence bent over her.

"Don't—leave——" She seemed unable to proceed, murmuring something that sounded like "sleepy." Then she tried again.

Tuppence bent lower still. It was only a breath.

"Mr.—Brown——" The voice stopped.

But the half-closed eyes seemed still to send an agonized message.

Moved by a sudden impulse, the girl said quickly: "I shan't leave the flat. I shall sit up all night."

A flash of relief showed before the lids descended once more. Apparently Mrs. Vandemeyer slept. But her words had awakened a new uneasiness in Tuppence. What had she meant by that low murmur, "Mr. Brown?" Tuppence caught herself nervously looking over her shoulder. The big wardrobe loomed up in a sinister fashion before her eyes. Plenty of room for a man to hide in that. . . . Half-ashamed of herself, Tuppence pulled it open and looked inside. No one—of course! She stooped down and looked under the bed. There was no other possible hiding-place.

Tuppence gave her familiar shake of the shoulders. It was absurd, this giving way to nerves! Slowly she went out of the room. Julius and Sir James were talking in a low voice. Sir James turned to her.

"Lock the door on the outside, please, Miss Tuppence, and take out the key. There must be no chance of any one entering that room."

The gravity of his manner impressed them, and Tuppence felt less ashamed of her attack of "nerves."

"Say," remarked Julius suddenly, "there's Tuppence's bright boy. I guess I'd better go down and ease his young mind. That's some lad, Tuppence."

"How did you get in, by the way?" asked Tuppence suddenly. "I forgot to ask."

"Well, Albert got me on the phone all right. I ran round for Sir James here, and we came right on. The boy was on the look out for us, and was just a mite worried about what might have happened to you. He'd been listening outside the door of the flat, but couldn't hear anything. Anyhow he suggested sending us up in the coal lift instead of ringing the bell. And sure enough we landed in the scullery and came right along to find you. Albert's still below, and must be just hopping mad by this time." With which Julius departed abruptly.

"Now then, Miss Tuppence," said Sir James, "you know this place better than I do. Where do you suggest we should take up our quarters?"

Tuppence considered for a moment or two.

"I think Mrs. Vandemeyer's boudoir would be the most comfortable," she said at last, and led the way there.

Sir James looked round approvingly.

"This will do very well, and now, my dear young lady, do go to bed and get some sleep."

Tuppence shook her head resolutely.

"I couldn't, thank you, Sir James. I should dream of Mr. Brown all night!"

"But you'll be so tired, child."

"No, I shan't. I'd rather stay up—really."

The lawyer gave in.

Julius reappeared some minutes later, having reassured Albert and rewarded him lavishly for his services. Having in his turn failed to persuade Tuppence to go to bed, he said decisively:

"At any rate, you've got to have something to eat right away. Where's the larder?"

Tuppence directed him, and he returned in a few minutes with a cold pie and three plates.

After a hearty meal, the girl felt inclined to pooh-pooh her fancies of half an hour before. The power of the money bribe could not fail.

"And now, Miss Tuppence," said Sir James, "we want to hear your adventures."

"That's so," agreed Julius.

Tuppence narrated her adventures with some complacence. Julius occasionally interjected an admiring "Bully." Sir James said nothing until she had finished, when his quiet "well done, Miss Tuppence," made her flush with pleasure.

"There's one thing I don't get clearly," said Julius. "What put her up to clearing out?"

"I don't know," confessed Tuppence.

Sir James stroked his chin thoughtfully.

"The room was in great disorder. That looks as though her flight was unpremeditated. Almost as though she got a sudden warning to go from some one."

"Mr. Brown, I suppose," said Julius scoffingly.

The lawyer looked at him deliberately for a minute or two.

"Why not?" he said. "Remember, you yourself have once been worsted by him."

Julius flushed with vexation.

"I feel just mad when I think of how I handed out Jane's photograph to him like a lamb. Gee, if I ever lay hands on it again, I'll freeze on to it like—like hell!"

"That contingency is likely to be a remote one," said the other dryly.

"I guess you're right," said Julius frankly. "And, in any case, it's the original I'm out after. Where do you think she can be, Sir James?"

The lawyer shook his head.

"Impossible to say. But I've a very good idea where she *has* been."

"You have? Where?"

Sir James smiled.

"At the scene of your nocturnal adventures, the Bournemouth nursing home."

"There? Impossible. I asked."

"No, my dear sir, you asked if anyone of the name of Jane Finn had been there. Now, if the girl had been placed there it would almost certainly be under an assumed name."

"Bully for you," cried Julius. "I never thought of that!"

"It was fairly obvious," said the other.

"Perhaps the doctor's in it too," suggested Tuppence.

Julius shook his head.

"I don't think so. I took to him at once. No, I'm pretty sure Dr. Hall's all right."

"Hall, did you say?" asked Sir James. "That is curious— really very curious."

"Why?" demanded Tuppence.

"Because I happened to meet him this morning. I've known him slightly on and off for some years, and this morning I ran across him in the street. Staying at the Métropole, he told me." He turned to Julius. "Didn't he tell you he was coming up to town?"

Julius shook his head.

"Curious," mused Sir James. "You did not mention his name this afternoon, or I would have suggested your going to him for further information with my card as introduction."

"I guess I'm a mutt," said Julius, with unusual humility. "I ought to have thought of the false name stunt."

"How could you think of anything after falling out of that tree?" cried Tuppence. "I'm sure anyone else would have been killed right off."

"Well, I guess it doesn't matter now, anyway," said Julius. "We've got Mrs. Vandemeyer on a string, and that's all we need."

"Yes," said Tuppence, but there was a lack of assurance in her voice.

A silence settled down over the party. Little by little the magic of the night began to gain a hold on them. There were sudden creaks in the furniture, imperceptible rustlings in the curtains. Suddenly Tuppence sprang up with a cry.

"I can't help it. I know Mr. Brown's somewhere in the flat! I can *feel* him."

"Sure, Tuppence, how could he be? This door's open into the hall. No one could have come in by the front door without our seeing and hearing him."

"I can't help it. I *feel* he's here!"

She looked appealingly at Sir James, who replied gravely:

"With due deference to your feelings, Miss Tuppence (and mine as well for that matter), I do not see how it is humanly possible for anyone to be in the flat without our knowledge."

The girl was a little comforted by his words.

"Sitting up at night is always rather jumpy," she confessed.

"Yes," said Sir James. "We are in the condition of people holding a séance. Perhaps if a medium were present we might get some marvellous results."

"Do you believe in spiritualism?" asked Tuppence, opening her eyes wide.

The lawyer shrugged his shoulders.

"There is some truth in it, without a doubt. But most of the testimony would not pass muster in the witness-box."

The hours drew on. With the first faint glimmerings of dawn, Sir James drew aside the curtains. They beheld, what few Londoners see, the slow rising of the sun over the sleeping city. Somehow, with the coming of the light, the dreads and fancies of the past night seemed absurd. Tuppence's spirits revived to the normal.

"Hooray!" she said. "It's going to be a gorgeous day. And we shall find Tommy. And Jane Finn. And everything will be lovely. I shall ask Mr. Carter if I can't be made a Dame!"

At seven o'clock Tuppence volunteered to go and make some tea. She returned with a tray, containing the teapot and four cups.

"Who's the other cup for?" inquired Julius.

"The prisoner, of course. I suppose we might call her that?"

"Taking her tea seems a kind of anti-climax to last night," said Julius thoughtfully.

"Yes, it does," admitted Tuppence. "But, anyway, here goes. Perhaps you'd both come, too, in case she springs on me, or anything. You see, we don't know what mood she'll wake up in."

Sir James and Julius accompanied her to the door.

"Where's the key? Oh, of course, I've got it myself."

She put it in the lock, and turned it, then paused.

"Supposing, after all, she's escaped?" she murmured in a whisper.

"Plumb impossible," replied Julius reassuringly.

But Sir James said nothing.

Tuppence drew a long breath and entered. She heaved a sigh of relief as she saw that Mrs. Vandemeyer was lying on the bed.

"Good morning," she remarked cheerfully. "I've brought you some tea."

Mrs. Vandemeyer did not reply. Tuppence put down the cup on the table by the bed and went across to draw up the blinds. When she turned, Mrs. Vandemeyer still lay without a movement. With a sudden fear clutching at her heart, Tuppence ran to the bed. The hand she lifted was cold as ice.

. . . Mrs. Vandemeyer would never speak now. . . .

Her cry brought the others. A very few minutes sufficed. Mrs. Vandemeyer was dead—must have been dead some hours. She had evidently died in her sleep.

"If that isn't the cruellest luck," cried Julius in despair.

The lawyer was calmer, but there was a curious gleam in his eyes.

"If it is luck," he replied.

"You don't think—but, say, that's plumb impossible—no one could have got in."

"No," admitted the lawyer. "I don't see how they could. And yet—she is on the point of betraying Mr. Brown, and—she dies. Is it only chance?"

"But how—"

"Yes, *how*! That is what we must find out." He stood there silently, gently stroking his chin. "We must find out," he said quietly, and Tuppence felt that if she was Mr. Brown she would not like the tone of those simple words.

Julius's glance went to the window.

"The window's open," he remarked. "Do you think—"

Tuppence shook her head.

"The balcony only goes along as far as the boudoir. We were there."

"He might have slipped out—" suggested Julius.

But Sir James interrupted him.

"Mr. Brown's methods are not so crude. In the meantime we must send for a doctor, but before we do so, is there anything in this room that might be of value to us?"

Hastily, the three searched. A charred mass in the grate indicated that Mrs. Vandemeyer had been burning papers on the eve of her flight. Nothing of importance remained, though they searched the other rooms as well.

"There's that," said Tuppence suddenly, pointing to a small, old-fashioned safe let into the wall. "It's for jewellery, I believe, but there might be something else in it."

The key was in the lock, and Julius swung open the door, and searched inside. He was some time over the task.

"Well," said Tuppence impatiently.

There was a pause before Julius answered, then he withdrew his head and shut to the door.

"Nothing," he said.

In five minutes a brisk young doctor arrived, hastily summoned. He was deferential to Sir James, whom he recognized.

"Heart failure, or possibly an overdose of some sleeping draught." He sniffed. "Rather an odour of chloral in the air."

Tuppence remembered the glass she had upset. A new thought drove her to the washstand. She found the little bottle from which Mrs. Vandemeyer had poured a few drops.

It had been three parts full. Now—*it was empty.*

XIV

A CONSULTATION

Nothing was more surprising and bewildering to Tuppence than the ease and simplicity with which everything was arranged, owing to Sir James's skillful handling. The doctor accepted quite readily the theory that Mrs. Vandemeyer had accidentally taken an overdose of chloral. He doubted whether an inquest would be necessary. If so, he would let Sir James know. He understood that Mrs. Vandemeyer was on the eve of departure for abroad, and that the servants had already left. Sir James and his young friends had been paying a call upon her, when she was suddenly stricken down and they had spent the night in the flat, not liking to leave her alone. Did they know of any relatives? They did not, but Sir James referred him to Mrs. Vandemeyer's solicitor.

Shortly afterwards a nurse arrived to take charge, and the other left the ill-omened building.

"And what now?" asked Julius, with a gesture of despair. "I guess we're down and out for good."

Sir James stroked his chin thoughtfully.

"No," he said quietly. "There is still the chance that Dr. Hall may be able to tell us something."

"Gee! I'd forgotten him."

"The chance is slight, but it must not be neglected. I think I told you that he is staying at the Métropole. I should suggest that we call upon him there as soon as possible. Shall we say after a bath and breakfast?"

It was arranged that Tuppence and Julius should return to the Ritz, and call for Sir James in the car. This programme was faithfully carried out, and a little after eleven they drew up before the Métropole. They asked for Dr. Hall, and a page-boy went in search of him. In a few minutes the little doctor came hurrying towards them.

"Can you spare us a few minutes, Dr. Hall?" said Sir James pleasantly. "Let me introduce you to Miss Cowley. Mr. Hersheimmer, I think, you already know."

A quizzical gleam came into the doctor's eye as he shook hands with Julius.

"Ah, yes, my young friend of the tree episode! Ankle all right, eh?"

"I guess it's cured owing to your skillful treatment, doc."

"And the heart trouble? Ha Ha!"

"Still searching," said Julius briefly.

"To come to the point, can we have a word with you in private?" asked Sir James.

"Certainly. I think there is a room here where we shall be quite undisturbed."

He led the way, and the others followed him. They sat down, and the doctor looked inquiringly at Sir James.

"Dr. Hall, I am very anxious to find a certain young lady for the purpose of obtaining a statement from her. I have reason to believe that she has been at one time or another in your establishment at Bournemouth. I hope I am transgressing no professional etiquette in questioning you on the subject?"

"I suppose it is a matter of testimony?"

Sir James hesitated a moment, then he replied:

"Yes."

"I shall be pleased to give you any information in my

power. What is the young lady's name? Mr. Hersheimmer asked me, I remember——" He half turned to Julius.

"The name," said Sir James bluntly, "is really immaterial. She would be almost certainly sent to you under an assumed one. But I should like to know if you are acquainted with a Mrs. Vandemeyer?"

"Mrs. Vandemeyer, of 20 South Audley Mansions? I know her slightly."

"You are not aware of what has happened?"

"What do you mean?"

"You do not know that Mrs. Vandemeyer is dead?"

"Dear, dear, I had no idea of it! When did it happen?"

"She took an overdose of chloral last night."

"Purposely?"

"Accidentally, it is believed. I should not like to say myself. Anyway, she was found dead this morning."

"Very sad. A singularly handsome woman. I presume she was a friend of yours, since you are acquainted with all these details."

"I am acquainted with the details because—well, it was I who found her dead."

"Indeed," said the doctor, starting.

"Yes," said Sir James, and stroked his chin reflectively.

"This is very sad news, but you will excuse me if I say that I do not see how it bears on the subject of your inquiry?"

"It bears on it in this way, is it not a fact that Mrs. Vandemeyer committed a young relative of hers to your charge?"

Julius leaned forward eagerly.

"That is the case," said the doctor quietly.

"Under the name of——?"

"Janet Vandemeyer. I understood her to be a niece of Mrs. Vandemeyer's."

"And she came to you?"

"As far as I can remember in June or July of 1915."

"Was she a mental case?"

"She is perfectly sane, if that is what you mean. I understood from Mrs. Vandemeyer that the girl had been with her on the *Lusitania* when that ill-fated ship was sunk, and had suffered a severe shock in consequence."

"We're on the right track, I think?" Sir James looked round.

"As I said before, I'm a mutt!" returned Julius.

The doctor looked at them all curiously.

"You spoke of wanting a statement from her," he said. "Supposing she is not able to give one?"

"What? You have just said that she is perfectly sane."

"So she is. Nevertheless, if you want a statement from her concerning any events prior to May 7, 1915, she will not be able to give it to you."

They looked at the little man, stupefied. He nodded cheerfully.

"It's a pity," he said. "A great pity, especially as I gather, Sir James, that the matter is important. But there it is, she can tell you nothing."

"But why, man? Darn it all, why?"

The little man shifted his benevolent glance to the excited young American.

"Because Janet Vandemeyer is suffering from a complete loss of memory."

"*What?*"

"Quite so. An interesting case, a *very* interesting case. Not so uncommon, really, as you would think. There are several very well known parallels. It's the first case of the kind that I've had under my own personal observation, and I must admit that I've found it of absorbing interest." There was something rather ghoulish in the little man's satisfaction.

"And she remembers nothing," said Sir James slowly.

"Nothing prior to May 7, 1915. After that date her memory is as good as yours or mine."

"Then the first thing she remembers?"

"Is landing with the survivors. Everything before that is a blank. She did not know her own name, or where she had come from, or where she was. She couldn't even speak her own tongue."

"But surely all this is most unusual?" put in Julius.

"No, my dear sir. Quite normal under the circumstances. Severe shock to the nervous system. Loss of memory proceeds nearly always on the same lines. I suggested a specialist, of course. There's a very good man in Paris—makes a study of these cases—but Mrs. Vandemeyer opposed the idea of publicity that might result from such a course."

"I can imagine she would," said Sir James grimly.

"I fell in with her views. There *is* a certain notoriety given to these cases. And the girl was very young—nineteen, I believe. It seemed a pity that her infirmity should be talked about—might damage her prospects. Besides, there is no special treatment to pursue in such cases. It is really a matter of waiting."

"Waiting?"

"Yes, sooner or later, the memory will return—as suddenly as it went. But in all probability the girl will have entirely forgotten the intervening period, and will take up life where she left off—at the sinking of the *Lusitania*."

"And when do you expect this to happen?"

The doctor shrugged his shoulders.

"Ah, that I cannot say. Sometimes it is a matter of months, sometimes it has been known to be as long as twenty years! Sometimes another shock does the trick. One restores what the other took away."

"Another shock, eh?" said Julius thoughtfully.

"Exactly. There was a case in Colorado——" The little man's voice trailed on, voluble, mildly enthusiastic.

Julius did not seem to be listening. He had relapsed into his own thoughts and was frowning. Suddenly he came out of his brown study, and hit the table such a resounding bang with his fist that every one jumped, the doctor most of all.

"I've got it! I guess, doc, I'd like your medical opinion on the plan I'm about to outline. Say Jane was to cross the herring pond again, and the same thing was to happen. The submarine, one sinking ship, every one to take to the boats—and so on. Wouldn't that do the trick? Wouldn't it give a mighty big bump to her subconscious self, or whatever the jargon is, and start it functioning again right away?"

"A very interesting speculation, Mr. Hersheimmer. In my own opinion, it would be successful. It is unfortunate that there is no chance of the conditions repeating themselves as you suggest."

"Not by nature, perhaps, doc. But I'm talking about art."

"Art?"

"Why, yes. What's the difficulty? Hire a liner——"

"A liner!" murmured Dr. Hall faintly.

"Hire some passengers, hire a submarine—that's the only difficulty, I guess. Governments are apt to be a bit hidebound over their engines of war. They won't sell to the first-comer. Still, I guess that can be got over. Ever heard of the word 'graft,' sir? Well, graft gets there every time! I reckon that we shan't really need to fire a torpedo. If every one hustles round and screams loud enough that the ship is sinking, it ought to be enough for an innocent young girl like Jane. By the time she's got a life-belt on her, and is being hustled into a boat, with a well-drilled lot of artistes doing the hysterical stunt on deck, why—she ought to be right back again where she was in May 1915. How's that for the bare outline?"

Dr. Hall looked at Julius. Everything that he was for the moment incapable of saying was eloquent in that look.

"No," said Julius, in answer to it, "I'm not crazy. The thing's perfectly possible. It's done every day in the States for the movies. Haven't you seen trains in collision on the screen? What's the difference between buying up a train and buying up a liner? Get the properties and you can go right ahead!"

Dr. Hall found his voice.

"But the expense, my dear sir." His voice rose. "The expense! It will be *colossal!*"

"Money doesn't worry me any," explained Julius simply.

Dr. Hall turned an appealing face to Sir James, who smiled slightly.

"Mr. Hersheimmer is very well off—very well off indeed."

The doctor's glance came back to Julius with a new and subtle quality in it. This was no longer an eccentric young fellow with a habit of falling off trees. The doctor's eyes held the deference accorded to a really rich man.

"Very remarkable plan. Very remarkable," he murmured. "The movies—of course! Your American word for the kinema. Very interesting. I fear we are perhaps a little behind the times over here in our methods. And you really mean to carry out this remarkable plan of yours."

"You bet your bottom dollar I do."

The doctor believed him—which was a tribute to his nationality. If an Englishman had suggested such a thing, he would have had grave doubts as to his sanity.

"I cannot guarantee a cure," he pointed out. "Perhaps I ought to make that quite clear."

"Sure, that's all right," said Julius. "You just trot out Jane, and leave the rest to me."

"Jane?"

"Miss Janet Vandemeyer, then. Can we get on the long distance to your place right away, and ask them to send her up; or shall I run down and fetch her in my car?"

The doctor stared.

"I beg your pardon, Mr. Hersheimmer. I thought you understood."

"Understood what?"

"That Miss Vandemeyer is no longer under my care."

XV

TUPPENCE RECEIVES A PROPOSAL

Julius sprang up.

"What?"

"I thought you were aware of that."

"When did she leave?"

"Let me see. To-day is Monday, is it not? It must have been last Wednesday—why, surely—yes, it was the same evening that you—er—fell out of my tree."

"That evening? Before, or after?"

"Let me see—oh yes, afterwards. A very urgent message arrived from Mrs. Vandemeyer. The young lady and the nurse who was in charge of her left by the night train."

Julius sank back again into his chair.

"Nurse Edith—left with a patient—I remember," he muttered. "My God, to have been so near!"

Dr. Hall looked bewildered.

"I don't understand. Is the young lady not with her aunt, after all?"

Tuppence shook her head. She was about to speak when a warning glance from Sir James made her hold her tongue. The lawyer rose.

"I'm much obliged to you, Hall. We're very grateful for all you've told us. I'm afraid we're now in the position of having to track Miss Vandemeyer anew. What about the nurse who accompanied her; I suppose you don't know where she is?"

The doctor shook his head.

"We've not heard from her, as it happens. I understood she was to remain with Miss Vandemeyer for a while. But what can have happened? Surely the girl has not been kidnapped."

"That remains to be seen," said Sir James gravely.

The other hesitated.

"You do not think I ought to go to the police?"

"No, no. In all probability the young lady is with other relations."

The doctor was not completely satisfied, but he saw that Sir James was determined to say no more, and realized that to try and extract more information from the famous K.C. would be mere waste of labour. Accordingly, he wished them good-bye, and they left the hotel. For a few minutes they stood by the car talking.

"How maddening," cried Tuppence. "To think that Julius must have been actually under the same roof with her for a few hours."

"I was a darned idiot," muttered Julius gloomily.

"You couldn't know," Tuppence consoled him. "Could he?" She appealed to Sir James.

"I should advise you not to worry," said the latter kindly. "No use crying over spilt milk, you know."

"The great thing is what to do next," added Tuppence the practical.

Sir James shrugged his shoulders.

"You might advertise for the nurse who accompanied the girl. That is the only course I can suggest, and I must confess I do not hope for much result. Otherwise there is nothing to be done."

"Nothing?" said Tuppence blankly. "And—Tommy?"

"We must hope for the best," said Sir James. "Oh yes, we must go on hoping."

But over her downcast head his eyes met Julius's, and almost imperceptibly he shook his head. Julius understood.

The lawyer considered the case hopeless. The young American's face grew grave. Sir James took Tuppence's hand.

"You must let me know if anything further comes to light. Letters will always be forwarded."

Tuppence stared at him blankly.

"You are going away?"

"I told you. Don't you remember? To Scotland."

"Yes, but I thought——" The girl hesitated.

Sir James shrugged his shoulders.

"My dear young lady, I can do nothing more, I fear. Our clues have all ended in thin air. You can take my word for it that there nothing more to be done. If anything should arise, I shall be glad to advise you in any way I can."

His words gave Tuppence an extraordinarily desolate feeling.

"I suppose you're right," she said. "Anyway, thank you very much for trying to help us. Good-bye."

Julius was bending over the car. A momentary pity came into Sir James's keen eyes, as he gazed into the girl's downcast face.

"Don't be too disconsolate, Miss Tuppence," he said in a low voice. "Remember, holiday-time isn't always all playtime. One sometimes manages to put in some work as well."

Something in his tone made Tuppence glance up sharply. He shook his head with a smile.

"No, I shan't say any more. Great mistake to say too much. Remember that. Never tell all you know—not even to the person you know best. Understand? Good-bye."

He strode away. Tuppence stared after him. She was beginning to understand Sir James's methods. Once before he had thrown her a hint in the same careless fashion. Was this a hint? What exactly lay behind those last brief words? Did he mean that, after all, he had not abandoned the case; that, secretly, he would be working on it still while——

Her meditations were interrupted by Julius, who abjured her to "get right in."

"You're looking kind of thoughtful," he remarked as they started off. "Did the old guy say anything more?"

Tuppence opened her mouth impulsively, and then shut it again. Sir James's words sounded in her ears: "Never tell all you know—not even to the person you know best." And like a flash there came into her mind another memory. Julius before the safe in the flat, her own question and the pause before his reply, "Nothing." Was there really nothing? Or had he found something he wished to keep to himself? If he could make a reservation, so could she.

"Nothing particular," she replied.

She felt rather than saw Julius throw a sideways glance at her.

"Say, shall we go for a spin in the park?"

"If you like."

For a while they ran on under the trees in silence. It was a beautiful day. The keen rush through the air brought a new exhilaration to Tuppence.

"Say, Miss Tuppence, do you think I'm ever going to find Jane?"

Julius spoke in a discouraged voice. The mood was so alien to him that Tuppence turned and stared at him in surprise. He nodded.

"That's so. I'm getting down and out over the business. Sir James to-day hadn't got any hope at all, I could see that. I don't like him—we don't gee together somehow—but he's pretty cute, and I guess he wouldn't quit if there was any chance of success—now, would he?"

Tuppence felt rather uncomfortable, but clinging to her belief that Julius also had withheld something from her, she remained firm.

"He suggested advertising for the nurse," she reminded him.

"Yes, with a 'forlorn hope' flavour to his voice! No—I'm about fed up. I've half a mind to go back to the States right away."

"Oh no!" cried Tuppence. "We've got to find Tommy."

"I sure forgot Beresford," said Julius contritely. "That's so. We must find him. But after—well, I've been day-dreaming ever since I started on this trip—and these dreams are rotten poor business. I'm quit of them. Say, Miss Tuppence, there's something I'd like to ask you."

"Yes?"

"You and Beresford. What about it?"

"I don't understand you," replied Tuppence with dignity, adding rather inconsequently: "And, anyway, you're wrong!"

"Not got a sort of kindly feeling for one another?"

"Certainly not," said Tuppence with warmth. "Tommy and I are friends—nothing more."

"I guess every pair of lovers has said that sometime or another," observed Julius.

"Nonsense!" snapped Tuppence. "Do I look the sort of girl that's always falling in love with every man she meets?"

"You do not. You look the sort of girl that's mighty often getting fallen in love with!"

"Oh!" said Tuppence, rather taken aback. "That's a compliment, I suppose?"

"Sure. Now let's get down to this. Supposing we never find Beresford and—and——"

"All right—say it! I can face facts. Supposing he's—dead! Well?"

"And all this business fiddles out. What are you going to do?"

"I don't know," said Tuppence forlornly.

"You'll be darned lonesome, you poor kid."

"I shall be all right," snapped Tuppence with her usual resentment of any kind of pity.

"What about marriage?" inquired Julius. "Got any views on the subject?"

"I intend to marry, of course," replied Tuppence. "That is, if"—she paused, knew a momentary longing to draw back, and then stuck to her guns bravely—"I can find some one rich enough to make it worth my while. That's frank, isn't it? I dare say you despise me for it."

"I never despise business instinct," said Julius. "What particular figure have you in mind?"

"Figure?" asked Tuppence, puzzled. "Do you mean tall or short?"

"No. Sum—income."

"Oh, I—I haven't quite worked that out."

"What about me?"

"You?"

"Sure thing."

"Oh, I couldn't!"

"Why not?"

"I tell you I couldn't."

"Again, why not?"

"It would seem so unfair."

"I don't see anything unfair about it. I call your bluff, that's all. I admire you immensely, Miss Tuppence, more than any girl I've ever met. You're so darned plucky. I'd just love to give you a real, rattling good time. Say the word, and we'll run round right away to some high-class jeweller, and fix up the ring business."

"I can't," gasped Tuppence.

"Because of Beresford?"

"No, no, *no!*"

"Well then?"

Tuppence merely continued to shake her head violently.

"You can't reasonably expect more dollars than I've got."

"Oh, it isn't that," gasped Tuppence with an almost hysterical laugh. "But thanking you very much, and all that, I think I'd better say no."

"I'd be obliged if you'd do me the favour to think it over until to-morrow."

"It's no use."

"Still, I guess we'll leave it like that."

"Very well," said Tuppence meekly.

Neither of them spoke again until they reached the Ritz.

Tuppence went upstairs to her room. She felt morally battered to the ground after her conflict with Julius's vigorous personality. Sitting down in front of the glass, she stared at her own reflection for some minutes.

"Fool," murmured Tuppence at length, making a grimace. "Little fool. Everything you want—everything you've ever hoped for, and you go and bleat out 'no' like an idiotic little sheep. It's your one chance. Why don't you take it? Grab it? Snatch at it? What more do you want?"

As if in answer to her own question, her eyes fell on a small snapshot of Tommy that stood on her dressing-table in a shabby frame. For a moment she struggled for self-control, and then abandoning all pretence, she held it to her lips and burst into a fit of sobbing.

"Oh, Tommy, Tommy," she cried, "I do love you so—and I may never see you again. . . ."

At the end of five minutes Tuppence sat up, blew her nose, and pushed back her hair.

"That's that," she observed sternly. "Let's look facts in the face. I seem to have fallen in love—with an idiot of a boy who probably doesn't care two straws about me." Here she paused. "Anyway," she resumed, as though arguing with an unseen opponent, "I don't *know* that he does. He'd never have dared to say so. I've always jumped on sentiment—and here I am being more sentimental than anybody. What idiots girls are! I've always thought so. I suppose I shall sleep with his photograph under my pillow, and dream about him all night. It's dreadful to feel you've been false to your principles."

Tuppence shook her head sadly, as she reviewed her backsliding.

"I don't know what to say to Julius, I'm sure. Oh, what a fool I feel! I'll have to say *something*—he's so American and thorough, he'll insist upon having a reason. I wonder if he did find anything in that safe——"

Tuppence's meditations went off on another tack. She reviewed the events of last night carefully and persistently. Somehow, they seemed bound up with Sir James's enigmatical words. . . .

Suddenly she gave a great start—the colour faded out of her face. Her eyes, fascinated, gazed in front of her, the pupils dilated.

"Impossible," she murmured. "Impossible! I must be going mad even to think of such a thing. . . ."

Monstrous—yet it explained everything. . . .

After a moment's reflection she sat down and wrote a note, weighing each word as she did so. Finally she nodded her head as though satisfied, and slipped it into an envelope which she addressed to Julius. She went down the passage to his sitting-room and knocked at the door. As she had expected, the room was empty. She left the note on the table.

A small page-boy was waiting outside her own door when she returned to it.

"Telegram for you, miss."

Tuppence took it from the salver, and tore it open carelessly. Then she gave a cry. The telegram was from Tommy!

XVI

FURTHER ADVENTURES OF TOMMY

From a darkness punctuated with throbbing stabs of fire, Tommy dragged his senses slowly back to life. When he at last opened his eyes, he was conscious of nothing but an excruciating pain through his temples. He was vaguely aware of unfamiliar surroundings. Where was he? What had happened? He blinked feebly. This was not his bedroom at the Ritz. And what the devil was the matter with his head?

"Damn!" said Tommy, and tried to sit up. He had remembered. He was in that sinister house in Soho. He uttered a groan and fell back. Through his almost-closed lids he reconnoitered carefully.

"He is coming to," remarked a voice very near Tommy's ear. He recognized it at once for that of the bearded and efficient German, and lay artistically inert. He felt that it would be a pity to come round too soon; and until the pain in his head became a little less acute, he felt quite incapable of collecting his wits. Painfully he tried to puzzle out what had happened. Obviously somebody must have crept up behind him as he listened and struck him down with a blow on the head. They knew him now for a spy, and would in all probability give him short shrift. Undoubtedly he was in a tight place. Nobody knew where he was, therefore he need expect no outside assistance, and must depend solely on his own wits.

"Well, here goes," murmured Tommy to himself, and repeated his former remark.

"Damn!" he observed, and this time succeeded in sitting up.

In a minute the German stepped forward and placed a glass to his lips, with the brief command "Drink." Tommy obeyed. The potency of the draught made him choke, but it cleared his brain in a marvellous manner.

He was lying on a couch in the room in which the meeting had been held. On one side of him was the German, on the other the villainous-faced doorkeeper who had let him in. The others were grouped together at a little distance away. But Tommy missed one face. The man known as Number One was no longer of the company.

"Feel better?" asked the German, as he removed the empty glass.

"Yes, thanks," returned Tommy cheerfully.

"Ah, my young friend, it is lucky for you your skull is so thick. The good Conrad struck hard." He indicated the evil-faced doorkeeper by a nod. The man grinned.

Tommy twisted his head round with an effort.

"Oh," he said, "so you're Conrad, are you? It strikes me the thickness of my skull was lucky for you too. When I look at you I feel it's almost a pity I've enabled you to cheat the hangman."

The man snarled, and the bearded man said quietly:

"He would have run no risk of that."

"Just as you like," replied Tommy. "I know it's the fashion to run down the police. I rather believe in them myself."

His manner was nonchalant to the last degree. Tommy Beresford was one of those young Englishmen not distinguished by any special intellectual ability, but who are emphatically at their best in what is known as a "tight place." Their natural diffidence and caution fall from them then like a glove. Tommy realized perfectly that in his own wits lay the only chance of escape, and behind his casual manner he was racking his brains furiously.

The cold accents of the German took up the conversation:

"Have you anything to say before you are put to death as a spy?"

"Simply lots of things," replied Tommy with the same urbanity as before.

"Do you deny that you were listening at the door?"

"I do not. I must really apologize—but your conversation was so interesting that it overcame my scruples."

"How did you get in?"

"Dear old Conrad here." Tommy smiled deprecatingly at him. "I hesitate to suggest pensioning off a faithful servant, but you really ought to have a better watchdog."

Conrad snarled impotently, and said sullenly, as the man with the beard swung round upon him:

"He gave the word. How was I to know?"

"Yes," Tommy chimed in. "How was he to know? Don't blame the poor fellow. His hasty action has given me the pleasure of seeing you all face to face."

He fancied that his words caused some discomposure among the group, but the watchful German stilled it with a wave of his hand.

"Dead men tell no tales," he said evenly.

"Ah," said Tommy, "but I'm not dead yet!"

"You soon will be, my young friend," said the German.

An assenting murmur came from the others.

Tommy's heart beat faster, but his casual pleasantness did not waver.

"I think not," he said firmly. "I should have a great objection to dying."

He had got them puzzled, he saw that by the look on his captor's face.

"Can you give us any reason why we should not put you to death?" asked the German.

"Several," replied Tommy. "Look here, you've been asking me a lot of questions. Let me ask you one for a change. Why didn't you kill me off at once before I regained consciousness?"

The German hesitated, and Tommy seized his advantage.

"Because you didn't know how much I knew—and where I obtained that knowledge. If you kill me now, you never will know."

But here the emotions of Boris became too much for him. He stepped forward waving his arms.

"You hell-hound of a spy," he screamed. "We will give you short shrift. Kill him! Kill him!"

There was a roar of applause.

"You hear?" said the German, his eyes on Tommy. "What have you to say to that?"

"Say?" Tommy shrugged his shoulders. "Pack of fools. Let them ask themselves a few questions. How did I get into this place? Remember what dear old Conrad said—*with your own password*, wasn't it? How did I get hold of that? You don't suppose I came up those steps haphazard and said the first thing that came into my head?"

Tommy was pleased with the concluding words of this speech. His only regret was that Tuppence was not present to appreciate its full flavour.

"That is true," said the working man suddenly. "Comrades, we have been betrayed!"

An ugly murmur arose. Tommy smiled at them encouragingly.

"That's better. How can you hope to make a success of any job if you don't use your brains?"

"You will tell us who has betrayed us," said the German. "But that shall not save you—oh, no! You shall tell us all that you know. Boris, here, knows pretty ways of making people speak!"

"Bah!" said Tommy scornfully, fighting down a singularly unpleasant feeling in the pit of his stomach. "You will neither torture me nor kill me."

"And why not?" asked Boris.

"Because you'd kill the goose that lays the golden eggs," replied Tommy quietly.

There was a momentary pause. It seemed as though Tommy's persistent assurance was at last conquering. They were no longer completely sure of themselves. The man in the shabby clothes stared at Tommy searchingly.

"He's bluffing you, Boris," he said quietly.

Tommy hated him. Had the man seen through him?

The German, with an effort, turned roughly to Tommy.

"What do you mean?"

"What do you think I mean?" parried Tommy, searching desperately in his own mind.

Suddenly Boris stepped forward, and shook his fist in Tommy's face.

"Speak, you swine of an Englishman—speak!"

"Don't get so excited, my good fellow," said Tommy calmly. "That's the worst of you foreigners. You can't keep calm. Now, I ask you, do I look as though I thought there were the least chance of your killing me?"

He looked confidently round, and was glad they could not hear the persistent beating of his heart which gave the lie to his words.

"No," admitted Boris at last sullenly, "you do not."

"Thank God, he's not a mind reader," thought Tommy. Aloud he pursued his advantage:

"And why am I so confident? Because I know something that puts me in a position to propose a bargain."

"A bargain?" The bearded man took him up sharply.

"Yes—a bargain. My life and liberty against——" He paused.

"Against what?"

The group pressed forward. You could have heard a pin drop.

Slowly Tommy spoke.

"The papers that Danvers brought over from America in the *Lusitania.*"

The effect of his words was electrical. Every one was on his feet. The German waved them back. He leaned over Tommy, his face purple with excitement.

"*Himmel!* You have got them, then?"

With magnificent calm Tommy shook his head.

"You know where they are?" persisted the German.

Again Tommy shook his head. "Not in the least."

"Then—then——" Angry and baffled, the words failed him.

Tommy looked round. He saw anger and bewilderment on every face, but his calm assurance had done its work—no one doubted but that something lay behind his words.

"I don't know where the papers are—but I believe that I can find them. I have a theory——"

"Pah!"

Tommy raised his hand, and silenced the clamours of disgust.

"I call it a theory—but I'm pretty sure of my facts—facts that are known to no one but myself. In any case what do you lose? If I can produce the papers—you give me my life and liberty in exchange. Is it a bargain?"

"And if we refuse?" said the German quietly.

Tommy lay back on the couch.

"The 29th," he said thoughtfully, "is less than a fortnight ahead——"

For a moment the German hesitated. Then he made a sign to Conrad.

"Take him into the other room."

For five minutes, Tommy sat on the bed in the dingy room next door. His heart was beating violently. He had risked all on this throw. How would they decide? And all the while that this agonized questioning went on within him, he talked flippantly to Conrad, enraging the cross-grained doorkeeper to the point of homicidal mania.

At last the door opened, and the German called imperiously to Conrad to return.

"Let's hope the judge hasn't put his black cap on," remarked Tommy frivolously. "That's right, Conrad, march me in. The prisoner is at the bar, gentlemen."

The German was seated once more behind the table. He motioned to Tommy to sit down opposite to him.

"We accept," he said harshly, "on terms. The papers must be delivered to us before you go free."

"Idiot!" said Tommy amiably. "How do you think I can look for them if you keep me tied by the leg here?"

"What do you expect, then?"

"I must have liberty to go about the business in my own way."

The German laughed.

"Do you think we are little children to let you walk out of here leaving us a pretty story full of promises?"

"No," said Tommy thoughtfully. "Though infinitely simpler for me, I did not really think you would agree to that plan. Very well, we must arrange a compromise. How would it be if you attached little Conrad here to my person. He's a faithful fellow, and very ready with the fist."

"We prefer," said the German coldly, "that you should remain here. One of our number will carry out your instructions minutely. If the operations are complicated, he will return to you with a report and you can instruct him further."

"You're tying my hands," complained Tommy. "It's a very delicate affair, and the other fellow will muff it up as likely as not, and then where shall I be? I don't believe one of you has got an ounce of tact."

The German rapped the table.

"Those are our terms. Otherwise, death!"

Tommy leaned back wearily.

"I like your style. Curt, but attractive. So be it, then. But one thing is essential, I must see the girl."

"What girl?"

"Jane Finn, of course."

The other looked at him curiously for some minutes, then he said slowly, and as though choosing his words with care:

"Do you not know that she can tell you nothing?"

Tommy's heart beat a little faster. Would he succeed in coming face to face with the girl he was seeking?

"I shall not ask her to tell me anything," he said quietly. "Not in so many words, that is."

"Then why see her?"

Tommy paused.

"To watch her face when I ask her one question," he replied at last.

Again there was a look in the German's eyes that Tommy did not quite understand.

"She will not be able to answer your question."

"That does not matter. I shall have seen her face when I ask it."

"And you think that will tell you anything?" He gave a short disagreeable laugh. More than ever, Tommy felt that there was a factor somewhere that he did not understand. The German looked at him searchingly. "I wonder whether, after all, you know as much as we think?" he said softly.

Tommy felt his ascendancy less sure than a moment before. His hold had slipped a little. But he was puzzled. What had he said wrong? He spoke out on the impulse of the moment.

"There may be things that you know which I do not. I have not pretended to be aware of all the details of your show. But equally I've got something up my sleeve that *you* don't know about. And that's where I mean to score. Danvers was a damned clever fellow——" He broke off as if he had said too much.

But the German's face had lightened a little.

"Danvers," he murmured. "I see——" He paused a minute, then waved to Conrad. "Take him away. Upstairs—you know."

"Wait a minute," said Tommy. "What about the girl?"

"That may perhaps be arranged."

"It must be."

"We will see about it. Only one person can decide that."

"Who?" asked Tommy. But he knew the answer.

"Mr. Brown——"

"Shall I see him?"

"Perhaps."

"Come," said Conrad harshly.

Tommy rose obediently. Outside the door his gaoler motioned to him to mount the stairs. He himself followed close behind. On the floor above Conrad opened a door and Tommy passed into a small room. Conrad lit a hissing gas burner and went out. Tommy heard the sound of the key being turned in the lock.

He set to work to examine his prison. It was a smaller room than the one downstairs, and there was something peculiarly airless about the atmosphere of it. Then he realized that there was no window. He walked round it. The walls were filthily dirty, as everywhere else. Four pictures hung crookedly on the wall representing scenes from "Faust." Marguerite with her box of jewels, the church scene, Siebel and his flowers, and Faust and Mephistopheles. The latter brought Tommy's mind back to Mr. Brown again. In this sealed and closed chamber, with its close-fitting heavy door, he felt cut off from the world, and the sinister power of the arch-criminal seemed more real. Shout as he would, no one could ever hear him. The place was a living tomb. . . .

With an effort Tommy pulled himself together. He sank on to the bed and gave himself up to reflection. His head ached badly; also, he was hungry. The silence of the place was dispiriting.

"Anyway," said Tommy, trying to cheer himself, "I shall see the chief—the mysterious Mr. Brown, and with a bit of luck in bluffing I shall see the mysterious Jane Finn also. After that——"

After that Tommy was forced to admit the prospect looked dreary.

XVII

ANNETTE

The troubles of the future, however, soon faded before the troubles of the present. And of these, the most immediate and pressing was that of hunger. Tommy had a healthy and vigorous appetite. The steak and chips partaken of for lunch seemed now to belong to another decade. He regretfully recognized the fact that he would not make a success of a hunger strike.

He prowled aimlessly about his prison. Once or twice he discarded dignity, and pounded on the door. But nobody answered the summons.

"Hang it all!" said Tommy indignantly. "They can't mean to starve me to death." A new-born fear passed through his mind that this might, perhaps, be one of those "pretty ways" of making a prisoner speak, which had been attributed to Boris. But on reflection he dismissed the idea.

"It's that sour faced brute Conrad," he decided. "That's a fellow I shall enjoy getting even with one of these days. This is just a bit of spite on his part. I'm certain of it."

Further meditations induced in him the feeling that it would be extremely pleasant to bring something down with a whack on Conrad's egg-shaped head. Tommy stroked his own head tenderly, and gave himself up to the pleasures of imagination. Finally a bright idea flashed across his brain. Why not convert imagination into reality? Conrad was undoubtedly the tenant of the house. The others, with the possible exception of the bearded German, merely used it as a rendezvous. Therefore, why not wait in ambush for Conrad behind the door, and when he entered bring down a chair, or one of the decrepit pictures, smartly on to his head. One would, of course, be careful not to hit too hard. And then—and then, simply walk out! If he met anyone on the way down, well——Tommy brightened at the thought of an encounter with his fists. Such an affair was infinitely more in his line than the verbal encounter of this afternoon. Intoxicated by his plan, Tommy gently unhooked the picture of the Devil and Faust, and settled himself in position. His hopes were high. The plan seemed to him simple but excellent.

Time went on, but Conrad did not appear. Night and day were the same in this prison room, but Tommy's wrist-watch, which enjoyed a certain degree of accuracy, informed him that it was nine o'clock in the evening. Tommy reflected gloomily that if supper did not arrive soon it would be a question of waiting for breakfast. At ten o'clock hope deserted him, and he flung himself on the bed to seek consolation in sleep. In five minutes his woes were forgotten.

The sound of the key turning in the lock awoke him from his slumbers. Not belonging to the type of hero who is famous for awakening in full possession of his faculties, Tommy merely blinked at the ceiling and wondered vaguely where he was. Then he remembered, and looked at his watch. It was eight o'clock.

"It's either early morning tea or breakfast," deduced the young man, "and pray God it's the latter!"

The door swung open. Too late, Tommy remembered his scheme of obliterating the unprepossessing Conrad. A moment later he was glad that he had, for it was not Conrad who entered, but a girl. She carried a tray which she set down on the table.

In the feeble light of the gas burner Tommy blinked at her.

He decided at once that she was one of the most beautiful girls he had ever seen. Her hair was a full rich brown, with sudden glints of gold in it as though there were imprisoned sunbeams struggling in its depths. There was a wild-rose quality about her face. Her eyes, set wide apart, were hazel, a golden hazel that again recalled a memory of sunbeams.

A delirious thought shot through Tommy's mind.

"Are you Jane Finn?" he asked breathlessly.

The girl shook her head wonderingly.

"My name is Annette, monsieur."

She spoke in a soft, broken English.

"Oh!" said Tommy, rather taken aback. *"Française?"* he hazarded.

"Oui, monsieur. Monsieur parle français?"

"Not for any length of time," said Tommy. "What's that? Breakfast?"

The girl nodded. Tommy dropped off the bed and came and inspected the contents of the tray. It consisted of a loaf, some margarine, and a jug of coffee.

"The living is not equal to the Ritz," he observed with a sigh. "But for what we are at last about to receive the Lord has made me truly thankful. Amen."

He drew up a chair, and the girl turned away to the door.

"Wait a sec," cried Tommy. "There are lots of things I want to ask you, Annette. What are you doing in this house? Don't tell me you're Conrad's niece, or daughter, or anything, because I can't believe it."

"I do the *service*, monsieur. I am not related to anybody."

"I see," said Tommy. "You know what I asked you just now. Have you ever heard that name?"

"I have heard people speak of Jane Finn, I think."

"You don't know where she is?"

Annette shook her head.

"She's not in this house, for instance?"

"Oh no, monsieur. I must go now—they will be waiting for me."

She hurried out. The key turned in the lock.

"I wonder who 'they' are," mused Tommy, as he continued to make inroads on the loaf. "With a bit of luck, that girl might help me to get out of here. She doesn't look like one of the gang."

At one o'clock Annette reappeared with another tray, but this time Conrad accompanied her.

"Good morning," said Tommy amiably. "You have *not* used Pear's soap, I see."

Conrad growled threateningly.

"No light repartee, have you, old bean? There, there, we can't always have brains as well as beauty. What have we for lunch? Stew? How did I know? Elementary, my dear Watson—the smell of onions is unmistakable."

"Talk away," grunted the man. "It's little enough time you'll have to talk in, maybe."

The remark was unpleasant in its suggestion, but Tommy ignored it. He sat down at the table.

"Retire, varlet," he said, with a wave of his hand. "Prate not to thy betters."

That evening Tommy sat on the bed, and cogitated deeply. Would Conrad again accompany the girl? If he did not, should he risk trying to make an ally of her? He decided that he must leave no stone unturned. His position was desperate.

At eight o'clock the familiar sound of the key turning made him spring to his feet. The girl was alone.

"Shut the door," he commanded. "I want to speak to you." She obeyed.

"Look here, Annette, I want you to help me get out of this." She shook her head.

"Impossible. There are three of them on the floor below."

"Oh!" Tommy was secretly grateful for the information. "But you would help me if you could?"

"No, monsieur."

"Why not?"

The girl hesitated.

"I think—they are my own people. You have spied upon them. They are quite right to keep you here."

"They're a bad lot, Annette. If you'll help me, I'll take you away from the lot of them. And you'd probably get a good whack of money."

But the girl merely shook her head.

"I dare not, monsieur; I am afraid of them."

She turned away.

"Wouldn't you do anything to help another girl?" cried Tommy. "She's about your age too. Won't you save her from their clutches?"

"You mean Jane Finn?"

"Yes."

"It is her you came here to look for? Yes?"

"That's it."

The girl look at him, then passed her hand across her forehead.

"Jane Finn. Always I hear that name. It is familiar."

Tommy came forward eagerly.

"You must know *something* about her?"

But the girl turned away abruptly.

"I know nothing—only the name." She walked towards the door. Suddenly she uttered a cry. Tommy stared. She had caught sight of the picture he had laid against the wall the night before. For a moment he caught a look of terror in her eyes. As inexplicably it changed to relief. Then abruptly she went out of the room. Tommy could make nothing of it. Did she fancy that he had meant to attack her with it? Surely not. He rehung the picture on the wall thoughtfully.

Three more days went by in dreary inaction. Tommy felt the strain telling on his nerves. He saw no one but Conrad and Annette, and the girl had become dumb. She spoke only in monosyllables. A kind of dark suspicion smouldered in her eyes. Tommy felt that if this solitary confinement went on much longer he would go mad. He gathered from Conrad that they were waiting for orders from "Mr. Brown." Perhaps, thought Tommy, he was abroad or away, and they were obliged to wait for his return.

But the evening of the third day brought a rude awakening.

It was barely seven o'clock when he heard the tramp of footsteps outside in the passage. In another minute the door was flung open. Conrad entered. With him was the evil-looking Number 14. Tommy's heart sank at the sight of them.

"Evenin', guv'nor," said the man with a leer. "Got those ropes, mate?"

The silent Conrad produced a length of fine cord. The next minute Number 14's hands, horribly dexterous, were winding the cord round his limbs, while Conrad held him down.

"What the devil——?" began Tommy.

But the slow, speechless grin of the silent Conrad froze the words on his lips.

Number 14 proceeded deftly with his task. In another minute Tommy was a mere helpless bundle. Then at last Conrad spoke:

"Thought you'd bluffed us, did you? With what you knew, and what you didn't know. Bargained with us! And all the time it was bluff! Bluff! You know less than a kitten. But your number's up now all right, you b——swine."

Tommy lay silent. There was nothing to say. He had failed. Somehow or other the omnipotent Mr. Brown had seen through his pretensions. Suddenly a thought occurred to him.

"A very good speech, Conrad," he said approvingly. "But wherefore the bonds and fetters? Why not let this kind gentleman here cut my throat without delay?"

"Garn," said Number 14 unexpectedly. "Think we're as green as to do you in here, and have the police nosing round? Not 'alf! We've ordered the carriage for your lordship tomorrow mornin', but in the meantime we're not taking any chances, see!"

"Nothing," said Tommy, "could be plainer than your words—unless it was your face."

"Stow it," said Number 14.

"With pleasure," replied Tommy. "You're making a sad mistake—but yours will be the loss."

"You don't kid us that way again," said Number 14. "Talking as though you were still at the blooming Ritz, aren't you?"

Tommy made no reply. He was engaged in wondering how Mr. Brown had discovered his identity. He decided that Tuppence, in the throes of anxiety, had gone to the police, and that his disappearance having been made public the gang had not been slow to put two and two together.

The two men departed and the door slammed. Tommy was left to his meditations. They were not pleasant ones. Already his limbs felt cramped and stiff. He was utterly helpless, and he could see no hope anywhere.

About an hour had passed when he heard the key softly turned, and the door opened. It was Annette. Tommy's heart beat a little faster. He had forgotten the girl. Was it possible that she had come to his help?

Suddenly he heard Conrad's voice:

"Come out of it, Annette. He doesn't want any supper to-night."

"*Oui, oui, je sais bien.* But I must take the other tray. We need the things on it."

"Well, hurry up," growled Conrad.

Without looking at Tommy the girl went over to the table, and picked up the tray. She raised a hand and turned out the light.

"Curse you"—Conrad had come to the door—"why did you do that?"

"I always turn it out. You should have told me. Shall I relight it, Monsieur Conrad?"

"No, come on out of it."

"*Le beau petit monsieur,*" cried Annette, pausing by the bed in the darkness. "You have tied him up well, *bien*? He is like a trussed chicken!" The frank amusement in her tone jarred on the boy; but at that moment, to his amazement, he felt her hand running lightly over his bonds, and something small and cold was pressed into the palm of his hand.

"Come on, Annette."

"*Maise me voilà.*"

The door shut. Tommy heard Conrad say:

"Lock it and give me the key."

The footsteps died away. Tommy lay petrified with amazement. The object Annette had thrust into his hand was a small penknife, the blade open. From the way she had studiously avoided looking at him, and her action with the light, he came to the conclusion that the room was overlooked. There must be a peep-hole somewhere in the walls. Remembering how guarded she had always been in her manner, he saw that he had probably been under observation all the time. Had he said anything to give himself away? Hardly. He had revealed a wish to escape and a desire to find Jane Finn, but nothing that could have given a clue to his own identity. True, his question to Annette had proved that he was personally unacquainted with Jane Finn, but he had never pretended otherwise. The question now was, did Annette really know more? Were her denials intended primarily for the listeners? On that point he could come to no conclusion.

But there was a more vital question that drove out all others. Could he, bound as he was, manage to cut his bonds? He essayed cautiously to rub the open blade up and down on the cord that bound his two wrists together. It was an awkward business, and drew a smothered "Ow" of pain from him as the knife cut into his wrist. But slowly and doggedly he went on sawing to and fro. He cut the flesh badly, but at last he felt the cord slacken. With his hands free, the rest was easy. Five minutes later he stood upright with some difficulty, owing to the cramp in his limbs. His first care was to bind up his bleeding wrist. Then he sat on the edge of the bed to think. Conrad had taken the key of the door, so he could expect little more assistance from Annette. The only outlet from the room was the door, consequently he would perforce have to wait until the two men returned to fetch him. But when they did . . . Tommy smiled! Moving with infinite caution in the dark room, he found and unhooked the famous picture. He felt an economical pleasure that his first plan would not be wasted. There was now nothing to do but to wait. He waited.

The night passed slowly. Tommy lived through an eternity of hours, but at last he heard footsteps. He stood upright, drew a deep breath, and clutched the picture firmly.

The door opened. A faint light streamed in from outside. Conrad went straight towards the gas to light it. Tommy deeply regretted that it was he who had entered first. It would have been pleasant to get even with Conrad. Number 14 followed. As he stepped across the threshold, Tommy brought the picture down with terrific force on his head. Number 14 went down amidst a stupendous crash of broken glass. In a minute Tommy had slipped out and pulled to the door. The key was in the lock. He turned it and withdrew it just as Conrad hurled himself against the door from the inside with a volley of curses.

For a moment Tommy hesitated. There was the sound of some one stirring on the floor below. Then the German's voice came up the stairs.

"*Gott im Himmel!* Conrad, what is it?"

Tommy felt a small hand thrust into his. Beside him stood Annette. She pointed up a rickety ladder that apparently led to some attics.

"Quick—up here!" She dragged him after her up the ladder. In another moment they were standing in a dusty garret littered with lumber. Tommy looked round.

"This won't do. It's a regular trap. There's no way out."

"Hush! Wait." The girl put her finger to her lips. She crept to the top of the ladder and listened.

The banging and beating on the door was terrific. The German and another were trying to force the door in. Annette explained in a whisper:

"They will think you are still inside. They cannot hear what Conrad says. The door is too thick."

"I thought you could hear what went on in the room?"

"There is a peep-hole into the next room. It was clever of you to guess. But they will not think of that—they are only anxious to get in."

"Yes—but look here—"

"Leave it to me." She bent down. To his amazement, Tommy saw that she was fastening the end of a long piece of string to the handle of a big cracked jug. She arranged it carefully, then turned to Tommy.

"Have you the key of the door?"

"Yes."

"Give it to me."

He handed it to her.

"I am going down. Do you think you can go half-way, and then swing yourself down *behind* the ladder, so that they will not see you?"

Tommy nodded.

"There's a big cupboard in the shadow of the landing. Stand behind it. Take the end of this string in your hand. When I've let the others out—*pull!*"

Before he had time to ask her anything more, she had flitted lightly down the ladder and was in the midst of the group with a loud cry:

"*Mon Dieu! Mon Dieu! Qu'est-ce qu'il y a?*"

The German turned on her with an oath.

"Get out of this. Go to your room!"

Very cautiously Tommy swung himself down the back of the ladder. So long as they did not turn round . . . all was well. He crouched behind the cupboard. They were still between him and the stairs.

"Ah!" Annette appeared to stumble over something. She stooped. "*Mon Dieu, voilà la clé!*"

The German snatched it from her. He unlocked the door. Conrad stumbled out, swearing.

"Where is he? Have you got him?"

"We have seen no one," said the German sharply. His face paled. "Who do you mean?"

Conrad gave vent to another oath.

"He's got away."

"Impossible. He would have passed us."

At that moment, with an ecstatic smile Tommy pulled the string. A crash of crockery came from the attic above. In a trice the men were pushing each other up the rickety ladder and had disappeared into the darkness above.

Quick as a flash Tommy leapt from his hiding-place and dashed down the stairs, pulling the girl with him. There was no one in the hall. He fumbled over the bolts and chain. At last they yielded, the door swung open. He turned. Annette had disappeared.

Tommy stood spell-bound. Had she run upstairs again? What madness possessed her! He fumed with impatience, but he stood his ground. He would not go without her.

And suddenly there was an outcry overhead, an exclamation from the German, and then Annette's voice, clear and high:

"*Ma foi*, he has escaped! And quickly! Who would have thought it?"

Tommy still stood rooted to the ground. Was that a command to him to go? He fancied it was.

And then, louder still, the words floated down to him:

"This is a terrible house. I want to go back to Marguerite. To Marguerite. To *Marguerite!*"

Tommy had run back to the stairs. She wanted him to go and leave her. But why? At all costs he must try and get her away with him. Then his heart sank. Conrad was leaping down the stairs, uttering a savage cry at the sight of him. After him came the others.

Tommy stopped Conrad's rush with a straight blow with his fist. It caught the other on the point of the jaw and he fell like a log. The second man tripped over his body and fell. From higher up the staircase there was a flash, and a bullet grazed Tommy's ear. He realized that it would be good for his health to get out of this house as soon as possible. As regards Annette he could do nothing. He had got even with Conrad, which was one satisfaction. The blow had been a good one.

He leapt for the door, slamming it behind him. The square was deserted. In front of the house was a baker's van. Evidently he was to have been taken out of London in that, and his body found many miles from the house in Soho. The driver jumped to the pavement and tried to bar Tommy's way. Again Tommy's fist shot out, and the driver sprawled on the pavement.

Tommy took to his heels and ran—none too soon. The front door opened and a hail of bullets followed him. Fortunately none of them hit him. He turned the corner of the square.

"There's one thing," he thought to himself, "they can't go on shooting. They'll have the police after them if they do. I wonder they dared to there."

He heard the footsteps of his pursuers behind him, and redoubled his own pace. Once he got out of these by-ways he would be safe. There would be a policeman about somewhere—not that he really wanted to invoke the aid of the police if he could possibly do without it. It meant explanations, and general awkwardness. In another moment he had reason to bless his luck. He stumbled over a prostrate figure, which started up with a yell of alarm and dashed off down the street. Tommy drew back into a doorway. In a minute he had the pleasure of seeing his two pursuers, of whom the German was one, industriously tracking down the red herring!

Tommy sat down quietly on the doorstep and allowed a few moments to elapse while he recovered his breath. Then he strolled gently in the opposite direction. He glanced at his watch. It was a little after half-past five. It was rapidly growing light. At the next corner he passed a policeman. The policeman cast a suspicious eye on him. Tommy felt slightly offended. Then, passing his hand over his face, he laughed. He had not shaved or washed for three days! What a guy he must look.

He betook himself without more ado to a Turkish Bath establishment which he knew to be open all night. He emerged into the busy daylight feeling himself once more, and able to make plans.

First of all, he must have a square meal. He had eaten nothing since midday yesterday. He turned into an A.B.C. shop and ordered eggs and bacon and coffee. Whilst he ate, he read a morning paper propped up in front of him. Suddenly he stiffened. There was a long article on Kramenin, who was described as the "man behind Bolshevism" in Russia, and who had just arrived in London—some thought as an unofficial envoy. His career was sketched lightly, and it was firmly asserted that he, and not the figurehead leaders, had been the author of the Russian Revolution.

In the centre of the page was his portrait.

"So that's who Number 1 is," said Tommy with his mouth full of eggs and bacon. "Not a doubt about it, I must push on."

He paid for his breakfast, and betook himself to Whitehall. There he sent up his name, and the message that it was urgent. A few minutes later he was in the presence of the man who did not here go by the name of "Mr. Carter." There was a frown on his face.

"Look here, you've no business to come asking for me in this way. I thought that was distinctly understood?"

"It was, sir. But I judged it important to lose no time."

And as briefly and succinctly as possible he detailed the experiences of the last few days.

Half-way through, Mr. Carter interrupted him to give a few

cryptic orders through the telephone. All traces of displeasure had now left his face. He nodded energetically when Tommy had finished.

"Quite right. Every moment's of value. Fear we shall be too late anyway. They wouldn't wait. Would clear out at once. Still, they may have left something behind them that will be a clue. You say you've recognized Number 1 to be Kramenin? That's important. We want something against him badly to prevent the Cabinet falling on his neck too freely. What about the others? You say two faces were familiar to you? One's a Labour man, you think? Just look through these photos, and see if you can spot him."

A minute later, Tommy held one up. Mr. Carter exhibited some surprise.

"Ah, Westway! Shouldn't have thought it. Poses as being moderate. As for the other fellow, I think I can give a good guess." He handed another photograph to Tommy, and smiled at the other's exclamation. "I'm right, then. Who is he? Irishman? Prominent Unionist M.P. All a blind, of course. We've suspected it—but couldn't get any proof. Yes, you've done very well, young man. The 29th, you say, is the date. That gives us very little time—very little time indeed."

"But——" Tommy hesitated.

Mr. Carter read his thoughts.

"We can deal with the General Strike menace, I think. It's a toss-up—but we've got a sporting chance! But if that draft treaty turns up—we're done. England will be plunged in anarchy. Ah, what's that? The car? Come on, Beresford, we'll go and have a look at this house of yours."

Two constables were on duty in front of the house in Soho. An inspector reported to Mr. Carter in a low voice. The latter turned to Tommy.

"The birds have flown—as we thought. We might as well go over it."

Going over the deserted house seemed to Tommy to partake of the character of a dream. Everything was just as it had been. The prison room with the crooked pictures, the broken jug in the attic, the meeting room with its long table. But nowhere was there a trace of papers. Everything of that kind had either been destroyed or taken away. And there was no sign of Annette.

"What you tell me about the girl puzzled me," said Mr. Carter. "You believe that she deliberately went back?"

"It would seem so, sir. She ran upstairs while I was getting the door open."

"H'm, she must belong to the gang, then; but, being a woman, didn't feel like standing by to see a personable young man killed. But evidently she's in with them, or she wouldn't have gone back."

"I can't believe she's really one of them, sir. She—seemed so different——"

"Good-looking, I suppose?" said Mr. Carter with a smile that made Tommy flush to the roots of his hair. He admitted Annette's beauty rather shamefacedly.

"By the way," observed Mr. Carter, "have you shown yourself to Miss Tuppence yet? She's been bombarding me with letters about you."

"Tuppence? I was afraid she might get a bit rattled. Did she go to the police?"

Mr. Carter shook his head.

"Then I wonder how they twigged me."

Mr. Carter looked inquiringly at him, and Tommy explained. The other nodded thoughtfully.

"True, that's rather a curious point. Unless the mention of the Ritz was an accidental remark?"

"It might have been, sir. But they must have found out about me suddenly in some way."

"Well," said Mr. Carter, looking round him, "there's nothing more to be done here. What about some lunch with me?"

"Thanks awfully, sir. But I think I'd better get back and rout out Tuppence."

"Of course. Give her my kind regards and tell her not to believe you're killed too readily next time."

Tommy grinned.

"I take a lot of killing, sir."

"So I perceive," said Mr. Carter dryly. "Well, good-bye. Remember you're a marked man now, and take reasonable care of yourself."

"Thank you, sir."

Hailing a taxi briskly Tommy stepped in, and was swiftly borne to the Ritz, dwelling the while on the pleasurable anticipation of startling Tuppence.

"Wonder what she's been up to. Dogging 'Rita' most likely. By the way, I suppose that's who Annette meant by Marguerite. I didn't get it at the time." The thought saddened him a little, for it seemed to prove that Mrs. Vandemeyer and the girl were on intimate terms.

The taxi drew up at the Ritz. Tommy burst into its sacred portals eagerly, but his enthusiasm received a check. He was informed that Miss Cowley had gone out a quarter of an hour ago.

XVIII

THE TELEGRAM

Baffled for the moment, Tommy strolled into the restaurant, and ordered a meal of surpassing excellence. His four days' imprisonment had taught him anew to value good food.

He was in the middle of conveying a particularly choice morsel of Sole à la Jeanette to his mouth, when he caught sight of Julius entering the room. Tommy waved a menu cheerfully, and succeeded in attracting the other's attention. At the sight of Tommy, Julius's eyes seemed as though they would pop out of his head. He strode across, and pumphandled Tommy's hand with what seemed to the latter quite unnecessary vigour.

"Holy snakes!" he ejaculated. "Is it really you?"

"Of course it is. Why shouldn't it be?"

"Why shouldn't it be? Say, man, don't you know you've been given up for dead? I guess we'd have had a solemn requiem for you in another few days."

"Who thought I was dead?" demanded Tommy.

"Tuppence."

"She remembered the proverb about the good dying

young, I suppose. There must be a certain amount of original sin in me to have survived. Where is Tuppence, by the way?"

"Isn't she here?"

"No, the fellows at the office said she'd just gone out."

"Gone shopping, I guess. I dropped her here in the car about an hour ago. But, say, can't you shed that British calm of yours, and get down to it? What on God's earth have you been doing all this time?"

"If you're feeding here," replied Tommy, "order now. It's going to be a long story."

Julius drew up a chair to the opposite side of the table, summoned a hovering waiter, and dictated his wishes. Then he turned to Tommy.

"Fire ahead. I guess you've had some few adventures."

"One or two," replied Tommy modestly, and plunged into his recital.

Julius listened spell-bound. Half the dishes that were placed before him he forgot to eat. At the end he heaved a long sigh.

"Bully for you. Reads like a dime novel!"

"And now for the home front," said Tommy, stretching out his hand for a peach.

"We-el," drawled Julius, "I don't mind admitting we've had some adventures too."

He, in his turn, assumed the rôle of narrator. Beginning with his unsuccessful reconnoitring at Bournemouth, he passed on to his return to London, the buying of the car, the growing anxieties of Tuppence, the call upon Sir James, and the sensational occurrences of the previous night.

"But who killed her?" asked Tommy. "I don't quite understand."

"The doctor kidded himself she took it herself," replied Julius dryly.

"And Sir James? What did he think?"

"Being a legal luminary, he is likewise a human oyster," replied Julius. "I should say he 'reserved judgment.' " He went on to detail the events of the morning.

"Lost her memory, eh?" said Tommy with interest. "By Jove, that explains why they looked at me so queerly when

I spoke of questioning her. Bit of a slip on my part, that! But it wasn't the sort of thing a fellow would be likely to guess."

"They didn't give you any sort of hint as to where Jane was?"

Tommy shook his head regretfully.

"Not a word. I'm a bit of an ass, as you know. I ought to have got more out of them somehow."

"I guess you're lucky to be here at all. That bluff of yours was the goods all right. How you ever came to think of it all so pat beats me to a frazzle!"

"I was in such a funk I had to think of something," said Tommy simply.

There was a moment's pause, and then Tommy reverted to Mrs. Vandemeyer's death.

"There's no doubt it was chloral?"

"I believe not. At least they call it heart failure induced by an overdose, or some such claptrap. It's all right. We don't want to be worried with an inquest. But I guess Tuppence and I and even the highbrow Sir James have all got the same idea."

"Mr. Brown?" hazarded Tommy.

"Sure thing."

Tommy nodded.

"All the same," he said thoughtfully, "Mr. Brown hasn't got wings. I don't see how he got in and out."

"How about some high-class thought transference stunt? Some magnetic influence that irresistibly impelled Mrs. Vandemeyer to commit suicide?"

Tommy looked at him with respect.

"Good, Julius. Distinctly good. Especially the phraseology. But it leaves me cold. I yearn for a real Mr. Brown of flesh and blood. I think the gifted young detectives must get to work, study the entrances and exits, and tap the bumps on their foreheads until the solution of the mystery dawns on them. Let's go round to the scene of the crime. I wish we could get hold of Tuppence. The Ritz would enjoy the spectacle of the glad reunion."

Inquiry at the office revealed the fact that Tuppence had not yet returned.

"All the same, I guess I'll have a look round upstairs," said

Julius. "She might be in my sitting-room." He disappeared.

Suddenly a diminutive boy spoke at Tommy's elbow:

"The young lady—she's gone away by train, I think, sir," he murmured shyly.

"What?" Tommy wheeled round upon him.

The small boy became pinker than before.

"The taxi, sir. I heard her tell the driver Charing Cross and to look sharp."

Tommy stared at him, his eyes opening wide in surprise. Emboldened, the small boy proceeded. "So I thought, having asked for an A.B.C. and a Bradshaw."

Tommy interrupted him:

"When did she ask for an A.B.C. and a Bradshaw?"

"When I took her the telegram, sir."

"A telegram?"

"Yes, sir."

"When was that?"

"About half-past twelve, sir."

"Tell me exactly what happened."

The small boy drew a long breath.

"I took up a telegram to No. 891—the lady was there. She opened it and gave a gasp, and then she said, very jolly like: 'Bring me up a Bradshaw, and an A.B.C., and look sharp, Henry. My name isn't Henry, but—"

"Never mind your name," said Tommy impatiently. "Go on."

"Yes, sir. I brought them, and she told me to wait, and looked up something. And then she looks up at the clock, and 'Hurry up,' she says. 'Tell them to get me a taxi,' and she begins a-shoving on of her hat in front of the glass, and she was down in two ticks, almost as quick as I was, and I seed her going down the steps and into the taxi, and I heard her call out what I told you."

The small boy stopped and replenished his lungs. Tommy continued to stare at him. At that moment Julius rejoined him. He held an open letter in his hand.

"I say, Hersheimmer"—Tommy turned to him—"Tuppence has gone off sleuthing on her own."

"Shucks!"

"Yes, she has. She went off in a taxi to Charing Cross in

the deuce of a hurry after getting a telegram." His eye fell on the letter in Julius's hand. "Oh; she left a note for you. That's all right. Where's she off to?"

Almost unconsciously, he held out his hand for the letter, but Julius folded it up and placed it in his pocket. He seemed a trifle embarrassed.

"I guess this is nothing to do with it. It's about something else—something I asked her that she was to let me know about."

"Oh!" Tommy looked puzzled, and seemed waiting for more.

"See here," said Julius suddenly, "I'd better put you wise. I asked Miss Tuppence to marry me this morning."

"Oh!" said Tommy mechanically. He felt dazed. Julius's words were totally unexpected. For the moment they benumbed his brain.

"I'd like to tell you," continued Julius, "that before I suggested anything of the kind to Miss Tuppence, I made it clear that I didn't want to butt in in any way between her and you——"

Tommy roused himself.

"That's all right," he said quickly. "Tuppence and I have been pals for years. Nothing more." He lit a cigarette with a hand that shook ever so little. "That's quite all right. Tuppence always said that she was looking out for——"

He stopped abruptly, his face crimsoning, but Julius was in no way discomposed.

"Oh, I guess it'll be the dollars that'll do the trick. Miss Tuppence put me wise to that right away. There's no humbug about her. We ought to gee along together very well."

Tommy looked at him curiously for a minute, as though he were about to speak, then changed his mind and said nothing. Tuppence and Julius! Well, why not? Had she not lamented the fact that she knew no rich men? Had she not openly avowed her intention of marrying for money if she ever had the chance? Her meeting with the young American millionaire had given her the chance—and it was unlikely she would be slow to avail herself of it. She was out for money. She had always said so. Why blame her because she had been true to her creed?

Nevertheless, Tommy did blame her. He was filled with a passionate and utterly illogical resentment. It was all very well to *say* things like that—but a *real* girl would never marry for money. Tuppence was utterly cold-blooded and selfish, and he would be delighted if he never saw her again! And it was a rotten world!

Julius's voice broke in on these meditations.

"Yes, we ought to gee along together very well. I've heard that a girl always refuses you once—a sort of convention."

Tommy caught his arm.

"Refuses? Did you say *refuses*?"

"Sure thing. Didn't I tell you that? She just rapped out a 'no' without any kind of reason to it. The eternal feminine, the Huns call it, I've heard. But she'll come round right enough. Likely enough, I hustled her some——"

But Tommy interrupted regardless of decorum.

"What did she say in that note?" he demanded fiercely.

The obliging Julius handed it to him.

"There's no earthly clue in it as to where she's gone," he assured Tommy. "But you might as well see for yourself if you don't believe me."

The note, in Tuppence's well-known schoolboy writing, ran as follows:

DEAR JULIUS,

It's always better to have things in black and white. I don't feel I can be bothered to think of marriage until Tommy is found. Let's leave it till then.

Yours affectionately,
TUPPENCE.

Tommy handed it back, his eyes shining. His feelings had undergone a sharp reaction. He now felt that Tuppence was all that was noble and disinterested. Had she not refused Julius without hesitation? True, the note betokened signs of weakening, but he could excuse that. It read almost like a bribe to Julius to spur him on in his efforts to find Tommy, but he supposed she had not really meant it that way. Darling Tuppence, there was not a girl in the world to touch her!

When he saw her—His thoughts were brought up with a sudden jerk.

"As you say," he remarked, pulling himself together, "there's not a hint here as to what she's up to. Hi—Henry!"

The small boy came obediently. Tommy produced five shillings.

"One thing more. Do you remember what the young lady did with the telegram?"

Henry gasped and spoke.

"She crumpled it up into a ball and threw it into the grate, and made a sort of noise like 'Whoop!' sir."

"Very graphic, Henry," said Tommy. "Here's your five shillings. Come on, Julius. We must find that telegram."

They hurried upstairs. Tuppence had left the key in her door. The room was as she had left it. In the fireplace was a crumpled ball of orange and white. Tommy disentangled it and smoothed out the telegram.

"Come at once, Moat House, Ebury, Yorkshire, great developments—TOMMY."

They looked at each other in stupefaction. Julius spoke first:

"You didn't send it?

"Of course not. What does it mean?"

"I guess it means the worst," said Julius quietly. "They've got her."

"What?"

"Sure thing! They signed your name, and she fell into the trap like a lamb."

"My God! What shall we do?"

"Get busy, and go after her! Right now! There's no time to waste. It's almighty luck that she didn't take the wire with her. If she had we'd probably never have traced her. But we've got to hustle. Where's that Bradshaw?"

The energy of Julius was infectious. Left to himself, Tommy would probably have sat down to think things out for a good half-hour before he decided on a plan of action. But with Julius Hersheimmer about, hustling was inevitable.

After a few muttered imprecations he handed the Bradshaw to Tommy as being more conversant with its mysteries. Tommy abandoned it in favour of an A.B.C.

"Here we are. Ebury, Yorks. From King's Cross. Or St. Pancras. (Boy must have made a mistake. It was King's Cross, not *Charing* Cross.) 12:50, that's the train she went by. 2:10, that's gone. 3:20 is the next—and a damned slow train too."

"What about the car?"

Tommy shook his head.

"Send it up if you like, but we'd better stick to the train. The great thing is to keep calm."

Julius groaned.

"That's so. But it gets my goat to think of that innocent young girl in danger!"

Tommy nodded abstractedly. He was thinking. In a moment or two, he said:

"I say, Julius, what do they want her for, anyway?"

"Eh? I don't get you."

"What I mean is that I don't think it's their game to do her any harm," explained Tommy, puckering his brow with the strain of his mental processes. "She's a hostage, that's what she is. She's in no immediate danger, because if we tumble on to anything, she'd be damned useful to them. As long as they've got her, they've got the whip hand of us. See?"

"Sure thing," said Julius thoughtfully. "That's so."

"Besides," added Tommy, as an afterthought, "I've great faith in Tuppence."

The journey was wearisome, with many stops and crowded carriages. They had to change twice, once at Doncaster, once at a small junction. Ebury was a deserted station with a solitary porter, to whom Tommy addressed himself:

"Can you tell me the way to the Moat House?"

"The Moat House? It's a tidy step from here. The big house near the sea, you mean?"

Tommy assented brazenly. After listening to the porter's meticulous but perplexing directions, they prepared to leave the station. It was beginning to rain, and they turned up the collars of their coats as they trudged through the slush of the road. Suddenly Tommy halted.

"Wait a moment." He ran back to the station and tackled the porter anew.

"Look here, do you remember a young lady who arrived by an earlier train, the 12:50 from London? She'd probably ask you the way to the Moat House."

He described Tuppence as well as he could, but the porter shook his head. Several people had arrived by the train in question. He could not call to mind one young lady in particular. But he was quite certain that no one had asked him the way to the Moat House.

Tommy rejoined Julius, and explained. Depression was settling down on him like a leaden weight. He felt convinced that their quest was going to be unsuccessful. The enemy had over three hours' start. Three hours was more than enough for Mr. Brown. He would not ignore the possibility of the telegram having been found.

The way seemed endless. Once they took the wrong turning and went nearly half a mile out of their direction. It was past seven o'clock when a small boy told them that "t' Moat House" was just past the next corner.

A rusty iron gate swinging dismally on its hinges! An overgrown drive thick with leaves. There was something about the place that struck a chill to both their hearts. They went up the deserted drive. The leaves deadened their footsteps. The daylight was almost gone. It was like walking in a world of ghosts. Overhead the branches flapped and creaked with a mournful note. Occasionally a sodden leaf drifted silently down, startling them with its cold touch on their cheek.

A turn of the drive brought them in sight of the house. That, too, seemed empty and deserted. The shutters were closed, the steps up to the door overgrown with moss. Was it indeed to this desolate spot that Tuppence had been decoyed? It seemed hard to believe that a human footstep had passed this way for months.

Julius jerked the rusty bell handle. A jangled peal rang discordantly, echoing through the emptiness within. No one came. They rang again and again—but there was no sign of life. Then they walked completely round the house. Everywhere silence, and shuttered windows. If they could believe the evidence of their eyes the place was empty.

"Nothing doing," said Julius.

They retraced their steps slowly to the gate.

"There must be a village handy," continued the young American. "We'd better make inquiries there. They'll know something about the place, and whether there's been any one there lately."

"Yes, that's not a bad idea."

Proceeding up the road, they soon came to a little hamlet. On the outskirts of it, they met a workman swinging his bag of tools, and Tommy stopped him with a question.

"The Moat House? It's empty. Been empty for years. Mrs. Sweeny's got the key if you want to go over it—next to the post office."

Tommy thanked him. They soon found the post office, which was also a sweet and general fancy shop, and knocked at the door of the cottage next to it. A clean, whole-some-looking woman opened it. She readily produced the key of the Moat House.

"Though I doubt if it's the kind of place to suit you, sir. In a terrible state of repair. Ceilings leaking and all. 'Twould need a lot of money spent on it."

"Thanks," said Tommy cheerily. "I dare say it'll be a wash-out, but houses are scarce nowadays."

"That they are," declared the woman heartily. "My daughter and son-in-law have been looking for a decent cottage for I don't know how long. It's all the war. Upset things terribly, it has. But excuse me, sir, it'll be too dark for you to see much of the house. Hadn't you better wait until to-morrow?"

"That's all right. We'll have a look around this evening, anyway. We'd have been here before only we lost our way. What's the best place to stay at for the night round here?"

Mrs. Sweeny looked doubtful.

"There's the Yorkshire Arms, but it's not much of a place for gentlemen like you."

"Oh, it will do very well. Thanks. By the way, you've not had a young lady here asking for this key to-day?"

The woman shook her head.

"No one's been over the place for a long time."

"Thanks very much."

They retraced their steps to the Moat House. As the front door swung back on its hinges, protesting loudly, Julius struck a match and examined the floor carefully. Then he shook his head.

"I'd swear no one's passed this way. Look at the dust. Thick. Not a sign of a footmark."

They wandered round the deserted house. Everywhere the same tale. Thick layers of dust apparently undisturbed.

"This gets me," said Julius. "I don't believe Tuppence was ever in this house."

"She must have been."

Julius shook his head without replying.

"We'll go over it again to-morrow," said Tommy. "Perhaps we'll see more in the daylight."

On the morrow they took up the search once more, and were reluctantly forced to the conclusion that the house had not been invaded for some considerable time. They might have left the village altogether but for a fortunate discovery of Tommy's. As they were retracing their steps to the gate, he gave a sudden cry, and stooping, picked something up from among the leaves, and held it out to Julius. It was a small gold brooch.

"That's Tuppence's!"

"Are you sure?"

"Absolutely. I've often seen her wear it."

Julius drew a deep breath.

"I guess that settles it. She came as far as here, anyway. We'll make that pub our head-quarters, and raise hell round here until we find her. Somebody *must* have seen her."

Forthwith the campaign began. Tommy and Julius worked separately and together, but the result was the same. Nobody answering to Tuppence's description had been seen in the vicinity. They were baffled—but not discouraged. Finally they altered their tactics. Tuppence had certainly not remained long in the neighbourhood of the Moat House. That pointed to her having been overcome and carried away in a car. They renewed inquiries. Had any one seen a car standing somewhere near the Moat House that day? Again they met with no success.

Julius wired to town for his own car, and they scoured the

neighbourhood daily with unflagging zeal. A grey limousine on which they had set high hopes was traced to Harrogate, and turned out to be the property of a highly respectable maiden lady!

Each day saw them set out on a new quest. Julius was like a hound on the leash. He followed up the slenderest clue. Every car that had passed through the village on the fateful day was tracked down. He forced his way into country properties and submitted the owners of the motors to a searching cross-examination. His apologies were as thorough as his methods, and seldom failed in disarming the indignation of his victims; but, as day succeeded day, they were no nearer to discovering Tuppence's whereabouts. So well had the abduction been planned that the girl seemed literally to have vanished into thin air.

And another preoccupation was weighing on Tommy's mind.

"Do you know how long we've been here?" he asked one morning as they sat facing each other at breakfast. "A week! We're no nearer to finding Tuppence, *and next Sunday is the 29th!*"

"Shucks!" said Julius thoughtfully. "I'd almost forgotten about the 29th. I've been thinking of nothing but Tuppence."

"So have I. At least, I hadn't forgotten about the 29th, but it didn't seem to matter a damn in comparison to finding Tuppence. But to-day's the 23rd, and time's getting short. If we're ever going to get hold of her at all, we must do it before the 29th—her life won't be worth an hour's purchase afterwards. The hostage game will be played out by then. I'm beginning to feel that we've made a big mistake in the way we've set about this. We've wasted time and we're no forrader."

"I'm with you there. We've been a couple of mutts, who've bitten off a bigger bit than they can chew. I'm going to quit fooling right away!"

"What do you mean?"

"I'll tell you. I'm going to do what we ought to have done a week ago. I'm going right back to London to put the case in the hands of your British police. We fancied ourselves as sleuths. Sleuths! It was a piece of damn-fool foolishness! I'm through! I've had enough of it. Scotland Yard for me!"

"You're right," said Tommy slowly. "I wish to God we'd gone there right away."

"Better late than never. We've been like a couple of babes playing 'Here we go round the Mulberry Bush.' Now I'm going right along to Scotland Yard to ask them to take me by the hand and show me the way I should go. I guess the professional always scores over the amateur in the end. Are you coming along with me?"

Tommy shook his head.

"What's the good? One of us is enough. I might as well stay here and nose round a bit longer. Something *might* turn up. One never knows."

"Sure thing. Well, so long. I'll be back in a couple of shakes with a few inspectors along. I shall tell them to pick out their brightest and best."

But the course of events was not to follow the plan Julius had laid down. Later in the day Tommy received a wire:

JOIN ME MANCHESTER MIDLAND HOTEL. IMPORTANT NEWS—
JULIUS.

At 7:30 that night Tommy alighted from a slow cross-country train. Julius was on the platform.

"Thought you'd come by this train if you weren't out when my wire arrived."

Tommy grasped him by the arm.

"What is it? Is Tuppence found?"

Julius shook his head.

"No. But I found this waiting in London. Just arrived."

He handed the telegraph form to the other. Tommy's eyes opened as he read:

JANE FINN FOUND. COME MANCHESTER MIDLAND HOTEL
IMMEDIATELY—PEEL EDGERTON.

Julius took the form back and folded it up.

"Queer," he said thoughtfully. "I thought that lawyer chap had quit!"

XIX

JANE FINN

"My train got in half an hour ago," explained Julius, as he led the way out of the station. "I reckoned you'd come by this before I left London, and wired accordingly to Sir James. He's booked rooms for us, and will be round to dine at eight."

"What made you think he'd ceased to take any interest in the case?" asked Tommy curiously.

"What he said," replied Julius dryly. "The old bird's as close as an oyster! Like all the darned lot of them, he wasn't going to commit himself till he was sure he could deliver the goods."

"I wonder," said Tommy thoughtfully.

Julius turned on him.

"You wonder what?"

"Whether that was his real reason."

"Sure. You bet your life it was."

Tommy shook his head unconvinced.

Sir James arrived punctually at eight o'clock, and Julius introduced Tommy. Sir James shook hands with him warmly.

"I am delighted to make your acquaintance, Mr. Beresford. I have heard so much about you from Miss Tuppence"—he smiled involuntarily—"that it really seems as though I already know you quite well."

"Thank you, sir," said Tommy with his cheerful grin. He scanned the great lawyer eagerly. Like Tuppence, he felt the magnetism of the other's personality. He was reminded of Mr. Carter. The two men, totally unalike so far as physical resemblance went, produced a similar effect. Beneath the weary manner of the one and the professional reserve of the other, lay the same quality of mind, keen-edged like a rapier.

In the meantime he was conscious of Sir James's close scrutiny. When the lawyer dropped his eyes the young man had the feeling that the other had read him through and through like an open book. He could not but wonder what the final judgment was, but there was little chance of learning that. Sir James took in everything, but gave out only what he chose. A proof of that occurred almost at once.

Immediately the first greetings were over Julius broke out into a flood of eager questions. How had Sir James managed to track the girl? Why had he not let them know that he was still working on the case? And so on.

Sir James stroked his chin and smiled. At last he said:

"Just so, just so. Well, she's found. And that's the great thing, isn't it? Eh! Come now, that's the great thing?"

"Sure it is. But just how did you strike her trail? Miss Tuppence and I thought you'd quit for good and all."

"Ah!" The lawyer shot a lightning glance at him, then resumed operations on his chin. "You thought that, did you? Did you really? H'm, dear me."

"But I guess I can take it we were wrong," pursued Julius.

"Well, I don't know that I should go so far as to say that. But it's certainly fortunate for all parties that we've managed to find the young lady."

"But where is she?" demanded Julius, his thoughts flying off on another tack. "I thought you'd be sure to bring her along?"

"That would hardly be possible," said Sir James gravely.

"Why?"

"Because the young lady was knocked down in a street

accident, and has sustained slight injuries to the head. She was taken to the infirmary, and on recovering consciousness gave her name as Jane Finn. When—ah!—I heard that, I arranged for her to be removed to the house of a doctor—a friend of mine, and wired at once for you. She relapsed into unconsciousness and has not spoken since."

"She's not seriously hurt?"

"Oh, a bruise and a cut or two; really, from a medical point of view, absurdly slight injuries to have produced such a condition. Her state is probably to be attributed to the mental shock consequent on recovering her memory."

"It's come back?" cried Julius excitedly.

Sir James tapped the table rather impatiently.

"Undoubtedly, Mr. Hersheimmer, since she was able to give her real name. I thought you had appreciated that point."

"And you just happened to be on the spot," said Tommy. "Seems quite like a fairy tale."

But Sir James was far too wary to be drawn.

"Coincidences are curious things," he said dryly.

Nevertheless Tommy was now certain of what he had before only suspected. Sir James's presence in Manchester was not accidental. Far from abandoning the case, as Julius supposed, he had by some means of his own successfully run the missing girl to earth. The only thing that puzzled Tommy was the reason for all this secrecy. He concluded that it was a foible of the legal mind.

Julius was speaking.

"After dinner," he announced, "I shall go right away and see Jane."

"That will be impossible, I fear," said Sir James. "It is very unlikely they would allow her to see visitors at this time of night. I should suggest to-morrow morning about ten-o'clock."

Julius flushed. There was something in Sir James which always stirred him to antagonism. It was conflict of two masterful personalities.

"All the same, I reckon I'll go round there to-night and see if I can't ginger them up to break through their silly rules."

"It will be quite useless, Mr. Hersheimmer."

The words came out like the crack of a pistol, and Tommy looked up with a start. Julius was nervous and excited. The hand with which he raised his glass to his lips shook slightly, but his eyes held Sir James's defiantly. For a moment the hostility between the two seemed likely to burst into flame, but in the end Julius lowered his eyes, defeated.

"For the moment, I reckon you're the boss."

"Thank you," said the other. "We will say ten o'clock then?" With consummate ease of manner he turned to Tommy. "I must confess, Mr. Beresford, that it was something of a surprise to me to see you here this evening. The last I heard of you was that your friends were in grave anxiety on your behalf. Nothing had been heard of you for some days, and Miss Tuppence was inclined to think you had got into difficulties."

"I had, sir!" Tommy grinned reminiscently. "I was never in a tighter place in my life."

Helped out by questions from Sir James, he gave an abbreviated account of his adventures. The lawyer looked at him with renewed interest as he brought the tale to a close.

"You got yourself out of a tight place very well," he said gravely. "I congratulate you. You displayed a great deal of ingenuity and carried your part through well."

Tommy blushed, his face assuming a prawn-like hue at the praise.

"I couldn't have got away but for the girl, sir."

"No." Sir James smiled a little. "It was lucky for you she happened to—er—take a fancy to you." Tommy appeared about to protest, but Sir James went on. "There's no doubt about her being one of the gang, I suppose?"

"I'm afraid not, sir. I thought perhaps they were keeping her there by force, but the way she acted didn't fit in with that. You see, she went back to them when she could have got away."

Sir James nodded thoughtfully.

"What did she say? Something about wanting to be taken to Marguerite?"

"Yes, sir. I suppose she meant Mrs. Vandemeyer."

"She always signed herself Rita Vandemeyer. All her friends spoke of her as Rita. Still, I suppose the girl must have been in the habit of calling her by her full name. And, at the moment she was crying out to her, Mrs. Vandemeyer was either dead or dying! Curious! There are one or two points that strike me as being obscure—their sudden change of attitude towards yourself, for instance. By the way, the house was raided, of course?"

"Yes, sir, but they'd all cleared out."

"Naturally," said Sir James dryly.

"And not a clue left behind."

"I wonder—" The lawyer tapped the table thoughtfully.

Something in his voice made Tommy look up. Would this man's eyes have seen something where theirs had been blind? He spoke impulsively:

"I wish you'd been there, sir, to go over the house!"

"I wish I had," said Sir James quietly. He sat for a moment in silence. Then he looked up. "And since then? What have you been doing?"

For a moment, Tommy stared at him. Then it dawned on him that of course the lawyer did not know.

"I forgot that you didn't know about Tuppence," he said slowly. The sickening anxiety, forgotten for a while in the excitement of knowing Jane Finn was found at last, swept over him again.

The lawyer laid down his knife and fork sharply.

"Has anything happened to Miss Tuppence?" His voice was keen-edged.

"She's disappeared," said Julius.

"When?"

"A week ago."

"How?"

Sir James's questions fairly shot out. Between them Tommy and Julius gave the history of the last week and their futile search.

Sir James went at once to the root of the matter.

"A wire signed with your name? They knew enough of you both for that. They weren't sure of how much you had learnt in that house. Their kidnapping of Miss Tuppence is the counter-move to your escape. If necessary they could seal your lips with a threat of what might happen to her."

Tommy nodded.

"That's just what I thought, sir."

Sir James looked at him keenly. "*You* had worked that out, had you? Not bad—not at all bad. The curious thing is that they certainly did not know anything about you when they first held you prisoner. You are sure that you did not in any way disclose your identity?"

Tommy shook his head.

"That's so," said Julius with a nod. "Therefore I reckon some one put them wise—and not earlier than Sunday afternoon."

"Yes, but who?"

"That almighty omniscient Mr. Brown, of course!"

There was a faint note of derision in the American's voice which made Sir James look up sharply.

"You don't believe in Mr. Brown, Mr. Hersheimmer?"

"No, sir, I do not," returned the young American with emphasis. "Not as such, that is to say. I reckon it out that he's a figurehead—just a bogy name to frighten the children with. The real head of this business is that Russian chap Kramenin. I guess he's quite capable of running revolutions in three countries at once if he chose! The man Whittington is probably the head of the English branch."

"I disagree with you," said Sir James shortly. "Mr. Brown exists." He turned to Tommy. "Did you happen to notice where that wire was handed in?"

"No, sir, I'm afraid I didn't."

"H'm. Got it with you?"

"It's upstairs, sir, in my kit."

"I'd like to have a look at it sometime. No hurry. You've wasted a week"—Tommy hung his head—"a day or so more is immaterial. We'll deal with Miss Jane Finn first. Afterwards, we'll set to work to rescue Miss Tuppence from bondage. I don't think she's in any immediate danger. That is, so long as they don't know that we've got Jane Finn, and that her memory has returned. We must keep that dark at all costs. You understand?"

The other two assented, and, after making arrangements for meeting on the morrow, the great lawyer took his leave.

At ten o'clock, the two young men were at the appointed spot. Sir James had joined them on the door-step. He alone appeared unexcited. He introduced them to the doctor.

"Mr. Hersheimmer—Mr. Beresford—Dr. Roylance. How's the patient?"

"Going on well. Evidently no idea of the flight of time. Asked this morning how many had been saved from the *Lusitania*. Was it in the papers yet? That, of course, was only what was to be expected. She seems to have something on her mind, though."

"I think we can relieve her anxiety. May we go up?"

"Certainly."

Tommy's heart beat sensibly faster as they followed the doctor upstairs. Jane Finn at last! The long-sought, the mysterious, the elusive Jane Finn! How wildly improbable success had seemed! And here in this house, her memory almost miraculously restored, lay the girl who held the future of England in her hands. A half groan broke from Tommy's lips. If only Tuppence could have been at his side to share in the triumphant conclusion of their joint venture! Then he put the thought of Tuppence resolutely aside. His confidence in Sir James was growing. There was a man who would unerringly ferret out Tuppence's whereabouts. In the meantime Jane Finn! And suddenly a dread clutched at his heart. It seemed too easy. . . . Suppose they should find her dead . . . stricken down by the hand of Mr. Brown?

In another minute he was laughing at these melodramatic fancies. The doctor held open the door of a room and they passed in. On the white bed, bandages round her head, lay the girl. Somehow the whole scene seemed unreal. It was so exactly what one expected that it gave the effect of being beautifully staged.

The girl looked from one to the other of them with large wondering eyes. Sir James spoke first.

"Miss Finn," he said, "this is your cousin, Mr. Julius P. Hersheimmer."

A faint flush flitted over the girl's face, as Julius stepped forward and took her hand.

"How do, Cousin Jane?" he said lightly.

But Tommy caught the tremor in his voice.

"Are you really Uncle Hiram's son?" she asked wonderingly.

Her voice, with the slight warmth of the Western accent, had an almost thrilling quality. It seemed vaguely familiar to Tommy, but he thrust the impression aside as impossible.

"Sure thing."

"We used to read about Uncle Hiram in the papers," continued the girl, in her low soft tones. "But I never thought I'd meet you one day. Mother figured it out that Uncle Hiram would never get over being mad with her."

"The old man was like that," admitted Julius. "But I guess the new generation's sort of different. Got no use for the family feud business. First thing I thought about, soon as the war was over, was to come along and hunt you up."

A shadow passed over the girl's face.

"They've been telling me things—dreadful things—that my memory went, and that there are years I shall never know about—years lost out of my life."

"You didn't realize that yourself?"

The girl's eyes opened wide.

"Why, no. It seems to me as though it were no time since we were being hustled into those boats. I can see it all now." She closed her eyes with a shudder.

Julius looked across at Sir James, who nodded.

"Don't worry any. It isn't worth it. Now, see here, Jane, there's something we want to know about. There was a man aboard that boat with some mighty important papers on him, and the big guns in this country have got a notion that he passed on the goods to you. Is that so?"

The girl hesitated, her glance shifting to the other two. Julius understood.

"Mr. Beresford is commissioned by the British Government to get those papers back. Sir James Peel Edgerton is an English Member of Parliament, and might be a big gun in the Cabinet if he liked. It's owing to him that we've ferreted you out at last. So you can go right ahead and tell us the whole story. Did Danvers give you the papers?"

"Yes. He said they'd have a better chance with me, because they would save the women and children first."

"Just as we thought," said Sir James.

"He said they were very important—that they might make

all the difference to the Allies. But, if it's all so long ago, and the war's over, what does it matter now?"

"I guess history repeats itself, Jane. First there was a great hue and cry over those papers, then it all died down, and now the whole caboodle's started all over again—for rather different reasons. Then you can hand them over to us right away?"

"But I can't."

"What?"

"I haven't got them."

"You—haven't—got them?" Julius punctuated the words with little pauses.

"No—I hid them."

"You *hid* them?"

"Yes. I got uneasy. People seemed to be watching me. It scared me—badly." She put her hand to her head. "It's almost the last thing I remember before waking up in the hospital. . . ."

"Go on," said Sir James, in his quiet penetrating tones. "What do you remember?"

She turned to him obediently.

"It was at Holyhead. I came that way—I don't remember why. . . ."

"That doesn't matter. Go on."

"In the confusion on the quay I slipped away. Nobody saw me. I took a car. Told the man to drive me out of the town. I watched when we got on the open road. No other car was following us. I saw a path at the side of the road. I told the man to wait."

She paused, then went on. "The path led to the cliff, and down to the sea between big yellow gorse bushes—they were like golden flames. I looked round. There wasn't a soul in sight. But just level with my head there was a hole in the rock. It was quite small—I could only just get my hand in, but it went a long way back. I took the oilskin packet from round my neck and shoved it right in as far as I could. Then I tore off a bit of gorse—My! but it did prick—and plugged the hole with it so that you'd never guess there was a crevice of any kind there. Then I marked the place carefully in my own mind, so that I'd find it again. There was a queer boulder in the path just there—for all the world like a dog sitting up begging. Then I went back to the road. The car was waiting, and I drove back. I just caught the train. I was a bit ashamed of myself for fancying things maybe, but, by and by, I saw the man opposite me wink at a woman who was sitting next to me, and I felt scared again, and was glad the papers were safe. I went out in the corridor to get a little air. I thought I'd slip into another carriage. But the woman called me back, said I'd dropped something, and when I stooped to look, something seemed to hit me—here." She placed her hand to the back of her head. "I don't remember anything more until I woke up in the hospital."

There was a pause.

"Thank you, Miss Finn." It was Sir James who spoke. "I hope we have not tired you?"

"Oh, that's all right. My head aches a little, but otherwise I feel fine."

Julius stepped forward and took her hand again.

"So long, Cousin Jane. I'm going to get busy after those papers, but I'll be back in two shakes of a dog's tail, and I'll tote you up to London and give you the time of your young life before we go back to the States! I mean it—so hurry up and get well."

XX

Too Late

In the street they held an informal council of war. Sir James
had drawn a watch from his pocket. "The boat train to
Holyhead stops at Chester at 12:14. If you start at once I
think you can catch the connection."

Tommy looked up, puzzled.

"Is there any need to hurry, sir? To-day is only the 24th."

"I guess it's always well to get up early in the morning,"
said Julius, before the lawyer had time to reply. "We'll make
tracks for the depot right away."

A little frown had settled on Sir James's brow.

"I wish I could come with you. I am due to speak at a meeting at two o'clock. It is unfortunate."

The reluctance in his tone was very evident. It was clear,
on the other hand, that Julius was easily disposed to put up
with the loss of the other's company.

"I guess there's nothing complicated about this deal," he
remarked. "Just a game of hide-and-seek, that's all."

"I hope so," said Sir James.

"Sure thing. What else could it be?"

"You are still young, Mr. Hersheimmer. At my age you will

probably have learnt one lesson. 'Never underestimate your adversary.' "

The gravity of his tone impressed Tommy, but had little effect upon Julius.

"You think Mr. Brown might come along and take a hand? If he does, I'm ready for him." He slapped his pocket. "I carry a gun. Little Willie here travels round with me everywhere." He produced a murderous-looking automatic, and tapped it affectionately before returning it to its home. "But he won't be needed this trip. There's nobody to put Mr. Brown wise."

The lawyer shrugged his shoulders.

"There was nobody to put Mr. Brown wise to the fact that Mrs. Vandemeyer meant to betray him. Nevertheless, *Mrs. Vandemeyer died without speaking.*"

Julius was silenced for once, and Sir James added on a lighter note:

"I only want to put you on your guard. Good-bye, and good luck. Take no unnecessary risks once the papers are in your hands. If there is any reason to believe that you have been shadowed, destroy them at once. Good luck to you. The game is in your hands now." He shook hands with them both.

Ten minutes later the two young men were seated in a first-class carriage *en route* for Chester.

For a long time neither of them spoke. When at length Julius broke the silence, it was with a totally unexpected remark.

"Say," he observed thoughtfully, "did you ever make a darned fool of yourself over a girl's face?"

Tommy, after a moment's astonishment, searched his mind.

"Can't say I have," he replied at last. "Not that I can recollect, anyhow. Why?"

"Because for the last two months I've been making a sentimental idiot of myself over Jane! First moment I clapped eyes on her photograph my heart did all the usual stunts you read about in novels. I guess I'm ashamed to admit it, but I came over here determined to find her and fix it all up, and take her back as Mrs. Julius P. Hersheimmer!"

"Oh!" said Tommy, amazed.

Julius uncrossed his legs brusquely and continued:

"Just shows what an almighty fool a man can make of himself! One look at the girl in the flesh, and I was cured!"

Feeling more tongue-tied than ever, Tommy ejaculated "Oh!" again.

"No disparagement to Jane, mind you," continued the other. "She's a real nice girl, and some fellow will fall in love with her right away."

"I thought her a very good-looking girl," said Tommy, finding his tongue.

"Sure she is. But she's not like her photo one bit. At least I suppose she is in a way—must be—because I recognized her right off. If I'd seen her in a crowd I'd have said 'There's a girl whose face I know' right away without any hesitation. But there was something about that photo"—Julius shook his head, and heaved a sigh—"I guess romance is a mighty queer thing!"

"It must be," said Tommy coldly, "if you can come over here in love with one girl, and propose to another within a fortnight."

Julius had the grace to look discomposed.

"Well, you see, I'd got a sort of tired feeling that I'd never find Jane—and that it was all plumb foolishness anyway. And then—oh, well, the French, for instance, are much more sensible in the way they look at things. They keep romance and marriage apart——"

Tommy flushed.

"Well, I'm damned! If that's——"

Julius hastened to interrupt.

"Say now, don't be hasty. I don't mean what you mean. I take it Americans have a higher opinion of morality than you have even. What I meant was that the French set about marriage in a business-like way—find two people who are suited to one another, look after the money affairs, and see the whole thing practically, and in a business-like spirit."

"If you ask me," said Tommy, "we're all too damned business-like nowadays. We're always saying, 'Will it pay?' The men are bad enough, and the girls are worse!"

"Cool down, son. Don't get so heated."

"I feel heated," said Tommy.

Julius looked at him and judged it wise to say no more.

However, Tommy had plenty of time to cool down before they reached Holyhead, and the cheerful grin had returned to his countenance as they alighted at their destination.

After consultation, and with the aid of a road map, they were fairly well agreed as to direction, so were able to hire a taxi without more ado and drive out on the road leading to Treaddur Bay. They instructed the man to go slowly, and watched narrowly so as not to miss the path. They came to it not long after leaving the town, and Tommy stopped the car promptly, asked in a casual tone whether the path led down to the sea, and hearing it did paid off the man in handsome style.

A moment later the taxi was slowly chugging back to Holyhead. Tommy and Julius watched it out of sight, and then turned to the narrow path.

"It's the right one, I suppose?" asked Tommy doubtfully. "There must be simply heaps along here."

"Sure it is. Look at the gorse. Remember what Jane said?"

Tommy looked at the swelling hedges of golden blossom which bordered the path on either side, and was convinced.

They went down in single file, Julius leading. Twice Tommy turned his head uneasily. Julius looked back.

"What is it?"

"I don't know. I've got the wind up somehow. Keep fancying there's some one following us."

"Can't be," said Julius positively. "We'd see him."

Tommy had to admit that this was true. Nevertheless, his sense of uneasiness deepened. In spite of himself he believed in the omniscience of the enemy.

"I rather wish that fellow would come along," said Julius. He patted his pocket. "Little William here is just aching for exercise!"

"Do you always carry it—him—with you?" inquired Tommy with burning curiosity.

"Most always. I guess you never know what might turn up."

Tommy kept a respectful silence. He was impressed by little William. It seemed to remove the menace of Mr. Brown farther away.

The path was now running along the side of the cliff, parallel to the sea. Suddenly Julius came to such an abrupt halt that Tommy cannoned into him.

"What's up?" he inquired.

"Look there. If that doesn't beat the band!"

Tommy looked. Standing out and half obstructing the path was a huge boulder which certainly bore a fanciful resemblance to a "begging" terrier.

"Well," said Tommy, refusing to share Julius's emotion, "it's what we expected to see, isn't it?"

Julius looked at him sadly and shook his head.

"British phlegm! Sure we expected it—but it kind of rattles me, all the same, to see it sitting there just where we expected to find it!"

Tommy, whose calm was, perhaps, more assumed than natural, moved his feet impatiently.

"Push on. What about the hole?"

They scanned the cliff-side narrowly. Tommy heard himself saying idiotically:

"The gorse won't be there after all these years."

And Julius replied solemnly:

"I guess you're right."

Tommy suddenly pointed with a shaking hand.

"What about that crevice there?"

Julius replied in an awestricken voice:

"That's it—for sure."

They looked at each other.

"When I was in France," said Tommy reminiscently, "whenever my batman failed to call me, he always said that he had come over queer. I never believed it. But whether he felt it or not, there *is* such a sensation. I've got it now! Badly!"

He looked at the rock with a kind of agonized passion.

"Damn it!" he cried. "It's impossible! Five years! Think of it! Bird's-nesting boys, picnic parties, thousands of people passing! It can't be there! It's a hundred to one against its being there! It's against all reason!"

Indeed, he felt it to be impossible—more, perhaps, because he could not believe in his own success where so many others have failed. The thing was too easy, therefore it could not be. The hole would be empty.

Julius looked at him with a widening smile.

"I guess you're rattled now all right," he drawled with some enjoyment. "Well, here goes!" He thrust his hand into the crevice, and made a slight grimace. "It's a tight fit. Jane's hand must be a few sizes smaller than mine. I don't feel anything—no—say, what's this? Gee whiz!" And with a flourish he waved aloft a small discoloured packet. "It's the goods all right. Sewn up in oilskin. Hold it while I get my penknife."

The unbelievable had happened. Tommy held the precious packet tenderly between his hands. They had succeeded!

"It's queer," he murmured idly, "you'd think the stitches would have rotted. They look just as good as new."

They cut them carefully and ripped away the oilskin. Inside was a small folded sheet of paper. With trembling fingers they unfolded it. The sheet was blank! They stared at each other, puzzled.

"A dummy?" hazarded Julius. "Was Danvers just a decoy?"

Tommy shook his head. That solution did not satisfy him. Suddenly his face cleared.

"I've got it! *Sympathetic ink!*"

"You think so?"

"Worth trying anyhow. Heat usually does the trick. Get some sticks. We'll make a fire."

In a few minutes the little fire of twigs and leaves was blazing merrily. Tommy held the sheet of paper near the glow. The paper curled a little with the heat. Nothing more.

Suddenly Julius grasped his arm, and pointed to where characters were appearing in a faint brown colour.

"Gee whiz! You've got it! Say, that idea of yours was great. It never occurred to me."

Tommy held the paper in position some minutes longer until he judged the heat had done its work. Then he withdrew it. A moment later he uttered a cry.

Across the sheet in neat brown printing ran the words:

WITH THE COMPLIMENTS OF MR. BROWN.

XXI

TOMMY MAKES A DISCOVERY

For a moment or two they stood staring at each other stupidly, dazed with the shock. Somehow, inexplicably, Mr. Brown had forestalled them. Tommy accepted defeat quietly. Not so Julius.

"How in tarnation did he get ahead of us? That's what beats me!" he ended up.

Tommy shook his head, and said dully:

"It accounts for the stitches being new. We might have guessed. . . ."

"Never mind the darned stitches. How did he get ahead of us? We hustled all we knew. It's downright impossible for anyone to get here quicker than we did. And, anyway, how did he know? Do you reckon there was a dictophone in Jane's room? I guess there must have been."

But Tommy's common sense pointed out objections.

"No one could have known beforehand that she was going to be in that house—much less that particular room."

"That's so," admitted Julius. "Then one of the nurses was a crook and listened at the door. How's that?"

"I don't see that it matters anyway," said Tommy wearily.

"He may have found out some months ago, and removed the papers, then——No, by Jove, that won't wash! They'd have been published at once."

"Sure thing they would! No, some one's got ahead of us today by an hour or so. But how they did it gets my goat."

"I wish that chap Peel Edgerton had been with us," said Tommy thoughtfully.

"Why?" Julius stared. "The mischief was done when we came."

"Yes——" Tommy hesitated. He could not explain his own feeling—the illogical idea that the K.C.'s presence would somehow have averted the catastrophe. He reverted to his former point of view. "It's no good arguing about how it was done. The game's up. We've failed. There's only one thing for me to do."

"What's that?"

"Get back to London as soon as possible. Mr. Carter must be warned. It's only a matter of hours now before the blow falls. But, at any rate, he ought to know the worst."

The duty was an unpleasant one, but Tommy had no intention of shirking it. He must report his failure to Mr. Carter. After that his work was done. He took the midnight mail to London. Julius elected to stay the night at Holyhead.

Half an hour after arrival, haggard and pale, Tommy stood before his chief.

"I've come to report, sir. I've failed—failed badly."

Mr. Carter eyed him sharply.

"You mean that the treaty——"

"Is in the hands of Mr. Brown, sir."

"Ah!" said Mr. Carter quietly. The expression on his face did not change, but Tommy caught the flicker of despair in his eyes. It convinced him as nothing else had done that the outlook was hopeless.

"Well," said Mr. Carter after a minute or two, "we mustn't sag at the knees, I suppose. I'm glad to know definitely. We must do what we can."

Through Tommy's mind flashed the assurance: "It's hopeless, and he knows it's hopeless!"

The other looked up at him.

"Don't take it to heart, lad," he said kindly. "You did your best. You were up against one of the biggest brains of the century. And you came very near success. Remember that."

"Thank you, sir. It's awfully decent of you."

"I blame myself. I have been blaming myself ever since I heard this other news."

Something in his tone attracted Tommy's attention. A new fear gripped at his heart.

"Is there—something more, sir?"

"I'm afraid so," said Mr. Carter gravely. He stretched out his hand to a sheet on the table.

"Tuppence——?" faltered Tommy.

"Read for yourself."

The typewritten words danced before his eyes. The description of a green toque, a coat with a handkerchief in the pocket marked P.L.C. He looked an agonized question at Mr. Carter. The latter replied to it:

"Washed up on the Yorkshire coast—near Ebury. I'm afraid—it looks very much like foul play."

"My God!" gasped Tommy. "*Tuppence!* Those devils—I'll never rest till I've got even with them! I'll hunt them down! I'll——"

The pity on Mr. Carter's face stopped him.

"I know what you feel like, my poor boy. But it's no good. You'll waste your strength uselessly. It may sound harsh, but my advice to you is: Cut your losses. Time's merciful. You'll forget."

"Forget Tuppence? Never!"

Mr. Carter shook his head.

"So you think now. Well, it won't bear thinking of—that brave little girl! I'm sorry about the whole business—confoundedly sorry."

Tommy came to himself with a start.

"I'm taking up your time, sir," he said with an effort. "There's no need for you to blame yourself. I dare say we were a couple of young fools to take on such a job. You warned us all right. But I wish to God I'd been the one to get it in the neck. Good-bye, sir."

Back at the Ritz, Tommy packed up his few belongings mechanically, his thoughts far away. He was still bewildered by the introduction of tragedy into his cheerful commonplace existence. What fun they had had together, he and Tuppence! And now—oh, he couldn't believe it—it couldn't be true! *Tuppence—dead!* Little Tuppence, brimming over with life! It was a dream, a horrible dream. Nothing more.

They brought him a note, a few kind words of sympathy from Peel Edgerton, who had read the news in the paper. (There had been a large headline: EX-V.A.D. FEARED DROWNED.) The letter ended with the offer of a post on a ranch in the Argentine, where Sir James had considerable interests.

"Kind old beggar," muttered Tommy, as he flung it aside.

The door opened, and Julius burst in with his usual violence. He held an open newspaper in his hand.

"Say, what's all this? They seem to have got some fool idea about Tuppence."

"It's true," said Tommy quietly.

"You mean they've done her in?"

Tommy nodded.

"I suppose when they got the treaty she—wasn't any good to them any longer, and they were afraid to let her go."

"Well, I'm darned!" said Julius. "Little Tuppence. She sure was the pluckiest little girl——"

But suddenly something seemed to crack in Tommy's brain. He rose to his feet.

"Oh, get out! You don't really care, damn you! You asked her to marry you in your rotten cold-blooded way, but I *loved* her. I'd have given the soul out of my body to save her from harm. I'd have stood by without a word and let her marry you, because you could have given her the sort of time she ought to have had, and I was only a poor devil without a penny to bless himself with. But it wouldn't have been because I didn't care!"

"See here," began Julius temperately.

"Oh, go to the devil! I can't stand your coming here and talking about 'little Tuppence.' Go and look after your cousin. Tuppence is my girl! I've always loved her, from the time we played together as kids. We grew up and it was just the same. I shall never forget when I was in hospital, and she came in in that ridiculous cap and apron! It was like a miracle to see the girl I loved turn up in a nurse's kit——"

But Julius interrupted him.

"A nurse's kit! Gee whiz! I must be going to Colney Hatch! I could swear I've seen Jane in a nurse's cap too. And that's plumb impossible! No, by gum, I've got it! It was her I saw talking to Whittington at that nursing home in Bournemouth. She wasn't a patient there! She was a nurse!"

"I dare say," said Tommy angrily, "she's probably been in with them from the start. I shouldn't wonder if she stole those papers from Danvers to begin with."

"I'm darned if she did!" shouted Julius. "She's my cousin, and as patriotic a girl as ever stepped."

"I don't care a damn what she is, but get out of here!" retorted Tommy also at the top of his voice.

The young men were on the point of coming to blows. But suddenly, with an almost magical abruptness, Julius's anger abated.

"All right, son," he said quietly, "I'm going. I don't blame you any for what you've been saying. It's mighty lucky you did say it. I've been the most almighty blithering darned idiot that it's possible to imagine. Calm down"—Tommy had made an impatient gesture—"I'm going right away now—going to the London and North Western Railway depot, if you want to know."

"I don't care a damn where you're going," growled Tommy.

As the door closed behind Julius, he returned to his suitcase.

"That's the lot," he murmured, and rang the bell.

"Take my luggage down."

"Yes, sir. Going away, sir?"

"I'm going to the devil," said Tommy regardless of the menial's feelings.

That functionary, however, merely replied respectfully:

"Yes, sir. Shall I call a taxi?"

Tommy nodded.

Where was he going? He hadn't the faintest idea. Beyond a fixed determination to get even with Mr. Brown he had no plans. He re-read Sir James' letter, and shook his head. Tuppence must be avenged. Still, it was kind of the old fellow.

"Better answer it, I suppose." He went across to the writing-table. With the usual perversity of bedroom stationery, there were innumerable envelopes and no paper. He rang. No one came. Tommy fumed at the delay. Then he remembered that there was a good supply in Julius's sitting-room. The American had announced his immediate departure, there would be no fear of running up against him. Besides, he wouldn't mind if he did. He was beginning to be rather ashamed of the things he had said. Old Julius had taken them jolly well. He'd apologize if he found him there.

But the room was deserted. Tommy walked across to the writing-table, and opened the middle drawer. A photograph, carelessly thrust in face upwards, caught his eye. For a moment he stood rooted to the ground. Then he took it out, shut the drawer, walked slowly over to an arm-chair, and sat down still staring at the photograph in his hand.

What on earth was a photograph of the French girl Annette doing in Julius Hersheimmer's writing-table?

XXII

IN DOWNING STREET

The Prime Minister tapped the desk in front of him with nervous fingers. His face was worn and harassed. He took up his conversation with Mr. Carter at the point it had broken off.

"I don't understand," he said. "Do you really mean that things are not so desperate after all?"

"So this lad seems to think."

"Let's have a look at his letter again."

Mr. Carter handed it over. It was written in a sprawling boyish hand.

"DEAR MR. CARTER,

Something's turned up that has given me a jar. Of course I may be simply making an awful ass of myself, but I don't think so. If my conclusions are right, that girl at Manchester was just a plant. The whole thing was prearranged, sham packet and all, with the object of making us think the game was up—therefore I fancy that we must have been pretty hot on the scent.

I think I know who the real Jane Finn is, and I've even

got an idea where the papers are. That last's only a guess, of course, but I've a sort of feeling it'll turn out right. Anyhow, I enclose it in a sealed envelope for what it's worth. I'm going to ask you not to open it until the very last moment, midnight on the 28th, in fact. You'll understand why in a minute. You see, I've figured it out that those things of Tuppence's are a plant too, and she's no more drowned than I am. The way I reason is this: as a last chance they'll let Jane Finn escape in the hope that she's been shamming this memory stunt, and that once she thinks she's free she'll go right away to the cache. Of course it's an awful risk for them to take, because she knows all about them—but they're pretty desperate to get hold of that treaty. *But if they know that the papers have been recovered by us*, neither of those two girls' lives will be worth an hour's purchase. I must try and get hold of Tuppence before Jane escapes.

I want a repeat of that telegram that was sent to Tuppence at the Ritz. Sir James Peel Edgerton said you would be able to manage that for me. He's frightfully clever.

One last thing—please have that house in Soho watched day and night.

Yours, etc.,
THOMAS BERESFORD."

The Prime Minister looked up.

"The enclosure?"

Mr. Carter smiled dryly.

"In the vaults of the Bank. I am taking no chances."

"You don't think"—the Prime Minister hesitated a minute—"that it would be better to open it now? Surely we ought to secure the document, that is, provided the young man's guess turns out to be correct, at once. We can keep the fact of having done so quite secret."

"Can we? I'm not so sure. There are spies all round us. Once it's known I wouldn't give that"—he snapped his fingers—"for the lives of those two girls. No, the boy trusted me, and I shan't let him down."

"Well, well, we must leave it at that, then. What's he like, this lad?"

"Outwardly, he's an ordinary clean-limbed, rather block-headed young Englishman. Slow in his mental processes. On the other hand, it's quite impossible to lead him astray through his imagination. He hasn't got any—so he's difficult to deceive. He worries things out slowly, and once he's got hold of anything he doesn't let go. The little lady's quite different. More intuition and less common sense. They make a pretty pair working together. Pace and stamina."

"He seems confident," mused the Prime Minister.

"Yes, and that's what gives me hope. He's the kind of diffident youth who would have to be *very* sure before he ventured an opinion at all."

A half smile came to the other's lips.

"And it is this—boy who will defeat the master criminal of our time?"

"This—boy, as you say! But I sometimes fancy I see a shadow behind."

"You mean?"

"Peel Edgerton."

"Peel Edgerton?" said the Prime Minister in astonishment.

"Yes. I see his hand in *this*." He struck the open letter. "He's here—working in the dark, silently, unobtrusively. I've always felt that if anyone was to run Mr. Brown to earth, Peel Edgerton would be the man. I tell you he's on the case now, but doesn't want it known. By the way, I got rather an odd request from him the other day."

"Yes?"

"He sent me a cutting from some American paper. It referred to a man's body found near the docks in New York about three weeks ago. He asked me to collect any information on the subject I could."

"Well?"

Carter shrugged his shoulders.

"I couldn't get much. Young fellow about thirty-five—poorly dressed—face very badly disfigured. He was never identified."

"And you fancy that the two matters are connected in some way?"

"Somehow I do. I may be wrong, of course."

There was a pause, then Mr. Carter continued:

"I asked him to come round here. Not that we'll get anything out of him he doesn't want to tell. His legal instincts are too strong. But there's no doubt he can throw light on one or two obscure points in young Beresford's letter. Ah, here he is!"

The two men rose to greet the new-comer. A half whimsical thought flashed across the Premier's mind. "My successor, perhaps!"

"We've had a letter from young Beresford," said Mr. Carter, coming to the point at once. "You've seen him, I suppose?"

"You suppose wrong," said the lawyer.

"Oh!" Mr. Carter was a little nonplussed.

Sir James smiled, and stroked his chin.

"He rang me up," he volunteered.

"Would you have any objection to telling us exactly what passed between you?"

"Not at all. He thanked me for a certain letter which I had written to him—as a matter of fact, I had offered him a job. Then he reminded me of something I had said to him at Manchester respecting that bogus telegram which lured Miss Cowley away. I asked him if anything untoward had occurred. He said it had—that in a drawer in Mr. Hersheimmer's room he had discovered a photograph." The lawyer paused, then continued: "I asked him if the photograph bore the name and address of a Californian photographer. He replied: 'You're on to it, sir. It had.' Then he went on to tell me something I *didn't* know. The original of that photograph was the French girl, Annette, who saved his life."

"What?"

"Exactly. I asked the young man with some curiosity what he had done with the photograph. He replied that he had put it back where he found it." The lawyer paused again. "That was good, you know—distinctly good. He can use his brains, that young fellow. I congratulated him. The discovery was a providential one. Of course, from the moment that the girl in Manchester was proved to be a plant everything was altered. Young Beresford saw that for himself without my having to tell it him. But he felt he couldn't trust his judgment on the subject of Miss Cowley. Did I think she was alive? I told him, duly weighing the evidence, that there was a very decided chance in favour of it. That brought us back to the telegram."

"Yes?"

"I advised him to apply to you for a copy of the original wire. It had occurred to me as probable that, after Miss Cowley flung it on the floor, certain words might have been erased and altered with the express intention of setting searchers on a false trail."

Carter nodded. He took a sheet from his pocket, and read aloud:

"COME AT ONCE, ASTLEY PRIORS, GATEHOUSE, KENT, GREAT DEVELOPMENTS—TOMMY."

"Very simple," said Sir James, "and very ingenious. Just a few words to alter, and the thing was done. And the one important clue they overlooked."

"What was that?"

"The page-boy's statement that Miss Cowley drove to Charing Cross. They were so sure of themselves that they took it for granted he had made a mistake."

"Then young Beresford is now?"

"At Gatehouse, Kent, unless I am much mistaken."

Mr. Carter looked at him curiously.

"I rather wonder you're not there too, Peel Edgerton?"

"Ah, I'm busy on a case."

"I thought you were on your holiday?"

"Oh, I've not been briefed. Perhaps it would be more correct to say I'm preparing a case. Any more facts about that American chap for me?"

"I'm afraid not. Is it important to find out who he was?"

"Oh, I know who he was," said Sir James easily. "I can't prove it yet—but I know."

The other two asked no questions. They had an instinct that it would be mere waste of breath.

"But what I don't understand," said the Prime Minister suddenly, "is how that photograph came to be in Mr. Hersheimmer's drawer?"

"Perhaps it never left it," suggested the lawyer gently.

"But the bogus inspector? Inspector Brown?"

"Ah!" said Sir James thoughtfully. He rose to his feet. "I mustn't keep you. Go on with the affairs of the nation. I must get back to—my case."

Two days later Julius Hersheimmer returned from Manchester. A note from Tommy lay on his table:

"DEAR HERSHEIMMER,

Sorry I lost my temper. In case I don't see you again, good-bye. I've been offered a job in the Argentine, and might as well take it.

Yours,
TOMMY BERESFORD."

A peculiar smile lingered for a moment on Julius's face. He threw the letter into the waste-paper basket.

"The darned fool!" he murmured.

XXIII

A Race Against Time

After ringing up Sir James, Tommy's next procedure was to make a call at South Audley Mansions. He found Albert discharging his professional duties, and introduced himself without more ado as a friend of Tuppence's. Albert unbent immediately.

"Things has been very quiet here lately," he said wistfully. "Hope the young lady's keeping well, sir?"

"That's just the point, Albert. She's disappeared."

"You don't mean as the crooks have got her?"

"They have."

"In the Underworld?"

"No, dash it all, in this world!"

"It's a h'expression, sir," explained Albert. "At the pictures the crooks always have a restoorant in the Underworld. But do you think as they've done her in, sir?"

"I hope not. By the way, have you by any chance an aunt, a cousin, a grandmother, or any other suitable female relation who might be represented as being likely to kick the bucket?"

A delighted grin spread slowly over Albert's countenance.

"I'm on, sir. My poor aunt what lives in the country has been mortal bad for a long time, and she's asking for me with her dying breath."

Tommy nodded approval.

"Can you report this in the proper quarter and meet me at Charing Cross in an hour's time?"

"I'll be there, sir. You can count on me."

As Tommy had judged, the faithful Albert proved an invaluable ally. The two took up their quarters at the inn in Gatehouse. To Albert fell the task of collecting information. There was no difficulty about it.

Astley Priors was the property of a Dr. Adams. The doctor no longer practised, had retired, the landlord believed, but he took a few private patients—here the good fellow tapped his forehead knowingly—"balmy ones! You understand!" The doctor was a popular figure in the village, subscribed freely to all the local sports—"a very pleasant, affable gentleman." Been there long? Oh, a matter of ten years or so— might be longer. Scientific gentleman, he was. Professors and people often came down from town to see him. Anyway, it was a gay house, always visitors.

In the face of all this volubility, Tommy felt doubts. Was it possible that this genial, well-known figure could be in reality a dangerous criminal? His life seemed so open and above-board. No hint of sinister doings. Suppose it was all a gigantic mistake? Tommy felt a cold chill at the thought.

Then he remembered the private patients—"balmy ones." He inquired carefully if there was a young lady amongst them, describing Tuppence. But nothing much seemed to be known about the patients—they were seldom seen outside the grounds. A guarded description of Annette also failed to provoke recognition.

Astley Priors was a pleasant red-brick edifice, surrounded by well-wooded grounds which effectually shielded the house from observation from the road.

On the first evening Tommy, accompanied by Albert, explored the grounds. Owing to Albert's insistence they dragged themselves along painfully on their stomachs, thereby producing a great deal more noise than if they had stood upright. In any case, these precautions were totally unnecessary. The grounds, like those of any other private house after nightfall, seemed untenanted. Tommy had imagined a possible fierce watchdog. Albert's fancy ran to a puma, or a tame cobra. But they reached a shrubbery near the house quite unmolested.

The blinds of the dining-room window were up. There was a large company assembled round the table. The port was passing from hand to hand. It seemed a normal, pleasant company. Through the open window scraps of conversation floated out disjointedly on the night air. It was a heated discussion on county cricket!

Again Tommy felt that cold chill of uncertainty. It seemed impossible to believe that these people were other than they seemed. Had he been fooled once more? The fair-bearded, spectacled gentleman who sat at the head of the table looked singularly honest and normal.

Tommy slept badly that night. The following morning the indefatigable Albert, having cemented an alliance with the greengrocer's boy, took the latter's place and ingratiated himself with the cook at Malthouse. He returned with the information that she was undoubtedly "one of the crooks," but Tommy mistrusted the vividness of his imagination. Questioned, he could adduce nothing in support of his statement except his own opinion that she wasn't the usual kind. You could see that at a glance.

The substitution being repeated (much to the pecuniary advantage of the real greengrocer's boy) on the following day, Albert brought back the first piece of hopeful news. There was a French young lady staying in the house. Tommy put his doubts aside. Here was confirmation of his theory. But time pressed. Today was the 27th. The 29th was the much-talked-of "Labour Day," about which all sorts of rumours were running riot. Newspapers were getting agitated. Sensational hints of a Labour *coup d'état* were freely reported. The Government said nothing. It knew and was prepared. There were rumours of dissension among the Labour leaders. They were not of one mind. The more far-seeing among them realized that what they proposed might well be a death-blow to the England that at heart they loved. They shrank from the starvation and misery a general strike would entail, and were willing to meet the Government half-way. But behind them were subtle, insistent forces at work, urging the memories of old wrongs, deprecating the weakness of half-and-half measures, fomenting misunderstandings.

Tommy felt that, thanks to Mr. Carter, he understood the position fairly accurately. With the fatal document in the hands of Mr. Brown, public opinion would swing to the side of the Labour extremists and revolutionists. Failing that, the battle was an even chance. The Government with a loyal army and police force behind them might win—but at a cost of great suffering. But Tommy nourished another and a preposterous dream. With Mr. Brown unmasked and captured he believed, rightly or wrongly, that the whole organization would crumble ignominiously and instantaneously. The strange permeating influence of the unseen chief held it together. Without him, Tommy believed an instant panic would set in; and, the honest men left to themselves, an eleventh-hour reconciliation would be possible.

"This is a one-man show," said Tommy to himself. "The thing to do is to get hold of the man."

It was partly in furtherance of this ambitious design that he had requested Mr. Carter not to open the sealed envelope. The draft treaty was Tommy's bait. Every now and then he was aghast at his own presumption. How dare he think that he had discovered what so many wiser and cleverer men had over-looked? Nevertheless, he stuck tenaciously to his idea.

That evening he and Albert once more penetrated the grounds of Astley Priors. Tommy's ambition was somehow or other to gain admission to the house itself. As they approached cautiously, Tommy gave a sudden gasp.

On the second floor window some one standing between the window and the light in the room threw a silhouette on the blind. It was one Tommy would have recognized anywhere! Tuppence was in that house!

He clutched Albert by the shoulder.

"Stay here! When I begin to sing, watch that window."

He retreated hastily to a position on the main drive, and began in a deep roar, coupled with an unsteady gait, the following ditty:

I am a Soldier
A jolly British Soldier;
You can see that I'm a Soldier by my feet . . .

It had been a favourite on the gramophone in Tuppence's hospital days. He did not doubt but that she would recognize it and draw her own conclusions. Tommy had not a note of music in his voice, but his lungs were excellent. The noise he produced was terrific.

Presently an unimpeachable butler, accompanied by an equally unimpeachable footman, issued from the front door. The butler remonstrated with him. Tommy continued to sing, addressing the butler affectionately as "dear old whiskers." The footman took him by one arm, the butler by the other. They ran him down the drive, and neatly out of the gate. The butler threatened him with the police if he intruded again. It was beautifully done—soberly and with perfect decorum. Anyone would have sworn that the butler was a real butler, the footman a real footman—only, as it happened, the butler was Whittington!

Tommy retired to the inn and waited for Albert's return. At last that worthy made his appearance.

"Well?" cried Tommy eagerly.

"It's all right. While they was a-running you out the window opened, and something was chucked out." He handed a scrap of paper to Tommy. "It was wrapped round a letter-weight."

On the paper were scrawled three words: "Tomorrow—same time."

"Good egg!" cried Tommy. "We're getting going."

"I wrote a message on a piece of paper, wrapped it round a stone, and chucked it through the window," continued Albert breathlessly.

Tommy groaned.

"Your zeal will be the undoing of us, Albert. What did you say?"

"Said we was a-staying at the inn. If she could get away, to come there and croak like a frog."

"She'll know that's you," said Tommy with a sigh of relief. "Your imagination runs away with you, you know, Albert.

Why, you wouldn't recognize a frog croaking if you heard it."
Albert looked rather crest-fallen.

"Cheer up," said Tommy. "No harm done. That butler's an
old friend of mine—I bet he knew who I was, though he
didn't let on. It's not their game to show suspicion. That's
why we've found it fairly plain sailing. They don't want to
discourage me altogether. On the other hand, they don't
want to make it too easy. I'm a pawn in their game, Albert,
that's what I am. You see, if the spider lets the fly walk out
too easily, the fly might suspect it was a put-up job. Hence
the usefulness of that promising youth, Mr. T. Beresford,
who's blundered in just at the right moment for them. But
later, Mr. T. Beresford had better look out!"

Tommy retired for the night in a state of some elation. He
had elaborated a careful plan for the following evening. He
felt sure that the inhabitants of Astley Priors would not interfere with him up to a certain point. It was after that that
Tommy proposed to give them a surprise.

About twelve o'clock, however, his calm was rudely
shaken. He was told that some one was demanding him in
the bar. The applicant proved to be a rude-looking carter
well coated with mud.

"Well, my good fellow, what is it?" asked Tommy.

"Might this be for you, sir?" The carter held out a very dirty
folded note, on the outside of which was written: "Take this
to the gentleman at the inn near Astley Priors. He will give
you ten shillings."

The handwriting was Tuppence's. Tommy appreciated her
quick-wittedness in realizing that he might be staying at the
inn under an assumed name. He snatched at it.

"That's all right."

The man withheld it.

"What about my ten shillings?"

Tommy hastily produced a ten-shilling note, and the man
relinquished his find. Tommy unfastened it.

DEAR TOMMY,

I knew it was you last night. Don't go this evening.
They'll be lying in wait for you. They're taking us away this
morning. I heard something about Wales—Holyhead, I
think.

I'll drop this on the road if I get a chance. Annette told me how you'd escaped. Buck up.

Yours,

TWOPENCE.

Tommy raised a shout for Albert before he had even finished perusing this characteristic epistle.

"Pack my bag! We're off!"

"Yes, sir." The boots of Albert could be heard racing upstairs.

Holyhead? Did that mean that, after all——Tommy was puzzled. He read on slowly.

The boots of Albert continued to be active on the floor above.

Suddenly a second shout came from below.

"Albert! I'm a damned fool! Unpack that bag!"

"Yes, sir."

Tommy smoothed out the note thoughtfully.

"Yes, a damned fool," he said softly. "But so's some one else! And at last I know who it is!"

XXIV

Julius Takes a Hand

In his suite at Claridge's, Kramenin reclined on a couch and dictated to his secretary in sibilant Russian.

Presently the telephone at the secretary's elbow purred, and he took up the receiver, spoke for a minute or two, then turned to his employer.

"Some one below is asking for you."

"Who is it?"

"He gives the name of Mr. Julius P. Hersheimmer."

"Hersheimmer," repeated Kramenin thoughtfully. "I have heard that name before."

"His father was one of the steel kings of America," explained the secretary, whose business it was to know everything. "This young man must be a millionaire several times over."

The other's eyes narrowed appreciatively.

"You had better go down and see him, Ivan. Find out what he wants."

The secretary obeyed, closing the door noiselessly behind him. In a few minutes he returned.

"He declines to state his business—says it is entirely private and personal, and that he must see you."

"A millionaire several times over," murmured Kramenin. "Bring him up, my dear Ivan."

The secretary left the room once more, and returned escorting Julius.

"Monsieur Kramenin?" said the latter abruptly.

The Russian, studying him attentively with his pale venomous eyes, bowed.

"Pleased to meet you," said the American. "I've got some very important business I'd like to talk over with you, if I can see you alone." He looked pointedly at the other.

"My secretary, Monsieur Grieber, from whom I have no secrets."

"That may be so—but I have," said Julius dryly. "So I'd be obliged if you'd tell him to scoot."

"Ivan," said the Russian softly, "perhaps you would not mind retiring into the next room——"

"The next room won't do," interrupted Julius. "I know these ducal suites—and I want this one plumb empty except for you and me. Send him round to a store to buy a penn'orth of peanuts."

Though not particularly enjoying the American's free and easy manner of speech, Kramenin was devoured by curiosity. "Will your business take long to state?"

"Might be an all night job if you caught on."

"Very good, Ivan. I shall not require you again this evening. Go to the theatre—take a night off."

"Thank you, your excellency."

The secretary bowed and departed.

Julius stood at the door watching his retreat. Finally, with a satisfied sigh, he closed it, and came back to his position in the centre of the room.

"Now, Mr. Hersheimmer, perhaps you will be so kind as to come to the point?"

"I guess that won't take a minute," drawled Julius. Then, with an abrupt change of manner: "Hands up—or I shoot!"

For a moment Kramenin stared blindly into the big automatic, then, with almost comical haste, he flung up his hands above his head. In that instant Julius had taken his

measure. The man he had to deal with was an abject physical coward—the rest would be easy.

"This is an outrage," cried the Russian in a high hysterical
voice. "An outrage! Do you mean to kill me?"

"Not if you keep your voice down. Don't go edging sideways
towards that bell. That's better."

"What do you want? Do nothing rashly. Remember my life
is of the utmost value to my country. I may have been maligned——"

"I reckon," said Julius, "that the man who let daylight into
you would be doing humanity a good turn. But you needn't
worry any. I'm not proposing to kill you this trip—that is, if
you're reasonable."

The Russian quailed before the stern menace in the
other's eyes. He passed his tongue over his dry lips.

"What do you want? Money?"

"No. I want Jane Finn."

"Jane Finn? I—never heard of her!"

"You're a darned liar! You know perfectly who I mean."

"I tell you I've never heard of the girl."

"And I tell you," retorted Julius, "that Little Willie here is
just hopping mad to go off!"

The Russian wilted visibly.

"You wouldn't dare——"

"Oh, yes, I would, son!"

Kramenin must have recognized something in the voice
that carried conviction, for he said sullenly:

"Well? Granted I do know who you mean—what of it?"

"You will tell me now—right here—where she is to be
found."

Kramenin shook his head.

"I daren't."

"Why not?"

"I daren't. You ask an impossibility."

"Afraid, eh? Of whom? Mr. Brown? Ah, that tickles you
up! There is such a person, then? I doubted it. And the mere
mention of him scares you stiff!"

"I have seen him," said the Russian slowly. "Spoken to
him face to face. I did not know it until afterwards. He was
one of a crowd. I should not know him again. Who is he

really? I do not know. But I know this—he is a man to fear."

"He'll never know," said Julius.

"He knows everything—and his vengeance is swift. Even I—Kramenin!—would not be exempt!"

"Then you won't do as I ask you?"

"You ask an impossibility."

"Sure that's a pity for you," said Julius cheerfully. "But the world in general will benefit." He raised the revolver.

"Stop," shrieked the Russian. "You cannot mean to shoot me?"

"Of course I do. I've always heard you Revolutionists held life cheap, but it seems there's a difference when it's your own life in question. I gave you just one chance of saving your dirty skin, and that you wouldn't take!"

"They would kill me!"

"Well," said Julius pleasantly, "it's up to you. But I'll just say this. Little Willie here is a dead cert, and if I was you I'd take a sporting chance with Mr. Brown!"

"You will hang if you shoot me," muttered the Russian irresolutely.

"No, stranger, that's where you're wrong. You forget the dollars. A big crowd of solicitors will get busy, and they'll get some high-brow doctors on the job, and the end of it all will be that they'll say my brain was unhinged. I shall spend a few months in a quiet sanitorium, my mental health will improve, the doctors will declare me sane again, and all will end happily for little Julius. I guess I can bear a few months' retirement in order to rid the world of you, but don't you kid yourself I'll hang for it!"

The Russian believed him. Corrupt himself, he believed implicitly in the power of money. He had read of American murder trials running much on the lines indicated by Julius. He had bought and sold justice himself. This virile young American, with the significant drawling voice, had the whip hand of him.

"I'm going to count five," continued Julius, "and I guess, if you let me get past four, you needn't worry any about Mr. Brown. Maybe he'll send some flowers to the funeral, but *you* won't smell them! Are you ready? I'll begin. One—two—three—four——"

The Russian interrupted with a shriek:

"Do not shoot. I will do all you wish."

Julius lowered the revolver.

"I thought you'd hear sense. Where is the girl?"

"At Gatehouse, in Kent. Astley Priors, the place is called."

"Is she a prisoner there?"

"She's not allowed to leave the house—though it's safe enough really. The little fool has lost her memory, curse her!"

"That's been annoying for you and your friends, I reckon. What about the other girl, the one you decoyed away over a week ago?"

"She's there too," said the Russian sullenly.

"That's good," said Julius. "Isn't it all panning out beautifully? And a lovely night for the run!"

"What run?" demanded Kramenin, with a stare.

"Down to Gatehouse, sure. I hope you're fond of motoring?"

"What do you mean? I refuse to go."

"Now don't get mad. You must see I'm not such a kid as to leave you here. You'd ring up your friends on that telephone first thing! Ah!" He observed the fall on the other's face. "You see, you'd got it all fixed. No, sir, you're coming along with me. This your bedroom next door here? Walk right in. Little Willie and I will come behind. Put on a thick coat, that's right. Fur lined? And you a Socialist! Now we're ready. We walk downstairs and out through the hall to where my car's waiting. And don't you forget I've got you covered every inch of the way. I can shoot just as well through my coat pocket. One word, or a glance even, at one of those liveried menials, and there'll sure be a strange face in the Sulphur and Brimstone Works!"

Together they descended the stairs, and passed out to the waiting car. The Russian was shaking with rage. The hotel servants surrounded them. A cry hovered on his lips, but at the last minute his nerve failed him. The American was a man of his word.

When they reached the car, Julius breathed a sigh of relief. The danger-zone was passed. Fear had successfully hypnotized the man by his side.

"Get in," he ordered. Then as he caught the other's side-long glance, "No, the chauffeur won't help you any. Naval man. Was on a submarine in Russia when the Revolution broke out. A brother of his was murdered by your people. George!"

"Yes, sir?" The chauffeur turned his head.

"This gentleman is a Russian Bolshevik. We don't want to shoot him, but it may be necessary. You understand?"

"Perfectly, sir."

"I want to go to Gatehouse in Kent. Know the road at all?"

"Yes, sir, it will be about an hour and a half's run."

"Make it an hour. I'm in a hurry."

"I'll do my best, sir." The car shot forward through the traffic.

Julius ensconced himself comfortably by the side of his victim. He kept his hand in the pocket of his coat, but his manner was urbane to the last degree.

"There was a man I shot once in Arizona——" he began cheerfully.

At the end of the hour's run the unfortunate Kramenin was more dead than alive. In succession to the anecdote of the Arizona man, there had been a tough from 'Frisco, and an episode in the Rockies. Julius's narrative style, if not strictly accurate, was picturesque!

Slowing down, the chauffeur called over his shoulder that they were just coming into Gatehouse. Julius bade the Russian direct them. His plan was to drive straight up to the house. There Kramenin was to ask for the two girls. Julius explained to him that Little Willie would not be tolerant of failure. Kramenin, by this time, was putty in the other's hands. The terrific pace they had come had still further un-manned him. He had given himself up for dead at every cor-ner.

The car swept up the drive, and stopped before the porch. The chauffeur looked round for orders.

"Turn the car first, George. Then ring the bell, and get back to your place. Keep the engine going, and be ready to scoot like hell when I give the word."

"Very good, sir."

The front door was opened by the butler. Kramenin felt

the muzzle of the revolver pressing against his ribs.

"Now," hissed Julius. "And be careful."

The Russian beckoned. His lips were white, and his voice was not very steady:

"It is I—Kramenin! Bring down the girl at once! There is no time to lose!"

Whittington had come down the steps. He uttered an exclamation of astonishment at seeing the other.

"You! What's up? Surely you know the plan——"

Kramenin interrupted him, using the words that have created many unnecessary panics:

"We have been betrayed! Plans must be abandoned. We must save our own skins. The girl! And at once! It's our only chance."

Whittington hesitated, but for hardly a moment.

"You have orders—from *him*?"

"Naturally! Should I be here otherwise? Hurry! There is no time to be lost. The other little fool had better come too."

Whittington turned and ran back into the house. The agonizing minutes went by. Then—two figures hastily huddled in cloaks appeared on the steps and were hustled into the car. The smaller of the two was inclined to resist and Whittington shoved her in unceremoniously. Julius leaned forward, and in doing so the light from the open door lit up his face. Another man on the steps behind Whittington gave a startled exclamation. Concealment was at an end.

"Get a move on, George," shouted Julius.

The chauffeur slipped in his clutch, and with a bound the car started.

The man on the steps uttered on oath. His hand went to his pocket. There was a flash and a report. The bullet just missed the taller girl by an inch.

"Get down, Jane," cried Julius. "Flat on the bottom of the car." He thrust her sharply forward, then standing up, he took careful aim and fired.

"Have you hit him?" cried Tuppence eagerly.

"Sure," replied Julius. "He isn't killed, though. Skunks like that take a lot of killing. Are you all right, Tuppence?"

"Of course I am. Where's Tommy? And who's this?" She indicated the shivering Kramenin.

"Tommy's making tracks for the Argentine. I guess he thought you'd turned up your toes. Steady through the gate, George! That's right. It'll take 'em at least five minutes to get busy after us. They'll use the telephone, I guess, so look out for snares ahead—and don't take the direct route. Who's this, did you say, Tuppence? Let me present Monsieur Kramenin. I persuaded him to come on the trip for his health."

The Russian remained mute, still livid with terror.

"But what made them let us go?" demanded Tuppence suspiciously.

"I reckon Monsieur Kramenin here asked them so prettily they just couldn't refuse!"

This was too much for the Russian. He burst out vehemently:

"Curse you—curse you! They know now that I betrayed them. My life won't be safe for an hour in this country."

"That's so," assented Julius. "I'd advise you to make tracks for Russia right away."

"Let me go, then," cried the other. "I have done what you asked. Why do you still keep me with you?"

"Not for the pleasure of your company. I guess you can get right off now if you want to. I thought you'd rather I tooled you back to London."

"You may never reach London," snarled the other. "Let me go here and now."

"Sure thing. Pull up, George. The gentleman's not making the return trip. If I ever come to Russia, Monsieur Kramenin, I shall expect a rousing welcome, and——"

But before Julius had finished his speech, and before the car had finally halted, the Russian had swung himself out and disappeared into the night.

"Just a mite impatient to leave us," commented Julius, as the car gathered way again. "And no idea of saying good-bye politely to the ladies. Say, Jane, you can get up on the seat now."

For the first time the girl spoke.

"How did you 'persuade' him?" she asked.

Julius tapped his revolver.

"Little Willie here takes the credit!"

"Splendid !" cried the girl. The colour surged into her face, her eyes looked admiringly at Julius.

"Annette and I didn't know what was going to happen to us," said Tuppence. "Old Whittington hurried us off. *We* thought it was lambs to the slaughter."

"Annette," said Julius. "Is that what you call her?"

His mind seemed to be trying to adjust itself to a new idea.

"It's her name," said Tuppence, opening her eyes very wide.

"Shucks!" retorted Julius. "She may think it's her name, because her memory's gone, poor kid. But it's the one real and original Jane Finn we've got here."

"What——?" cried Tuppence.

But she was interrupted. With an angry spurt, a bullet embedded itself in the upholstery of the car just behind her head.

"Down with you," cried Julius. "It's an ambush. These guys have got busy pretty quickly. Push her a bit, George."

The car fairly leapt forward. Three more shots rang out, but went happily wide. Julius, upright, leant over the back of the car.

"Nothing to shoot at," he announced gloomily. "But I guess there'll be another little picnic soon. Ah!"

He raised his hand to his cheek.

"You are hurt?" said Annette quickly.

"Only a scratch."

The girl sprang to her feet.

"Let me out! Let me out, I say! Stop the car. It is me they're after. I'm the one they want. You shall not lose your lives because of me. Let me go." She was fumbling with the fastenings of the door.

Julius took her by both arms, and looked at her. She had spoken with no trace of foreign accent.

"Sit down, kid," he said gently. "I guess there's nothing wrong with your memory. Been fooling them all the time, eh?"

The girl looked at him, nodded, and then suddenly burst into tears. Julius patted her on the shoulder.

"There, there—just you sit tight. We're not going to let you quit."

Through her sobs the girl said indistinctly:

"You're from home. I can tell by your voice. It makes me home-sick."

"Sure I'm from home. I'm your cousin—Julius Hersheimmer. I came over to Europe on purpose to find you—and a pretty dance you've led me."

The car slackened speed. George spoke over his shoulder: "Cross-roads here, sir. I'm not sure of the way."

The car slowed down till it hardly moved. As it did so a figure climbed suddenly over the back, and plunged head first into the midst of them.

"Sorry," said Tommy, extricating himself.

A mass of confused exclamations greeted him. He replied to them severally:

"Was in the bushes by the drive. Hung on behind. Couldn't let you know before at the pace you were going. It was all I could do to hang on. Now then, you girls, get out!"

"Get out?"

"Yes. There's a station just up that road. Train due in three minutes. You'll catch it if you hurry."

"What the devil are you driving at?" demanded Julius. "Do you think you can fool them by leaving the car?"

"You and I aren't going to leave the car. Only the girls."

"You're crazed, Beresford. Start staring mad! You can't let those girls go off alone. It'll be the end of it if you do."

Tommy turned to Tuppence.

"Get out at once, Tuppence. Take her with you, and do just as I say. No one will do you any harm. You're safe. Take the train to London. Go straight to Sir James Peel Edgerton. Mr. Carter lives out of town, but you'll be safe with him."

"Darn you!" cried Julius. "You're mad. Jane, you stay where you are."

With a sudden swift movement, Tommy snatched the revolver from Julius's hand, and levelled it at him.

"Now will you believe I'm in earnest? Get out, both of you, and do as I say—or I'll shoot!"

Tuppence sprang out, dragging the unwilling Jane after her.

"Come on, it's all right. If Tommy's sure—he's sure. Be quick. We'll miss the train."

They started running.

Julius's pent-up rage burst forth.

"What the hell——"

Tommy interrupted him.

"Dry up! I want a few words with you, Mr. Julius Hersheimmer."

XXV

Jane's Story

Her arm through Jane's, dragging her along, Tuppence reached the station. Her quick ears caught the sound of the approaching train.

"Hurry up," she panted, "or we'll miss it."

They arrived on the platform just as the train came to a standstill. Tuppence opened the door of an empty first-class compartment, and the two girls sank down breathless on the padded mats.

A man looked in, then passed on to the next carriage. Jane started nervously. Her eyes dilated with terror. She looked questioningly at Tuppence.

"Is he one of them, do you think?" she breathed.

Tuppence shook her head.

"No, no. It's all right." She took Jane's hand in hers. "Tommy wouldn't have told us to do this unless he was sure we'd be all right."

"But he doesn't know them as I do!" The girl shivered. "You don't understand. Five years! Five long years! Sometimes I thought I should go mad."

"Never mind. It's all over."

"Is it?"

The train was moving now, speeding through the night at a gradually increasing rate. Suddenly Jane Finn started up.

"What was that? I thought I saw a face—looking in through the window."

"No, there's nothing. See." Tuppence went to the window, and lifting the strap let the pane down.

"You're sure?"

"Quite sure."

The other seemed to feel some excuse was necessary:

"I guess I'm acting like a frightened rabbit, but I can't help it. If they caught me now they'd——" Her eyes opened wide and staring.

"Don't!" implored Tuppence. "Lie back, and *don't think.* You can be quite sure that Tommy wouldn't have said it was safe if it wasn't."

"My cousin didn't think so. He didn't want us to do this."

"No," said Tuppence, rather embarrassed.

"What are you thinking of?" said Jane sharply.

"Why?"

"Your voice was so—queer!"

"I *was* thinking of something," confessed Tuppence. "But I don't want to tell you—not now. I may be wrong, but I don't think so. It's just an idea that came into my head a long time ago. Tommy's got it too—I'm almost sure he has. But don't *you* worry—there'll be time enough for that later. And it mayn't be so at all! Do what I tell you—lie back and don't think of anything."

"I'll try." The long lashes drooped over the hazel eyes.

Tuppence, for her part, sat bolt upright—much in the attitude of a watchful terrier on guard. In spite of herself she was nervous. Her eyes flashed continually from one window to the other. She noted the exact position of the communication cord. What it was that she feared, she would have been hard put to it to say. But in her own mind she was far from feeling the confidence displayed in her words. Not that she disbelieved in Tommy, but occasionally she was shaken with doubts as to whether anyone so simple and honest as he was could ever be a match for fiendish subtlety of the arch-criminal.

If they once reached Sir James Peel Edgerton in safety, all would be well. But would they reach him? Would not the silent forces of Mr. Brown already be assembling against them? Even that last picture of Tommy, revolver in hand, failed to comfort her. By now he might be overpowered, borne down by sheer force of numbers. . . . Tuppence mapped out her plan of campaign.

As the train at length drew slowly into Charing Cross, Jane Finn sat up with a start.

"Have we arrived? I never thought we should!"

"Oh, I thought we'd get to London all right. If there's going to be any fun, now is when it will begin. Quick, get out. We'll nip into a taxi."

In another minute they were passing the barrier, had paid the necessary fares, and were stepping into a taxi.

"King's Cross," directed Tuppence. Then she gave a jump. A man looked in at the window, just as they started. She was almost certain it was the same man who had got into the carriage next to them. She had a horrible feeling of being slowly hemmed in on every side.

"You see," she explained to Jane, "if they think we're going to Sir James, this will put them off the scent. Now they'll imagine we're going to Mr. Carter. His country place is north of London somewhere."

Crossing Holborn there was a block, and the taxi was held up. This was what Tuppence had been waiting for.

"Quick," she whispered. "Open the right-hand door!"

The two girls stepped out into the traffic. Two minutes later they were seated in another taxi and were retracing their steps, this time direct to Carlton House Terrace.

"There," said Tuppence, with great satisfaction, "this ought to do them. I can't help thinking that I'm really rather clever! How that other taxi man will swear! But I took his number, and I'll send him a postal order to-morrow, so that he won't lose by it if he happens to be genuine. What's this thing swerving——Oh!"

There was a grinding noise and a bump. Another taxi had collided with them.

In a flash Tuppence was out on the pavement. A police-man was approaching. Before he arrived Tuppence had handed the driver five shillings, and she and Jane had merged themselves in the crowd.

"It's only a step or two now," said Tuppence breathlessly. The accident had taken place in Trafalgar Square.

"Do you think the collision was an accident, or done deliberately?"

"I don't know. It might have been either."

Hand-in-hand, the two girls hurried along.

"It may be my fancy," said Tuppence suddenly, "but I feel as though there was some one behind us."

"Hurry!" murmured the other. "Oh, hurry!"

They were now at the corner of Carlton House Terrace, and their spirits lightened. Suddenly a large and apparently intoxicated man barred their way.

"Good evening, ladies," he hiccupped. "Whither away so fast?"

"Let us pass, please," said Tuppence imperiously.

"Just a word with your pretty friend here." He stretched out an unsteady hand, and clutched Jane by the shoulder. Tuppence heard other footsteps behind. She did not pause to ascertain whether they were friends or foes. Lowering her head, she repeated a manoeuvre of childish days, and butted their aggressor full in the capacious middle. The success of these unsportsman like tactics was immediate. The man sat down abruptly on the pavement. Tuppence and Jane took to their heels. The house they sought was some way down. Other footsteps echoed behind them. Their breath was coming in choking gasps as they reached Sir James's door. Tuppence seized the bell and Jane the knocker.

The man who had stopped them reached the foot of the steps. For a moment he hesitated, and as he did so the door opened. They fell into the hall together. Sir James came forward from the library door.

"Hullo! What's this?"

He stepped forward, and put his arms round Jane as she swayed uncertainly. He half carried her into the library, and laid her on the leather couch. From a tantalus on the table he poured out a few drops of brandy, and forced her to drink them. With a sigh she sat up, her eyes still wild and frightened.

"It's all right. Don't be afraid, my child. You're quite safe."

Her breath came more normally, and the colour was returning to her cheeks. Sir James looked at Tuppence quizzically.

"So you're not dead, Miss Tuppence, any more than that Tommy boy of yours was!"

"The Young Adventurers take a lot of killing," boasted Tuppence.

"So it seems," said Sir James dryly. "Am I right in thinking that the joint venture has ended in success, and that this"—he turned to the girl on the couch—"is Miss Jane Finn?"

Jane sat up.

"Yes," she said quietly, "I am Jane Finn. I have a lot to tell you."

"When you are stronger——"

"No—now!" Her voice rose a little. "I shall feel safer when I have told everything."

"As you please," said the lawyer.

He sat down in one of the big arm-chairs facing the couch. In a low voice Jane began her story.

"I came over on the *Lusitania* to take up a post in Paris. I was fearfully keen about the war, and just dying to help somehow or other. I had been studying French, and my teacher said they were wanting help in a hospital in Paris, so I wrote and offered my services, and they were accepted. I hadn't got any folk of my own, so it made it easy to arrange things.

"When the *Lusitania* was torpedoed, a man came up to me. I'd noticed him more than once—and I'd figured it out in my own mind that he was afraid of somebody or something. He asked me if I was a patriotic American, and told me he was carrying papers which were just life or death to the Allies. He asked me to take charge of them. I was to watch for an advertisement in the *Times*. If it didn't appear, I was to take them to the American Ambassador.

"Most of what followed seems like a nightmare still. I see it in my dreams sometimes. . . . I'll hurry over that part. Mr. Danvers had told me to watch out. He might have been shadowed from New York, but he didn't think so. At first I had no suspicions, but on the boat to Holyhead I began to get uneasy. There was one woman who had been very keen to look after me, and chum up with me generally—a Mrs. Vandemeyer. At first I'd been only grateful to her for being so kind to me; but all the time I felt there was something about her I didn't like, and on the Irish boat I saw her talking to some queer-looking men, and from the way they looked I saw that they were talking about me. I remembered that she'd been quite near me on the *Lusitania* when Mr. Danvers gave me the packet, and before that she'd tried to talk to him once or twice. I began to get scared, but I didn't quite see what to do.

"I had a wild idea of stopping at Holyhead, and not going on to London that day, but I soon saw that that would be plumb foolishness. The only thing was to act as though I'd noticed nothing, and hope for the best. I couldn't see how they could get me if I was on my guard. One thing I'd done already as a precaution—ripped open the oilskin packet and substituted blank paper, and then sewn it up again. So, if anyone did manage to rob me of it, it wouldn't matter.

"What to do with the real thing worried me no end. Finally I opened it out flat—there were only two sheets—and laid it between two of the advertisement pages of a magazine. I stuck the two pages together round the edge with some gum off an envelope. I carried the magazine carelessly stuffed into the pocket of my ulster.

"At Holyhead I tried to get into a carriage with people that looked all right, but in a queer way there seemed always to be a crowd round me shoving and pushing me just the way I didn't want to go. There was something uncanny and frightening about it. In the end I found myself in a carriage with Mrs. Vandemeyer after all. I went out into the corridor, but all the other carriages were full, so I had to go back and sit down. I consoled myself with the thought that there were other people in the carriage—there was quite a nice-looking man and his wife sitting just opposite. So I felt almost happy about it until just outside London. I had leaned back and closed my eyes. I guess they thought I was asleep, but my eyes weren't quite shut, and suddenly I saw the nice-looking man get something out of his bag and hand it to Mrs. Vandemeyer, and as he did so he *winked*. . . .

"I can't tell you how that wink sort of froze me through and through. My only thought was to get out in the corridor as quick as ever I could. I got up, trying to look natural and easy. Perhaps they saw something—I don't know—but suddenly Mrs. Vandemeyer said 'Now,' and flung something over my nose and mouth as I tried to scream. At the same moment I felt a terrific blow on the back of my head. . . ."

She shuddered. Sir James murmured something sympathetically. In a minute she resumed:

"I don't know how long it was before I came back to consciousness. I felt very ill and sick. I was lying on a dirty bed. There was a screen round it, but I could hear two people talking in the room. Mrs. Vandemeyer was one of them. I tried to listen, but at first I couldn't take much in. When at last I did begin to grasp what was going on—I was just terrified! I wonder I didn't scream right out there and then.

"They hadn't found the papers. They'd got the oilskin packet with the blanks, and they were just mad! They didn't know whether I'd changed the papers, or whether Danvers had been carrying a dummy message, while the real one was sent another way. They spoke of"—she closed her eyes— "torturing me to find out!

"I'd never known what fear—really sickening fear—was before! Once they came to look at me. I shut my eyes and pretended to be still unconscious, but I was afraid they'd hear the beating of my heart. However, they went away again. I began thinking madly. What could I do? I knew I wouldn't be able to stand up against torture very long.

"Suddenly something put the thought of loss of memory into my head. The subject had always interested me, and I'd read an awful lot about it. I had the whole thing at my fingertips. If only I could succeed in carrying the bluff through, it might save me. I said a prayer, and drew a long breath. Then I opened my eyes and started babbling in *French*!

"Mrs. Vandemeyer came round the screen at once. Her face was so wicked I nearly died, but I smiled up at her doubtfully, and asked her in French where I was.

"It puzzled her, I could see. She called the man she had

been talking to. He stood by the screen with his face in shadow. He spoke to me in French. His voice was very ordinary and quiet, but somehow, I don't know why, he scared me worse than the woman. I felt he'd see right through me, but I went on playing my part. I asked again where I was, and then went on that there was something I *must* remember—*must* remember—only for the moment it was all gone. I worked myself up to be more and more distressed. He asked me my name. I said I didn't know—that I couldn't remember anything at all.

"Suddenly he caught my wrist, and began twisting it. The pain was awful. I screamed. He went on. I screamed and screamed, but I managed to shriek out things in French. I don't know how long I could have gone on, but luckily I fainted. The last thing I heard was his voice saying: 'That's not bluff! Anyway, a kid of her age wouldn't know enough.' I guess he forgot American girls are older for their age than English ones, and take more interest in scientific subjects.

"When I came to, Mrs. Vandemeyer was sweet as honey to me. She'd had her orders, I guess. She spoke to me in French—told me I'd had a shock and been very ill. I should be better soon. I pretended to be rather dazed—murmured something about the 'doctor' having hurt my wrist. She looked relieved when I said that.

"By and by she went out of the room altogether. I was suspicious still, and lay quite quiet for some time. In the end, however, I got up and walked round the room, examining it. I thought that even if anyone *was* watching me from somewhere, it would seem natural enough under the circumstances. It was a squalid, dirty place. There were no windows, which seemed queer. I guessed the door would be locked, but I didn't try it. There were some battered old pictures on the walls, representing scenes from *Faust*."

Jane's two listeners give a simultaneous "Ah!" The girl nodded.

"Yes—it was the place in Soho where Mr. Beresford was imprisoned. Of course, at the time I didn't even know if I was in London. One thing was worrying me dreadfully, but my heart gave a great throb of relief when I saw my ulster lying carelessly over the back of a chair. *And the magazine was still rolled up in the pocket!*

"If only I could be certain that I was not being overlooked! I looked carefully round the walls. There didn't seem to be a peep-hole of any kind—nevertheless I felt kind of sure there must be. All of a sudden I sat down on the edge of the table, and put my face in my hands, sobbing out a *'Mon Dieu! Mon Dieu!'* I've got very sharp ears. I distinctly heard the rustle of a dress, and slight creak. That was enough for me. I was being watched!

"I lay down on the bed again, and by and by Mrs. Vandemeyer brought me some supper. She was still sweet as they make them. I guess she'd been told to win my confidence. Presently she produced the oilskin packet, and asked me if I recognized it, watching me like a lynx all the time.

"I took it and turned it over in a puzzled sort of way. Then I shook my head. I said that I felt *ought* to remember something about it, that it was just as though it was all coming back, and then, before I could get hold of it, it went again. Then she told me that I was her niece, and that I was to call her 'Aunt Rita.' I did obediently, and she told me not to worry—my memory soon would soon come back.

"That was an awful night. I'd made my plan whilst I was waiting for her. The papers were safe so far, but I couldn't take the risk of leaving them there any longer. They might throw that magazine away any minute. I lay awake waiting until I judged it must be about two o'clock in the morning. Then I got up as softly as I could, and felt in the dark along the left-hand wall. Very gently, I unhooked one of the pictures from its nail—Marguerite with her casket of jewels. I crept over to my coat and took out the magazine, and an odd envelope or two that I had shoved in. Then I went to the washstand, and damped the brown paper at the back of the picture all round. Presently I was able to pull it away. I had already torn out the two stuck-together pages from the magazine, and now I slipped them with their precious enclosure between the picture and its brown paper backing. A little gum from the envelopes helped me to stick the latter up again. No one would dream the picture had ever been tampered with. I rehung it on the wall, put the magazine back in my coat pocket, and crept back to bed. I was pleased with my hiding-place. They'd never think of pulling to pieces one of their own pictures. I hoped that they'd come to the conclusion that Danvers had been carrying a dummy all along, and that, in the end, they'd let me go.

"As a matter of fact, I guess that's what they did think at first and, in a way, it was dangerous for me. I learnt afterwards that they nearly did away with me then and there—there was never much chance of their 'letting me go'—but the first man, who was the boss, preferred to keep me alive on the chance of my having hidden them, and being able to tell where if I recovered my memory. They watched me constantly for weeks. Sometimes they'd ask me questions by the hour—I guess there was nothing they didn't know about the third degree!—but somehow I managed to hold my own. The strain of it was awful, though . . .

"They took me back to Ireland, and over every step of the journey again, in case I'd hidden it somewhere *en route*. Mrs. Vandemeyer and another woman never left me for a moment. They spoke of me as a young relative of Mrs. Vandemeyer's whose mind was affected by the shock of the *Lusitania*. There was no one I could appeal to for help without giving myself away to *them*, and if I risked it and failed—and Mrs. Vandemeyer looked so rich, and so beautifully dressed, that I felt convinced they'd take her word against mine, and think it was part of my mental trouble to think myself 'persecuted'—I felt that the horrors in store for me would be too awful once they knew I'd been only shamming."

Sir James nodded comprehendingly.

"Mrs. Vandemeyer was a woman of great personality. With that and her social position she would have had little difficulty in imposing her point of view in preference to yours. Your sensational accusations against her would not easily have found credence."

"That's what I thought. It ended in my being sent to a sanitorium at Bournemouth. I couldn't make up my mind at first whether it was a sham affair or genuine. A hospital nurse had charge of me. I was a special patient. She seemed so nice and normal that at last I determined to confide in her. A merciful providence just saved me in time from falling into the trap. My door happened to be ajar, and I heard her talking to some one in the passage. *She was one of them!* They still fancied it might be a bluff on my part, and she was put in charge of me to make sure! After that, my nerve went completely. I dared trust nobody.

"I think I almost hypnotized myself. After a while, I almost forgot that I was really Jane Finn. I was so bent on playing the part of Janet Vandemeyer that my nerves began to play me tricks. I became really ill—for months I sank into a sort of stupor. I felt sure I should die soon, and that nothing really mattered. A sane person shut up in a lunatic asylum often ends by becoming insane, they say. I guess I was like that. Playing my part had become second nature to me. I wasn't even unhappy in the end—just apathetic. Nothing seemed to matter. And the years went on.

"And then suddenly things seemed to change. Mrs. Vandemeyer came down from London. She and the doctor asked me questions, experimented with various treatments. There was some talk of sending me to a specialist in Paris. In the end, they did not dare risk it. I overheard something that seemed to show that other people—friends—were looking for me. I learnt later that the nurse who had looked after me went to Paris, and consulted a specialist, representing herself to be me. He put her through some searching tests, and exposed her loss of memory to be fraudulent; but she had taken a note of his methods and reproduced them on me. I dare say I couldn't have deceived the specialist for a minute—a man who has made a lifelong study of a thing is unique—but I managed once again to hold my own with them. The fact that I'd not thought of myself as Jane Finn for so long made it easier.

"One night I was whisked off to London at a moment's notice. They took me back to the house in Soho. Once I got away from the sanitorium I felt different—as though something in me that had been buried for a long time was waking up again.

"They sent me in to wait on Mr. Beresford. (Of course I didn't know his name then.) I was suspicious—I thought it was another trap. But he looked so honest, I could hardly believe it. However, I was careful in all I said, for I knew we could be overheard. There's a small hole, high up in the wall.

"But on the Sunday afternoon a message was brought to the house. They were all very disturbed. Without their knowing, I listened. Word had come that he was to be killed. I needn't tell the next part, because you know it. I thought I'd have time to rush up and get the papers from their hiding-place, but I was caught. So I screamed out that he was escaping, and I said I wanted to go back to Marguerite. I shouted the name three times very loud. I knew the others would think I meant Mrs. Vandemeyer, but I hoped it might make Mr. Beresford think of the picture. He'd unhooked one the first day—that's what made me hesitate to trust him."

She paused.

"Then the papers," said Sir James slowly, "are still at the back of the picture in that room."

"Yes." The girl had sunk back on the sofa exhausted with the strain of the long story.

Sir James rose to his feet. He looked at his watch.

"Come," he said, "we must go at once."

"To-night?" queried Tuppence, surprised.

"To-morrow may be too late," said Sir James gravely. "Besides, by going to-night we have the chance of capturing that great man and super-criminal—Mr. Brown!"

There was dead silence, and Sir James continued:

"You have been followed here—not a doubt of it. When we leave the house we shall be followed again, but not molested, *for it is Mr. Brown's plan that we are to lead him.* But the Soho house is under police supervision night and day. There are several men watching it. When we enter that house, Mr. Brown will not draw back—he will risk all, on the chance of obtaining the spark to fire his mine. And he fancies the risk not great—since he will enter in the guise of a friend!"

Tuppence flushed, then opened her mouth impulsively.

"But there's something you don't know—that we haven't told you." Her eyes dwelt on Jane in perplexity.

"What is that?" asked the other sharply. "No hesitations, Miss Tuppence. We need to be sure of our going."

But Tuppence, for once, seemed tongue-tied.

"It's so difficult—you see, if I'm wrong—oh, it would be

dreadful." She made a grimace at the unconscious Jane. "Never forgive me," she observed cryptically.

"You want me to help you out, eh?"

"Yes, please. You know who Mr. Brown is, don't you?"

"Yes," said Sir James gravely. "At last I do."

"At last?" queried Tuppence doubtfully. "Oh, but I thought——" She paused.

"You thought correctly, Miss Tuppence. I have been morally certain of his identity for some time—ever since the night of Mrs. Vandemeyer's mysterious death."

"Ah!" breathed Tuppence.

"For there we are up against the logic of facts. There are only two solutions. Either the choral was administered by her own hand, which theory I reject utterly, or else——"

"Yes?"

"Or else it was administered in the brandy you gave her. Only three people touched that brandy—you, Miss Tuppence, I myself, and one other—Mr. Julius Hersheimmer!"

Jane Finn stirred and sat up, regarding the speaker with wide astonished eyes.

"At first, the thing seemed utterly impossible. Mr. Hersheimmer, as the son of a prominent millionaire, was a well known figure in America. It seemed utterly impossible that he and Mr. Brown could be one and the same. But you cannot escape from the logic of facts. Since the thing was so— it must be accepted. Remember Mrs. Vandemeyer's sudden and inexplicable agitation. Another proof, if proof was needed.

"I took an early opportunity of giving you a hint. From some words of Mr. Hersheimmer's at Manchester, I gathered that you had understood and acted on that hint. Then I set to work to prove the impossible possible. Mr. Beresford rang me up and told me, what I had already suspected, that the photograph of Miss Jane Finn had never really been out of Mr. Hersheimmer's possession——"

But the girl interrupted. Springing to her feet, she cried out angrily:

"What do you mean? What are you trying to suggest? That

Mr. Brown is *Julius?* Julius—my own cousin!"

"No, Miss Finn," said Sir James unexpectedly. "Not your cousin. The man who calls himself Julius Hersheimmer is no relation to you whatsoever."

XXVI

MR. BROWN

Sir James' words came like a bomb-shell. Both girls looked equally puzzled. The lawyer went across to his desk, and returned with a small newspaper cutting, which he handed to Jane. Tuppence read it over her shoulder. Mr. Carter would have recognized it. It referred to the mysterious man found dead in New York.

"As I was saying to Miss Tuppence," resumed the lawyer, "I set to work to prove the impossible possible. The great stumbling-block was the undeniable fact that Julius Hersheimmer was not an assumed name. When I came across this paragraph my problem was solved. Julius Hersheimmer set out to discover what had become of his cousin. He went out West, where he obtained news of her and her photograph to aid him in his search. On the eve of his departure from New York he was set upon and murdered. His body was dressed in shabby clothes, and the face disfigured to prevent identification. Mr. Brown took his place. He sailed immediately for England. None of the real Hersheimmer's friends or intimates saw him before he sailed—though indeed it would hardly have mattered if they had, the impersonation was so perfect. Since then he had been hand and glove with those sworn to hunt him down. Every secret of theirs has been known to him. Only once did he come near disaster. Mrs. Vandemeyer knew his secret. It was no part of his plan that that huge bribe should ever be offered to her. But for Miss Tuppence's fortunate change of plan, she would have been far away from the flat when we arrived there. Exposure stared him in the face. He took a desperate step, trusting in his assumed character to avert suspicion. He nearly succeeded—but not quite."

"I can't believe it," murmured Jane. "He seemed so splendid."

"The real Julius Hersheimmer *was* a splendid fellow! And Mr. Brown is a consummate actor. But ask Miss Tuppence if she also has not had her suspicions."

Jane turned mutely to Tuppence. The latter nodded.

"I didn't want to say it, Jane—I knew it would hurt you. And, after all, I couldn't be sure. I still don't understand why, if he's Mr. Brown, he rescued us."

"Was it Julius Hersheimmer who helped you to escape?"

Tuppence recounted to Sir James the exciting events of the evening, ending up: "But I can't see *why!*"

"Can't you? I can. So can young Beresford, by his actions. As a last hope Jane Finn was to be allowed to escape—and the escape must be managed so that she harbours no suspicions of its being a put-up job. They're not averse to young Beresford's being in the neighbourhood, and, if necessary, communicating with you. They'll take care to get him out of the way at the right minute. Then Julius Hersheimmer dashes up and rescues you in true melodramatic style. Bullets fly—but don't hit anybody. What would have happened next? You would have driven straight to the house in Soho and secured the document which Miss Finn would probably have entrusted to her cousin's keeping. Or, if he conducted the search, he would have pretended to find the hiding-place already rifled. He would have had a dozen ways of dealing with the situation, but the result would have been the same. And I rather fancy some accident would have happened to both of you. You see, you know rather an inconvenient

amount. That's a rough outline. I admit I was caught nap-
ping; but somebody else wasn't."

"Tommy," said Tuppence softly.

"Yes. Evidently when the right moment came to get rid of
him—he was too sharp for them. All the same, I'm not too
easy in my mind about him."

"Why?"

"Because Julius Hersheimmer is Mr. Brown," said Sir
James dryly. "And it takes more than one man and a revolver to hold up Mr. Brown. . . ."

Tuppence paled a little.

"What can we do?"

"Nothing until we've been to the house in Soho. If Beresford has still got the upper hand, there's nothing to fear. If
otherwise, our enemy will come to find us, and he will not
find us unprepared!" From a drawer in the desk, he took a
service revolver, and placed it in his coat pocket.

"Now we're ready. I know better than even to suggest going
without you, Miss Tuppence——"

"I should think so indeed!"

"But I do suggest that Miss Finn should remain here. She
will be perfectly safe, and I am afraid she is absolutely worn
out with all she has been through."

But to Tuppence's surprise Jane shook her head.

"No. I guess I'm going too. Those papers were my trust. I
must go through with this business to the end. I'm heaps
better now anyway."

Sir James's car was ordered round. During the short drive
Tuppence's heart beat tumultuously. In spite of the momentary qualms of uneasiness respecting Tommy, she
could not but feel exultation. They were going to win!

The car drew up at the corner of the square and they got
out. Sir James went up to a plain-clothes man who was on
duty with several others, and spoke to him. Then he rejoined
the girls.

"No one has gone into the house so far. It is being watched
at the back as well, so they are quite sure of that. Anyone
who attempts to enter after we have done so will be arrested
immediately. Shall we go in?"

A policeman produced a key. They all knew Sir James

well. They had also had orders respecting Tuppence. Only the third member of the party was unknown to them. The three entered the house, pulling the door to behind them. Slowly they mounted the rickety stairs. At the top was the ragged curtain hiding the recess where Tommy had hidden that day. Tuppence had heard the story from Jane in her character of "Annette." She looked at the tattered velvet with interest. Even now she could almost swear it moved—as though *some one* was behind it. So strong was the illusion that she almost fancied she could make out the outline of a form. . . . Supposing Mr. Brown—Julius—was there waiting. . . .

Impossible of course! Yet she almost went back to put the curtain aside and make sure. . . .

Now they were entering the prison room. No place for any one to hide here, thought Tuppence, with a sigh of relief, then chided herself indignantly. She must not give way to this foolish fancying—this curious insistent feeling that *Mr. Brown was in the house.* . . . Hark! What was that? A stealthy footstep on the stairs? There *was* some one in the house! Absurd! She was becoming hysterical.

Jane had gone straight to the picture of Marguerite. She unhooked it with a steady hand. The dust lay thick upon it, and festoons of cobwebs lay between it and the wall. Sir James handed her a pocket-knife, and she ripped away the brown paper from the back. . . . The advertisement page of a magazine fell out. Jane picked it up. Holding apart the frayed inner edges she extracted two thin sheets covered with writing!

No dummy this time! The real thing!

"We've got it," said Tuppence. "At last. . . ."

The moment was almost breathless in its emotion. Forgotten the faint creakings, the imagined noises of a minute ago. None of them had eyes for anything but what Jane held in her hand.

Sir James took it, and scrutinized it attentively.

"Yes," he said quietly, "this is the ill-fated draft treaty!"

"We've succeeded," said Tuppence. There was awe and an almost wondering unbelief in her voice.

Sir James echoed her words as he folded the paper carefully and put it away in his pocket-book, then he looked curiously around the dingy room.

"It was here that our young friend was confined for so long, was it not?" he said. "A truly sinister room. You notice the absence of windows, and the thickness of the close-fitting door. Whatever took place here would never be heard by the outside world."

Tuppence shivered. His words woke a vague alarm in her. What if there *was* some one concealed in the house? Some one who might bar that door on them, and leave them to die like rats in a trap? Then she realized the absurdity of her thought. The house was surrounded by police who, if they failed to reappear, would not hesitate to break in and make a thorough search. She smiled at her own foolishness—then looked up with a start to find Sir James watching her. He gave her an emphatic little nod.

"Quite right, Miss Tuppence. You scent danger. So do I. So does Miss Finn."

"Yes," admitted Jane. "It's absurd—but I can't help it."

Sir James nodded again.

"You feel—as we all feel—*the presence of Mr. Brown.* Yes"—as Tuppence made a movement—"not a doubt of it— *Mr. Brown is here. . . .*"

"In this house?"

"In this room. . . . You don't understand? *I am Mr. Brown. . . .*"

Stupefied, unbelieving, they stared at him. The very lines of his face had changed. It was a different man who stood before them. He smiled a slow cruel smile.

"Neither of you will leave this room alive! You said just now we had succeeded. *I* have succeeded! The draft treaty is mine." His smile grew wider as he looked at Tuppence. "Shall I tell you how it will be? Sooner or later the police will break in, and they will find three victims of Mr. Brown— three, not two, you understand, but fortunately the third will not be dead, only wounded, and will be able to describe the attack with a wealth of detail! The treaty? It is in the hands of Mr. Brown. So no one will think of searching the pockets of Sir James Peel Edgerton!"

He turned to Jane.

"You outwitted me. I make my acknowledgments. But you will not do it again."

There was a faint sound behind him, but, intoxicated with success, he did not turn his head.

He slipped his hand into his pocket.

"Checkmate to the Young Adventurers," he said, and slowly raised the big automatic.

But, even as he did so, he felt himself seized from behind in a grip of iron. The revolver was wrenched from his hand, and the voice of Julius Hersheimmer said drawlingly:

"I guess you're caught redhanded with the goods upon you."

The blood rushed to the K.C.'s face, but his self-control was marvellous, as he looked from one to the other of his two captors. He looked longest at Tommy.

"You," he said beneath his breath. "*You!* I might have known."

Seeing that he was disposed to offer no resistance, their grip slackened. Quick as a flash his left hand, the hand which bore the big signet ring, was raised to his lips. . . .

" '*Ave, Cæsar! te morituri salutant,*' " he said, still looking at Tommy.

Then his face changed, and with a long convulsive shudder he fell forward in a crumpled heap, whilst an odour of bitter almonds filled the air.

XXVII

A Supper Party at the Savoy

The supper party given by Mr. Julius Hersheimmer to a few friends on the evening of the 30th will long be remembered in catering circles. It took place in a private room, and Mr. Hersheimmer's orders were brief and forcible. He gave carte blanche—and when a millionaire gives carte blanche he usually gets it!

Every delicacy out of season was duly provided. Waiters carried bottles of ancient and royal vintage with loving care. The floral decorations defied the seasons, and fruits of the earth as far apart as May and November found themselves miraculously side by side. The list of guests was small and select. The American Ambassador, Mr. Carter, who had taken the liberty, he said, of bringing an old friend, Sir William Beresford, with him, Archdeacon Cowley, Dr. Hall, those two youthful adventurers, Miss Prudence Cowley and Mr. Thomas Beresford, and last, but not least, as guest of honour, Miss Jane Finn.

Julius had spared no pains to make Jane's appearance a success. A mysterious knock had brought Tuppence to the door of the apartment she was sharing with the American girl. It was Julius. In his hand he held a cheque.

"Say, Tuppence," he began, "will you do me a good turn? Take this, and get Jane regularly togged up for this evening. You're all coming to supper with me at the Savoy. See? Spare no expense. You get me?"

"Sure thing," mimicked Tuppence. "We shall enjoy ourselves! It will be a pleasure dressing Jane. She's the loveliest thing I've ever seen."

"That's so," agreed Mr. Hersheimmer fervently.

His fervour brought a momentary twinkle to Tuppence's eye.

"By the way, Julius," she remarked demurely, "I—haven't given you my answer yet."

"Answer?" said Julius. His face paled.

"You know—when you asked me to—marry you," faltered Tuppence, her eyes downcast in the true manner of the early Victorian heroine, "and wouldn't take no for an answer. I've thought it well over——"

"Yes?" said Julius. The perspiration stood on his forehead.

Tuppence relented suddenly.

"You great idiot!" she said. "What on earth induced you to do it? I could see at the time you didn't care a twopenny dip for me!"

"Not at all. I had—and still have—the highest sentiments of esteem and respect—and admiration for you——"

"H'm!" said Tuppence. "Those are the kind of sentiments that very soon go to the wall when the other sentiment comes along! Don't they, old thing?"

"I don't know what you mean," said Julius stiffly, but a large and burning blush overspread his countenance.

"Shucks!" retorted Tuppence. She laughed, and closed the door, reopening it to add with dignity: "Morally, I shall always consider I have been jilted!"

"What was it?" asked Jane as Tuppence rejoined her.

"Julius."

"What did he want?"

"Really, I think, he wanted to see you, but I wasn't going to let him. Not until to-night, when you're going to burst upon every one like King Solomon in his glory! Come on! *We're going to shop!"*

To most people the 29th, the much-heralded "Labour Day," had passed much as any other day. Speeches were made in the Park and Trafalgar Square. Straggling processions, singing the *Red Flag*, wandered through the streets in a more or less aimless manner. Newspapers which had hinted at a general strike, and the inauguration of a reign of terror, were forced to hide their diminished heads. The bolder and more astute among them sought to prove that peace had been effected by following their counsels. In the Sunday papers a brief notice of the sudden death of Sir James Peel Edgerton, the famous K.C., had appeared. Monday's papers dealt appreciatively with the dead man's career. The exact manner of his sudden death was never made public.

Tommy had been right in his forecast of the situation. It had been a one-man show. Deprived of their chief, the organization fell to pieces. Kramenin had made a precipitate return to Russia, leaving England early on Sunday morning. The gang had fled from Astley Priors in a panic, leaving behind, in their haste, various damaging documents which compromised them hopelessly. With these proofs of conspiracy in their hands, aided further by a small brown diary taken from the pocket of the dead man which had contained a full and damning résumé of the whole plot, the Government had called an eleventh-hour conference. The Labour leaders were forced to recognize that they had been used as a cat's paw. Certain concessions were made by the Government, and were eagerly accepted. It was to be Peace, not War!

But the Cabinet knew by how narrow a margin they had escaped utter disaster. And burnt in on Mr. Carter's brain was the strange scene which had taken place in the house in Soho the night before.

He had entered the squalid room to find that great man, the friend of a lifetime, dead—betrayed out of his own mouth. From the dead man's pocket-book he had retrieved the ill-omened draft treaty, and then and there, in the presence of the other three, it had been reduced to ashes. . . . England was saved!

And now, on the evening of the 30th, in a private room at the Savoy, Mr. Julius P. Hersheimmer was receiving his guests.

Mr. Carter was the first to arrive. With him was a choleric-looking old gentleman, at sight of whom Tommy flushed up to the roots of his hair. He came forward.

"Ha!" said the old gentleman, surveying him apoplecti-cally. "So you're my nephew, are you? Not much to look at—but you've done good work, it seems. Your mother must have brought you up well after all. Shall we let bygones be bygones, eh? You're my heir, you know; and in future I pro-pose to make you an allowance—and you can look upon Chalmers Park as your home."

"Thank you, sir, it's awfully decent of you."

"Where's this young lady I've been hearing such a lot about?"

Tommy introduced Tuppence.

"Ha!" said Sir William, eyeing her. "Girls aren't what they used to be in my young days."

"Yes, they are," said Tuppence. "Their clothes are differ-ent, perhaps, but they themselves are just the same."

"Well, perhaps you're right. Minxes then—minxes now!"

"That's it," said Tuppence. "I'm a frightful minx myself."

"I believe you," said the old gentleman, chuckling, and pinched her ear in high good-humour. Most young women were terrified of the "old bear," as they termed him. Tup-pence's pertness delighted the old misogynist.

Then came the timid archdeacon, a little bewildered by the company in which he found himself, glad that his daughter was considered to have distinguished herself, but unable to help glancing at her from time to time with nervous appre-hension. But Tuppence behaved admirably. She forbore to cross her legs, set a guard upon her tongue, and steadfastly refused to smoke.

Dr. Hall came next, and he was followed by the American Ambassador.

"We might as well sit down," said Julius, when he had

introduced all his guests to each other. "Tuppence, will you——"

He indicated the place of honour with a wave of his hand. But Tuppence shook her head.

"No—that's Jane's place! When one thinks of how she's held out all these years, she ought to be made the queen of the feast to-night."

Julius flung her a grateful glance, and Jane came forward shyly to the allotted seat. Beautiful as she had seemed before, it was as nothing to the loveliness that now went fully adorned. Tuppence had performed her part faithfully. The model gown supplied by a famous dressmaker had been entitled "A tiger lily." It was all golds and reds and browns, and out of it rose the pure column of the girl's white throat, and the bronze masses of hair that crowned her lovely head. There was admiration in every eye, as she took her seat.

Soon the supper party was in full swing, and with one accord Tommy was called upon for a full and complete explanation.

"You've been too darned close about the whole business," Julius accused him. "You let on to me that you were off to the Argentine—though I guess you had your reasons for that. The idea of both you and Tuppence casting me for the part of Mr. Brown just tickles me to death!"

"The idea was not original to them," said Mr. Carter gravely. "It was suggested, and the poison very carefully instilled, by a past-master in the art. The paragraph in the New York paper suggested the plan to him, and by means of it he wove a web that nearly enmeshed you fatally."

"I never liked him," said Julius. "I felt from the first that there was something wrong about him, and I always suspected that it was he who silenced Mrs. Vandemeyer so appositely. But it wasn't till I heard that the order for Tommy's execution came right on the heels of our interview with him that Sunday that I began to tumble to the fact that he was the big bug himself."

"I never suspected it at all," lamented Tuppence. "I've always thought I was so much cleverer than Tommy—but he's undoubtedly scored over me handsomely."

Julius agreed.

"Tommy's been the goods this trip! And, instead of sitting there as dumb as a fish, let him banish his blushes, and tell us all about it."

"Hear! hear!"

"There's nothing to tell," said Tommy, acutely uncomfortable. "I was an awful mug—right up to the time I found that photograph of Annette, and realized that she was Jane Finn. Then I remembered how persistently she had shouted out that word 'Marguerite'—and I thought of the pictures, and—well, that's that. Then of course I went over the whole thing to see where I'd made an ass of myself."

"Go on," said Mr. Carter, as Tommy showed signs of taking refuge in silence once more.

"That business about Mrs. Vandemeyer had worried me when Julius told me about it. On the face of it, it seemed that he or Sir James must have done the trick. But I didn't know which. Finding that photograph in the drawer, after that story of how it had been got from him by Inspector Brown, made me suspect Julius. Then I remembered that it was Sir James who had discovered the false Jane Finn. In the end, I couldn't make up my mind—and just decided to take no chances either way. I left a note for Julius, in case he was Mr. Brown, saying I was off to the Argentine, and I dropped Sir James's letter with the offer of the job by the desk so that he would see it was a genuine stunt. Then I wrote my letter to Mr. Carter and rang up Sir James. Taking him into my confidence would be the best thing either way, so I told him everything except where I believed the papers to be hidden. The way he helped me to get on the track of Tuppence and Annette almost disarmed me, but not quite. I kept my mind open between the two of them. And then I got a bogus note from Tuppence—and I knew!"

"But how?"

Tommy took the note in question from his pocket and passed it round the table.

"It's her handwriting all right, but I knew it wasn't from her because of the signature. She'd never spell her name 'Two-pence,' but anyone who'd never seen it written might quite easily do so. Julius *had* seen it—he showed me a note of hers to him once—but *Sir James hadn't!* After that everything was plain sailing. I sent off Albert post-haste to Mr. Carter. I pretended to go away, but doubled back again. When Julius came bursting up in his car, I felt it wasn't part of Mr. Brown's plan—and that there would probably be trouble. Unless Sir James was actually caught in the act, so to speak, I knew Mr. Carter would never believe it of him on my bare word——"

"I didn't," interposed Mr. Carter ruefully.

"That's why I sent the girls off to Sir James. I was sure they'd fetch up at the house in Soho sooner or later. I threatened Julius with the revolver, because I wanted Tuppence to repeat that to Sir James, so that he wouldn't worry about us. The moment the girls were out of sight I told Julius to drive like hell for London, and as we went along I told him the whole story. We got to the Soho house in plenty of time and met Mr. Carter outside. After arranging things with him we went in and hid behind the curtain in the recess. The policemen had orders to say, if they were asked, that no one had gone into the house. That's all."

And Tommy came to an abrupt halt.

There was silence for a moment.

"By the way," said Julius suddenly, "you're all wrong about that photograph of Jane. It *was* taken from me, but I found it again."

"Where?" cried Tuppence.

"In that little safe on the wall in Mrs. Vandemeyer's bedroom."

"I knew you found something," said Tuppence reproachfully. "To tell you the truth, that's what started me off suspecting you. Why didn't you say?"

"I guess I was a mite suspicious too. It had been got away from me once, and I determined I wouldn't let on I'd got it until a photographer had made a dozen copies of it!"

"We all kept back something or other," said Tuppence thoughtfully. "I suppose secret service work makes you like that!"

In the pause that ensued, Mr. Carter took from his pocket a small shabby brown book.

"Beresford has just said that I would not have believed Sir James Peel Edgerton to be guilty unless, so to speak, he was caught in the act. That is so. Indeed, not until I read the entries in this little book could I bring myself fully to credit the amazing truth. This book will pass into the possession of Scotland Yard, but it will never be publicly exhibited. Sir James's long association with the law would make it undesirable. But to you, who know the truth, I propose to read certain passages which will throw some light on the extraordinary mentality of this great man."

He opened the book, and turned the thin pages.

". . . It is madness to keep this book. I know that. It is documentary evidence against me. But I have never shrunk from taking risks. And I feel an urgent need for self-expression. . . . The book will only be taken from my dead body. . . .

". . . From an early age I realized that I had exceptional abilities. Only a fool underestimates his capabilities. My brain power was greatly above the average. I know that I was born to succeed. My appearance was the only thing against me. I was quiet and insignificant—utterly nondescript. . . .

". . . When I was a boy I heard a famous murder trial. I was deeply impressed by the power and eloquence of the counsel for the defence. For the first time I entertained the idea of taking my talents to that particular market. . . . Then I studied the criminal in the dock. . . . The man was a fool— he had been incredibly, unbelievably stupid. Even the eloquence of his counsel was hardly likely to save him. I felt an immeasurable contempt for him. . . . Then it occurred to me that the criminal standard was a low one. It was the wastrels, the failures, the general riff-raff of civilization who drifted into crime. . . . Strange that men of brains had never realized its extraordinary opportunities. . . . I played with the idea. . . . What a magnificent field—what unlimited possibilities! It made my brain reel. . . .

". . . I read standard works on crime and criminals. They all confirmed my opinion. Degeneracy, disease—never the deliberate embracing of a career by a far-seeing man. Then I considered. Supposing my utmost ambitions were realized—that I was called to the bar, and rose to the height of my profession? That I entered politics—say, even, that I became Prime Minister of England? What then? Was that power? Hampered at every turn by my colleagues, fettered by the democratic system of which I should be the mere figurehead! No—the power I dreamed of was absolute. An autocrat! A dictator! And such power could only be obtained by working outside the law. To play on the weaknesses of human nature, then on the weaknesses of nations—to get together and control a vast organization, and finally to overthrow the existing order, and rule! The thought intoxicated me. . . .

". . . I saw that I must lead two lives. A man like myself is bound to attract notice. I must have a successful career which would mask my true activities. . . . Also I must cultivate a personality. I modelled myself upon famous K.C.'s. I reproduced their mannerisms, their magnetism. If I had chosen to be an actor, I should have been the greatest actor living! No disguises—no grease paint—no false beards! Personality! I put it on like a glove! When I shed it, I was myself, quiet, unobtrusive, a man like every other man. I called myself Mr. Brown. There are hundreds of men called Brown—there are hundreds of men looking just like me. . . .

". . . I succeeded in my false career. I was bound to succeed. I shall succeed in the other. A man like me cannot fail. . . .

". . . I have been reading a life of Napoleon. He and I have much in common. . . .

". . . I make a practice of defending criminals. A man should look after his own people. . . .

". . . Once or twice I have felt afraid. The first time was in Italy. There was a dinner given. Professor D——, the great alienist, was present. The talk fell on insanity. He said, 'A great many men are mad, and no one knows it. They do not know it themselves.' I do not understand why he looked at me when he said that. His glance was strange. . . . I did not like it. . . .

". . . The war has disturbed me. . . . I thought it would further my plans. The Germans are so efficient. Their spy system, too, was excellent. The streets are full of these boys in khaki. All empty-headed young fools. . . . Yet I do not know. . . . They won the war. . . . It disturbs me. . . .

". . . My plans are going well. . . . A girl butted in—I do not think she really knew anything. . . . But we must give up the Esthonia. . . . No risks now. . . .

". . . All goes well. The loss of memory is vexing. It cannot be a fake. No girl could deceive ME! . . .

". . . The 29th. . . . That is very soon. . . ." Mr. Carter paused.

"I will not read the details of the *coup* that was planned. But there are just two small entries that refer to the three of you. In the light of what happened they are interesting.

". . . By inducing the girl to come to me of her own accord, I have succeeded in disarming her. But she has intuitive flashes that might be dangerous. . . . She must be got out of the way. . . . I can do nothing with the American. He suspects and dislikes me. But he cannot know. I fancy my armour is impregnable. . . . Sometimes I fear I have underestimated the other boy. He is not clever, but it is hard to blind his eyes to facts. . . ."

Mr. Carter shut the book.

"A great man," he said. "Genius, or insanity, who can say?"

There was silence.

Then Mr. Carter rose to his feet.

"I will give you a toast. The Joint Venture which has so amply justified itself by success!"

It was drunk with acclamation.

"There's something more we want to hear," continued Mr. Carter. He looked at the American Ambassador. "I speak for you also, I know. We'll ask Miss Jane Finn to tell us the story that only Miss Tuppence has heard so far—but before we do so we'll drink her health. The health of one of the bravest of America's daughters, to whom is due the thanks and gratitude of two great countries!"

XXVIII

AND AFTER

"That was a mighty good toast, Jane," said Mr. Hersheimmer, as he and his cousin were being driven back in the Rolls-Royce to the Ritz.

"The one to the joint venture?"

"No—the one to you. There isn't another girl in the world who could have carried it through as you did. You were just wonderful!"

Jane shook her head.

"I don't feel wonderful. At heart I'm just tired and lonesome—and longing for my own country."

"That brings me to something I wanted to say. I heard the Ambassador telling you his wife hoped you would come to them at the Embassy right away. That's good enough, but I've got another plan. Jane—I want you to marry me! Don't get scared and say no at once. You can't love me right away, of course, that's impossible. But I've loved you from the very moment I set eyes on your photo—and now I've seen you I'm simply crazy about you! If you'll marry me, I won't worry you any—you shall take your own time. Maybe you'll never come to love me, and if that's the case I'll manage to set you free.

But I want the right to look after you, and take care of you."

"That's what I want," said the girl wistfully. "Some one who'll be good to me. Oh, you don't know how lonesome I feel!"

"Sure thing I do. Then I guess that's all fixed up, and I'll see the archbishop about a special license tomorrow morning."

"Oh, Julius!"

"Well, I don't want to hustle you any, Jane, but there's no sense in waiting about. Don't be scared—I shan't expect you to love me all at once."

But a small hand was slipped into his.

"I love you now, Julius," said Jane Finn. "I loved you that first moment in the car when the bullet grazed your cheek. . . ."

Five minutes later Jane murmured softly:

"I don't know London very well, Julius, but is it such a very long way from the Savoy to the Ritz?"

"It depends how you go," explained Julius unblushingly. "We're going by way of Regent's Park!"

"Oh, Julius—what will the chauffeur think?"

"At the wages I pay him, he knows better than to do any independent thinking. Why, Jane, the only reason I had the supper at the Savoy was so that I could drive you home. I didn't see how I was ever going to get hold of you alone. You and Tuppence have been sticking together like Siamese twins. I guess another day of it would have driven me and Beresford stark staring mad!"

"Oh. Is he——?"

"Of course he is. Head over ears."

"I thought so," said Jane thoughtfully.

"Why?"

"From all the things Tuppence didn't say!"

"There you have me beat," said Mr. Hersheimmer. But Jane only laughed.

In the meantime, the Young Adventurers were sitting bolt upright, very stiff and ill at ease, in a taxi which, with a singular lack of originality, was also returning to the Ritz via Regent's Park.

A terrible constraint seemed to have settled down between them. Without quite knowing what had happened, everything seemed changed. They were tongue-tied—paralysed. All the old *camaraderie* was gone.

Tuppence could think of nothing to say.

Tommy was equally afflicted.

They sat very straight and forbore to look at each other.

At last Tuppence made a desperate effort.

"Rather fun, wasn't it?"

"Rather."

Another silence.

"I like Julius," essayed Tuppence again.

Tommy was suddenly galvanized into life.

"You're not going to marry him, do you hear?" he said dictatorially. "I forbid it."

"Oh!" said Tuppence meekly.

"Absolutely, you understand."

"He doesn't want to marry me—he really only asked me out of kindness."

"That's not very likely," scoffed Tommy.

"It's quite true. He's head over ears in love with Jane. I expect he's proposing to her now."

"She'll do for him very nicely," said Tommy condescendingly.

"Don't you think she's the most lovely creature you've ever seen?"

"Oh, I dare say."

"But I suppose you prefer sterling worth," said Tuppence demurely.

"I—oh, dash it all, Tuppence, you know!"

"I like your uncle, Tommy," said Tuppence, hastily creating a diversion. "By the way, what are you going to do, accept Mr. Carter's offer of a Government job, or accept Julius's invitation and take a richly remunerated post in America on his ranch?"

"I shall stick to the old ship, I think, though it's awfully good of Hersheimmer. But I feel you'd be more at home in London."

"I don't see where I come in."

"I do," said Tommy positively.

Tuppence stole a glance at him sideways.

"There's the money, too," she observed thoughtfully.

"What money?"

"We're going to get a cheque each. Mr. Carter told me so."

"Did you ask how much?" inquired Tommy sarcastically.

"Yes," said Tuppence triumphantly. "But I shan't tell you."

"Tuppence, you are the limit!"

"It has been fun, hasn't it, Tommy? I do hope we shall have lots more adventures."

"You're insatiable, Tuppence. I've had quite enough adventures for the present."

"Well, shopping is almost as good," said Tuppence dreamily. "Think of buying old furniture, and bright carpets, and futurist silk curtains, and a polished dining-table, and a divan with lots of cushions——"

"Hold hard," said Tommy. "What's all this for?"

"Possibly a house—but I think a flat."

"Whose flat?"

"You think I mind saying it, but I don't in the least! *Ours*, so there!"

"You darling!" cried Tommy, his arms tightly round her. "I was determined to make you say it. I owe you something for the relentless way you've squashed me whenever I've tried to be sentimental."

Tuppence raised her face to his. The taxi proceeded on its course round the north side of Regent's Park.

"You haven't really proposed now," pointed out Tuppence. "Not what our grandmothers would call a proposal. But after listening to a rotten one like Julius's, I'm inclined to let you off."

"You won't be able to get out of marrying me, so don't you think it."

"What fun it will be," responded Tuppence. "Marriage is called all sorts of things, a haven, and a refuge, and a crowning glory, and a state of bondage, and lots more. But do you know what I think it is?"

"What?"

"A sport!"

"And a damned good sport too," said Tommy.